EXTINCTION CHRONICLES
PANDORA'S BOX

EXTINCTION CHRONICLES
PANDORA'S BOX

E. THOMAS PALMER

LitPrime Solutions
21250 Hawthorne Blvd
Suite 500, Torrance, CA 90503
www.litprime.com
Phone: 1 (209) 788-3500

Published by LitPrime Solutions   03/05/2021

ISBN: 978-1-954886-16-2(sc)
ISBN: 978-1-954886-17-9(e)

Library of Congress Control Number: 2021904084

CONTENTS

W HEN HE HEARD THE TWIG snap, Jonathan sprang to his feet. Crouching low, he stepped back from the fire; disappearing into the darkness. Remaining in a defensive posture, he waited. Whomever or whatever was out there knew it had made a mistake and now remained silent and motionless. It was a life and death standoff. The surrounding forest was more than silent; it was devoid of all sound. The unknown hunter could not approach without revealing itself; and Jonathan could not retreat without risking his life.

Long, deathly-silent minutes passed. Neither Jonathan, nor his unseen adversary, was willing to yield their slim advantage. Finally, a voice in the darkness whispered, "I'm a friend. I didn't know anyone was out here. Please don't kill me. I'll retreat."

The voice was a delicate mix of fear and feminine beauty. Jonathan secreted his weapon in the overhanging length of his jacket sleeve. This could still be a trick, but it had been a year since he had spoken directly to another human. "I'm a friend. I won't harm you. Come forward. . . slowly," he replied.

Still hidden by the shroud of darkness, Jonathan remained crouched outside the glow of the campfire until she came into view. He wasn't afraid of an ambush by others who may still be hidden. No one ever traveled in groups at night, especially hunters. Besides, his weapon was loaded and ready for any sudden betrayal.

"I'm unarmed," she said as she tossed her weapons towards the fire.

"You should never relinquish your weapons. You don't know

who I am or what I'm capable of." He remained in the dark fringes of the campfire.

"I'm at your mercy sir. I've lost my way and your fire drew me here."

"You *ARE* a very foolish girl," he chastised. Stepping into the dim outer glow of the fire, he paused while they sized each other up.

"I would hope for some civility in all of the madness that has consumed our world. There must be hope if we're to remain human." The commanding conviction in her voice revealed this statement was not meant as a plea; it was her belief.

The words echoed in his ears like rolling thunder. A portent of what would be lost if he faltered or strayed from his goal. She could be a friend, a true friend. He advanced into the brighter glow so she could see him more clearly.

"My name is Erin. I have a campsite somewhere around here. I lost my way and have been wandering for hours until I smelled the smoke from your fire. I didn't know there were any other humans in this area. I've not seen anybody for several months."

"No hunting parties?" He eased back into the shadows.

"No."

"What about raptors or spiders?" he pressed.

Erin's reply was a flat, cold statement. "The raptors came in and cleared out all the humans and other food animals and moved on. There aren't any spiders either." Brightening a bit, she added, "It's been six or seven months now, so I feel pretty safe here."

"Trey," he said, moving into the full firelight.

She looked him directly in the eyes. "Trey, what's your story?"

Her stare was unsettling and somehow inviting. *Don't think about sex. She's beautiful and you've not been with a woman for years. Be alert. You must survive. Redirect your thoughts you idiot. REDIRECT!!!* "Tell me, how many humans were here before the raptors?"

"We were a large group, a little over two hundred." She paused, studying his eyes. "Mostly adults, but there were fifteen children. We were trying to establish a sanctuary of sorts. But the raptors came before we could effectively fortify our defenses. We lost over a hundred in the first week. The children were among the first."

She choked back sorrow and rage before continuing. "We managed to kill about twenty of the raptors, but they just kept coming." A single tear rolled down her cheek as her eyes glazed.

Jonathon knew this horror first hand and waited for the right moment to speak. "I've never seen them hunt in packs as large as you've described. This is a bad turn of events."

"I believe they've adapted a strategy to their already formidable hunting skills." Anger flashed in her eyes as her voice faltered, "We weren't ready for such a unified assault. It was an eradication effort and they were well prepared. It was so savage. I was the only lucky one. I had a small cave to hide in. Bushes protect its entrance. There was so much carnage that they missed my scent. I don't know how many survived… if any."

The news was very alarming. Jonathan pulled back his sleeve revealing his weapon. Erin fell backwards. Fear etched her face. Regaining her composure, she calmed herself.

Erin judged the distance to her weapons and could see the futility of an attempted defensive move. There would be no escape. He'd been right; she was a foolish girl. "So," she said, resigned to her fate, "will it be rape or murder or both?"

"What are you talking about?" he said as he placed the weapon back into its holster.

"I'm sorry. When you. . . never mind. I was wrong. You are a friend. Thank you. This kindness helps me keep my hope alive." Erin began to cry.

Jonathan rushed to her side to comfort her. With his arm around her shoulder he pressed her head to his chest and stroked her hair. He rocked her gently, remembering all the terrors he'd survived. Absently, he kissed her hair as he rocked to settle his own fears as much as hers.

Erin reached around and pulled the pistol from the holster and eased herself from his comforting embrace. Pointing the gun in his face, she asked, "Who's the foolish one now?"

Jonathan remained in stunned silence as she handed him his gun.

After their little exchange she returned to the comfort of his embrace. They sat silently in the firelight as the evening waned. There was companionship to be had here and they both needed human contact. Neither moved again until they both found sleep; comforted by the warm embrace of their renewed hope and friendship.

The sound of pots and pans woke him from the best sleep he'd had in months. He raised himself onto an elbow to watch her as she made a meager breakfast of dried fish and some over ripe fruit.

Without turning to face him, she said, "So you're finally awake. I've made some breakfast, but your supplies are pretty slim. Here," she said as she proffered the plate.

She smiled at him as she began to eat. It smelled good as he dug in ravenously. *It's amazing how having someone to share a meal with makes the food taste better. I wonder if she would agree to travel with me. She must be told who I am. Then she can make up her mind. Not many humans care for my company.*

The two of them chatted until the meal was finished. Jonathan began to fashion some spears and a bow for her. Her weapons were poor at best. They found several feathers and made some arrows together.

"Is there any water around here? I'm almost out and you have none." He shook his canteen to judge its depleted contents.

"I'm disoriented," she said, "but there is a pond close by. I just don't know which direction."

"You came from over there. We'll retrace you path and find your camp."

"I'm not very adept at tracking. I can't help you."

"How have you managed to stay alive? If we're going to travel together, you'll have to learn. I can start teaching you right now. The relative safety of these woods will allow us time to practice without losing our lives."

"You want to travel with me?" Tears welled in her eyes.

"Sure, why not? You're intelligent, a good cook. . . and beautiful."

Dragging her fingers through her matted, tangled hair she asked, "You think I'm beautiful?"

"When's the last time you looked in a mirror? Erin, you are among the most beautiful women I've ever seen."

She hugged him and wiped away her tears. "Let's get started on the tracking lessons. There's so much I need to learn. I want to be a partner, not baggage."

They tracked her path and discovered where she'd made a wrong turn. Sometime after lunch, they found her camp. From there she could direct him to the pond. Her camp was well provisioned and they wouldn't need to hunt for several days. Jonathan relaxed completely as he shed the weight from years of running and hiding.

It was just before dusk when he remembered his dirty utensils. "Take me to the pond. I need to clean my utensils before they become contaminated."

"Sure, follow me. It's only ten or fifteen minutes from here." Gathering up her own utensils, she headed into the forest. The path was clear and Jonathan followed after collecting his gear.

When he arrived, he found her naked and waist deep in the water. She was washing the dirt from her body and wringing water from her hair. She turned to look him in the eyes. "Why is your mouth hanging open?" she smiled. "I thought you said you'd seen other women before?"

Jonathan blushed and spun around, giving her some privacy. "I'm sorry. I had no idea you would be, um, ah. . . not dressed."

"Did anyone ever tell you that you're cute when you blush? You had better hurry up and get in here. I've heard some very strange noises coming from the pond, but it's safe at this time. I always bathe at this time."

Not being someone to risk unnecessary danger, Jonathan

reluctantly stripped off his clothes and waded into the pond. He couldn't even remember the last time he ventured into open water. There were too many *things* lurking below.

"How do you know it's safe?" he asked as the water rose above his ankles.

"When the others were still alive, we dragged the pond with a large net. It stretched from edge to edge. The group dragged the pond several times. We got a few very peculiar things out of here, but it's been safe since then. Sometimes at night I hear things through the forest, but nothing ever comes to bother me. I just make sure that I'm bathed before it gets too dark. Make sure to wash your clothes while we're here. We can dry them by the campfire."

This was a surreal turn of events. This young woman had unabashedly exposed her nakedness, displaying a complete trust in him. It rekindled his almost lost hope in human salvation. They were not unlike Adam and Eve.

Traveling naked and unarmed through the forest was both exciting and frightening. He struggled to remain calm as Erin, unconcerned about her nudity, weapons and surroundings, led the way.

Hanging their clothes on a line Erin had strung; they set it near the fire. Content, they sat and ate dried fish and some greens. They talked about all manner of things until darkness consumed the forest.

The two became very close over the next several weeks. Jonathan wasn't sure that it was love, but it didn't matter, he was willing to stay with her for the rest of his natural days. She expressed the same feelings. He knew it was time for him to reveal his identity.

"Erin."

"Yes Trey."

"There's something I must reveal. I've kept a secret from you because I fear for my life. I wander the forests because it's the only way I can survive."

"I don't understand. The forests are sure death to anyone who stays too long. If it wasn't for luck and my cave, I'd have been dead long ago."

"I have something that I must show you."

Fear and concern showed on her face as she slid up next to him. She watched as he reverently unbundled a stack of composition books. They were the type students used to use for essays. He wiped imaginary dirt from the cover of the one he selected and offered it to her. This was a pivotal moment in their relationship and he knew he would either have her love or lose her in the next few minutes.

"I want you to read this first entry here," he said as he opened the book. "This is who I am. It's why I stay hidden and live alone. I'll understand if you want me to leave. As close as we've become, this may destroy everything that we have."

She accepted the open book and the puzzled look never left her face as she read.

September 14, 2016 Journal Entry 5:37PM
Jonathan Crenshaw III

Where do I begin? I'm so tired of running. I'm tired of hiding from the world and what it's become. My past, no my grandparents' past, will haunt me until those who hunt me find me and kill me. . . or I die at the hands of any one of a number of unspeakable creatures. It will not be swift nor will it be pleasant in either circumstance. I yearn for a chance at a normal life, but Pandora's Box has long since been opened and there is no way to close it until we come to our senses. . . or become extinct as a species.

The calamitous certainty of mankind's voracious appetite and greed has seen to our destruction by our own hand. There are those among the survivors who blame me for my grandparents' discovery. The fact is that they did not unleash this calamity upon the earth. Greedy, self-serving politicians, businessmen and other nefarious individuals have brought about the very real possibility of mankind's

xv

extinction. Over fifty-thousand years of evolution and innovation. . . gone in the blink of an eye.

Telling the story as factually as possible is the only way I know to vindicate my family's name and help us survive as a species. Perhaps someday, someone will find these journals and the truth will be known.

Truth can only experience clarity with the passage of time. History is rewritten in many variations, but the facts will still remain. I know this is a childish dream; I may even be accused of writing a fantasy to support my family. The revisionists will only hold sway on the truth until they are out of power or dead; killed by what has become of our earth and our species. No one of the original group remains. All the voices are silenced. Only I am left. . . a grim, and almost hopeless guardian of the truth.

I live each day dreaming of a better world. What recourse do I have? I am the last unaltered human who knows the whole truth. The truth as it really was and again will be. The truth *IS* and I must write it down before it's lost forever. If we are to survive as a species, we must eventually learn from our mistakes. Fifty thousand years of history should mean something. Now that's a childish dream! Yet I find it amazing that at twenty-two, I still am able to dream.

The powerbrokers and all those they accuse of being the villains, and what they proffered as the truth will all fade from this world and time will cleanse the truth. Then and only then will my writing be proven as honest. We have chosen to play God; may God have mercy on our souls. Perhaps extinction may be a merciful end to our existence.

I'm so, so tired. This probably sounds like the ramblings of a mad man. I can no longer

be sure. Is the madness within me. . . or is the real madness the world that surrounds me? There has to be a way to salvage what's left of the human race. I have faith that we can survive, but what will become of our species?

I hear them in the distance. They're hunting for me again today.

I must have left a marker somewhere, some small thing or scent to betray me. I can't afford to slip up. There may be others like me out there, but it's too risky to search for them. I'll resume the journal when I find more time. This will be all for now. I'll be on the run for several days before I can eliminate my trail and find a precious few moments of peace. . . and evade the death that awaits me each day.

I just want the world to know that I loved my grandparents and what they thought could be a gift to the world. At one time their discovery was actually capable of being the greatest gift mankind could have ever known. We have done this to ourselves and we must undo it, or someday we will be the fossils that another species will collect and display in a museum.

Beethoven, Mozart, Manet, Monet, Van Gogh all wrought beauty from their vision and genius and made the world a better place. Their works have enriched the lives of millions upon millions of people, yet what we have wrought from greed and foisted upon the world as beauty will be our ruination and damnation.

Why can't we leave well enough alone? What is it about our species that must dominate and conquer everything in its path? I'm not thinking clearly. I can hear them in the distance. They're moving away. Maybe I won't have to run tonight. The earth has been a crucible since its formation. The strong survive and dominate. The weak are their fodder.

Strength and intelligence are the keys. Common sense and careful judgment is needed to temper our propensity towards avarice and self-destruction. Only this will bring our species back from the brink.

I must close now. The noise has faded into the distance, now only a dim echo of the terror it brings. I must sleep while I can and find a new place to hide in the morning. The humans and dinosaurs will hunt until dusk and the other mutated creatures will hunt by night. I am left to wander in the faint light before dawn, when few creatures or men venture out. I will survive.

Erin flipped nervously through sever al more pages after. She'd heard of his grandparents and what they had done to the world. She should hate this man, but she sensed that it wasn't the correct response.

"Can you tell me the whole story? This is a large stack of books, there has to be more in here than your ancestry."

A sigh of relief escaped his lips as he took the journal. "Most of what I will tell you is in these journals. There are a few personal family things that I can share, but this will be the unvarnished truth. My grandparents only discovered the technology; our government and military unleashed the devastation on the world. It was not my grandparents.

"I was twelve when it first began. All those years ago my life was homework and weekends, school and summer vacation. On Saturday's I played baseball in the park with the other kids. There was kick the can, hide and seek, playing war or cowboys and Indians. Like all kids, I didn't have a care. The world was my neighborhood. . . all those years ago."

"What are your plans? If you live alone, how are you going to get the truth out there?"

"Good question. I have the entire history documented in my journals. If I die before I can begin my work, at least there are the journals."

"For someone who's made a life surviving the forests, you have a lousy plan. If someone discovers your journals, most likely they'll use the paper for starting fires. Or worse yet, for cleaning up after. . . well you understand."

"I must make the truth known if I'm to save the human race. We are worth saving and only I can do it. Only I know the truth." They sat naked, facing each other in the glow of the firelight. Nervous and anxious, he held her hands. After long moments of searching, he found his resolve. The time was now and he began his tale of discovery, betrayal and destruction. "This is how it all began. . ."

CHAPTER ONE

. . . AND SO, IT BEGINS.

B OTH OF THEM WERE ANXIOUS about the dig. The university expected results. Would they be able to deliver again this year? Grant money and equipment were in jeopardy with a poor showing; so much hung in the balance from one year to the next.

It was late afternoon when the Crenshaw's arrived in town. It was a long drive, but worth the effort. No matter where they traveled in, this place, this town, was their favorite spot. It was situated only forty-five minutes from where they usually scouted for fossils.

Over the years the town had become a favorite hangout for them. It provided the warmth and comfort of human contact and shelter when the weather turned really bad. There was a decent general store and a bar with a dance floor. A single road went through the center of town. The post office was across the street from the diner and next to the sheriff's office. They loved the old western Americana feel of the place.

After twenty years of research and fossil collecting, most of the town's people knew them by name, or recognized them on the street. This was a vignette of America as it had been since the first settlers moved westward and staked a personal claim to their right of life, liberty and the pursuit of happiness brought about by their strength of will and a proud, self-sufficient attitude.

Parking in front of the diner, they noticed the sheriff's truck across the street. "I wonder if Bob's around." Ellen looked up and down the street, but didn't see him anywhere. "He's probably in his office. Let's grab a bite to eat first and then we can visit."

"I am pretty hungry. That's a good idea. Lead on my dear."

They entered the diner, waiting at the hostess station. It wasn't long before Nancy came up with a broad smile across her face. "Is it that time already?" she asked. Their table had a view of the main street, yet out of the sun. They enjoyed watching the activity of the town.

"It seems like it's always that time. It's so good to see you again. How are the kids Nancy?"

"They're kids." Her voice was resigned to that fate.

"Enough said." Ellen understood the meaning in her tone. "Your oldest will be getting out of high school soon, won't he?"

"He starts his senior year in the fall. That boy's gonna be the death of me yet. The girls just won't leave him alone or maybe it's the other way around." Nancy set the table as they continued to chat.

"Is Bob around?" asked Jonathan. "I see his truck, but we seemed to have missed him."

"He's in his office. He just called and ordered a late lunch."

Sensing an opportunity to escape the girl talk, Jonathan rose from the table and said, "Ladies, if you'll excuse me, I have an appointment with my favorite lawman."

Throwing open the sheriff's door, Jonathan cried out, "I did it! I did it! Arrest me!"

Bob was taken with such surprise that he didn't recognize Jonathan at first. Once he recognized this loud intruder, he jumped from his seat giving each other a bear hug and their typical, I'm stronger than you, handshake.

"How the hell are you? I can't believe it's been a year already. Is Ellen with you?"

"Like American Express, I don't leave home without her."

"She's a fine-looking woman. . . too good for the likes of you, he laughed. I'm gonna get her for myself one of these years."

"Yeah, yeah, I don't believe you could handle her. That wonderful woman is almost too much for me, but she tolerates me, so I hang around."

"The way I hear it, she's just waitin' 'til you kick off so she can come to me without hurtin' your feelings"

"Where'd you hear such nonsense? I know, in one of your dreams, you old rascal."

"Could be at that," replied Bob stifling a laugh.

Changing the subject completely, Jonathan said, "We're tired and hungry and Nancy won't serve us until you get your sorry backside over to the diner. Put some hustle into it. I'm starving."

They laughed all the way across the street and were still going at it as they sat down at the table. There were more hugs and kisses with Ellen as the two men sat down for lunch.

"So, tell me Ellen, how many kids this year?"

"Just ten… but they're really good. We're expecting a lot from them if we find a good site. How's Grace?"

"That's right, you wouldn't have heard. She got married just a month after you two left last summer. They'd been dating for quite some time and decided to tie the knot. They moved down to Colorado. I hear from her all the time. He's a good man, and I'm happy for her.

"She's due in three more months." She finally got the photo from pocket. Here's a picture of Grace and her husband on their wedding day.

"That's great news," said Ellen, accepting the photo. "They're a beautiful couple. The baby is going to be gorgeous. How was the ceremony? She looks beautiful in that wedding dress."

"It was a simple affair. They didn't want to wait. They'd been making plans between themselves for several months and then they just up and did it. I was happy that they took care of all the details."

Bob sat down at the table as Jonathan asked, "What are you up to now that Grace is gone?"

"I'm trying to keep myself busy with Nancy here," he quipped as she walked past to the table. Nancy swished some menus at him and missed. "She's been playing hard to get because she knows where all the bodies are buried. Ellen, I'm really waiting for you to come to your senses and move out here to God's country and hook up with me."

Ellen looked at Jonathan to see his reaction. Jonathan joked, "Well you could do worse."

"I've already done worse," she shot back.

After twenty years of coming here, the relationships they developed a friendly, homelike atmosphere. These people were counted among their closest friends. Each summer the time went by entirely too quickly, having to leave again. It was like that every year. This playful banter was part of their arrival ritual.

The conversation remained light while waited for lunch. Jonathan sipped at his iced tea and Ellen talked almost nonstop. A year's absence offered a lot of news to catch up on. Ellen was in all her glory. Bob was having a good time too. He really loved the two of them and enjoyed the time they spent together.

Nancy brought their food. Hours as they continued sharing their stories. Nancy joined them whenever she could. By the time they'd finished it was as if they had never left. This was a fabulous extended family for the four of them.

"We'll be back soon. The kids will be arriving shortly and we need to pick them up."

"Where you gonna dig this year?"

"Don't know yet Bob. We'll scout around for a couple of days. If we catch a break, we'll be pretty close. It'll be the luck of the draw. You know it always is."

"The reason I asked is that we've got a pretty good band playing on Saturday night. Why don't you two come into town so I can swing this pretty lady around the dance floor all night long?"

"Sounds good to me Bob," she replied. "How about you Jonathan, are you up to it?"

He grabbed his lower back and in his best old man voice said, "No… you young- uns have fun. I'll manage not to fall down being alone at the campsite and all. Don't fret about me. You two just go on and enjoy yourselves."

Not one to miss an opportunity, Bob chimed in, "You're mine on Saturday night."

"No wait! I've just had a miraculous recovery. My old back is as fit as a fiddle. If there's going to be any swinging around the dance floor, I'll be doing the swinging."

"Just a couple of dances then?"

"Deal." Jonathan extended his hand.

"Have I just been auctioned off to the low bidder?" protested Ellen.

"It's not like that at all dear. You don't know what this scoundrel told me earlier. He wants you for his own. He wants you to leave me."

"Well why didn't you tell me this earlier?" she said as she put her arm through Bob's. "You can have as many dances as you'd like." Casting a glance over her shoulder, she smirked at Jonathan.

Bob and Jonathan looked at each other but couldn't think of anything to say.

"This is kind of nice, two handsome men fighting for my affections. Nancy I'll toss you the scraps when I'm through."

Nancy was laughing so hard there were tears in her eyes.

"I can't wait for Saturday night. I sure hope you two can get into town. I haven't had this much fun in a long time."

Hugs and kisses were exchanged as they attempted their departure. Saturday night was yet unresolved, but definitely added to their schedule.

CHAPTER TWO

J ONATHAN AND ELLEN ARRIVED AT their customary location for a field survey. Nothing had changed much in a year. It never did. There were about four good hours left before dusk. There would be enough time to pitch their tent and organize some of their equipment, but the majority of the work would have to wait until morning.

They wanted to get out and scout around while they still had light. There had been unusually heavy rains for three days prior to their arrival and several good storms had saturated the area in the past few weeks. Many fossils were newly exposed, newly buried or simply washed away to become untold treasures never to be discovered. Still, the Bad Lands always held surprises for any who wished to look closely enough.

Working quickly and efficiently, they had their supplies off the truck. Twenty years of practice made it almost effortless. Jonathan began setting up the tent while Ellen prepared the cots and bedding. She had developed a technique of preparing all the bedding in. No matter when they arrived, once Jonathan had the tent ready, she was only a matter of minutes from having both cots up and made. The campsite seemed to materialize out of the ground.

"All done here," she called.

"Be right in dear. I forgot to fill the lantern before we left. I'll only be a couple of minutes."

"Take your time. I'm not ready for bed yet. We still have to scout the area."

"I've got some zucchini on the cook stove ready to slice. Would you like a light snack before we head out?"

"Not yet. We just finished lunch a little over an hour ago." *That man could eat twenty-four seven if I let him get away with it.*

"Let's get moving then. I'll fix you something when we get back. Deal?"

"Deal."

For no particular reason, they headed west. They walked back and forth, covering over an acre before Ellen found a small fragment of bone. "Pretty slim pickings dear," she commented while offering up the tiny fragment.

"Not necessarily. We've got a lot of territory to cover before I agree to choose another site. The rain may have uncovered some wonderful bones. Don't be so quick to discount this site. Each year we manage to find something good enough to satisfy the university and more than cover expenses. Why should this year be any different?" *I hope we have good luck. We need that grant money.*

"I'm not that confident, John. There's something about this site that bothers me. It's like a premonition. It feels different somehow."

"Don't get all superstitious on me, Ellen. We're scientists and by virtue of our education and experience. . . logical. There's no logic in superstition."

"I didn't say I was superstitious, I said I had an uneasy feeling about this site. In case you didn't notice, they're two separate things all together. I'm going out tomorrow and check out that formation over there." Ellen pointed to a small hill to the east. It was a short walk from the camp. "Let's head back to camp. All this walking has made me hungry."

"Whatever you want dear. The light will be fading in a couple of hours anyway." They walked the short distance to the camp while continuing their search for fragments.

Jonathan was preparing the stove when he said, "Do you want the zucchini?"

"Sure," she answered. "Do we have any tomatoes? I'd love some sliced and wrapped with the zucchini and butter if there's no olive oil, oh yeah, and some garlic for a little punch."

So much for a light snack, he thought. "I'll get right on it."

They continued their conversation as Jonathan prepared the vegetables. "You want a beer?"

"Perfect. Just leave mine in the bottle. I don't need a glass out here," answered Ellen, ducking into the tent.

"Like I didn't already know that," he retorted over his shoulder. *I guess she figures after saying she doesn't need a glass for the thousandth time, I still don't remember.*

He went over to the cooler and returned to the tent with her beer. The bottle was cold, water dripping from bottle. Jonathan watched for a few moments as the drops collected on the front of Ellen's shirt. Disappearing through the tent flap, the sounds of cooking could be heard. It was only a short time later that the tantalizing aroma of tomato, zucchini and garlic filled the air.

As soon as he finished Jonathan brought the food. "Here you go," he said as he placed her plate and another cold bottle of beer on the table/desk.

She didn't hesitate to begin eating. Looking up from her plate she said, "This is fantastic dear. It sure hits the spot." She took a long pull from her bottle. The water dripping from the bottle ran down her cleavage. She let out what he considered to be a very seductive little squeal. He followed its trail until it disappeared from view.

"Slow down dear, you'll end up getting tipsy." Grinning slyly, he added, "I'd be forced to take advantage of you in your uninhibited state." *Or any other state for that matter* continued his unspoken conversation.

Draining the bottle as if answering a challenge, Ellen tossed it angrily beside her cot and said, "Service around here is terrible. Where's another beer? I want to see the manager immediately. I demand some form of compensation for the shabby service I'm receiving. I'm paying good money here and I haven't been getting any value for the money spent!"

Sensing her game was beginning; he rushed outside to get another beer. Now cloaked in his new role as a bad waiter, he approached with a beer and said, "I'm so sorry Miss. This one is on the house. Is there anything else that I might offer you?" He was boldly staring down the front of her shirt and licking his lips.

"As a matter of fact, there is," she continued as a sly smile curled the corners of her mouth. "I would like to know when this joint closes. I demand some personal attention, and I think that you're just the man to give it to me."

"I'd love to give it to you, Miss. How, I mean where would you like it?" He was still holding the bottle of beer.

"I'd love for you to give it to me right her. . . right now." Ellen grabbed him by the shirt and dragged him onto her cot. She straddled his prone body and downed the third beer in one long, continuous swallow. Grinding herself onto him, she added, "This better be good or I'm reporting this joint to the Better Business Bureau."

"I'll make sure that you're happy, just don't report me, Miss. I'll do anything that you say."

"That's exactly what I wanted to hear."

"You're one hot dame, lady. I want you to keep coming back here so I can give you my personal service all the time."

They stood only long enough for his pants to fall to the floor. He stepped out of them as he watched her rip her blouse off. Lying back on the cot she raised her hips so he wouldn't have any difficulty removing her pants.

After thirty minutes of soft caresses and carefully avoiding touching any of her hot spots directly, they fell together in a loving embrace. They shared each other intimately and ultimately finished the game she'd started.

Jonathan kissed her hair and whispered his heart felt love. He was barely able to drag himself over to his cot. Managing to throw the covers up over his shoulders, he slipped into a deep satisfying sleep.

CHAPTER THREE

THEY HAD ESTABLISHED PATTERNS OF behavior over the last twenty-five years – a protocol of sorts. Ellen would rise early and scout for promising sites. Jonathan would rise a short time later and prepare himself for the day. By the time he was cleaned and pressed, with breakfast just coming from the camp stove; Ellen would return to camp.

In spite of the previous night's adventurous game, she remained true to her pattern. This new day, like all the others, found Ellen dressed and out of camp just as the sun crested the horizon. Ellen really liked the tranquility of the early morning. It made the task more gratifying for her. She relished the sounds of nature and the solitude. Her focus seemed to intensify. A short distance ahead, she could see the object of her trek. It was a bleak, barren hillside, not that significantly different from the rest of the surrounding territory, save for the wash she'd seen last night.

The hillside was taller and steeper than it had appeared from the distance. She worked her way around the east side to see if there was a safe place to work her way up the loose soil. To her amazement, there was a ridge of soil that formed a small trail up the side of the hill. A crescent shaped gouge had been washed from the face, forming a curved recess into the east face. She was struck with the image of a scythe, broad at the base, curving away to a point at the tip.

The rising sun showed the wash to be deeper than expected. Ellen worked her way up the impromptu path to the opening. Looking up, she estimated that it was at least ten feet tall and curved up several more feet to the left. The top narrowed, until the two sides almost touched, as it curved away. The image of the scythe played at the back of her mind. Uncharacteristically, she felt a sense of foreboding. It was the same apprehensive feeling that she tried to explain to Jonathan the night before. Pausing in front of the opening, she shook off the foreboding sensation, steeling herself for the task ahead.

She stepped tentatively into the opening and tested the sidewalls with her pick. They were firm – almost rock in their solidity, yet the pick could pull the compacted soil away with some effort. The opening itself was nearly twelve feet wide by a quick estimate.

Cautiously, she edged her way deeper into the cleft. It must have washed out nearly thirty feet by her estimate. The deepening shadows caused the foreboding sensation to return. Ellen could not see the end of the passageway, even with the early morning light giving an ambient glow through the opening at the top of the passage. The cleft didn't provide the light she needed. She needed to take some photographs and do some measuring before she got too far into this.

Ellen took the flashlight from her pack and fingered the switch. The wash was interesting because they had never encountered any other geological formations similar to this anywhere in the region. She wondered why so much loose soil was moved in such a peculiar fashion.

Geologically, the area was pretty much the same for endless miles in every direction. The significance of this formation meant this was an anomaly worthy of careful study. Wondering if soil samples were necessary, she stared into the darkness.

With flashlight in hand, she moved farther into the opening. It actually widened after about twenty feet. The curve to the surface was not as severe this far in, and the morning light was able to penetrate. It infused the cave with a soft amber glow. It would eventually brighten as the sun rose even farther.

The walls were very solid this far in and Ellen realized that she was in no danger of their collapse. Still, she probed the walls for any loose material. It was still hard pack, yet it could be shoveled or picked away with some effort. Being able to access the inside of the hill like this was a unique opportunity. She didn't want to miss anything.

Now, at least thirty feet in, she noticed that the soil at the back was still loose and dark with residual moisture. Casting the light left and right, she checked to see if the soil was damp all over. The moisture appeared to be concentrated in a space roughly ten feet wide and eight feet to ten feet high.

She removed her backpack and untied her collapsible shovel. Ellen started to dig at the loose soil; mindful of the danger of the soil sliding in on her. Shoveling small amounts, she tossed them behind her in an arc, spreading soil out evenly across the floor of the passage. She didn't need to trip on a pile of dirt if she needed to make a hasty retreat. Jonathan had no idea of where she was and there would be no way to call out loud enough for anyone to hear. Safety first.

After ten or so scoops with no unexpected slides, she decided to take larger amounts with each pass. Still, the soil didn't slide so she was content that all would be fine. She glanced at her watch to see how long she'd been gone. It was getting late and Jonathan would probably have breakfast ready by now. Picking up her flashlight, she glanced at her watch a second time, judging her remaining time.

Ellen worked quickly with the skill of a surgeon. She had gained experience and ability with her twenty-five years of practice. She knew what she doing as the soil yielded to her continual efforts.

The soil gave way much sooner than she had anticipated. A slide started directly in front of her. With cat-like reflexes, she jumped back from the movement and was prepared to leave the passage if the soil started to pull from the walls. Nothing happened. It was only a small slide – barely moving a yard of material.

As Ellen picked up her shovel to continue, the sun had risen high enough to allow the light to stream in from the upper opening. The shadows stopped about half way up the wall. Searching for the best place to resume shoveling, she saw it at the edge of the light. Swinging the flashlight to center on what she'd seen, shock, excitement and fear planted her to her spot as if she were rooted like a tree. Ellen stood transfixed by what the slide had revealed. In all her experience she was not prepared for what was buried there.

Tentatively, Ellen stepped into the loose soil. She reached to touch it, but apprehension held her fast. She was afraid, yet professionally curious. Her mind was swimming with insane thoughts. She was – for the very first time in twenty-five years of experience – at loss for what she should do.

This unexpected situation had confounded her. Without taking her eyes from the back wall, she felt for the sidewalls as she backed out of the passage. Jonathan needed to see this. Maybe he'd heard or seen something similar in his travels before they had met, perhaps a story from a colleague. Between them and their combined experience, they could figure out what to do.

Once outside and down the hillside, she took off at a full run. Ellen was middle aged, but years in the field had kept her in top physical shape, not lean but muscular. She would make camp in no time. Morning sunlight splashed across her eyes as she ran. It went unnoticed as her thoughts focused intently on the situation.

CHAPTER FOUR

JONATHAN HAD RISEN ABOUT HALF an hour after Ellen. He mused over how excited she had been last night. Chuckling over her youthful zeal and his good fortune, he busied himself with emptying the remaining equipment and supplies from the truck before he started breakfast.

It wasn't his usual morning routine, but something told him that after last night's game, Ellen would not be back on time this morning. He enjoyed camp preparation as much as she enjoyed her early morning surveys. That was one of the reasons they made such a great team. Besides being in love and enjoying each other's company, they both liked to do separate tasks that made the camp set up move efficiently.

Everything that they required was laid out in Jonathan's typical fashion. There was water heating on the camp stove to do dishes after breakfast. He'd just filled a pitcher with the first pot of hot water so that he might finish a shave before breakfast.

He was just pouring water into the washbasin when Ellen came hurtling around the side of the tent. She was moving so fast that she couldn't avoid the collision. The table, washbasin, pitcher and Jonathan sprawled unceremoniously in a soggy heap on the ground. He was livid at the frantic, erratic assault to his morning routing.

Ellen grabbed at him frantically as he struggled to get back to his feet and out of the rapidly forming mud. Partially dragging him to his feet, she lost her grip on his wet shirt. He fell back, twisting to catch his balance and ended up face first in the mud. She covered her mouth with both hands and began to laugh. Jonathan was ready to explode with rage.

Ellen's laughter calmed him down as quickly as it had enraged him. The sound of her voice, her laughter was one of his greatest joys. He surveyed his wet and muddied clothes as he sat there, assessing the situation.

He must have made a proper sight, laying face first in the mud before his first cup of coffee. It was his only thought at the moment. Jonathan chuckled to himself. *We should have gotten a picture of this. And she was the one that had a sense of foreboding.*

Warily, he accepted Ellen's outstretched hand for a second time. He was not sure yet, if this was a joke or something more serious. The only things he required now were a clean change of clothes, some breakfast, and a plausible explanation.

He searched her eyes as he rose to his feet. This was not like the Ellen he knew. She seemed preoccupied or distant somehow. He wasn't sure, and it concerned him. She was clearly agitated about something. There was still a trace of excitement in her eyes – even now that she had calmed a bit. Was it fear or was it excitement?

They both moved to the tent so Jonathan could clean off the mud and change his clothes. There was a period of silence that hung in the air like a barrier. Jonathan didn't know just what to say or just how to say it.

Ellen broke the silence. "I'm sorry dear. I didn't mean to knock you down like that. I thought that you would be finishing breakfast, not trying to shave in the middle of the road. I'm really hungry you know." She knew the words sounded weak but she didn't want to allow the excitement to overcome her. Besides, she thought, *you should have seen yourself lying in the fresh mud like that. I'd have given anything for a camera.*

"What gives anyway? That was a little out of the ordinary wouldn't you say? After all, I spent my morning prepping the camp and you come tearing around the tent like your pants are on fire. We both changed our routines a little. The way I see it, your change was a bit too extreme." He knew he sounded angry, but then again, he was. . . just a little. *And this better be a damn good answer,* he mused, *or I'll dump you in the mud just to get even.* He chuckled silently to himself as he imagined her being extricated from the same prone, mud soaked position that he recently experienced.

"I said that I was sorry." Her eyes were pleading. "What more do you want from me?" she angrily complained. *I've got serious things to discuss and you revert to being a child. Oh the things women must endure at times.*

"Wait a minute. We don't need to fight over this. I only want to know why you were acting like that. It scared me. For a moment you seemed possessed. I've never seen you like that in all of our years together. We've been in some pretty tough scrapes over the years and you have always maintained a calm head. I'm sorry for getting angry. I guess it was a reflex action for having been half drowned and then covered in mud."

Ellen started laughing again at the image of Jonathan in the mud. She knew he hated things like that. It was one thing to get filthy dirty while doing your job, but quite another to be pushed into the mud. The dirt was the same, but the circumstances were very different.

She continued to laugh until Jonathan turned his back to her. Reaching out to comb her fingers through the back of his hair she soothed him. "I really didn't mean to laugh honey. The sight of you like that was just too comical. I can't remember the last time anything like that has happened to you. Maybe it never has." *And just think; I got to be the one to do it to you. Joy.*

The look on his face was unreadable. "Apology accepted, although you still hurt my feelings. . . and my pride. Now are you going to tell me what in blue blazes is going on here, or will I have to introduce you to the mud pits of Camp Crenshaw? I hear that they are quite therapeutic."

Ellen looked him up and down and decided he really meant it. She began to relate her experience so he would be brought up to speed. "You have always known how I enjoy my morning walks. It's part of who I am. Today started out no differently. I went east to see that formation. You know the one we saw last night. The one that I thought had been washed away by the rain."

"I remember. Did you get that far this morning?"

"It's more than that. I got there and the hillside was washed out like I thought. The rain had exposed a cave or something. There is a huge cleft in the side of the hill at the top. When you see it, it will remind you of a scythe. I'm not sure it's a cave, or was a cave, but the rest of the area is stone and inside is soil."

For his part, Jonathan did not interrupt so she wouldn't miss the slightest detail.

"Anyway, after I'd tested the soil by rapidly removing larger amounts, nothing happened. The loose soil at the back of the cave didn't slide. I assumed, while damp, it was dry enough to hold itself from randomly sliding when all of a sudden it started towards me. I sprang back and watched as the soil slid from the back, or what I thought was the back of the cave."

Jonathan stopped what he was doing when she said that. It was an unusual phrasing. It left something completely unsaid. He didn't interrupt her storyline; cutting the last of the vegetables as she proceeded.

"That's when I saw it sticking from the soil. Well not sticking from the soil as much as exposed by the slide."

Jonathan almost dropped the pan of eggs and vegetables when she told him what she'd seen. He couldn't have heard her correctly. Turning abruptly as he regained the balance of the frying pan, he asked her to repeat herself so that he could be sure of what he was hearing.

Ellen repeated her previous statement verbatim. She didn't elaborate beyond the original statement. Not a single word was added or subtracted.

Ellen had seemed out of control when she first thundered through the camp, but now that he fully understood the circumstances, he was convinced that things could have been a whole lot worse for him than a dip in the mud.

He was about to throw out the eggs and race to the hillside when she reached over and grabbed his arm to stop him. "Don't you dare think that you're going to waste valuable supplies just because you want to charge right off and investigate this thing in the cave? Whatever it is, it's been there for a while. It'll last until we finish these wonderful eggs. The veggies are a nice touch. Too bad we don't have any cheese. Did you pour the juice yet dear?"

This was the Ellen that he knew and loved. She was clearly in charge of her emotions again. Everything had its' proper time for her. It was now proper time to eat and relax. They might be gone for a very long time, and they needed a good meal to sustain themselves.

"We're supposed to be up here scouting for a dig site for the students. They'll be here at the end of the week. We've got to keep this secret. I love those kids but we can't trust them with anything like this," reminded Ellen. "Mmm, these are so good. Did you use olive oil this morning?"

"I just might agree with you about scouting if you would take me to see *it*," said Jonathan, looking up from his plate. "The oil was infused with chilies."

"Good choice on the oil. It adds a zest to all the flavors. I'm sorry honey. Let's leave right now. It's not that far, but I would prefer to drive if you don't mind?"

Looking up from his plate, he motioned that he was just going to finish the last couple of bites and be right there. Cramming the last of his meal into his mouth; he rose to join her. Walking briskly to catch up, he tossed the empty plate and silverware into the dishwater on his way to their truck. *Relax, she says, but only if I let you is what she means.*

They left shortly after packing some of their more specialized tools. Neither knew what they were facing, but they also didn't want to keep going back and forth all day. Planning what to do next made it seem like their first time out in the field to them. It was exhilarating.

Ellen particularly enjoyed the cloak and dagger sensation she derived from all of this. It took her mind away from speculating about what she had discovered or where it had come from.

Jonathan was more unperturbed about the whole thing. After all of the flap about the tyrannosaur, 'Sue,' several years earlier, he didn't trust anything to luck anymore. Deep in thought, he said, "First things first."

"What did you say dear?"

"Nothing. . . just thinking out loud. We need to see this treasure before we can assess what actions to take. There may be several options open, but we don't know yet."

"Well I do, I've seen it. You'll be just as surprised as I was. Trust me on this one. It may not turn into anything grandiose, but I'm putting my money on a major find."

Jonathan turned to look at her. Ellen reached over and squeezed his cheeks together so his lips pursed. She then pursed hers in a mock kiss. "I love you dear, but wait just a bit more. You'll see for yourself."

"We're here. Turn in right here and drive around over there," she pointed, "so the truck is from the road." They stopped the truck on the west side just short of the natural walkway up the hill.

They moved about their work wordlessly. After many years of loading and unloading, each knew their task and how to assist without getting in the way. In very little time the tools and equipment were sorted into practical piles. Each representing a specific utility or function. A couple of the piles were just stuff that was seldom used, but necessary, especially if you were a thousand miles from nowhere and you didn't have a particular item with you.

He turned and said, "All right. What next?"

"Now we unpack the backpacks and get over to my cave or whatever it is."

"I'll follow. . . you lead."

"You following automatically results from me leading. . . doesn't it?" *What an idiot. Sometimes I just don't know.*

"Not necessarily. I could be walking beside you the whole way."

Ellen smiled at him, shouldering her backpack. *Point well taken, but being at my side is not very likely today Jonathan my dear. Catch me if you can.*

"I think we're ready dear," said Jonathan. He grabbed her hand and gently squeezed it. She returned the squeeze with a little one of her own.

At the foot of the pathway, she said, "It isn't dangerous, but it is narrow enough that you'd slip if you lost concentration." She added, "I would think that it would be similar to falling into mud," and quickly stepped just beyond his reach, avoiding a pinch on her bottom. She set a brisk pace up the narrow path.

Jonathan followed her lead, ignoring the jibe. This was her show and he was only an eager spectator. They moved up the face the short distance to the wash. They were not more than fifteen feet above ground level. He thought Ellen was correct in her assessment of this path though. You could take a nasty little tumble if you weren't careful.

"Here we are," she said. "And it's about time too." *I just want some kind of resolution so I can get back to normal. You better come up with something good my love. This thing is already driving me crazy.* There was an edge of excitement in her voice as she looked back at him. Jonathan recognized the gleam in her eye. Ellen was like a bloodhound on the trail, nothing would deter her from her goal. She moved into the cleft to allow Jonathan to enter beside her. Having already removed her flashlight, she was fingering it in her right hand.

"Lead on my beloved," he said as his hand swept forward in a chivalrous gesture. She stepped into the passage. The mid-day sun helped fill the cleft with a wash of muted light. The sunlight had taken on the color of the hillside. It was quite pretty inside the cave.

They both moved slowly, examining the walls as they went. He was curious, and she was searching for clues as to what lay at the end of the passage or why it was there at all.

"I wonder why this hill washed out like this. I've never seen anything like it before. It was a strong rain, but it shouldn't have done anything like this. Did you notice any of the other hills this morning? Was there any sign of something like this elsewhere?" He never looked at her; he spoke while probing the walls with his pick.

"No dear. This is the only one that I know of. After I found this and what is back there," she gestured with her flashlight down the remaining length of the passage, "I really didn't go looking around much."

"Yeah, I guess you're right," he replied. "I'm really curious about this washout. It really baffles me." Shaking his head slightly, he moved forward with Ellen ahead of him.

"Watch your footing here," she said pointing her flashlight to the ground. This is where I threw all the soil I was shoveling. It's spread thinly all over. I wouldn't want you to slip." *Besides, without any mud, it wouldn't be nearly as funny.*

"Thanks. We're just about there aren't we?"

"We are here." The sunlight was not as bright as she had anticipated. Ellen turned on her flashlight as Jonathan was removing his from his pack.

In the ruddy light, Jonathan saw it, the thing that had caused all of Ellen's excitement. As the arc of her flashlight finally illuminated the back wall of the cave, he began to see details. He stood transfixed. His mouth hung open unprofessionally. Squinting, he tried to focus more clearly. Finally, he managed to fumble his own flashlight from the pack. Turning it on with equal clumsiness, he added its' light to Ellen's.

He was still dumbfounded.

They moved closer at the same instant. That motion seemed to break the spell they had been in. They looked at each other and, without additional words, continued towards the object.

"What in blue blazes is that?" he asked in hushed tones. His whisper was almost reverent.

She looked at him in bewilderment. She only shrugged her shoulders. Her hands went into the universal gesture of 'I don't know' at the same time. *That's why you're here you idiot. If I knew the answer, I'd have told you instead of dragging you back here.*

He removed his pack and fished through its contents until he acquired the proper tools. He moved onto the mound of soil that sloped in front of the object. As he leaned in and touched it, he jerked his hand away as if he had been electrocuted. He stared mutely at his hand.

The sudden motion had frightened her. "What's wrong?" she screamed.

"Nothing," he said examining his hand.

"Then why are you kneeling there rubbing your hand?" she demanded.

"Really honey, there's nothing wrong. This thing is warm. It scared me. I was expecting something stone cold and the warmth came as a sensory shock. Really, that's all."

Though he never stopped rubbing his hands though. It appeared as if he were trying to rid his flesh of something sticky that refused to be wiped off.

Ellen reached out to touch it herself. Tentatively she extended her arm, placing her palm fully onto it. She flinched in surprise. It really was warm. She backed up, bumping into Jonathan, who was still vigorously rubbing his hands, and shined her flashlight up to the curved open crest of the passage. The sunlight was dim, even for midday. The only way the sun could have warmed this thing was if it had direct light on it for several hours. Even then, it wouldn't be warm all the way down here at floor level.

"What do you make of this?" she asked.

"I'm not sure. After the initial shock wore off, I've been pondering several alternatives. Nothing seems to add up. I'm temporarily stumped." He stood up and brushed the cold soil from his pants. The disparity of temperature was disquieting.

"Maybe it's sitting on some kind of thermal vent or something. It would account for this very peculiar washout. Steam may have caused this curved crevice as it blew out all the surrounding soil."

"I don't know Ellen. There's no known thermal activity in this area. Besides, there's no evidence of a vent around here. That much steam would have been escaping for a long time. Someone would have spotted it before this. Still, it's a slim possibility at best. There has to be some other plausible explanation. I won't discount yours though. There's no trail of running water. Steam hitting this thing would condense and the water would run out the front of the cave. Look at the floor. A vent would probably have ripped a hole somewhere up through this floor. We don't have any idea how big this thing is, but moisture would have to work its way around it somewhere. There's no evidence of that happening."

Ellen looked a little crest fallen.

"Right now, it's as good an idea as any," he was quick to add. "We can speculate and work on other theories as we proceed. Agreed?"

Jonathan returned with his backpack and a small battery-operated lantern. The light was bright and it filled the area. They could start working without worrying for a while. The fresh batteries would last almost four hours.

He began to clear away as high as he could reach. Ellen cleared the debris and worked sideways to get an idea of how big this thing was. It was after about two hours that they had finally removed all the loose soil and were chipping away at the rock-like hard pack on the walls of the crevice.

Without a wheelbarrow, they began to haul the loose soil to the front of the cave and tossed it down the hillside a shovel full at a time. It would be two more hours before they finished. As slow as the work was going, the end result was worth the effort.

From best guesstimates, they both figured it to be about ten feet wide and at least twelve feet high. They stood back to inspect their handiwork. They were both impressed with what they saw.

They broke for a late lunch. Food and the brief rest sustained them for the rest of the afternoon.

CHAPTER FIVE

Steve Groves assembled everyone in the quad. As a teacher's aide for Dr. Crenshaw, he was responsible for preparing the equipment and the students for this year's field trip. They knew they were going to the Bad Lands and were excited. The conversations were light and centered on the pending trip as they waited for Steve to begin.

Dr. Crenshaw always selected the student with the highest test scores, field knowledge and practical application to be the team lead. Steve was a postgraduate student and had been one of the brightest students Jonathan had ever taught. Choosing him for the second time to lead the field trip was an easy decision.

Steve checked the list of all the students who were scheduled for the field trip. They were preparing for the long drive to the Crenshaw's campsite. He had previously handed out a list of supplies that each student would be responsible for acquiring on their own. It made them more responsible with their tools when they invested their own money in them.

There were ten students in all. Each wanted to come for their own personal reasons, but the common bond was that they all loved dinosaurs and searching for fossils. That was the primary pre-requisite for the Drs. Crenshaw. They didn't want to be babysitting a bunch of young kids who wanted to come fossil hunting for a good time. The Crenshaw's didn't do this to entertain anybody. What they required was dedicated young men and women who understood that a little hard work meant nothing if it was a labor of love.

"Does everyone understand their assignments?" Steve finally

asked when he finished his review of the papers. "Remember, you've had two weeks to collect your supplies. The list I just gave you is only a final check against what you should already have. Study it carefully against your supplies and make sure you've missed nothing. There is nowhere to get decent supplies once we've reached the site. Do I make myself clear?"

They all indicated that they understood. A hand went up, but then went back down again. There were a few puzzled expressions and tentative questions that were not asked. Each of the ten understood their individual assignments.

After pointing to a couple of the students who looked as if they were about to ask a question, and getting no response, Steve decided to end the meeting. "I guess this concludes our business. Remember, everyone is to meet at the Student Union because we leave on Friday morning at 6:00AM sharp. We can only wait ten minutes. Anyone later than 6:00AM should not bother to come, because the rest of us will be gone. Please contact me if anyone is missing any of their tools. I can direct you to the best sources for anything on your list. I'll be in my dorm room for another hour if you need some assistance. That's all then, I'll see you Friday morning at 5:50AM. Bring all your supplies. Should you forget them, it tells me that you're really not that interested. We will not wait until you retrieve the forgotten items. You've had two full weeks to prepare."

When he returned to his room he found that a telegram had been delivered. The old saying about only bad news arrives by telegram rattled around in his head as he stared at the envelope, but didn't actually begin to read it. He opened it apprehensively, and read. After a brief scan, he shouted, "Yes!" He waved his arms and the paper in the air. Looking at it again, he crumpled it to his lips and kissed it. "This is it! I knew it would happen someday! I've worked so hard and this is the big payoff!"

"Hey! Keep it down up there," an angry voice yelled up the stairwell. "People are trying to study. Have a little courtesy."

Kevin Henderson came into the room to check out all the

commotion. "Hey Steve, what's with all the noise? You don't say two words all week, and now you're the town crier. Is everything okay?"

"Is everything okay?" exclaimed Steve. "Look at this!" Thrusting the telegram into Kevin's face, he waved it back and forth while Kevin strained to catch a glimpse of it.

Snatching it from Steve's hand in mid wave, Kevin began to read. "Wow! This is big! We need to party tonight! I've got a couple of young ladies all lined up. Just say the word and we're out of here."

"I can't believe it. The Crenshaw's want me to head up the dig! This is so good. I don't even have my doctorate yet. Oh man, it would be so cool if we found something big. I could write my own ticket. It would mean the fast track to anywhere!"

Kevin removed Steve's hands from the front of his shirt. "I know you're happy and everything, but you don't have to rip my clothes off."

"Sorry, Kevin." Steve apologized as he attempted to brush smooth the freshly wrinkled shirt. "I'm just so excited."

"Really? I hadn't noticed at all."

"Call the girls. You did say you had girls didn't you?"

"You heard that? I couldn't tell if you were even listening. Yes I have two girls."

"We are out of here! Where do you want to go? This is a major celebration. It has to be just right."

"Have you been to that new place on the other side of the campus?

"No I haven't been there yet. I heard that it's great though. On Wednesdays they have live jazz."

"Steve, this is Wednesday! I don't remember the name, but I have a card on my nightstand. It's stuck under the edge of my lamp. You can't miss it. I'll go downstairs and call the girls. Call and make reservations for 8:00 p.m. That should be more than enough time to put this thing in gear."

Kevin ran down the stairs to use the payphone while Steve fell backwards onto his bed. He held the telegram up at arm's length and grinned his biggest, proudest grin.

Steve went to the payphone at the end of the hallway and quickly punched in the number. As the phone rang, he thought about the trip and all that it meant.

"Blue Parrot... May I help you?"

"Yes. I'd like to make reservations for four at 8:00 o'clock tonight. Do you have anything available? Non-smoking."

"We can seat your party at 8:00 sir. Name please."

"Groves."

"I have it taken care of Mr. Groves."

Mr. Groves, Steve mused. *I could really get used to the sound of that.* "Thank you," he said as he hung up the phone.

Kevin returned to the room as Steve lay on his bed thinking about everything happening so quickly. "We set?" he asked.

"All taken care of. . . I hope you have money. I can't cover all four of us?"

"I'm cool man. The girls are excited. We'll drive over around 7:00 to pick them up. We can talk a bit before we leave. Who's playing anyway?"

"She said it was a new trio for them, but they are supposed to be very good. They're a fusion group with rock overtones and jazz underpinnings. I got seats away from the music so we can talk, but they're supposed to be close enough to get the good music. Does the girl I'm getting like to dance? Girls tend to like rock better than jazz. This sounds like the perfect group tonight."

"More than just dance buddy. You're going to be one lucky dude tonight."

Steve sat at the edge of his bed contemplating what Kevin had said. It was going to be a very good night indeed. "Oh my God," he said as he thought, *I don't have anything to wear. I need to do some ironing. I should have a clean shirt somewhere.* He began to rummage through his drawers until he found just the right shirt. There was a good jacket hanging in his closet. It was casual enough to wear to the club without looking stuffy. Finding a freshly washed pair of jeans finished the ensemble.

CHAPTER SIX

THE CRENSHAW'S BEGAN A NEW day at the site. Yesterday, after the morning's excitement, they had driven into town and sent a telegram to Steve Groves. Steve would oversee the dig and manage all aspects of it, from the camp set up to organizing the search teams. He had the knowledge and the experience. It was time he had his trial by fire. They knew he was up to the challenge. It would provide them with the much-needed cover to proceed on their own, all the while accomplishing the work that the school was funding. It was a masterful plan.

Working quietly, they were each lost in personal thoughts. Suddenly Ellen dropped a shovel full of soil across Jonathan's feet. Giggling a little, she said, "Sorry sweetheart. I was distracted."

"What could possibly be more distracting than this?" he said, waving his shovel at the metal monstrosity before them.

"I was just thinking that Steve ought to be receiving the telegram about now. There's no way he would have gotten it yesterday. I was just wondering how he'd react. . . that's all."

"He's pretty level headed dear. He's sitting in his dorm room right now making final plans for the trip. There's not a carefree bone in his body. He's rock steady, you can count on that." Jonathan puffed his chest a bit when he spoke about Steve. He'd chosen paleontology as his career path and Jonathan was proud to assist in any way possible.

"Now that we've cleared out a lot of this debris, I think I know why this has washed out the way it has. This definitely was a cave for millions of years. I'll bet it hasn't been filled with soil for more than two or three thousand years, if that much."

"I think you're right Jonathan. This soil is compressed but it's not what you'd expect. It should be solid rock, just like everything else around here."

"If I'm right, we should be able to dig our way around to the left or right by early next week. The only problem is going to be what we will do with all the soil we'll be removing."

He picked up his shovel while contemplating the problem and began the arduous task of removing as much of the soil packed across the face of this thing as he could. He decided to work to his right. The passageway was wide at the back of the cave, but the huge metal slab was exposed where it was closest to the perceived wall at the right.

Three long hours had passed before he stopped for lunch. Jonathan had removed several yards of earth and was making excellent headway. It was strenuous, yet invigorating. The damp soil of the hillside would serve as cover for now. No one would really know how much had been removed by the rain. They should be able to throw it straight down the hill for at least two days. As the sun slowly dried everything out, it wouldn't be too obvious what they were doing.

Once the amount of damp, darker soil exceeded what the sun had dried, they would have to develop another plan. Jonathan held out hope that he could get the majority of the work done before everything outside was too dry. It would mean much less soil to bag and cart if we broadcast it down the edge of the path.

"What's for lunch today?" asked Ellen.

"I'm gonna throw a couple of sandwiches together and a quick soup. I've got some chicken stock and noodles. All I need to do is add the vegetables."

"Sounds delicious," she replied. "What kind of sandwiches?"

"We have a real nice smoked ham on Jewish rye with baby Swiss or I could make grilled cheese. I have Smoked Gouda or Havarti."

"I'll have my grilled cheese with Havarti. I know how much you like Smoked Gouda. I don't want to eat it all. We probably can't get any out here anyway."

"I'll ask Steve to bring some. There's no need to deprive yourself of your favorite cheese."

"Good point. I'll take the Havarti today and the Smoked Gouda tomorrow."

The whole meal took about thirty minutes to prepare. Jonathan was a whiz at the camp stove. The soup was a perfect accent to the sandwich. The portions were filling; yet small enough to keep from getting over full and lethargic. They cleaned everything up and returned to the site.

"Hey, look at this! I think I've reached a corner!" Jonathan called. His voice was edgy with excitement and the exertion of his labor. The excitement was always evident, no matter how tired he was.

Ellen rushed back from the entrance to see what he had found. "You were right! This was the closest corner after all! Now we should really be making some headway."

She bent down, with flashlight in hand, to inspect the corner more closely. Reaching her hand in around the corner, she brushed soil from the newly exposed surface. Even this completely buried side was warm. The mere touch of it made her extremely uncomfortable. Her flesh crawled with the sensation of touching warm metal freshly excavated from the cold earth. It was eerie and she felt as if someone (or something) was watching her. She didn't like it.

Ellen had her arm in the opening she had created. She was clearing soil in a sweeping arc from her elbow, exposing as much surface as possible without using her shovel. She was almost in a little farther than her elbow when she stopped abruptly. Ellen didn't jerk her arm out of the small opening, but she did give Jonathan a very peculiar look.

"What's wrong? I know that look. Are you all right?"

"I'm fine. There's something on the surface of this thing. I can feel it. It just surprised me. . . that's all. We need to get this thing cleared out. I don't like this thing. It scares me. It doesn't belong here, yet here it is!" Her tone was starting to get anxious. Not much would push either of them over the edge right now.

"Okay. Can you describe what you feel?" asked Jonathan calmly.

"It's a texture of sorts. I can't tell exactly what I'm feeling, but it is definitely a texture or a pattern?"

They were both tired from all of the work. Besides the strain of the physical work, there was the additional stress of the situation. The two of them were doing the work of the crew they would normally have had. This task really made them feel their age at times.

Jonathan moved in at the corner and started bringing the soil down in large scoops. He wanted to get a large enough space around the corner so that they might at least be able to get in to take a look. He caught his second wind as his shovel moved the earth relentlessly. Large chunks of hard pack fell like snowflakes from the wall.

Ellen was having trouble keeping up with him. She'd gone back to get the wheelbarrow and when she returned, he was standing, buried in about a foot of loose soil and pieces of hard pack. "Slow down dear. I don't want you to hurt yourself. We have the time to get this done properly. Just relax."

"I can't Ellen. I feel the same way you do about this... this thing. Right now I wish that you'd never discovered it. What's more irritating than anything else is that I'm driven to discover what it is. It's my professional curiosity. The irony is that at the same time I want to run away, I want to stand and discover. It's an interesting paradox, wouldn't you say? We have no way of knowing what we have here. I don't saying that the initial prospects don't seem all that inviting."

"I thought that it was just me," sighed Ellen heavily. "I'm so glad to hear you say that. I was sure that you thought that I was crazy for being afraid of a metal slab, or box, or whatever this damn thing is. . . even if it was buried in living rock and had no reason for being there."

Each maintained an even pace for another hour before Jonathan finally declared that the opening around the corner was large enough for what he wanted. He had successfully cleared enough room for them both to stand facing the newly exposed side. There was about four feet of space in all. They could use their flashlights with enough room to examine the surface carefully.

As excited as they both were, they paused for a quick snack and some cool water. The rest, and food and water were revitalizing. The impromptu picnic was exactly what they needed. The dirt was cool and soft, providing a comfortable seat. Besides, they both wanted a clear head when they returned for a closer look at the newly exposed side.

Jonathan leaned with his back against the cave wall, his hands comfortably holding his raised knee. His head was resting against the wall. He looked peaceful with his eyes closed and his chest raised and lowered with the steady rhythm of his breathing. Ultimately, with a heavy sigh of resignation he said, "I'm ready dear. . . how about you?"

Ellen had been ready for several minutes, but she didn't want to rush Jonathan. She took comfort in watching him relax and ponder the possibilities. "I'm ready dear," she responded. She was in no rush. The tension had been diminished, but it had not been eliminated. Anxiety held her hostage to dreams of glory and fear.

They both moved into the opening. Ellen went in first; it was her discovery. She shined her light down towards the area she had felt earlier. The whole exposed portion of the surface was covered with strange markings. They were beautiful and intricately carved. Both cleared soil from the carvings with their hands and brushes. They looked at each other in amazement.

This thing, now a two-sided chunk of metal, was even more of an enigma than before. One unadorned, highly polished surface and one extremely ornate surface only served to fuel new speculations. Many thoughts raced through their minds as they looked from the markings to each other and back again.

They each started to speak at the same time, and Jonathan put up his hand and asked, "Would you like to go first?"

"I don't know what to think dear. My head is spinning with possibilities. This is getting out of control." *I sure hope you have something magic to say or I'm going to go crazy and you just might join me on my journey.*

"Let's just step away from this and take time to regroup. We need to calm down a bit and get back to some basic investigative practices. We're running blind here and it only compounds our anxiety and frustration."

"I'll buy that. Move out of the way so I can get out of here," she said, nudging him in the leg. *Well it wasn't magic, but it'll do just fine.*

"These marking are unlike anything I've ever seen. Yet when you think about them, they seem familiar."

Sitting in silence, they considered the possibilities. Ellen spoke first. "They remind me of pictographs. Perhaps even hieroglyphics?"

"That's it. That's what was at the fringes of my thoughts, but I couldn't put a name to it. You've done it dear. Congratulations."

"Jonathan?" she asked tentatively. "Do you suppose this is a language?"

"I wouldn't discount that probability. They're very ornate. It's a very strong possibility dear."

"Why did I ever wander over here in the first place?" After long moments Ellen continued, "We're done for the night," she said with conviction. "Let's go back to camp and relax. I need to unwind. This tension is getting to me."

"Consider it done dear. Why don't you sit here and rest while I gather up all the supplies? It won't take that long."

"That would be great dear," she responded. Now that she was committed to resting, her body relented to the physical and mental strain. The tiredness washed over her as she sank to the floor in almost total exhaustion.

CHAPTER SEVEN

S TEVE RETURNED TO HIS ROOM after a thoroughly enjoyable evening. Kevin was coming up the stairs behind him, still humming the last piece of music they'd heard before leaving the club.

"Thanks Kevin. Those were two very nice young ladies. I had a great time; they helped make this celebration special. I think that they had a good time too."

"I'm sure they did. They think that you're going to be famous. I have to admit I am a little jealous. Dinosaurs are so cool." Kevin studied him from head to toe for a moment before he shouted, "YOU ARE THE MAN!" and then he high fived Steve.

"Come on, lay off," said Steve as his face and neck tuned crimson.

"No, I mean it pal. You could have had anything you wanted tonight."

"All I want is some sleep. I have to get up early tomorrow and make new plans. This is going to change everything I had scheduled. I haven't even started yet and already it means more work."

Each drifted away, Kevin into their room and Steve down to the study room to make additional plans before going to bed. *I can't get caught up in all this. I'll be a legend in my own mind. Don't be a fool. Take the praise, but don't let it go to your head. This is going to be more difficult than I'd imagined. It's what I've wanted for all these years and now I can see how much more it really is and how easy it is to fall prey to self-delusion.*

Opening his notepad, Steve began to make additional notes in preparation for his new task as team leader. It was 3:00 am before he went to bed.

"Ellen? Do you remember that Steve and the crew will be here Friday?"

"How could I forget? I was hoping to be farther along than this!" She was letting herself become agitated. "What have we gotten ourselves in to?"

In the three days since Steve's telegram, the Crenshaw's had completely excavated the face and the right side of what was shaping up to be a metal box instead of a slab. They had worked their way around the first corner and had reached the next corner of the right side. The top was now evident, but not yet cleared off. As of yet, neither could determine which section represented the front or the back. They only knew for sure was that it was a rectangle, not a cube.

During lunch breaks and short rest periods, Ellen studied the markings on the surface. They were intricate and beautifully rendered. They reminded her of hieroglyphs the more she studied them. She had never studied Egyptian art or writing, but these markings seemed familiar in a way. Jonathan had the same feeling about them; however, he was reluctant to put words to his thoughts. He knew so little about the box at this point, and he didn't want to make any false assumptions. He never made ungrounded, unsubstantiated postulations.

"Jonathan, can you come over here for a minute? I want you to see this. I've found a repeating image."

When Jonathan came around the corner, Ellen was busily brushing away soil from the grooves formed by some of the images. He asked, "What is it dear? What have you found?"

"Look at this." She pointed to a large image that repeated itself at least five times on the surface in front of her. "I haven't even checked the entire surface yet. I've looked at this for a couple of days now and all of a sudden there they were." She pointed to the other locations as she spoke.

"I see. Do you think it's some kind of language? These are clearly pictographs. There are too many other symbols here for this to be exclusively pictographs. Maybe they're nothing more than ornamentation, you know, like the drawings around ancient Greek vases and such." Shaking his head in new bewilderment, he continued. "This puzzle is becoming more complex the more soil we remove. Let's get back to work. We've got a lot to do before the kids arrive tomorrow."

"That's a good point, but something's nagging me. There's more to this than simple decorations. I want to stop early tonight. I'm going to take some photographs of this side of the box," she said. "I want the images to overlap like a series of panoramic photographs, so I can create an entire image. I can study them at night. Somewhere, there's a clue in these images. It'll take some time, but I'll figure it out."

"Good idea. It's getting late and we need to meet the crew before ten o'clock tomorrow morning. They have a map to the diner in town. I'll go alone if you'd like to stay and study your photos."

"That's tempting, but I'll go in with you. I need to get some supplies anyway. It won't look right if both of us aren't there, we have always met the kids together. We need to congratulate Steve properly." Ellen placed the palm of her hand on Jonathans' chest and smiled coquettishly.

"Fair enough… I was only trying to help, you know that." *I hate when she does that. She knows damn well I can never refuse her when she smiles like that. Someday I'm going to just say no… but not today.*

"I know dear. Thank you." She kissed him on the cheek, letting her hand linger on his chest for a moment more before she went to get her camera. She was anxious to get her photos before the light was too dim.

Jonathan busied himself with cleaning up the tools and staying out of Ellen's way. He made a feeble attempt at leveling the floor of the cave, but his heart wasn't in it. . . and it wasn't necessary anyway.

Ellen was placing the photos on the ground next to her, as she created the photo mosaic of the wall. She stopped shooting to rummage through her backpack for a marker. Quickly deciding on a system, she numbered the edges of the photos. She' be able to reassemble the entire map if the photos became mixed.

Dawn arrived at least three hours earlier than anticipated as far as Jonathan was concerned. Ellen was already up and out of the tent before he rose. He looked around the tent to see if she was there just as she rounded the corner. "Is that for me?" she cheerily inquired.

"Punctual as always my love, were you up at the cave?"

"Not this morning. I don't want that on my mind when we meet Steve and the kids."

"I don't blame you. Let's get an early start so we can scout a couple of places for them to begin their summer of fun."

"That's a great idea. It's better than leaving them to search for themselves. They could end up too close to us and then where would be?"

"Let's go farther down the road. Should we need to make any trips into town, then we wouldn't be passing by their site all the time." Jonathan waved his fork in the general direction of the road as he swallowed a last mouthful of food.

"Anytime you're ready dear. Breakfast was great. The ham wasn't too salty and had just the right touch of smokiness."

"As soon as we're done with the dishes we can head out. Two hands make the work go faster," he said rising from the table.

"What? And ruin these lovely hands. Dishes are man's work. My job is to look as ravishing as possible at all times."

"Well my love, if you must know my deepest secrets: I am never turned on more than having a woman doing dishes with me."

"How can I refuse such an offer?" she laughed. "I'll dry."

CHAPTER EIGHT

T HE CRENSHAW'S PULLED INTO A parking spot in front of the diner around 9:30AM. There was plenty of time to shop for supplies and meet the kids. Ellen crossed the road and went over to the General Store. She stocked up on batteries and other sundries. She even remembered to pick up an extra bar of soap.

The clerk was helping her load the supplies in the truck when she saw the caravan of students pull up to the diner. Tipping the clerk for his help, she rushed off to greet them. *Well the adventure begins,* she thought as she made her way towards the diner. Jonathan was just coming out of the diner as she approached.

"How was the drive Steve?" he asked. "No problems I hope."

"No problems at all Dr. Crenshaw. We made good time."

Ellen hugged him and patted his back. "I'm just glad that you're all here safe and sound. It looks to be a great summer. Jonathan… Dr. Crenshaw and I have found some promising sites to investigate. We want your opinion on them."

All thirteen of them settled into the diner. The conversation was animated and congratulations were handed around. Nancy brought Steve a cupcake with "boss man" written on top. Everyone had a good laugh. Steve took it in stride and laughed louder than anyone. Too soon, it was time to get started again.

There was room enough in the truck, so Steve road along with the Crenshaw's. The rest followed closely. He had many questions about what the potential sites may yield. His mind was racing faster than he could speak. It was important to him that he made a credible first show as site leader.

"What makes you think that we have found anything Steve?" probed Ellen.

"Well actually I'm sort of hoping that you haven't found anything. I was afraid that you may have unearthed something really good and then I would take over and. . . oh damn. Look, I'm really sorry. I know you guys aren't like that. I just wanted this first dig to be my sole endeavor. I didn't mean to imply that you would set me up for success. Hell, I'm so embarrassed now that I don't know what I mean. Look, I'll shut up now and then you won't have any more reasons to throw me off of the team."

"Don't be silly, Steve," replied Ellen. She squeezed his hand reassuringly. "We know and trust you and your capabilities. If we thought that we would have to set you up for success then we wouldn't be the team leader. This is your *baby* from start to finish. We don't want to hear any more talk about you being embarrassed. We're not offended in the least. We were your age once and can still remember the thrill of our first dig. It's just the first time jitters. Shrug it off."

"Thanks, Dr. Crenshaw. I appreciate all that you two are doing. I just wish that there was some way that I could repay this debt."

"Well Steve," said Jonathan, "maybe there will be an opportunity for you to help us out in the near future. We could then call the debt paid in full. You know, just one colleague helping another. You can start by calling us Ellen and Jonathan before we go any further. You are soon to be our peer. It wouldn't feel right to us to have you still referring to either of us as Dr. Crenshaw."

"Thank you, Doctor, I mean Jonathan. It'll take some time to get used to this. Not a minute goes by that I'm not learning something new. It's already been an experience. The others seem to treat me differently. How did you handle that on your first time?"

"Well I can't speak for Ellen, but I took it in stride. You're an affable young man. Accept the fact that people will treat you differently from now on. You're in charge. Act like it, but don't lord it over people. A lot of first timers think that yelling or demanding is the only way to show authority. It's a big mistake. I can guarantee that it's the sure road to failure. Your team will respect you for fair treatment and despise you if you become an egomaniac. Just be Steve Groves and you'll do just fine."

"That's sound advice. I should have known that intuitively from being around the two of you for these last few years. You've always treated each team member as an equal. There were a few times that I disagreed with you, but you were always fair with everyone. No one ever got any special treatment. I remember it all now. You've been teaching by example. Maybe you should have hit me with a two by four to get me to notice it sooner. Thanks again."

"Are we almost there? These areas seem to be the kind of place that we would normally look for."

"As a matter of fact, Steve, one of the places we thought you might wish to start is around the next bend. The road forks there and the dirt road to the left had some interesting looking formations, although Jonathan and I haven't gone to any of the places. We scouted them from the truck as we drove by. We didn't want any previous knowledge about the area to filter your decision."

The truck rumbled to a stop on the rocks and sand. The slowing motion brought him back to reality. "This is nice," Steve said while appraising the area with the same critical eye that the Crenshaw's had taught him. "There could be some good stuff here. I don't know if you could have picked a better spot. Look at those fragments over there. He ran over to a small pile of washed out debris.

Ellen and Jonathan looked at each other. The rain had exposed as much in this area as it had where they were working. It was only dumb luck that Ellen had stumbled on to her discovery. Had they been in an area like this, they would have had no reason to leave and explore elsewhere. It instilled a new vigor to continue, despite the apprehensions of the box and its eerie warmth.

"Come over here you guys. Take a look at this!" He was very excited at a fragment he was holding in his hand.

As Jonathan walked up Steve handed him the small leg bone and asked, "Is that what I think it is?"

"That depends on what you think it is. Tell me and then I'll answer you."

"I think it's the leg bone of a baby raptor. Look at the knee joint. This could have come right from a textbook photo."

"That's exactly what it is. It's quite a nice find. It's good to see you have a good memory."

"Thanks. I wonder what else is just lying about." Steve began to laugh.

"What's so funny?" asked Ellen.

"Nothing really, I was just imagining what it would be like if all fossils were just lying out in the open like this one." He held the miniature leg bone before his eyes and continued, "I got a visual of a forest of leg bones with rib cages as shrubs and . . . well you get the picture. Excuse me for a minute. I want the others to see this. The new people will get their first taste of fossil hunting."

"Sure Steve, go ahead. We understand your excitement," said Ellen.

"Thanks, you two. I can't tell you how much I appreciate this." Steve called the rest of the students. "Come on over here! You have to see this!"

They all came and formed a semi-circle around Steve.

"What's up?" asked one of the female members. Steve remembered that her name was Janet B something or other.

"This was just lying here on the ground. It's a leg bone from a baby raptor." He passed it around so all could see it and touch it. Smiles erupted on everyone's faces. They'd all handled fossils in class, but this was the first in field experience for some of them. It was very exciting.

"Not all fossils are this easy to find, but once you've trained your eyes, you can find treasures under your feet almost every time you look down. I don't want to give anyone the wrong impression, but if you have patience and practice, small finds like this sometimes develop into larger more significant discoveries."

Now there's an understatement if I ever heard one, thought Jonathan.

Ellen mused silently, *from the mouths of babes.*

"How long do you search before you give up on a site," asked Janet?

"Sometimes you work a site for days with little or no hope, then out of the clear blue, a real find. Other times you never give up and you never find anything. It's the luck of the draw.

"This area is a real treasure trove of fossils. You can search almost anywhere in this area of the country and turn up something. I know this doesn't answer your question precisely, but I personally don't see the need to give up on any site. There's always something to learn, even when you come up empty handed."

Jonathan remained silent, but was thinking, *Well said Steve. Ellen and I are going to be very proud of you. You keep up this pace and you'll find a place for yourself in paleontology.*

"Anyway, I just thought that you'd be interested in seeing the leg bone. We should have a good summer. With luck, this will be the first of many discoveries. Let's get the trucks in here and get the camp set up. You all have your assignments. If anyone has a question, just ask. I'm available."

When Steve turned back, Ellen said, "That was wonderful. You did a fine job."

"That's right Steve. Keep up the good work. It'll take you places," added Jonathan. "We should probably head out. You've got a lot of work ahead of you this evening. We'll only be in the way."

"No you won't," implored Steve. He was apprehensive about assuming the reins. "Why don't you stay for supper? We can go over some of the plans that I've been formulating."

"Excuse me Steve," interrupted one of the students. "We can't seem to find three of the bed rolls. Do you know where they're packed?"

"Sorry," he apologized. "They need my help. I'll only be a moment."

They both knew better and blended into the background. Steve wouldn't even notice that they weren't standing there anymore. Unnoticed and unmissed, they went to their truck.

A couple of students came over and helped load some burlap bags into the Crenshaw's truck. Jonathan wished them a successful summer and closed his door. "Tell Steve we said goodbye. . . when he's not so busy. There's no need to interrupt him just now. Wait a while."

"Sure thing Dr. Crenshaw," said one of the students. The other one checked the tailgate and tapped twice on the roof. Jonathan understood the all-clear signal and drove off.

Steve was deeply involved with his team as the Crenshaw's left. The decision had been made to work this site, and he plunged right into the task and never looked back.

Returning to the camp, the students told Steve that the Crenshaw's had given their warm wishes for success and good luck and that they would be back to check on his progress a couple of times a week.

"Thanks," he said. Steve stopped long enough to look around and see if the Crenshaw's were gone or just leaving. He noticed that the dust raised by their truck was almost completely settled. It was just as well; he was too busy to be with them anyway.

With ten people setting up camp, Steve was amazed that it didn't take any time. The natural flood lines were easy to follow. Equipment and tents were all placed on high ground, even though there was no rain in the immediate forecast.

Steve walked around the campsite; pleased that things had gone so smoothly. Six of the team members had been on last summer's dig. Their experience helped the others transition into a camp rhythm rather quickly.

"Everyone, gather around please," Steve called as he motioned everyone him. "We're not going to start searching for anything until tomorrow. Tonight we're going to party. It's been a long hard drive and we need to unwind. I know that I want to work some of the road kinks out of my spine. You all probably feel the same. The camp looks great. You've all done a fine job. Let's have some fun."

Steve grabbed his duffle bag. Rifling through the contents, he didn't smile until he felt the object of his search. Removing his hand from the bag, he raised it in triumph. He revealed a cold bottle of champagne. A second package revealed enough glassed for everyone.

He popped the champagne and filled all the glasses. With his glass raised in a toast, Steve said, "I know this is premature, but whether we find anything or not, we'll have made a success of this summer by working as a team and doing something that we all love. There's nothing like sharing a good time with friends." Cheers went up as they raised their glasses in the toast to their potential success.

Steve felt this was a positive start. He hadn't bought their friendship with the champagne, but he had sent a clear message that he understood. He hoped that they would realize that just last week he was one of them.

The champagne bottle was empty. Someone had turned on a radio and the music was playing softly. Steve had set each of them a task that brought the camp's final details together quickly. A neat and efficient camp made the work easier. It was the small details that helped. Little things like having a battery-operated lamp from the post that held up the curtains for the latrines helped at night. The isolated location meant no ambient city light. It was more than just dark at night; it was pitch black.

Steve could hardly wait until dark. He loved the night sky. The stars were truly magnificent. You could see the entire night sky as God had intended it to be seen. The Milky Way looked like a river of light as it snaked through the night sky. He knew Ellen loved the sunrise, but his passion was the night sky. This area gave him a sense of being connected with the universe.

As the sun began to set, the camp setup was completed. Supper was on the camp stoves and the music had been turned up. People were beginning to dance and laughter could be heard here and there. Steve looked out over the area that tomorrow would be the dig site. He could barely contain his excitement.

Watching as the last few dishes were cleaned and dried, Steve joined the festivities. Relaxing a bit, he wanted to set a deadline for when the party was to end. Everyone needed to be fresh and ready for the work that the new day would bring. Tomorrow was his big day. He'd gotten a good start with the champagne, but now he must show them the leadership that was requisite.

As the darkness deepened, he gave the end of day assignments and wished everybody a good night's sleep. They would be up early tomorrow and needed to be rested. He took a final look at his beloved night sky before he entered his tent.

Lying alone in his tent was a new experience for Steve. He'd always had someone else in the tent with him. There was always that conversation that ended a day. Now he felt the solitude pressing in on him. Leadership at any level was lonely. People needed you to be resolute and ready to face any situation. Steve wasn't over dramatic in his thinking, just rational.

Trying to find sleep, he wondered how Ellen and Jonathan were doing. This was a monumental decision for them. He wasn't sure that he'd ever get used to calling them by their first names.

Unaccustomed to being alone, Steve finally went back outside to spend a little time stargazing. He sat in a chair just outside the tent and leaned back heavily and rested his head on the chair's canvas back. The entire night sky spread out before his eager eyes. These were the things he remembered most about digs.

This was not unlike Ellen's morning walks. The night sky cleared his head and allowed him to focus his thoughts. Stargazing helped him focus on the important things in life, and the beautiful sky and nature's bounty was his reward. Family and friends were the real wealth of the world. Of course, money and fame wouldn't hurt. Smiling, he went into his tent.

His smile continued to spread across his face as satisfaction warmed his soul. What more could someone ask for in life? He had a good education and he'd found a career that he was passionate about. Whether there was money or not, he knew in his heart that he'd always be happy as long as he could sit under a night sky like the one tonight.

Tomorrow, and all that it would bring would arrive soon enough.

He crawled into his cot and pulled the covers up. Steve reassured himself that he'd find a pattern and quickly acclimate to being alone. So many thoughts raced through his mind that he wasn't sure he'd ever get to sleep. The champagne and the long trip finally took their toll on him. His eyelids seemed to be made of lead. Sleep was fitful for him, but he rested well enough.

CHAPTER NINE

Ellen and Jonathan arrived back at their campsite ten minutes after their last goodbye. It was only a few miles, but in this country, it might as well be another planet. There was still more than enough work ahead of them, and they needed the privacy that Steve's leadership would afford them.

The summer sun would give them at least four more hours of bright light and two to three hours of fading light. The two of them could still get in plenty of work before it would be too dark to continue. Neither of them wanted the lantern light acting as a beacon from the opening in the top of the cave. They were willing to accept some reasonable risk, and bright lights were not on the list.

Jonathan unloaded the burlap bags as Ellen walked back to her favorite spot in front of the metal slab. By the time Jonathan had finished with his unloading and carrying the bags up to the cave Ellen had settled in for an evening of careful analysis. She had her magnifying glass with her as she studied the images more closely. Concentrating so intently on the images, she almost lost her balance and fell backwards. Ellen managed to place her hands behind her as she lowered herself to a seated position.

Jonathan saw her as she caught her balance. "Are you all right? You didn't hurt yourself did you?"

Ellen just sat there in stunned silence. She didn't even acknowledge his presence. She couldn't take her eyes away from the pictographs. Pointing mutely with her magnifying glass, she finally turned to face him.

"What is it? What am I supposed to see?"

Ellen looked up and just stared up at him with a blank look on her face. "Take a look for yourself," she finally muttered, extending the magnifying glass to Jonathan. Her eyes still locked on the pictographs. Reaching over her shoulder, he took it and studied her position for a moment.

Jonathan had only seen this level of excitement from her on one other occasion. It had been the time she had discovered a fossilized egg, and it had been completely intact. The baby dinosaur was just emerging. Caught up in the moment and euphoria of the discovery, she just froze, too excited to even shout her joy. Later, she had explained how the overwhelming excitement had simply left her speechless. Judging from where she was sitting he positioned the magnifying glass about two feet up the side. He focused in on the section that she had most likely been studying.

Moving in closely to the box he eased in front of her and focused the glass. "I don't believe this," he said aloud. "There's something wrong here."

"I know, dear," Ellen responded. "This doesn't make any sense at all. I don't know what to make of this. This is getting more and more fantastic as we go along. What are we looking at?"

"I don't know Ellen." The silence was deafening. Neither spoke for what seemed an eternity. They continued to stare at the spot Ellen had discovered.

"This is not just a slab of cast metal. This section has been extensively machined to a very precise tolerance. Look at that!", he finally exclaimed. "I've never seen anything like it; at least not by today's standards. I think that the government might be able to produce something like this, but I'm not entirely sure. Furthermore, why would the government bury something like this in the middle of nowhere?

"I'm going to find the other corner of this thing before we continue down this side. I have a hunch about this, but it's only a guess. I want to see the other side before I say anything. What do you say that we get started?"

"I'm all for that," she chimed in. Rising to her feet, she pocketed the magnifying glass and went to get the wheelbarrow.

Ellen was caught up in the challenge once again. This was a riddle that needed to be solved. "We need to get this done as soon as possible. You know. . . if we threw a tarp over the opening, we could work well into the night without casting any light. What do you think?"

"Brilliant! Simply brilliant! I love you," he said, hugging her. He pecked her on the cheek as he turned to leave for the truck. Shouting over his shoulder, "I'll only be a minute. Don't go anywhere."

Where would I go? she thought as her gaze followed him out of the cave.

They moved the tarp to the top of the hill and stretched it out along the crack that formed the upper opening. They didn't want to get too close to the edge of the opening because they had no idea of how unstable this section was after the rains. It was living stone, yet the support had now thinned considerably.

The tarp was wide enough to be thrown across the opening. The plan was to stake it down with rocks along the edges. They wouldn't have to move them very far when they were ready to remove the tarp. The idea was a complete success. It stretched across with ten feet on each side of the crevice. It was now secure from anything but a very strong wind.

The Crenshaw's worked with a renewed vigor well into the night. The tarp completely blocked the light from the top opening. They were deep enough into the cave that no amount of light shown from the mouth. Adding to that, the mouth faced east and it couldn't be seen from the road. Both of them had no intention of stopping until they had reached the left corner of this 'thing.'

Their goal came with remarkable ease. The soil, even though compacted, was removed easily. They had cleared the entire face from base to top. Their original assessment of its size was holding true. The surface of the face was smooth and finished everywhere. There were no markings like those found on the right side.

An unexpected side benefit was the placement of the damp soil. The temperature cooled slightly and the soil would retain most of its moisture. They could start fresh in the morning with a damp dark hillside. Jonathan didn't want to start bagging soil yet.

It was past 10:00 PM and they both needed to stop. The work had been strenuous, yet it was satisfying to see the entire surface exposed like this. Both of them were still unsure of what it was that they were looking at. They didn't even try to speculate. Walking slowly, they left the cave hand in hand. It was a pleasant leisurely pace and they shared their excitement and each other's company as they looked at the night sky. The narrow path had been traversed so many times now that each footstep was second nature. They got back to the tent without mishap; settling in for some much-needed sleep.

Ellen slept comfortably. Her breathing became slow and steady only moments after curling into her favorite sleeping position. A smile remained on her face even in sleep. Jonathan, however, had a troubled sleep. He could not shake the images of what he had seen. They kept returning from his sub-conscious. The machining was too perfect. It wasn't natural. He'd found a new puzzle to solve and it gnawed at him.

His dreams became almost nightmares as the days' events twisted and turned in his head. The sleeping mind brings up all manner of fantastic and surreal imagery. Most of the time you don't remember any of them, but the haunting feelings they evoke stays with you after you wake. Eventually sleep found him. Even as he slept, a solution was formulating in his sub-conscious mind. These dreams and their residual effects would be no different for Jonathan when he rose the next morning. He'd had these nights before and they always left him drawn and unfocused.

CHAPTER TEN

THE MORNING DAWNED BRIGHT AND promising. Steve felt like a new man after his first night as team leader. The camp was set up and no one seemed ill at ease with him. Most of them were used to the routine from previous digs. As long as he didn't stumble or over step his authority he would be just fine. The camp was busy with the morning preparations. After stepping from his tent, he stretched his arms and legs. He looked around and saw that everything was running smoothly already.

"Good morning everyone. . . how was your night?" he asked. Breakfast was just ready to be served. Many of the tools had already been sorted and laid out. He glanced at his watch to make sure that he hadn't overslept. So much had already been done that he found himself amazed at everyone's efficiency.

What he saw from the four rookies impressed him. They were just as busy as the rest of the team and appeared to be working comfortably. All hands were busy with something. There appeared to be no wasted effort.

"You guys eat first," he said turning to the two cooks. "You earned first place in line. I'll serve."

They smiled as they picked up their plates and utensils. "Thanks Steve," each said as they passed. They both had worked a dig before and they knew it would be a while before lunch was served. Their portions were large enough to last the mornings work schedule.

The rest lined up and followed their lead. As they all sat around the table, diverse conversations were struck up between mouthfuls. The newbies wanted to know more about the routine and the most experienced told a few white lies about the workload. Each outrageous statement was met with laughter.

People assigned to breakfast clean up went about their duties while Steve outlined what he had planned for the day. He'd gone over fossil samples with each of them before they left the campus. Now they were in the field; this was the real thing. He was confident in each of them because of their knowledge and desire. His praise was spartan, but real.

Almost everyone was very nervous on their first dig. As they found small bone fragments and developed confidence, they would become more enthusiastic. He enjoyed watching that transition in a student. Some would be consumed with paleontology while others did well, but would never be more than assistants.

Each of the new people had been assigned to an experienced partner for the first four days. Training could be more or less depending on individual progress, yet four days was the norm. No one was ever assigned to permanent camp duty. Ellen and Jonathan had taught him that it made the new students feel inferior if they were not allowed out of camp to search with the team.

The solution was basic. Steve posted a duty roster and each person checked off their name when their assigned task was completed. Aside from illness, there were no substitutions allowed. He'd set up an excel spreadsheet and each student's name systematically rotated through every task. It was fair and unbiased.

Steve took one of the new people for himself. He was so full of enthusiasm that he wanted it to rub off on somebody. . . anybody.

He still found himself in disbelief over his situation. Leadership was a prize he definitely coveted, but he had never expected it this soon. If he died right now, he felt that he would surely go straight to fossil hunting heaven.

With breakfast complete, and the students picking up their tools, Steve announced the mornings plans. "Everybody," he called. "This will be the plan for this morning. I want each team to spread out in this general direction," waving his arm to the west. "Every team should keep roughly fifty feet apart. If you don't know what fifty feet looks like, it's the distance from where we are right now to the vehicles, pointing to the cars behind him. "Are we all clear on this?"

"I understand what you're asking, but why?" asked one of the new students.

"Good question. George." He pointed to one of the others and asked, "Can you answer that?"

"Sure. We're trying to locate any areas that show promise without overlapping our efforts. We can cover a lot of area with five teams and we'll know if we should move to another area or search farther away from the campsite."

"That's right. We need to be as thorough as possible. I want every little object checked. Don't be afraid to ask. We found a leg bone of a baby raptor just casually yesterday. Perhaps it was a good omen. Who knows what we'll find with honest effort? It really doesn't matter as long as we each do our assigned task to the best of our abilities. Are there any other questions?"

"Yes," said the young lady assigned as his partner. "There are eleven of us, counting you, and you'll be fielding all the questions and looking at all the suspected fossils, wouldn't it be more expedient if I were paired with one of the senior team members? You could still teach and without the distraction of a new student at your side."

"Good point. I like your idea. Initially the Crenshaw's were to be the leaders so I automatically took a partner. Frank, you are currently odd man out; you have just acquired a new partner."

"Whatever you say Steve. . . let's go find some dinosaur bones!"

"Don't rush off too soon. I have one more direction to give. I would like the teams to be five wide to cover roughly two hundred fifty feet. Each team will start at the left side of their fifty-by-fifty grid and work from left to right. By the end of the day we should easily cover a range of field that will be two hundred fifty feet long and one hundred feet wide.

"I just remembered that I have a hundred-foot tape in my truck. Frank, would you get it out of the glove box for me?"

Steve sketched the grid on a napkin. Being careful to lay in landmarks in each grid, it made it simpler for the others to quickly grasp his intentions. They all gathered around as he dashed off the picture. The senior team members would make certain that the grid was examined as efficiently as possible.

"Frank, I want you and your partner to lay out the tape so each team can mark their grid corners. When you're finished, you two can take the last grid at the top. The grid will square itself after the first couple of markers are located."

Seeing that everyone really understood and not just agreed with his statements, Steve continued, "I want you to be aware of all your tools. There aren't any stores to purchase replacements. If you lose a tool, it's lost. It will hinder progress when you make a discovery. Please, please keep them in your pockets and pouches, checking all the time to make sure that you didn't drop or forget something as you move from place to place. Nothing is more aggravating than the inability to complete a task because of a careless mistake. That's it for now. Good hunting."

The group fanned out across the grid and began their searching with enthusiasm. Each team took their relative positions and turned to face Steve for final approval. Some were spot on and others had to be moved left or right slightly. All in all, he was pleased with his grid and the students caught on immediately. A plan was no good if it was too complicated to implement.

Steve hoped for an early discovery to keep the morale and momentum up. His eyes scanned the group as the all squatted or knelt in their respective quadrants. As if anticipating his expectations, almost simultaneously, three people shouted that they'd found something. He was up in a flash and rushed to the nearest pair to check on their discovery.

It was a turtle shell fragment. This was important because it indicated that there was water near this area all those millions of years ago. The other two pairs had also found shell fragments including a small tooth fragment.

Things were looking up as he went from team to team. This was a promising beginning to the dig. The new people got to see what it was they were looking for and there had been a discovery with in ten minutes of starting the search.

Steve returned to the makeshift worktable. He'd eventually have to clean up his paperwork to allow the rest of the team to have a decent lunch table. Once seated, he began to calculate the easiest method to utilize the table without having to clean between each meal.

Ultimately, he separated one of the tables and just designated it as his. It was the most expedient solution. The solution offered Steve the opportunity to work outside of his tent and face the team while they worked.

CHAPTER ELEVEN

E LLEN HAD RISEN EARLIER THAN Jonathan. She stood outside the tent for a few minutes and watched as the rising sun painted the sky in shimmering bands of magenta, orange and yellow. As the sun rose higher, cerulean blue filled the remainder of the sky. Eventually she went up the hill and pulled back the tarp. *This is going to work out well*, she thought.

Progress had gone so well the night before, now she toyed with the idea of taking a day off. Ellen knew that Jonathan would be all business today. She also knew that he wasn't wrong in feeling that way. There was so much to accomplish and time was against them. Still, she felt more than just a little naughty at the thought.

Taking the five-foot-long probe, she tested the edge of the gaping wound in the hilltop. It was remarkably stable. The only debris that she could loosen was almost at the very edge. Even directly at the edge, it yielded only minute amounts of loose rock. It meant that they only need concern themselves with avoiding the direct opening. They would be able to move the tarp about with even more ease than she already experienced.

Smelling breakfast on the stove, she made her way back down the hill. Jonathan was up earlier than usual this morning. He was more anxious than he let on. It didn't matter. She was hungry and food was waiting.

"Why good morning dear," she said coyly as she moved over to smell the food. "How was your night? Mine was absolutely fabulous."

Before he could answer, she was behind him. She circled her arms around his waist and pressed herself up against his back. Kissing the back of his neck, she softly said, "I love you Jonathan Crenshaw."

Turning, without breaking the embrace, he kissed her on the lips. "I love you too. What's up? This is definitely out of the ordinary."

"I know. I was just thinking about you while moving the tarp. I just wanted to tell you before the day got the better of us."

Jonathan smiled broadly. He loved Ellen more than he loved his work, and he was eternally committed to his work. Placing his large hands on her hips, he eased her back to arm's length. "You know what I think?" he asked with a crooked smile.

"Why no Dr. Crenshaw?" she answered as she swayed in his grip.

"Well let me tell you. I think that we have done a stellar job of removing as much soil as we have. I also think that we need a break." He inhaled deeply, swelling his chest. The crooked smile remained.

"Do tell, Dr. Crenshaw," she said heavily, fluttering her eyelashes.

"I think that we should adjourn to yonder tent my lady. I will show you sights that will amaze and entertain you."

"Oh how you do go on Dr. Crenshaw. I might surely blush if you continue." Fluttering her eyelashes, she turned her head aside in mock embarrassment.

They both laughed as they fell back into each other's arms. They kissed passionately before heading to the tent. This would be the break in the tension that they were desperately searching for. Whatever it was that they had unearthed, it definitely had a disquieting effect on both of them. Finding security in each other's arms was not only a distraction, but also an anchor to reality.

Emerging from the tent a while later, Ellen pulled her robe closed and tied it loosely. She smelled the food and went over to the cook stove. The food was covered and still warm. She served herself a large portion. Between mouthfuls, she called over her shoulder, "The foods still warm dear. Want any?"

"Sure. After the workout you gave me, if I don't eat soon, I'll pass out." He threw back the tent flap and stood in the opening as naked as the day he was born.

Ellen smiled to herself. She loved when he said things like that. He knew how to make her feel feminine. What was even more important was that he truly meant every word of every compliment he had ever given her. Approaching her from behind, he said, "We need to get started soon," and then he leaned over and kissed her cheek.

"You were fantastic." He reached around to get his plate and filled with food. When he finished, he said, "That was a great breakfast, even if I was the chef. If you're finished, I can take your plate dear." Reaching over the table, he attempted to grab it.

"Thanks, dear," she said, turning the plate away from his outstretched hand. "I'll get it myself. I want to eat a little more."

"Let me have your plate when you're finished, I'd like to let it soak for a few minutes before I wash it. I can nibble right from the pan. You know, like a guy."

"You know how I hate that." *More disgusting guy habits. . . when will they ever end? They're so inventive when it comes to thinking up stupid habits to irritate women. It's not a God given talent. I swear they teach each other new methods when they have their guy's nights. It's a male conspiracy.*

"Yeah, I know. I just figured that I could get the dishes done by the time you were finished and then all I would have to wash was the pan."

"Okay, you win. It's a good idea. Just don't let it go to your head too often. If I let you, you would eat all your meals from a pan."

"What's your point?" *Pan or plate, the foods the same isn't it? Women are so damned fussy about the silliest things. She even hates when I eat with my hands. I don't get it. We were born with the perfect utensils at the ends of our arms, so why not use them?*

"Men!" she said mockingly. "God created women because no one else would have you and your disgusting habits."

"Well I'm glad that God created you." He hugged her and kissed the back of her neck.

Ellen brushed playfully at her neck as if she were shooing a fly.

"Go on with you. And put some clothes on! We'll be out of here and in the cave in less than twenty minutes.

"When are we going to see Steve and the rest of the students? Do you think we should go right after lunch or just before supper?" she questioned.

"I would prefer just before supper. It would help us to make up some of this morning's mysteriously lost time. There, all the dishes are finished." He winked and smiled at her. She playfully snapped him with a damp dishtowel. It left a red welt on his bare backside.

"Ouch! That hurt," he whined as he rubbed the welt and scuttled into the tent.

"Next time you should be more considerate and dress for a meal." *Although it was kind of cute and I love how his butt jiggles when he walks. The mud was still funnier. I can't wait to tell the grandkids how Grandpa fell face first into a mud puddle.*

Steve's teams fanned out across the rock outcroppings that formed the grids and campsite. There was an abundance of small fossil bones to be seen everywhere. The abundance of fossils would help the new member's transition more quickly. It was only a matter of minutes before each person was bent over inspecting something. If this rapid pace continued, Steve would soon have to call everyone back to inspect what each had found. In his own experience, he had seen this happen only once before.

By 9:30, they all had small pouches full of fossilized treasures. Steve could see that it was time to call everyone in. Calling to the teams in one at a time; they all gathered around the large table that Steve had set up for this very purpose. Each in turn emptied their pouches on to the table.

As Steve walked around the table, he was able to identify many small dinosaur teeth, bones, and bone fragments. A pattern started to emerge from all the fossil remains spread before him.

Steve had everyone continue to sort down his or her individual piles while he went back to his tent for a reference book. He wanted to be very sure of what he already suspected. It served no purpose to announce something with little to no supporting evidence; just to retract it later because your suppositions were in error.

He brought the book back and went to the nearest pile. Flipping through a few pages he stopped. With deliberate care, he moved the fragments, pausing occasionally to scrutinize a particular selection. Finally, he picked up a bone fragment and went back to the book. Setting the fragment down, he grabbed what looked like a broken bit of tooth. Returning to the book for confirmation; he looked up and had a strange almost smile on his lips. Everyone was starting to get excited. Maybe they had found something important.

Steve moved to the next pile, checking repeatedly against the textbook. Closing the book, he remained standing in front of the two piles he'd just separated. Everyone gathered in front of the two piles as he instructed, "I want you to look at these fragments." He pushed the pieces that he'd selected from the piles closer to the center of the table.

After getting everyone's attention, he continued, "These are the kind of things that I want you to sort from your piles. I need to look at each pile when you're finished. Don't mix them with any other pile. I want them all separated by individual grid. Let's get started everyone."

"What's going on? Have we found something?" asked an excited newcomer.

"It's too early to tell. We must sort the rest of your collections to see if a pattern emerges. From there we can formulate a hypothesis. Do you understand?"

"Yes. There are no quick answers and you don't speculate on one fragment. You must have empirical data to arrive at the proper conclusion."

"Very good," he complimented. "You've learned your lessons well. I'm happy to hear that you've been listening to Dr. Crenshaw's lectures." Steve smiled and turned, facing everyone.

"It's just that you seemed to be on to something, and I got a little excited," answered the student.

"Well I might be on to something, then we can all get excited, but not before we finish the work before us. Two of the piles aren't enough to establish a clear picture. The sooner we complete the sorting, the sooner we'll have our answer." *I can only dream that I'm right. This looks to be a major find. I need to keep everyone subdued until we can be sure. I need to check the terrain. I hope this isn't a mass death caused by a flash flood or some other similar natural catastrophe.*

Steve watched with quiet enthusiasm as each pile began to reveal the fossils he was hoping for. This was the first step in the formation of a hypothesis. As the search continued over the next few days, he felt confident that his original speculation would prove to be a valid theory.

CHAPTER TWELVE

THE CRENSHAW'S RESUMED THEIR DIGGING immediately after their delayed breakfast. They were both anxious to get completely around to the right side of this remarkable metal thing. For all intent and purposes, it would have to be called a box. Neither knew exactly what it might be, but as the excavation continued, it resembled a huge metal box.

Earth and debris practically flew from the cave. Jonathan had remarked earlier as to how young he felt. Ellen agreed. They each knew it was the excitement. Both of them kept up an almost frantic pace throughout the morning. The passageway along the right side of the box was forming as nicely as the one. This one was even a foot or so wider. It was lunchtime before they stopped to assess what their efforts had wrought.

The metal pole Ellen had brought to probe the top turned into a real asset. Jonathan used it to pry large sections of the compacted soil from farther up the box and the opening they were creating. It was the main reason that the work went so quickly.

"We can stop for lunch now dear. We've done quite a bit."

Jonathan just stood there, tired yet invigorated. "You're right dear. Let's grab a bite and hurry back. This is going so much better than I could have hoped for."

"You could stay here and clear away some of this loose stuff while I get lunch. You obviously don't want to stop."

"Good idea. I'll get this area ready for you. You should be able to start fine cleaning the box yet today. Make me a couple of sandwiches, please." He had already picked up his shovel and continued to dig.

"You know what I like." Lost in his work, he called out just before she exited the cave, "Thanks honey."

"No problem dear. I'll be right back. Slow down a little so you can digest without cramping."

"Thanks honey. Right as usual. I'll cool down a little with a slower pace. Don't be long, I'm hungry now that we've talked about food."

Ellen was as excited as Jonathan, maybe now they might be able to determine just what it was that she had discovered. It would be comforting to put a real name to the object. She hated speculation. They both did. They were scientists and they dealt in quantifiable matters. Scientists only speculated when they were trying to form a new theory, but they would abandon it if it could not be proven. This was too big to abandon.

Ellen finished making the last sandwich and grabbed a jug of sun-brewed tea. She headed back to the cave to eat with Jonathan and to resolve this mystery.

"Look at this Ellen. The marks on this side are exactly the same as the left side. That means that they are primarily decorative. We'll have to see both sides in total to be sure."

Handing Jonathan his sandwiches and tea, Ellen studied the markings. They were the same as on the left side. Except they were mirror imaged. "Did you take any measurements?" she asked.

"Yes dear. The big one down there is exactly 337 mm from the base. Its' counterpart is exactly 337 mm from the base. I'm pleased to say that all five of the markings are all in the exact same position as these. It's a fine piece of craftsmanship. I checked both the x and y-axis of each figure; they're the same in all cases."

"You're probably right. You've got a good eye when it comes to judging close tolerances. Although, school's still out on the decorative aspect. We still don't know if it's a language or not."

"Eat up. Those are two of the finest sandwiches that I've ever made."

Jonathan realized that he was still holding his sandwiches and the jug of tea. He knew Ellen had gone through a lot of trouble to make them and he had not even said "Thank You." Or did he? "They look great dear." Taking a mouthful of sandwich, he continued, "Mm mmm. . . these are great, thanks."

"All right already! Apology accepted." She rolled her eyes. "I could see how intent you were when I walked in. If I don't know you after all these years, then I haven't been too observant."

"I am sorry. I was thinking of how remarkable it was that this much effort was put into something that was just intended to be buried." They both looked up at each other, shouting out at the same time, "It's a casket!"

"Do you really think so? It's so huge. It's logical but not practical." Ellen began to mumble different scenarios to herself before Jonathan could even reply.

"It may be some sort of time capsule. The markings are confusing me; it's as ornate as an Egyptian sarcophagus. If this were a monument it should have markings all the way around it. So far, they are only on the two sides. Casket or sarcophagus is still the best guess. I like it."

"Well I don't. We don't speculate, we know. Consider the monuments in King of Prussia at Valley Forge. They're impressive and only carved on one side in a lot of cases. Maybe in every case, you know we never really stopped to look that closely. Let's get busy. The sooner we uncover this thing the sooner we will know." Ellen was satisfied making her point.

"You're right. Although the sarcophagus angle feels right somehow."

"Dear, this is at least sixty-five million years old. This rock is from the Cretaceous period. We can't make a direct correlation to the designs from a few thousand years ago.

"I think you might take a different perspective if this were not already buried. Remember, this was a cave at one time, not a grave site," Jonathan replied.

"Maybe you're right," he offered. "We don't have any insight into funerary rites from millions of years ago. There are, however, a lot of cave burials throughout human history. Don't be so quick to dismiss an idea. I'm almost through here. It won't take much longer to reach the corner. I need a moment to answer the call of nature first."

Jonathan moved to the front of the cave entrance where they had placed a makeshift toilet. The bend in the cave walls provided for privacy while still allowing full conversation.

"Don't be long. I need to go myself."

"If you need to go now, I can go outside."

"No dear, I can wait." *Why do men have a need for urinating in the outdoors? It's just one more of their disgusting habits. All the saints must surely be women.*

Ellen began the careful task of removing the bits of crusted debris from the raised markings. She didn't believe that it was possible to damage this monstrosity in any way. Years of cleaning debris from dinosaur bones had given her a careful touch. She was thankful that she didn't need her dental tools to pick away some of the more stubborn particles. They seemed to come away with a good brushing.

"Your turn dear... don't be long," he said.

She smiled to herself. *He could take hours in the bathroom doing God knows what, but if I take two minutes he's there asking if everything was all right. Truly. . . the saints are definitely all women.* Chuckling at her private thoughts, she turned so he wouldn't notice her smirking. "I won't be long," she said.

Jonathan was already involved with something and waved his acknowledgement to something he never heard. The metal pole struck deep into the compacted soil and with a swift wrenching motion, debris cascaded from the top of the box. Leaning the pole against the side of the cave, Jonathan began to fill the wheelbarrow.

Repeating the process, he's managed to fill the wheelbarrow to a large heaping mound. Picking up the handles, he realized that he'd definitely overfilled it. It was manageable, yet he'd need to move slowly or risk dumping the whole thing. *Too much wasted labor old man. Take it easy next time.*

"My, aren't we the manly man this afternoon?" chided Ellen as she saw the amount of soil in front of the cave. "Don't strain yourself," she said in a more concerned voice this time. "We can't afford to have you down for the count when we're this close."

"I already realize my mistake. I need to concentrate on keeping the load steady, so if you don't mind occupying yourself with something useful, I'd appreciate it."

"Well, I never," Ellen said indignantly. She knew she had only been teasing him. He should have known that. *What a spoiled brat!*

Jonathan cringed at the rebuke. It had come out all wrong and now he'd need to apologize. Concentrating on the load for the moment, he eased the wheelbarrow down the passage. Apologies would have to wait until this was finished.

Returning, Jonathan said, "I'm sorry dear. I know you were teasing me. What I said came out all wrong. I meant no disrespect. I was concentrating so hard on not spilling the wheelbarrow that I spoke in haste. Can you forgive me?"

Ellen kissed his cheek and returned to her work.

Jonathan grinned from ear to ear. They still loved each other and he was satisfied that she was happy again. He may have even been forgiven, but it didn't matter. She was happy and that was the most important thing to him.

CHAPTER THIRTEEN

S TEVE SAT ALONE IN HIS tent with his open journal, just starting the days' entries. It had been a remarkable day on many levels. He paused, staring at the empty page before he began to write. His pen danced in circles waiting impatiently for him to compose his thoughts. Finally, the pen touched the paper and the words began to flow.

June 17, 1999. This is the first full day at the dig site. I was excited when Ellen and Jonathan had shown it to me. (Side note: I'm instructed to call them by their first names now.) The first day's work consisted of gathering a large assortment of fragments. I'm formulating a hypothesis concerning these specimens. A full 70% of them are raptor. This many fragments of the same species at one location is peculiar.

There are so many that you could easily speculate that this was some sort of nesting area. That theory flies in the face of everything that we've ever been taught about raptors. I checked the specimens very carefully. I'm sure of my identification. I'll speak to Ellen and Jonathan tomorrow. The size of the fossils would indicate a wide range of ages. The very young and juvenile samples make up the majority of the group. There are many larger fragments that show there were also more than a handful of adults.

I hope this proves to be the find I think it is. The team

agreed that we don't have enough information to draw an accurate conclusion. We really need to find a complete adult bone or some portion of a skeleton. That's the final proof I need to bear out my newly forming hypothesis.

It's long been speculated that raptors hunted in packs like modern day lions; however, the plethora of fossil evidence at this site has led me to speculate that they also had a strong family bond as a pack. More than that, this was a social group with an established a territory This looks to be a communal nesting area where all of the young were raised and trained to hunt. My God, just to see it written down is mind boggling. I need more evidence.

With the entry complete, Steve closed his journal and slid the chair back. Propping his feet on the desk, he leaned back in the chair. He began mulling over the collection strategies he might employ.

Leaning forward, Steve searched for some writing paper. He needed to sketch the work area so he could more easily visualize the teams in their search patterns. Starting all ten in a straight line heading out away from the center of camp would be the quickest approach. They would each place a flag at their starting points. They would then sweep left from the center of the camp. Each of them would search a small grid of five feet by five feet by placing flags at the corners.

Different colored flags would indicate the corners of the grid so they could easily be distinguished from the fossil flags. The flags will be marked with the description and number of any collected fossil. They would need a format meeting to determine the best notations. Everyone needs to use the same method.

Steve closed his eyes, focusing on a mental picture of the collection process.

The pattern would be color coded for easy reference. Many fragments in a grid would be colored red. A few fragments would be green, and little or no fragments would have no color.

Steve sat at his desk contemplating his plan. The sounds of the camp faded as silence filled his tent. He closed his eyes again and watched the events play out in an imaginary movie. It seemed to run smoothly.

It was getting very late and neither Ellen nor Jonathan had taken a break for supper. They were so involved in what they were doing that they hadn't noticed the hours slipping by. Stopping for a moment's conversation interrupted the silence of their routine.

"What time is it dear? I left my watch in the tent after making lunch."

"What did you say?" Jonathan looked up to see Ellen pointing to her wrist, where her watch should have been.

"It's eight-thirty-seven," he responded after a quick glance at his watch. Already returning to digging.

"Don't you think we should stop for a bite to eat?"

"What's that you say?" he asked.

"I said we're going to stop for supper. We've worked straight through."

"I guess so. I'm hungry. Why don't we stop for supper?"

"That's a good idea dear. I don't know why I didn't think of it?" *He's an idiot savant and deaf to boot.*

"What did I do?" He could tell by the tone in her voice that she wasn't happy about something. "Do we have time for me to finish here? I'm almost to the next corner. I can feel it."

"Sure. I'll be in the tent. If you're not there in thirty minutes you're not eating tonight."

"No problem dear. I'll be there." He still wasn't sure what he'd said or done, but he knew enough to be there in thirty minutes or else. He set the beeper on his watch for twenty minutes. That would allow enough time to get down to the tent and still get washed up. Shrugging his shoulders, he could only guess that maybe things weren't going as she had expected. He'd find out soon enough.

History dictated that a good supper meant a minor infraction. A paper plate, a can of beans, and a can opener meant sleeping alone tonight. Not even a paper plate meant sleeping outside the tent.

Ellen was a beautiful, loving wife and mother, but when he screwed up it was hell to pay. It was just the stress of the situation. He was feeling it himself. Jonathan remembered how good they had felt after their little interlude. That would help break the tension. Yes, that would be his plan of action.

"You're here early. I gave you half an hour." *He wants sex again tonight.*

"I know. Is there anything that I can do to help?" *Whatever I can do to get sex tonight will be fine with me.*

"Not really dear. Just get washed up. I'll only be a little bit." *Nice try playboy.*

"Whatever you say dear." He patted her bottom as he went to get cleaned up. He hadn't seen a paper plate anywhere. He smiled broadly. *There still may be a ray of hope for sex or maybe just a little fondling. Whatever, anything would be fine with him tonight.*

Supper was a simple affair, but Ellen always seemed to make even boiled water taste good. He wondered how he always managed to stay thinner than a lot of his colleagues at the university. Especially the way Ellen cooked. Once you started eating something that she prepared, you didn't want to stop until you almost exploded. Drying his face and hands, he went back out to the cook-stove.

"Here, take this." Ellen said as she handed him a pan. Watching him juggle the pan, she quickly added, "Careful. . . it's hot."

Jonathan had already figured that out. His hand wasn't burned, but it was pretty hot. He went back to the stove to get the plates and utensils. Ellen had already brought the coffee to the table.

Jonathan sat down beside her, instead of across from her.

"What's on your mind?" she asked coyly. *You might get sex if you're particularly good tonight and I'm not too tired. I'll be keeping track of your every move hot shot.*

"Oh, nothing dear. I just want to make up for whatever it was that I said or did." *Play the sympathy card too soon and the door gets slammed in your face every time.*

"It was nothing dear. It's been a really long day. I'm tired and irritable. You didn't hear me ask you about supper and then you said, 'How about a supper break?' I was just a little put off, that's all."

"I'm sorry dear." Caressing her thighs, he said softly, "Is there anything else you might want me to do?"

Ellen grabbed his hand and placed it back on the table. She held it gently as she smiled. "Can I have a rain check on that request?" She squeezed his hand as she asked.

"Sure dear. I just thought. . ." *Damn and that was my best shot.*

Interrupting, she said, "I know dear. It's a lovely thought, but I'm way too tired to have that much fun. I will take a cuddle though, if you don't mind."

"Not at all. . . a cuddle it shall be." *Close enough to count for sex and I get brownie points for being a good boy. Life is good. I have to work on my timing or ask the right questions. Then again, can you ever ask the right questions? They're always changing the questions; it's a woman's prerogative.*

"We were supposed to go see Steve tonight."

"I know. If you hadn't said anything, I'd still be up there," filling his mouth as he motioned towards the hill.

"I feel relaxed enough to get in another couple of hours studying those markings. Are you're up to it?" she asked.

"I sure am," swallowing his last mouthful. "I'm just about at the other corner. I can see a little of it. I just need to break through. The soil is more compacted around that end of the box. It takes more effort to remove it."

"The markings on both sides seem to be more than decorations. It's difficult to explain what I'm feeling. I think that they might be informational somehow. They're arranged in a text fashion. I don't know for sure because this is still pure conjecture on my part." said Ellen.

"Wasn't it you who said, 'We must not speculate, we must know?'"

"Yes, it was. I'm getting a feeling from this. It's intuitive. I can't explain it. I guess I noticed something sub-consciously that I haven't been able to bring to the surface yet."

"Let's get the tarp over the top. It'll be dark soon. I don't want to wander around up there in the dark any more than I have to."

"Don't be such a baby," she chided.

"I'm not. If one of us gets hurt and we have to bring people in, our secret's out."

"Good point. I didn't think about that. Let's go." They headed for the hilltop in silence. Jonathan took the time to drop everything into the water to let them soak while they were gone. Supper dishes would have wait for now.

Getting the tarp in position, they entered the cave and turned on a fuel burning lantern. They wanted to save the battery lantern for emergency situations. Jonathan dug while Ellen sketched and made rubbings; planning to study both the rubbings and photographs.

It was shortly after 10:00 p.m. when Jonathan succeeded at clearing the corner. Rushing around the other side of the box, he came to get Ellen. She would want to see this. Jonathan stopped abruptly in his tracks; she was nowhere to be found.

He called towards the cave entrance. Perhaps she was momentarily detained at the portable latrine. There was no answer. He went down the passage to where the toilet sat. No Ellen.

Jonathan was scared. She never wandered off like this. The only time that she ever left anywhere on her own was when she took her morning walks. There were never any other exceptions in twenty-five years of working together.

CHAPTER FOURTEEN

RUSHING BACK INSIDE, HE GRABBED his flashlight. Standing on the pathway, he scanned the hillside for indications that she'd slipped and fell. There were no telltale signs or slide marks down the hillside. And still there was no Ellen anywhere to be found.

He hurried down to the tent, still no Ellen. He didn't want to panic, but this was the most difficult situation that he'd ever encountered. Jonathan felt the intense pain of fear and potential loss constricting his heart and clouding his judgment. He called out into the darkness, circling around after each call so his voice carried in several directions. He tried to stop at eight different points for each call, but in his panic, he couldn't be sure if he'd stopped even once.

"ELLEN!" he called at the top of his lungs. He strained with every fiber of his being to hear her respond. Struggling to control the sound of his ragged breathing, he heard nothing but the night sounds as they closed in around him. Now he was fully panicked. He walked away from the camp and continued to call out to her. If she had fallen, he might hear her muffled cry for help if he was farther from the camp.

Jonathan searched the full area around the camp. There were no traces of her tracks anywhere. She clearly had not left the campsite on foot. The truck was still on the other side of the tent.

His mind raced with all manner of wild speculations. He quickened his pace back to the camp. Maybe she had fallen asleep in the truck. It made sense. She wouldn't hear his calls clearly. And once he left camp, she wouldn't hear him at all. His heart ached already and he wasn't even sure if she was gone or hurt, unable to move or call out.

He reached the truck and in anticipation of seeing her sleeping form he flung open the door. She wasn't there. He scrambled into the back of the truck. Again, she wasn't there. He cried out her name in anguish. Jonathan felt alone, confused. Anxiety was pressing in on his chest to the point of debilitating pain; his breathing was becoming even more ragged. His heartbeat thundered in his ears. Tears welled in his eyes.

Suddenly, from the cave came a beacon of hope. Through the pounding in his ears, he heard her call his name. It was music carried on the night air. "I'm here," he called back to her through his tears. "I'm coming," he shouted as best he could.

Jonathan managed the path up to the entrance, through teary eyes. He embraced her when he got there. Jonathan held on to her, like a drowning man holds onto a life ring. He just cried. "I love you; I love you; I love you."

"What's the matter dear?" she asked as she broke his embrace. "What's happened? Is every one all right? No one is hurt or worse? Answer me." Ellen was experiencing panic of her own.

"I've been looking for you for almost half an hour. You were nowhere to be found and you can ask me what's wrong?"

"I'm sorry dear." She returned the embrace. Understanding washed over her and she didn't want to let go of him. "I hadn't realized that it had been that long. I never left the cave though. You have to believe me."

"I'm not stupid. I came around where you were working, and you weren't there. How can you say that you didn't leave the cave? I thought you were lying somewhere hurt or unconscious, unable to call for help." *This better be a damn good explanation after what you just put me through. I'll make some mud and show you exactly how angry I am.*

"I've discovered the most amazing thing!" Ellen could barely contain her excitement, even in the presence of Jonathan's anguish. "This is beyond anything that you've ever experienced! I can hardly control myself. Look at me; I'm shaking like a schoolgirl on her first date. Jonathan, this is the most fantastic discovery of all time! Follow me."

Leading him back down the passage, just as she had done only a few days earlier, Ellen had once again made a promise of an outstanding, outrageous discovery. He was so overjoyed to see her again that he blindly followed her lead.

Guiding him by his hand, she took him back into the cave and around to the side of the box where she had been working. "Let me start at the beginning. You know that I said that I thought that these markings were instructional somehow. Well they are. I haven't figured the whole thing out yet, but what I found is beyond description."

"Well, that I can believe," he interrupted. "This whole situation is beyond description. The skill level of its construction defies most available modern technologies. Is it a government secret? Maybe. Is it extra-terrestrial? Maybe. Is it sixty-five million years old? Maybe. Is this whole mess crazy? Definitely!"

"Well dear, so far you're correct. This is definitely crazy," she said flatly. "I can answer all of your other questions to a certain degree. This is definitely not government. Even you have to give me that one. It may indeed be sixty-five million years old. I'll even go with extra-terrestrial."

"What'd you just say?" interrupting her. "You think this is how old?"

"If you will allow me to finish, I can answer that question. It may be sixty-five million years old and it may even be extra-terrestrial. Let me show you. What I've found is going to take a while to analyze. I need your full co-operation on this. I am sorry that you couldn't find me," she stoked his cheek with her palm to emphasize her sincerity, "but soon you'll know why. You mustn't be this upset. I'm all right."

"Upset! You scared the shit out of me. You tell me some wild fanciful story and then you expect me to calmly say, 'Okay dear, whatever you say. I'll be fine.' Well I don't think so." Jonathan pacing the entire time he was ranting. Now he abruptly rounded on her and yelled, "I just want to know what in the hell is going on here." *You're this close to being on the receiving end of a swift kick in the butt.*

"I'm trying to explain the unexplainable. I have to show you to have you fully understand. What I have to show you is so fantastic that you'll become excited and agitated at the same time. That's why I need you to calm down. I know that you won't be able to be calm later on."

"Well you're pretty damn calm for having experienced the moment of a lifetime," he snapped defensively.

"I've had time to deal with it. Granted, not much time, but still, I have been afforded that small luxury, whereas you've not. We are scientists above all else Jonathan. It's our nature to study and understand through that study. This is something that will call upon everything you've ever learned or heard. It's phenomenal! Just trust me on this." *I guess he's right. I should have called him before I disappeared. At least he'd have known where I was. He gets sex tonight for being a good sport about this.*

"I'm okay now. Let's get on with it." Jonathan knew he'd been beaten on this issue. Physically and mentally he was drained from his earlier fear of losing her. His scientific instinct was taking over. Professional curiosity would win out over whimsy or emotion every time.

Jonathan knew she was not given to idle fancy. She was here and safe. And she had a very peculiar story to tell. Whatever she was about to reveal, she firmly believed that it was as fantastic as she had described it. The level of excitement she revealed could not be faked.

"Step over here." She pointed to a place on the ground where she wished him to stand and scraped a line in the soil with her boot.

"What next?"

"Can you see well enough from there? I'm going to be working down here nearer the floor of the cave."

"I can see clearly," he said moving into position.

"As you know, I've been making rubbings of these figures here. These are the same ones that appear on the other side in mirror image. I started my rubbings when one of the figures depressed. It remained depressed. It was this one here." She pointed to the one that would be lower left of the pentagonal form they made.

"It startled me. After thinking about it for a bit, I surmised that this must be some form of locking device."

"Wait a minute. You did all of this with me just around the corner, and you couldn't say a word to me?" A sense of indignation surged through him briefly. *And I thought we shared everything. What other secrets are you keeping?*

"I was going to call you when it first happened, but at that moment I became intently curious about the other markings. I pressed on the one just up from it and nothing happened. As I sat there the first one returned to the surface. I pressed it again, and it recessed again. It had to be timed somehow, that much was obvious.

"Speculations began to run through my mind about the nature of control devices. This could be operated by any number of mechanical or electrical devices. I had to figure out something to get to the next step.

"I moved up to the one in the center top and pressed it. It depressed. Now I have two out of the five depressed. I guessed that the pattern was alternating – like tightening or loosening lug nuts on a tire – so I skipped the next marking and went to the one in the lower right corner. It also depressed. I then moved up to the one at the upper left. It too depressed. Once the last one was depressed it happened. All five rose as a group, curving in towards the center of the grouping, but not touching. They looked like the faucet handles you find on an outside spigot, and so I pulled on them. Nothing happened. I pushed and they all went back down and remained flush with the surface.

"That's when I was going to call you over and show you what I'd found. It might have been nothing, but it was definitely strange. Instead, I went through the sequence again and they all protruded from the surface just as they had done the first time. This time I put my fingers in between them – like I was turning on a faucet – and turned to the left. You know lefty loosey, righty tighty. Nothing happened. They didn't even move.

"I figured why not try clockwise this time. They began to move slowly. They stopped and opened out like a flower in bloom. A door-type device slid away and exposed the center space formed by the five symbols as they are here on the surface. A cylinder rose up from the center. On it was an indentation where a hand was to be placed. I guessed that it was like the hand locks they use on some of the government labs at the university. You've seen them. You place your whole hand on the plate and it's scanned. This one was strange though. It has only three digits, not five. It was also an indented area in the surface, not a flat scanning surface.

"I put my thumb in the first space, my index and middle finger into the center space, both my ring and little fingers into the last space. The whole thing just opened up." Ellen gestured again, with a sweep of her hand to encompass the area she described.

Jonathan remained silent for a time. His brain was assimilating everything he'd heard. As fanciful as the story appeared, he knew his wife to be a keen observer. There was entirely too much detail for this to be a practical joke. Truth was the only explanation.

Finally, he spoke. "Are you telling me that you found a doorway into this thing? Why wouldn't you call me over for something like this? I don't understand."

"I was so overcome with excitement that I didn't think to call you. I had already not called for you on two separate occasions and I just didn't call this time either. I remember fumbling for my flashlight and after I shined it into the opening I went inside. It was exactly where we found that almost invisible seam that had been machined so well. We just needed to look harder to find the whole outline of the door. Now that I know it's there, I can see it easily." She traced her finger along the outline. Jonathan could also see it clearly now.

"Okay. I'm with you right up to where you go inside. Ellen, we've been together for more than half of our lives, I know how over-excitement freezes you up sometimes, and I understand it. Nothing you're saying correlates with Ellen Crenshaw's normal behavioral patterns. Remember how you were when you discovered this thing. Are you sure that you that you didn't fall down and bump your head, and you just think all of this happened?" *Oh shit, I should never have said that. When will I learn? There's that look! Oh well, brace yourself old man, here it comes.*

"You son-of-a bitch!" She needed him to believe her. . . to believe *in* her. All she was getting was his cool logical approach to the situation. She continued to unleash her pent up emotions. "Don't you think that I know the difference between a fall and reality? What the hell kind of scientist do you take me for?

"You already said you went looking for me. I have to assume you looked over here first. Did you see my unconscious, prone body laying here on the ground, you dumb ass? Show me a bump on my head smart ass! Go ahead find one!" Ellen began pulling sections of her hair apart, exposing her scalp. After a few of the frantic hair-pulling she continued, "You can't because there isn't one to find. All I wanted was some understanding and support. And you feed me shit. Give me a minute while I get my shovel. I'll show you what a bump on the head looks like!"

"I'm sorry dear." He was clearly staggered by the sudden intensity of her outburst. Jonathan knew he was in trouble when he opened his mouth. He grabbed her arm as she tried to rush past him.

She stopped immediately and forcibly yanked her arm from his grip. "Sorry my ass! I'll show you the meaning of sorry!"

Scrambling for a mental safe haven, he continued in a placating tone, "You're knocking me off my feet with this unbelievable story. I'm trying to believe everything that you're saying, but this pushes the envelope a little too far. Look at it from my viewpoint. . ."

Abruptly cutting him off in mid-sentence, she retorted, "All right smart ass. Watch this! Prepare to experience my view point."

Ellen reached down and deftly depressed the images in their proper sequence. They rose just as she had described them.

"I'll be damned," was all he said. His mouth managed to remain open after he spoke.

Now that the images protruded, exactly as she'd described them, she inserted her fingers between the raised figures just as she described. Turning them slowly clockwise they began to open like a blooming flower. The panel slid away and the cylinder rose up reveling the three-fingered hand image that was either engraved or molded into the top surface of the cylinder.

"Would you like the honor of opening the door? You know, you could wake up from this dream at any moment." *I'm going to shove you in the mud as soon as I can pour the water.*

"I'm so sorry, Ellen. This is beyond my wildest imaginings. I understand why you didn't call for me. I admit, this holds your attention." He rambled a few more sentences before he shut up.

He looked at her eyes and placed his fingers into the imprint like she had described. The side of the wall began to move. It shifted out of the way, like an iris, forming an opening large enough for both of them to step through. He turned to Ellen and extended his hand.

"Do you want me or a flashlight?" she asked coldly. *I'm not through with you yet buster, so don't expect any kindness for the rest of this century.*

"Huh? What? Oh yeah. Both, if you don't mind." He didn't turn away from the door. Jonathan half expected something to lunge out, grabbing them both.

Ellen stepped into the opening just ahead of him. She had her flashlight on and handed his to him as she passed him on her way in.

The experience was every bit as unnerving the second. Jonathan was only half a step behind her. He'd already turned his light on. "You had better step in a little farther or the door will get you," she added.

CHAPTER FIFTEEN

As SILENTLY AS IT HAD opened, it closed. They were entombed in this box of unknown origin, in the middle of nowhere. No one knew where they were. They would never be found in time. Jonathan slammed himself against the inside of the box as if sheer desire would be enough to cause the door to open again. Relentlessly, he beat his fists against the unyielding metal. Panic had consumed him. He was on the verge of hyperventilating.

Grabbing him by the shoulders, Ellen shook him abruptly to get his attention focused on her. "I told you that I needed you to be relaxed. You are clearly too tense. Look at you, you're panicked." Her voice was calm and soothing with just the right amount of disdain. "I've been in here and gotten out again. When *you* think about it rationally, there is no reason to worry." *This is your first lesson in sorry, asshole.*

Breathing heavily, he rasped, "Okay, what next? I'm not in very good shape right now."

Smiling up at him, she asked, "Would you move a little to your left before you have your heart attack? There's something I have to do and you're in my way sweetheart."

As he stepped aside, she said, "That's enough." She shined her flashlight on a panel just behind Jonathan. It had the same hand imprint as the one that rose up on the cylinder. This one was placed at a more reasonable height from the floor. Placing her hand onto it, the door opened silently. *This is your second lesson in 'I'm sorry' big boy. You had better learn to trust me or next time I'll throw you in here with no instructions on how to get out.*

Jonathan lurched out into the night air of the cave. He rushed through the opening so forcefully that he slammed into the cave wall. Ellen stepped from the opening with a broad smile across her face. "Well, that's all for the tour this evening. Watch your step please. Make sure that you tell the management if there was anything in particular that you enjoyed. I know that they're always interested in your comments and making any improvements to make your experience more enjoyable."

Jonathan's mouth hung slack. He was at a total loss for words, just standing there, staring in disbelief. His concentration was distorted to the point that he didn't even hear Ellen's sarcastic remarks.

"Let's get back to the tent. We can see Steve tomorrow and formulate some new plans. We've both had more than our share of adventure for one day." His voice was raspy and his breath was still somewhat shallow, but improving.

They walked silently back to the tent; Jonathan was slowly recovering from his panic attack. Ellen walked with a self-satisfied smugness to her obvious swagger. What could they say that they hadn't already experienced?

Somehow Jonathan suddenly found himself standing in front of their tent. He glanced over his shoulder to look back in the direction of the cave. Ellen brushed past him and entered the tent. Jonathan trailed behind her. He stood next to his cot and began undressing. As he folded his pants, he noticed that he was already wearing pajamas. Where did they come from? They were both prepared for bed, and no words other than 'I love you' followed by a kiss, were spoken to close the rift.

All would be mended by morning light. They didn't fight very often and he knew this was a minor fight. It would never be spoken of again until it would be a party story, they could both enjoy retelling to everyone's amusement.

Steve had spent the last several hours studying and editing his plans. There were papers scattered all across his desk. There was no improving on what he'd already accomplished. He decided it was time for bed. Preoccupied with the plan, he lay there staring at the empty space above his head. Eventually he settled in for the night.

It was after 2:00 a.m. before he drifted off to sleep. He didn't realize that he had even fallen asleep until the 6:00 a.m. alarm rousted him. Steve knew that he hadn't slept very long, but he felt strangely refreshed. The resolution of potential problems gave him peace of mind. The plans framework would allow him to make slight modifications as he went along.

The smell of bacon and eggs wafted into his tent. He quickly dressed; gathering his thoughts and his papers before joining the rest of the world. A satisfied smirk formed on his lips as he scanned the camp and the site. It was going to be a wonderful day.

It was 10:00 a.m. before the Crenshaw's left for Steve's site. They'd gotten up early to look at the box again. They ate a light breakfast and formulated several plans. Neither was very hungry. The task was too daunting for the two of them alone. They had decided that they would need to recruit Steve's assistance; no matter what direction this was heading.

As the truck's engine roared to life, Ellen said, "I'm sorry about last night. You hurt my feelings and you needed to be knocked down a peg or two." *Know it all.*

"Well you did a fine job of it." His tone was flat. Still smarting from last night's humiliation, he didn't wish to discuss it. Especially now that Ellen revealed that she'd done it on purpose. *I deserve better than this.*

"Jonathan, I don't want this to put a wedge between us." *Especially since I now have the upper hand.*

Enraged by her attitude, Jonathan responded, "Shut up Ellen." *Shut up bitch is what I'd love to say. I may be crazy, but I'm not that stupid.*

"Shut up? Who the hell do you think you're talking to? I'm not some dog to be ordered around like that!" *You petty, pompous ass.*

"Oh sure, it's okay to tear me to shreds, but don't dare come after you. I get it now. You have the box and don't need anyone else. Is that it Ellen. . . Well?" After no response the second time he muttered, "I thought as much." *Gotcha!*

"You're crazy as a loon." *You'll be what, five years old this fall?*

"Go ahead, make it personal. If you can't win intellectually; attack the person."

"How dare you?" *Shit, I hate it when he's right.*

Slamming on the brakes and sliding the truck off the road, Jonathan turned to face her directly, "Look, we've been married for thirty years and have a wonderful son and two beautiful grandchildren. We've been together in the field for twenty-five years. I don't like what you've become since this box has been unearthed. Cut the bullshit or I'm history. If you don't believe me, just try me." *If you push just one more button, I'm on the next plane to anywhere. Go ahead and make my day lady.*

Ellen hadn't expected the ultimatum he just delivered. She began to cry when she realized the full implications of what he'd just said. Through the years they had their fair share of quarrels, its human nature to disagree. This was no different to her than a garden-variety argument. Jonathan seemed to believe it was a direct attack on their marriage or his manhood or both. "You really mean that don't you?" she said as she began to sob uncontrollably.

"Yes, I do. We talked a lot when we were first married and then it tapered off. I accepted that and as we grew more comfortable with each other I really never considered it a problem until now." He couldn't tell if she could hear him through all the crying, but he continued. It was important that he explain his anxieties.

"Since this box has entered our lives, we've both changed. I don't like what I see. I love you very much and would dread not having you in my life, but if we don't start talking again, I don't see any other way but to leave. It may be a knee jerk reaction, but honest communication is proof of our love for each other. At least it is to me."

Ellen sat red eyed and sniffling. Her crying was subsiding as she listened. She was too numb to speak or think. Her whole life was falling apart. Looking out the side window, she just stared at the landscape.

"Well, I guess that's it then. You'd rather have me leave than work through this. Have I really been all that bad Ellen?"

Jonathan stared at her for an indefinite amount of time. All he knew was the silence seemed to last an eternity. Their whole life was crumbling before his eyes and she was just sitting and starring out the window. Giving up all hope, he reached for the ignition to re-start the truck.

"You can't go," she finally blurted out. "I don't want you to leave. Let's just blow that damn thing up and forget we ever found it in the first place." She grabbed onto the front of his shirt and looking him squarely in the eyes whispered, "Please don't do this. We need and love each other. We'll get through this. I know we will."

"You know we can't do that Ellen."

"You're not even willing to try?" She was desperate to understand what was happening.

"No not that, I'm talking about the box. An explosion that size would bring Bob out here before the dust settled. Someone would eventually find the remains and then we. . . well I don't know what. I just know that it's not an option."

Releasing the front of his shirt, her hands just dropped, and her shoulders sagged. "Well I guess that's it. We're going to have to tell Johnny."

"That's it!" yelled Jonathan excitedly. Kissing her full on the mouth, he said, "We should have thought of this sooner. You're brilliant. We need to tell Johnny." Jonathan started the truck and gravel flew everywhere as he wheeled the truck around and headed into town to call their son.

By the time they arrived in town, Ellen had finally understood what Jonathan was getting at. He'd changed horses in mid-stream and completely lost her for a while. They'd both made their hasty apologies and agreed to settle the matter fully at a later date. For now, there were more pressing matters to be dealt with. She kissed him, and meant it, as he got out to use the pay phone.

They were a bit cryptic about what was going on. Young Jonathan knew not to ask too many questions over the phone. From experience he knew by their tone that they were on to something big and that they would fill him in when they felt more secure. He was convinced that they were soliciting his help for something. All he could do was wait for a call back.

Now that a major hurdle had been successfully negotiated, they headed back to visit with Steve and his team. When the Crenshaw's finally arrived, they noticed the grid of markers placed around the camp. Steve had learned well. The team was clearly sweeping the grid looking for something. It appeared to be an efficient technique. Seeing Steve by the main tent, they approached.

"Good morning Steve," came Jonathan's voice from around the corner of the tent.

"Good morning dear." Ellen's greeting followed immediately.

"Hi. How are you guys? I missed you yesterday." Glancing down at his watch, he remarked, "And it's almost noon. Are you two planning on never seeing me on time? There's so much that I need to show you. . . to tell you! It's very exciting!"

"Really?" questioned Ellen. "What has happened in the span of one short day?"

"You won't believe what I am about to show you! It's so exciting!"

They both chuckled to themselves. They glanced at each other when they saw that Steve wasn't looking. The poor boy had no idea how everything now seemed so insignificant to them.

"You must remember that we're only here as advisors," Jonathan admonished. "This is your dig. We don't wish to interfere in any fashion. We will answer your questions, but we won't guide you in any way. You're going to succeed or fail on your own merit. We meant what they said when we offered you this opportunity."

"I understand completely, Jonathan. I fully understood the terms when you first presented them. I only wish for you to confirm some of our initial findings. I know my identifications are correct, however, I want your confirmation before I move on to the next step. I won't try to get unnecessary help from you. This shouldn't take long at all. By the way, have you guys established a site yet? I think that I ended up with the best potential on this outing. No offense, but I've stumbled on to something really big here."

"That's great, Steve." Ellen embraced him with a quick, professional hug around the waist returning the embrace he was giving her around the shoulders. "When do we get to see your preliminary findings?"

"Right now. I have everything in the tent, if you would care to follow me."

"Thank you, my boy," boomed Jonathan's voice. "I couldn't be prouder than if you were my own son. It has been a pleasure having you with us all of these years. Now you have enough experience, and courage to venture out on your own. Ellen is very proud of you also. We were just commenting about that on the way here."

"Thank you. That means a lot to me. . . especially coming from both of you. It's been my pleasure to work with you all of these years. I wouldn't be where I am today without you guys." He shook Jonathan's hand heartily. They patted themselves on the backs before they released their grip.

Throwing open the tent flap, Steve let them both inside. He tied it off before he came in. The slight breeze would keep the tents heat manageable, especially with three of them inside. He went over to his makeshift desk and gathered some of his belongings.

"You guys want anything to drink before we get started?" They both shook their heads no while reading some of the notes on his desk.

Carefully, Steve unrolled the cloth containing the previous day's samples. He laid it out before them.

"These are magnificent. You got these here? These are all raptor. Did you find a mass death site? Was it a flash flood? How are the bodies dispersed?"

"Yes, these were all collected here. No, we have no evidence of a mass death site. There are no bodies as of yet."

Ellen interrupted. "You haven't found anything resembling a mass death site?"

"No, and I don't think that I will. Let me explain. These came from a general search of the grounds yesterday. These samples came from all over the place. I too, came to the conclusion that they were all raptor. That's what I wanted you guys to verify that for me. Now that I know you agree with me; I can show you what else has been uncovered."

He handed them another carefully wrapped bundle. It was wrapped the way that they had taught him to wrap delicate bone fragments. Jonathan eased the wrappings open, slowly, methodically. He laid the bone fragments out for closer inspection. He immediately noticed the small cuts covering the bone's surface. There were several larger cuts and the clear indication that this fragment was bitten as a whole piece from the animal that had been killed.

"What are we looking at Steve?"

"Well, this is what I have so far. I have laid a grid around the area surrounding the campsite. We have found very young and juvenile fragments spread throughout the area. Also, we have some teeth fragments from adult raptors as well.

"After carefully examining the dispersal patterns of all the samples, I checked for evidence of washout from the rain. This area is slightly elevated from the surrounding terrain. Any washout would have carried the fragments away. It would not have scattered them over this section.

"Then there is the bone sample that you have before you. I have seven such samples. They were all collected within fifty yards of one another. That's the largest fragment that we've found so far. As you can see, there are several different sized teeth abrasions on the surface. Something very small was chewing on that bone. Imagine the power of the young jaws that could mark the bone that deeply. You can also see juvenile markings as well."

CHAPTER SIXTEEN

With all the evidence spread before them, the unspoken question hung heavily in the tent. Urging him to his conclusion, Ellen asked, "What's your point in all of this?"

Jonathan looked up from the sample and said, "I think I understand where you're taking this. Tell us. If it's what I think it is, it's very intriguing. You will knock the academic world for a loop when you publish."

Steve began with a new enthusiasm, "I believe that the raptors were every bit as social, and maternal, as the herbivores. The initial evidence indicates that this area encompassed a wide spread social group. Look at the bone. It's the same as one that you would give a dog to chew. I believe, and intend to prove, that these animals cared for their young.

"I've been thinking about how lions hunt in packs and then the young come in and share in the feast. There may have been too many youngsters to let them wander around from one kill to the next. It's my contention that food fragments were brought back to a centralized nesting area, or nursery, and given to the young and juvenile animals to feast on.

"It would serve many purposes. First and foremost, it would provide nourishment. It would also help develop chewing skills. Youngsters could learn to slice the meat away from the bone as well as exercise their jaw muscles."

"That's fascinating. What drew you to these conclusions?" Jonathan pressed.

"The mounting evidence," Steve defended.

"Don't get me wrong. I don't disagree. If I was faced with this same evidence, I'd draw the same conclusions. I only want you to understand that the rest of the academic world will soon be split in their thinking. Even though they weren't here to see what you saw, they will have an opinion. Some will agree with you, some will not. You must gather as much empirical data as you can. Do you have enough film to document this for permanent records? There will be those who don't trust photographs, most will."

"Is it always like this?"

"No, only when you change course in mid-stream. You, Steve, have come up with something quite radical. You'll definitely make a name or a reputation for yourself. I hope you're up to the challenge. We both think you're a very capable young man.

"Once you present this evidence and the conclusions that you draw from it, you'll be placing yourself in the eye of the storm. You will, fortunately, experience a short period of calm before the storm begins to rage around you, before it consumes you. I envy you and at the same time I am glad not to be in your shoes."

"Jonathan, you're frightening the boy."

"Good, because it's going to get a lot worse before it gets better."

"Thank you both. It's sound advice. I hope I'm up to the challenge. I'll proceed non-the-less. The evidence is what it is. I can't deny it because I am scared of the consequences by presenting it. Did I mention that we're taking measurements inside each grid to show the concentration of bone fragments? Three of the ten grids already have concentration spots on slightly mounded ground of very young to baby bone fragments. I believe that these mounds are the actual nests."

"That's the spirit! Now get out there and search for more evidence. What you have is very strong, but you'll need much more if you want to win this argument."

Turning to Ellen, he said, "I believe it's time that we left Steve to his task. Let's get back before the day is gone. It will be lunchtime soon, if it's not already."

"Why don't you stay here for lunch? They'll begin preparation shortly."

"Thank you for the invitation, but we must return to our own work," said Ellen. Seeing the disappointment on his face she quickly added, "There is still much that we must talk about. May we come by tomorrow? We'll even stay for lunch."

"That'll be great," he brightened. "I'll have much more by tomorrow. Your faith in me is not unfounded. Thank you again. I won't let you down."

"Steve, you could never let us down. You've long since proven yourself to us. You wouldn't be here if we thought you couldn't do the job. Am I right Ellen?"

"He's right Steve. You just be yourself, that's the most anyone can ask of you."

Steve walked them back to their truck. They said a few more good-byes. As they drove away Steve turned his thoughts to his work and the Crenshaw's returned to formulating their own plans.

There was still much to do before they could show him what Ellen had found. Not the least of which was saving their marriage. Much had been said that should have remained unspoken. Neither felt that the damage was irreparable, yet they were adult enough to know time was going to be a key factor. And the pressing issue of the box was yet to be fully resolved.

They drove back to their campsite in silence. Both were deep in thought. Steve had found an excellent site and it would bring a lot of publicity for him and the school. They needed to figure out a way to exploit the situation. There was always a solution to a problem and sometimes it was convoluted. They were confident that they would resolve this dilemma as they always did. This problem was too basic to overwhelm them.

While Jonathan prepared lunch he kept looking up the hillside. The box drew his attention like a magnet. There was something wonderful, yet frightening about it. The intellect needed to create it must have been staggering.

"What do you think dear? Got any brainstorms?" he asked Ellen.

"Not yet Jonathan, but it's not for lack of trying."

"How do you want your eggs Ellen?"

"In a nest, please. You remember how we used to serve them for Johnny?"

"How could I forget? It was the only way he would eat them for three years. Do you mind if I cut the center out of the bread with a knife, or do you want me to dirty a glass?"

"I believe that I would like you to cut a box shape out of the center before you toss in the egg," quipped Ellen.

"That's it dear! You've done it again."

"What are you talking about?"

"All we have to do is remove the box and transport it as if it were just another fossil. Don't you see? We should treat the box as if it were no big deal. It could be a new way of transporting fossils. We could say that it's hermetically sealed to protect the delicate nature of the fragments. It's an experiment to try and prevent covering everything in layer after layer of plaster."

"You're going to have to stop giving me credit for your ideas. I'll accept the inspiration, but nothing more than that. You're right though, a driver would neither know, nor care about the box. Freight is just freight to them, nothing more and nothing less. The only change I'd make to your idea is to not disclose anything about the box. We'll just seal the whole thing up in a giant crate and ship it away. It's clean and simple. And no one will know there's a metal box inside."

"We need to finish uncovering this monstrosity before we go back inside. You know as well as I do, that once inside, we'll never move another shovel full of dirt."

"I know, but I really want to study whatever we find in there."

"I'll make you a deal. I'll go back inside with you, right after lunch. We'll stay inside for half an hour. We're not sure of the air supply yet. No matter what we do or don't find, that will be the last time we enter the box until we show Steve. As your kind and generous husband, I ask you, is that a fair deal?"

"You stink, you know that? I have to admit the air supply thing is right. I was in there for about half an hour and it was becoming oppressive. With the two of us in there, it would only allow us about ten to fifteen minutes." *Damn it, he was right two times in one morning. The world is spinning out of control.*

"I see that you feel the deal is more than fair." *At least things seem like they're getting back to normal.*

"I hate it when you're so damned right. We better come up empty handed, or it will be hell to pay."

"You're beautiful when you're crazed," he said with that silly grim he had when he was right.

"Shut up and give me my eggs." She grabbed the plate from his hand in mock anger. When the eggs started to slide from the edge of the plate, they both laughed as Ellen twisted and turned, saving her lunch in the process.

"You are a woman of many talents. I didn't know that you could juggle too."

She stared intently at him. She wasn't angry, only embarrassed. However, they did need to find an appropriate location to study it more closely. Someplace that was far from prying eyes, and probing questions. They often took several weeks off after a summer dig. Nobody ever asked where they went or what they did. That had always offended them in the past, but now she was grateful for the established pattern.

Wiping egg yolk from the corner of her mouth, she said, "That was good dear. Thank you for a fine lunch."

"You're welcome. Ready? Let's get going."

"After you. It's your plan. Lead on my captain."

"Very funny sweetheart." *God, I love this woman more than life itself. I know I could never bring myself to leave her. Why did I ever open that can of worms? I have a big mouth.*

CHAPTER SEVENTEEN

ARRIVING AT THE CAVE, THEY felt the same apprehension as before. They had wanted this to be a great discovery in its own right. Both were justifiably afraid that this might be some lost military secret or something else. At the same time, they didn't want to be sending signals out into space, inviting whomever or whatever down for milk and cookies.

Ellen manipulated the figures for a third time now and watched silently as the door opened. With flashlights and lantern in hand, they stepped inside. They stepped clear as the door silently closed behind them.

"There must be a way to keep that thing open. I don't have a strong wish to die in here." Jonathan was already edgy. *Maybe I suffer from claustrophobia and don't know it.*

"Why don't you open the door every now and again, to let the air in?" she asked. *It's such a simple solution. Why didn't you think of it?*

She turned and started closely examining the walls. The door had the hand shaped locking mechanism and a few markings. They were probably the instructions on how to keep the door open. There were several other markings that reminded her of hazard signs. Ellen made a mental note to stay away from any area that was marked similarly. Looking around, she wondered why this room was so much smaller than the box itself. That was confusing. It was as if this were a false back or something. It was clearly a much smaller part of the whole.

Jonathan had moved to the other side of the small room. His

attention was focused on more of the highly precise lines that had earlier turned out to be the seams of the door into this room.

He was hoping that he had found another door. After carefully studying the entire surface area, he didn't see any lock or similar pattern of figures to indicate an opening mechanism. "Well, I don't know what to make of all this Ellen. We're in a small portion of the box. I don't understand any of it. Do you have any ideas?"

"Maybe. Come here and look at these markings. What contemporary thing do they remind you of?"

"Warning signs… High voltage signs… Danger signs? Hell, I don't even know what answer you're looking for."

"That's exactly the answer I'm looking for. That's the same thing that I thought when I saw them. These markings are near the door, but not at or on the door. I think that the power supply might be behind this plate."

"What do you mean, plate?"

"There is a line that goes all the way around these symbols. Look. There are no other lines near them, just this one." She traced the line completely around the plate so he could see it.

"I believe that any of the lines that we find are separate pieces placed together in a very precise manner for a particular purpose. I want to try and open this. It has to work like the outside door. Those lines were actually the door itself."

"Why don't you start like you did last time?" Jonathan suggested. "The pattern may repeat throughout this box. It doesn't make sense that every sealed door or access panel would have a different kind of lock."

Ellen excitedly began the manipulating the figures before Jonathan had finished his sentence. These were in a different pattern than the outside of the door. They were evenly spaced and in a straight line. Again, there were five of them like the pentagonal grouping on the outside of the box. She had tried several combinations, when suddenly the panel itself rose from the surface of the inner box. She stepped back quickly.

Jonathan was distracted; the other lines he was tracing had drawn his attention away from Ellen. Her sudden movement drew his attention. As he turned, he saw the panel rise from the surface. He moved closer to watch its progress. There might be a clue to be found that would explain this new panel or whatever it was.

The panel moved at least ten centimeters away from the surface. It didn't expose anything that was behind it. It was obviously a heavy plate, based on its thickness. He tried to pull on it, but nothing happened. He pushed on it and it glided slowly back into position.

"Why'd you do that?" complained Ellen. "What if I can't get it open again?"

"Well it'll have to wait. Our half hour is up."

"Are you sure? My watch seems to have stopped."

"Nice try dear. It won't fly around here," Jonathan stated flatly.

"No seriously. Look for yourself. Check yours."

"I'll be damned. I just checked my watch a moment ago and it was running. Try to open that panel again."

"Maybe it emits an EM pulse or something when it's activated. We don't have a clue as to what powers this thing. It can't be purely mechanical. There's no noise when things happen with the door and this panel."

"Now that the panel is closed, my watch is running again. Open it up and I'll check my watch."

The panel glided noiselessly open while Jonathan exclaimed that his watch had stopped again. This was another clue in what soon would become a long line of clues.

"You know how much I want to stay in here Jonathan?" Her eyes and voice were pleading.

"Yes, dear I know, but we need to get Johnny to take a look at this. He's a computer whiz and might have this figured out in no time. Let's just do what we do best and get this box out of this cave and onto a truck. We have enough friends and contacts to get us through the worst of times. Come on, you agreed."

"I know, but that doesn't mean I like it." Ellen pouted while stepping through the door.

They both went about the business of unearthing the last of the box once the door closed. They could figure out how to get it down the hillside once they were finished.

CHAPTER EIGHTEEN

THERE WERE SMALL FLAGS POPPING up all over the grid. It was obvious that he had a very bountiful site. He called the two students from the farthest two grids. He assigned them the task of photographing and logging each item that had been flagged. It was a formidable task. Steve wondered if he needed a couple more students for the job. There were more and more fossils being flagged as the survey progressed. At this rate, he was going to run out of flags.

Steve wished that he knew how to reach either Jonathan or Ellen. He could send them in to town and solicit some help from the locals. Considering how much money the university would spend for a discovery like this made the idea plausible. The publicity alone would offset any expenditure. Student applications would increase from the news telecasts alone. The university could then start its own private media blitz for alumni donations.

"Well, what do you think?"

Steve was startled by one of the assigned cataloging students. "What did you say?" he fumbled.

"I just wanted to know if you approved of the cataloging method I'm using," she said, extending her tablet to him.

Steve took the tablet. He studied it intently. He wrote a couple of notes in the margins and handed it back to her. "That's very nice. You're doing a fine job. Have you done this kind of work before?"

"Well, I helped out with inventory at my father's company almost every year. He had some pretty good forms to use. I changed one of them around a little so that I could use it for the fossils. There would have been a lot of other useless information otherwise."

"That's remarkable. I would like you to change it a little bit more. If you change it the way I have noted in the margins, I think we'll have a winner. When you're done could you please bring me a copy of the form before it's filled in? I would like to take it into town and have some copies made. I would seriously like to use this as my permanent cataloging form, with your permission of course."

"I'd be honored. I only did it to make my job a little easier. I figured that if I could get the work done simply, I could do more in the same time it takes when using the old form."

"Then it's settled. As soon as you finish the form, I'll run in to town and have them copied. I'll go during lunch so that we don't lose that much time. Thank you very much. Do you think we should call it the Inventory and Cataloging Form, Brogdon 1.0?"

"Now I think you're being silly." *He's so cute.*

"No, I'm very serious Miss Brogdon. This is your work and I think it should bear your name. I'll put it down in the lower left corner like companies do on their internal forms. There's nothing worse than someone else taking credit for the work you've done. I won't steal or use any one's ideas or work. If I can't use it out in the open, then I shouldn't be using it at all."

"I appreciate that you want to give me credit. Although I think that if you want to give me credit, you should just tell everyone that I did it. And you can call me Janet."

"Perhaps you don't understand. I want to use this form from now on. It's to become my one and only method of cataloging and saving information in the field. Someday, when computers are easier to carry and their battery power will last a full day, I can incorporate your form into the database and then all you would need to do is key in the information right on the spot."

"Thank you for that kindness. That means a lot to me. I'll clean this up and have it back to you shortly." Miss Brogdon, Janet, hurried from Steve's tent. She was going to have the form done before lunch, if it killed her. Janet was very excited about his praise. He had such a sincere look about him. It engendered a certain trust. She felt compelled to help him in any way that she could.

Janet had only met one other person with that endearing quality before. It had been a fruitful relationship. She had learned so much from it. Now she met Steve, and she recognized the same air of authority. She didn't sense arrogance; it was more of a self-assured composure. It was his bearing, his stature. He seemed to stand taller than other people. This may be his first dig as team leader, but he had a natural ability to lead and she saw that people followed him easily and willingly.

Steve turned his attention to the items that were being flagged. There were more and more raptor fragments being discovered. There were just too many of them for this to be anything other than a nursery. Three new leg bones had recently been discovered. They were all from baby raptors. A rib and spinal section from a juvenile had been flagged at one of the outer most grids. His hopes for a partial or complete raptor were increasing with each new flag.

He reminded himself that this was only the second day. The fossil remains that he had were evidence enough for his theory. Steve just wanted a complete raptor to top off this already amazing cache of fossils. Working as quickly as the amount of information allowed, Steve continued to chart the finds on his grid paper. There was a total of seven mound-like hot spots now. They were not laid out in any particular pattern, but it might be too soon to determine that portion of his supposition.

It was apparent that the areas that showed only small amounts of fossils were like garbage heaps. All turtle shell or other bone fragments. The commonality in each of these areas was the teeth marks ranging in sizes from the very small young to those of juvenal raptors. There could be no doubting the mounting evidence of a nursery and communal environment.

"Lunch is ready," shouted the cook. Soon the whole crew was headed for the tables. They sat around chatting about what they were finding. Everyone was excited about the preponderance of flagged fossils.

Steve heard all the commotion and came out of his tent. Everyone was about half way through lunch. He'd nearly missed it. Janet stepped up carrying a plate of food; giving him a shy smile as she handed him the plate.

"Thank you, Janet."

"I hope it's enough. I can get more, there's plenty."

"No, this will be fine. It's very considerate of you. Thank you, again."

"I just wanted to show my appreciation for using my form. Actually, when I get done making the changes it'll be our form. This will be our first collaboration." She swayed her hips, batted her eyelashes, pulling on loose strands of hair, smiling shyly as she walked away.

Steve felt his neck getting warm and soon the warmth had spread to his face. He shuffled his foot back and forth in the dirt. He found himself out of his element.

"I want everyone to know that I'm going in to town shortly," Steve announced. "If anyone needs me to pick something up, let me know in the next five minutes. Write it down, along with your name. I'll distribute everything when I get back."

Steve laid a pad of paper and a pen on the end of the table. He began to eat the large portion of the amazing stew Janet had given him. Even at the rapid pace he was consuming the stew, he was enjoying the meal. There was a hint of something just in the background. He wished that he had the time to sit and casually savor the subtle marriage of the vegetable and meat flavors, but that wasn't going to happen.

CHAPTER NINETEEN

Jonathan and Ellen had noticed Steve's truck as they pulled into the parking spot just beyond the General Store. They looked up and down the street, but they saw no trace of him.

"He must be in the store getting supplies," said Ellen. "Let's go in and talk to him. We're going to need his help on this. There's no other way around it."

"You're right dear."

"There he is. He's coming out of the Post Office," she said.

"Steve!" shouted Ellen. "Over here!" She yelled again, waving her arms to attract his attention.

Steve saw them and waved back. He called out something that neither of them understood.

Now that she had his attention, she signaled him to cross over and meet them at the store. He nodded his compliance. She smiled broadly as he drew near. Jonathan stepped forward to take his hand.

"What are you doing in town Steve? I thought you'd be up to your eyeballs in fossils by now.

"Well, actually I am. That's why I'm here." He handed each of them the form that he'd just copied. "One of the students did this. That's her name there on the bottom, in the corner there," he said pointing out Janet's name. "I thought that it was a nice touch."

"This is good. Did you get the rights to use it?"

"She only wants me to tell the others that it was hers. I told her that her name was going on the form and that was all I would hear about it. She said that she would be honored. . . and here I am making a hundred copies.

"Also, I stopped over to the hardware store to pick up a couple hundred of those little wire gas line flags. They're a special-order item, so I bought this 250' roll of heavy-duty wire, some wire cutters and a roll of this orange surveying tape. Anyway, I'm out and this is the closest thing I could think of that would work."

"That was good thinking Steve. There's something that Ellen and I need to discuss with you. It's a matter of grave urgency. Before we say anything, we need you to swear an oath of utter secrecy and total allegiance. Are you up to it?"

"That's a strange request."

"Yes or no, what'll it be?" Jonathan pressed.

"Okay. I swear that I will not reveal or cause to be revealed anything that you are going to tell me."

"Steve, we need your help in removing something that we found. No one must ever know that we have a separate site from yours. We're going to join you at your site and complain of no success. The others have no idea that we've already been digging for two weeks."

"My god what is it?" Steve was lost in thought and excitement. "Two weeks?"

"We're going to get some supplies and then call Johnny. It's to the point that we're going to need his help as well. We have a pretty amazing story and an even more amazing find. You'll understand the need for total secrecy once you see what we've found. Let's go inside and grab a cup of coffee while Ellen calls Johnny."

Jonathan unraveled the threads of his story as they sat in the back booth of the diner. He left nothing out, including even the smallest details in his story. They wanted to ensure that Steve had the most complete story possible. They both were hoping that Steve might pick up a lead somewhere, something that they had missed.

"Jonathan, I'm having difficulty dealing with this. This is either the most amazing discovery of all time or you two are a pair of totally certifiable grade 'A' crackpots. I don't know which. What do you want from me? I want to see this box of yours and at the same time I want to run screaming into the night."

"I've already told you what we want, what we expect. Do you actually believe I, we, would contrive a story like this as a gag?"

"It could be a hazing of sorts; this IS my first dig and everything."

"We swear that this is on the level. You don't have the slightest idea of how huge this is. Your apprehension won't be resolved until you see it. And keep your voice down, you look terrible."

"Well there's a brilliant observation." *What the hell are you two up to?*

"Don't get smart with me. For now, shut up and listen."

"I'm sorry Jonathan. I have no intention of offending you or Ellen. Do you know what a bomb you've just dropped on me? How did you expect me to react? Be reasonable."

"You're right. I didn't mean to be so harsh. You'll understand when you see it."

"I hope so. This is too strange to comprehend." *This better be a gag. It's too strange to be the truth.*

"Well, how are my two men handling this?" interjected Ellen. She pulled up a chair and motioned for a Nancy to bring some coffee. "I can see Steve's in a state of shock."

"That's an understatement." *I'm lucky to still be conscious.*

"All in all, dear, I think it went well."

"Would you like some cream Ellen?"

"No thanks. Could you leave the pot? I'll pay for it now if you'd like."

"No problem. Jonathan already paid while you were on the phone. He figured you'd want me to leave the pot. I brewed this one fresh for you."

"Thanks Nancy." *Starting early? Well I guess that's permissible. There aren't any ground rules to making peace.*

"It was nothing. It's just my job."

"Well thanks anyway." Ellen slipped her a five-dollar tip.

When Nancy left, Ellen continued, "Well, we have enough coffee, and I'm sure that there are questions that you want answered. Fire away. We'll leave when we run out of coffee or questions."

"I'm not sure where to begin," Steve said. "This is fantastic. It almost defies words." Steve began to ask any and every question that came to mind. The Crenshaw's answered those that they deemed fit. The others would be more suitably answered at the site. He was in no position to argue.

Jonathan looked at his watch. They'd been sitting there for two hours. It was time well spent, but no work was getting done. "When are you expected back at the site Steve?"

"I never said. They know I'll be back when I'm finished."

"Perfect. Let's give you the thrill or shock of your lifetime."

CHAPTER TWENTY

I T WAS ONLY THE THIRD day of his first dig and mentally things were spinning out of control. This was almost more than Steve could deal with. He'd understood Jonathan's story and even picked up on a couple of small details. Steve was adept at puzzle solving. Now he sat in lonely silence as he drove to the Crenshaw's site.

"This doesn't look like anything out of the ordinary," commented Steve as he stepped from his truck. He let his eyes wander freely around the camp. There was nothing that even hinted at what they were describing.

"Thank you for your observation. We've tried hard to maintain a natural, normal appearance. That was a daunting task. We solved our biggest hurdle by scattering some of the soil we removed all along the trail as we drove in and out. Most of it is just dumped down the hillside for the first week. It hasn't interfered with access to the cave and you can't really see any of it from here."

Putting his arm around Steve's shoulder, Jonathan said, "Let's get going. The sooner he sees this, the better we'll all feel." Turning to Steve, he continued, "Trust me son, you won't believe any of this until you actually touch it. Even then, you're going to doubt your own senses."

The three of them headed for the cave. As they rounded the side of the hill, Steve could see the soil that had been removed. It must have been twenty or thirty yards. There was no way of calculating the amount that had been scattered about.

Jonathan guided him up the well-traveled path to the mouth of the cave. They all paused before they entered. Steve was apprehensive.

He peered down the crescent shaped corridor. The sun did a fine job of illuminating the way. He could see that it had been well traveled. Steve edged cautiously closer, unsettled by what the Crenshaw's had told him.

"Do you mind if I use the toilet?" he asked flatly.

"Not at all. We'll be around the curve there," said Ellen. "That way you'll have a bit of privacy."

"That would be great," he said. "I'll only be a moment."

"Take your time."

"I guess that I'm just nervous," added Steve. He felt like he had to keep the conversation going until they left. He rocked a little from one foot to the next while he talked. They got the message.

"We'll wait for you." She and Jonathan walked down the passage until they were out of sight.

"Well what do you think?" she whispered.

"I think that he'll be just fine once we get this initial contact over with. He's made of tough stuff. I have confidence in him," whispered Jonathan.

"It's not that I don't trust him. He just seems too nervous."

"I didn't exactly ease into the conversation back at the diner. I just slapped him in the face with it."

"That wasn't very fair to the boy."

"I figured that if we were on campus and had all the time in the world, we could be nice and gentle. We're not, so I wasn't. It's that simple."

"Well I guess so. Is this another one of your guy things?" *Boys will always be boys. I can't imagine the pleasure they derive from taunting one another like that.*

"In a way," he chuckled. "If he couldn't handle a little rough treatment over this, how do you figure he would bear up once he announces the findings from his dig sight?"

"I see your point. I wasn't questioning your motivation, just your method."

"Thanks for the vote of confidence. I thought you knew me better than that. Do you actually think that I would jeopardize this find to play macho games with Steve? You really hurt me with that one."

"Don't be a baby. You just misunderstood me. I don't think you're trying to spoil everything. I just wouldn't have done it in the same fashion. I would have been more subtle. Then I would have shown him the box almost casually and picked up the pieces from there. It's the same end game, different rules."

"Well you left to call Johnny, and I handled Steve like a guy. We're here and Steve is more than willing to help. You're right. It's the same end game. I guess we'll never know which approach would have been the best. I'll tell you what, the next time we get into something this far over our heads, you can have at the volunteers. Then at least, we'll know if subtle is more correct than harsh reality. Does that sound fair to you?"

"Shut up already," she said as she playfully poked him in the ribs. She cupped her hand over her mouth as she realized her voice was raised.

There would be no point in carrying this conversation any further. Whatever method was used, this was the moment of truth. Once Steve saw the box, they would need to do or say whatever was necessary to secure his full co-operation. They had his promise, but that was sight unseen.

"I hope that I didn't keep you long. I am a little nervous right now and, well you know."

Smiling her reassurance, Ellen grabbed his hand and headed down the passage. Steve let himself be led. He felt as excited as he did when he first theorized about the raptor nesting sight. His heart pounded wildly as each leaden footstep brought him closer to the unknown. It was very exhilarating and very frightening.

"Even in the bright daylight, we need a little light back here," she said as she let go of his hand and went to turn on the lantern. The light filled the area. Steve covered his eyes reflexively.

"What the hell is that?" he said after acclimating to the light.

"This is our prize, Steve. Do you like it?" Jonathan watched his movements carefully. Jonathan glanced at Ellen and they smiled at each other. They knew from this first reaction that Steve was not going to be any problem at all. It was relaxing to have that pressure removed.

"Come on boy, it won't bite."

"Listen to you, Mister Bravery. I believe that it was you who was scared out of his wits just a few nights ago."

"I only want him to move in a little closer so that he may start a preliminary study of the box. I'm curious to hear his speculations on its' origin and its' purpose. Doesn't that interest you too?"

"Of course, it does." *Nice save my love.*

"Fair enough," he responded.

Steve didn't say another word; he just stared at the box, eyes and mouth wide open. They watched as he hesitantly edged forward, his hand outstretched, anticipating the contact of the metal. He looked as if he wasn't breathing. There was a slight youthful grin on his face. The kind a child gets when he discovers a great treasure from a pile of junk.

His hand stayed motionless, mere millimeters from the surface of the box. He let the metal identify itself. His fingertips sensed more warmth than he had anticipated. Jonathan had said that it was warm to the touch, but he assumed that he'd been mistaken. Even metal that was somewhat warm often felt cool to the touch.

"Has this been in direct sunlight?" Steve asked.

"No. The dim light you see now is all that you get from the opening at the top." Jonathan pointed to where the open crevasse curved away.

In the beginning, we were sure that this fissure was caused by thermal erosion. It was later that we discovered that this had actually been a cave at one time. From the lack of soil compaction, it was easy to speculate that rainwater had worn away the cave roof and eventually the hillside collapsed in on itself and filled the cave with soil. The rain eventually washed a lot of the soil out of the caves natural opening."

"Do you have any questions Steve?" asked Ellen.

"Not really. I must have missed this part of the story at the diner earlier."

"I don't think so Steve. As I recall, I forgot to tell you. Ellen's so much better at remembering all the facts. Even the inanest observations come in handy on occasion."

CHAPTER TWENTY-ONE

THE WORK AT STEVE'S SITE proceeded as if he were there. There were enough experienced people to carry out his directives effectively. The preponderance of flags was becoming unmanageable. There was an air of excitement. The students intuitively understood they were part of something big, really big. Conversations around the camp ranged from casual enthusiasm to outright exuberance.

The new members were the most excited. Naturally, all were excited, but the more experienced students had seen, or heard, of many good discoveries getting lost or overlooked in academic quibbling. Those who held current popularity and power were reluctant to fall from grace when something big or new came along.

It had been close to three hours since lunch and Steve hadn't returned. The group took notice of his absence. Being engaged in their work, they paid little attention to his absence. They understood he would return when his business was completed. If there was a serious problem, he'd use the cell phone to contact them. Sara Higgins was the first to hear Steve's phone ring. She was responsible to answer it as part of her duties of prepping for the next meal. "This is Sara Higgins; may I help you?"

"Hi Sara, it's Steve. I'm running very late. There was more to do than I had anticipated. Can you let everyone know that I won't be back until supper time?"

"Sure Steve. Is there anything in particular that you want, or special instructions?"

"Not really. Just keep up the good work. I'm bringing extra film and supplies to make more flags. Any other developments I need to know about?"

"It's good that you're bringing more flags; we're just about out. There is so much stuff here that we're not sure what to do with it all. We just keep flagging, tagging and bagging. It's all we can do to keep up with the cataloging."

"I figured that might be the case. I made at least a hundred copies of Janet's cataloging form. That should speed up the process. I'll distribute them when I return.

"The Crenshaw's were in town and I told them of our discovery. As it turns out, they are not having any success at all. They let me have their whole supply of flags too, plus I have the supplies that I'd already purchased. I have to go. I'll see all of you at suppertime. We can knock off after supper and make flags for tomorrow. Bye now."

Steve ended the call and turned back to Jonathan and Ellen. He was content with the alibi and knew Sara believed his story. Now he had more pressing issues to deal with. Multitudes of scenarios raced through his mind. "I've taken care of everything at the site. They're not expecting me before suppertime. That gives me a couple more hours."

"Well Steve," Jonathan said, putting his arm over Steve's shoulder. "Let me show you the way. If you thought the outside was intriguing, then you'll just love the inside."

Ellen keyed the figures and the door glided silently open. Steve lost all color in his face. He had not anticipated this. The craftsmanship on this box was magnificent. Jonathan had said how precise everything was, but he didn't even see the doorway until it opened only a few feet in front of him.

"There are several linear patterns that I want you to look at for me. I believe the cuts in the box determine its function." Jonathan continued his conversation as he entered the box. He turned to Steve only to find him still just outside the door. He was staring through the opening with a bewildered look on his face.

"Get in here," Jonathan motioned. "You can study the outside later. What I need you to look at is in here."

"Uh. . . yeah. . . in there. I'm coming."

"Hurry up. The door is about to close. We don't know how to keep it open all of the time. That's just one of the things we need for you to figure out, if it's even possible."

Stepping numbly through the doorway, Steve found himself inside the small room. He made a mental note that the room was significantly smaller than the overall dimensions of the box as a whole.

He noticed that the Crenshaw's were busy studying the interior walls very closely. He looked over Ellen's shoulder and watched her trace the outline of the panel that was near the door. He marveled at how it seemed to grow from the surface after she initiated the proper key sequence.

His attention turned to Jonathan, who was tracing the fine lines on one of the walls with his finger. Soon he was involved in what was going on around him, and he forgot to be frightened.

"What do you think?" asked Ellen. "Personally, I think it's an access panel of some kind. These markings remind me of some warning or danger sign. Don't you agree?"

"Actually, I do." He leaned in a little to facilitate a very close inspection of the surface of the panel. "Is this all it does? I mean does it only pop out of the wall and nothing more?"

"We don't know. I accidentally found the combination to the outside door. I applied the same key pattern to these markings and this panel appeared. That's all we have so far."

"That's very interesting," he said as his face practically scraped along the wall. He was scrutinizing even the smallest detail of the metal surface by shining his flashlight on the wall and looking sideways down the surface.

"What on earth are you doing?" asked Ellen.

"It's really quite simple. Have you ever lost anything small on the floor, maybe something easily lost in a pattern? If you lay your head on the floor, you can look across it. Even the smallest object stands out against the expanse of the flat surface. I used to find stuff like that when I was a kid. I'm applying the same method here to see any imperfections in the surface of the wall."

"Well?"

"Well nothing. It's as smooth as glass for as far as I can see. I need to move along this wall a little farther to inspect more of the surface, but so far, nothing."

"It's a darn good technique, if you ask me," said Jonathan. "Keep up the good work. You might try gently dragging a fingernail across the surface. You know what I mean, like when you're trying to find the edge of a roll of tape?"

"Thanks. Got it," he answered, waving his hand back towards Jonathan's voice. He looked up at Ellen, "I think that this is some form of a control panel. Look closely and you will see many fine lines in the surface. They look to be joints rather than scratches in the metal."

Ellen moved in as close as she could without smashing her nose. She took out her magnifying loop and moved skillfully along the surface. "I see what you mean. These separations could be almost anything though."

"I think that they're keys of some sort. Maybe like a touch pad. Have you tried using them that way?"

"How could we? You've only just discovered them. We've had so much to do removing the soil from the exterior that we had to limit the time that we spend in here. That reminds me, we need to open the door before we run out of air. She placed her hand into the three-fingered imprint and the door glided silently open. The rush of incoming air was refreshing. They all inhaled deeply.

Steve noticed that one of the small squares created by the lines on the panel rose slightly above the rest. He waved her over to the box as he bent closer. "Do you just press the thing or is there some other process involved?"

"Wait, Steve. What if it's a lock and we can't get out. Let me go outside first, and then you can press the button."

Jonathan was not so lost in concentration that he was oblivious to the conversation. He moved over to where the two of them were standing. He asked, "Have either of you considered that it might be an internal lock. That once outside, you can never get in again until the person inside unlocks the door?"

"Well no. I didn't consider that," Steve said.

"It wouldn't make any sense," reasoned Ellen. "If there were an air supply, I might agree with you. I don't believe that it's a lock. I'm going outside. If I can't get it open from out there you can just open it from in here. Just to be safe, let's synchronize our watches. I'll wait ten seconds after the door closes before I try and re-open it. It takes about fifteen seconds for me to work the controls. If the door doesn't open in thirty seconds after it closes, then you should open it from inside. Does that sound okay to both of you?"

"I hope you're right. Remember, our watches will be stopped. I'm not fond of dying. I think it's highly over-rated. I believe that I will ever participate in death, no matter how old I get."

Ellen stepped through the door and waited for it to close again. They had pushed the button before she went out. Once closed she waited the agreed upon ten seconds before she tried the lock. The schedule was perfect. At exactly twenty-five seconds after the door had closed, she completed the control sequence. Nothing happened. She became frightened.

Inside, Jonathan and Steve waited an eternity that was only twenty-five seconds long. They too became frightened. Jonathan tried the hand control. Nothing happened. The silence was deafening.

"Well the only thing new is the button. Push it Steve."

Steve did as he was asked. The button eased gently back to the surface after the slightest touch.

"Now push on the panel itself. It will become flush with the surface as well."

Again, Steve did as he was directed. The panel disappeared onto the surface. Jonathan placed his hand into the lock. The door opened quickly and silently. The rush of air was almost non-existent, but for Jonathan and Steve it was like food and water to a starving man. They both fell through the doorway simultaneously. They almost tripped themselves on their way to freedom.

"Now that was scary," admitted Jonathan.

"How did you know what to do?" asked Steve.

"What makes you think that I knew what to do? This was a first for me too."

Steve staggered back with the shock of the realization. "Oh my God!" he gasped. "We could have been locked in there forever! I don't even want to think about it right now."

"So, what did you do to get out?" inquired Ellen.

"I did all the steps backwards. It was the only thing that I could think of. I was almost in a state of panic. Now we know one more thing about this monster. I'll wager that we'll find many amazing things in the near future. This box has a lot of secrets to reveal. I can feel it."

"I'm sure of it," said Steve. "At least know that the button locks the door from accidentally opening from either side. What could this be used for that you would need that kind of security?" He was still leaning with his hands on his knees for support.

Steve was no worse for the wear, but he looked haggard. His breathing had returned to normal and a decent color returned to his face, albeit somewhat more pale than normal. "That's enough to turn anyone into a certified claustrophobic."

"Well, you're both fine, and unharmed. It's almost time for us to leave and Steve needs to get back to his site. Let's call it a day."

Bolting upright, he pleaded, "How can I leave this? This is the most important discovery of all time. We need to research this until we know absolutely all there is to know."

Ellen and Jonathan just smiled; they'd already traveled this road. They knew only too well, the pitfalls that followed that line of thinking. Steve would come to understand that it would not be practical to try and study the box out here. This needed to be done in the proper environment, discretely and in total secrecy.

"Steve, we've devised a plan to remove the box from this location. We plan to secret it away under the guise of a new fossil transport container. We've already contacted Johnny and he's helping with the arrangements.

"No one knows about this site. If we start trucking in enough research equipment to study this here, it will draw unnecessary attention to our secret. Can you imagine the media blitz that the University would launch once they got wind of our equipment requisitions?

"We don't have to tell a driver anything. He just needs to pick up the box and move it away. We'll have it delivered to a location that is convenient to have it picked up by a second truck and moved to its final destination." Jonathan paused to let Steve absorb the information.

"That's a good plan. I understand the need for secrecy. It's just so damn exciting. How do you keep from shouting from the mountain tops?" *Why can't you let me study this on my own? Please.*

"It's not easy Steve," said Ellen. "It took a lot for us to even approach you," she said emphatically. She searched his eyes for a sign of understanding.

"I don't mean to sound insulting, Steve. It's just that we haven't any idea of what we have here and we don't want to lose it before we can find out. I know you understand. I can see it in your eyes. The guarantee of losing everything can only come from telling the wrong person, or even the right person at the wrong time. I hope you can appreciate just how much we've gone through. The amount of work Jonathan put in on removing the soil alone is enough to warrant our permanent possession."

"Ellen, I couldn't agree more. I'm just caught up in the excitement. As I said earlier, I'll do whatever it takes to see this project through. I'll never get a chance like this again. I'm not about to toss this out the window."

"Thank you dear," she said as she hugged him. "We knew you were the right choice."

"You won't regret this Steve," added Jonathan. "This is going to be as big as your nursery site. By the way, we still need to get back there before the others think we've died and fallen off the face of the earth."

"No problem. I'll catch up to you later," Steve said half-heartedly. *I feel like a little boy being sent to his room for stealing a cookie. It's not fair.*

CHAPTER TWENTY-TWO

They walked back to the campsite in silence. Steve wanted to ask as many questions as he could, but he knew there would be a better time and place. Sliding into his truck, he turned the key and shut the door. The dull thud of the door echoed in his ears. He was sealing himself off from the world's greatest discovery in history.

His foot found the gas pedal. Turning to look through the rear window, he accelerated rapidly and spun the wheel to redirect his motion as well as his thoughts. The Crenshaw's were right; he needed to find focus and quickly. Ellen and Jonathan would be right behind him as soon as they broke camp.

Checking his rearview mirror, he didn't see them pulling onto the road. He just kept driving. His mind was racing and driving was calming his nerves.

They arrived at Steve's site about half an hour before they had planned. Their intentions were to arrive just far enough behind him to allow him to catch up on the day's events. It was their hope that this would refocus his attention and get him back on track.

Ellen and Jonathan went straight into Steve's tent and didn't come out for nearly ten minutes. The rest of the camp assumed that the Crenshaw's were getting settled in. Nobody really expected an explanation. That was just as well, because if they asked, they weren't going to be told the truth anyway.

Steve left his tent as soon as the Crenshaw's arrived. Calling everyone over to the large table took a few minutes. It gave Steve a chance to answer a few site questions and take care of additional camp business.

Once they were assembled, he started, "May I have your attention please?" Silence settled over the group. "The Crenshaw's have had little to no luck in finding a proper dig site. I've invited them here to work with us. We can use their expertise in sorting through the monumental number of fossils.

"This in no way will jeopardize, or minimize, your contributions. They fully understand the scale of our operation. They've agreed to act as consultants only. This is still my site, and as such, everyone will share equally in any and all discoveries that we have already made or will make.

"I want you to rely on the Crenshaw's for questions or information if they are more readily available than me. As you know, camp business sometimes keeps me from answering a question immediately. As consultants, they will be at your disposal, so use them where you can.

"The camp will continue to operate on the same schedule. I believe I've covered everything. I'm through, unless there are any questions." He paused long enough to look each person in the eye. No one needed additional clarification.

"Okay, since there aren't any questions, thank you very much for your co-operation. Let's get an early supper tonight. From what I see here, you've earned a night off. I have refreshments in the back of the truck. We'll organize the flag making after we eat and then have a little fun."

No one moved. "Well, let's get started," he prodded. The group broke up and returned to their individual grids to continue their work.

The Crenshaw's had stepped from the tent shortly after Steve had called everyone to order, only approaching him after he'd finished. They were very impressed with the way that he handled the whole thing. He was developing into a fine leader. "Is there anything that we can do to help?" asked Ellen. "We should show them that we are going to pull our own weight around here."

"I wouldn't have asked, but if you insist, could you help with the beer from the truck? There are at least two cases in the back and some ice for the coolers. I also got a bunch of different six packs. There should be something for everyone."

"That'll be just fine," beamed Jonathan. "Whatever I can do to help is fine with me. Ellen, maybe you can help with supper?" Without waiting for a response, he continued, "Some of these kids have never experienced your gift with a camp stove. I'm sure that they'd want you to be permanent cook once they've tried your stew. Hot stew and cold beer are a great combo. I'll be right back with the beer, and then I'll help you with the stew. I'm getting more ravenous as we speak." He kissed her on the cheek and headed over to get the beer.

A couple of the students joined him at the truck. Between the three of them, they succeeded in bringing all the beer and ice in one load.

"I think this should go in a tub instead of coolers," suggested Jonathan. "We're going to finish it tonight anyway. I'll get the tub if you two bring the ice."

"Sure thing Dr. Crenshaw," they replied.

Perhaps it was the solitude that added to the overall sense of dread that permeated everything. It hung cloistered in the air while they worked in the cave. Jonathan hadn't realized just how much he had missed camp activity. For a moment he just stood silently and took in the camp and all the activity. He'd been so caught up in Ellen's discovery that he'd not considered the isolation. Now that he was back in a camp full of people, he felt whole again.

A sense of wellbeing enveloped him. He knew that he and Ellen weren't going to have any more trouble. It was the isolation and the situation that brought the little trials of life to the surface like festering boils. Too many things had been said and now he could talk privately with Ellen and discuss this revelation. With his luck he'd only be a dollar short and a day late.

Jonathan watched as the two boys brought the ice and beer over to the table where he'd set the tub. "Steve told me of your raptor discoveries," said Jonathan. "Are there really that many fossils here?"

"Yes," answered the first student. "We've cataloged well over three hundred already, and there's a lot more to go," he continued proudly. Jonathan could see the team spirit twinkle in his eyes as he looked at his friend who nodded in enthusiastic agreement.

"Over three hundred," Jonathan replied. "That's phenomenal! How do you keep up the pace? My wife and I have never worked such a prolific site in all of our twenty-five years in the field. It must be very exciting."

The second young man responded, "It's very exciting. Steve tells us that he's going to present this as a raptor nursery. He showed us the patterns we were establishing with our flags. He updates the map every hour, when he's here. I believe that he's right on the money with this one." Turning to his friend, he asked, "Don't you?"

"Yeah," was the quick answer. "We have four distinct age groups of the same raptors scattered all over here. It's the most reasonable explanation that I can think of. "Although," he continued, "we don't have any eggs yet. Maybe there aren't any to be found. We may have found a nest though. The ground is right. There are many young fossils around this one particular mound. We'll need a little more before we can accept it as a nest. It's the closest thing that we have right now. Even though there are many mounds already, only this one has all the most details of a nest."

"Consider the erosion of sixty-five million years boys. A significant amount of earth has been overlaid onto this terrain and then over the millennia, it's been stripped away millimeter by millimeter, until you arrived. You've all seen the various layers in the striations along the face of the hillsides."

"We'll learn. Sometimes it's easy to miss the obvious large things when you are searching for hidden small things," commented the closest young man.

During the conversation, they had slowly walked out into the collection grids, and the two students were pointing to different discoveries to emphasize their statements.

They made their way back to the table where Jonathan had put the tub. Ellen motioned for him to put it on the ground, out of the way. They filled it with beer and ice. It wouldn't take long for the beer to regain its' chill.

"I've got to help my wife with supper boys. It won't be long before it's ready. I have a couple of Frisbees and a football in my truck if you're interested. Maybe we can get a game together after supper. There's gonna be plenty of sunlight left by the time we're finished."

"Hey, thanks man, I mean Dr. Crenshaw. Sorry. That's a great idea. We'll get the stuff and fool around while we're waiting for supper. Maybe you can get away and join us?"

"That's okay boys," he said. "I can wait until supper's done. I'll stand a better chance against you when you're tired and stuffed."

They both laughed. Jonathan gave them the keys to the storage chest in the back of the truck. It didn't take any time at all to get the toys and return the keys. It took even less time for them to form impromptu teams and start up touch football.

Jonathan and Ellen smiled at each other. They knew that this was a good idea. She seemed to understand the need for company as keenly as Jonathan had. They didn't discuss it, yet they seemed to sense the completeness that they had discovered.

"You were having quite a conversation with those two. Anything I need to hear about?"

"Not really sweetheart. They're enjoying themselves and are enthusiastic about the dig. Steve's got a very fine team here. Are you about finished?" he asked as he spooned into the stew pot. *Man, how I love her cooking.*

"It'll be at least ten more minutes dear," she answered as she slapped his hand. "Get out of here if you're just going to pick at the food like that. Why don't you join the others? I've got everything under control." *His eating habits are going to be the death of me yet.*

"Are you sure? I'm fine right here. I promised that I'd play after they'd eaten their fill and gotten a little slower."

"Why would you say something like that? After all that we've been through in the last two weeks, I'd think that you'd be anxious to show off your strength. You sound like a frail old man." Pinching his backside, she added, "And I know better than that. Go away. Go show those kids a thing or two."

"Anything you say dear. I shall return the vanquishing hero. I will bring home the heads of my enemies spiked on long poles. All who view them shall tremble in fear of my wrath."

"What planet are you on?" *Boys will be boys, and now he's fifty-five going on six or seven. I swear some days…*

"Just trying to make you happy, dear." *Besides, I'm hot for your body.*

"Have some fun. Don't get hurt. Return hungry and happy. Those are my only orders. If you think you can handle them, then you'll make me happy."

"You got it. Try not to miss me too much. After all, I'll be all the way down by the road. That's at least seventy-five yards away. I shall travel the distance as a labor of love."

"Have you been drinking? I haven't seen you pick up a beer yet."

"I'm drunk on love, my dear." *That and the thought of you and me between the sheets.*

"We'll get the tent set up after you have destroyed those kids at football. You can show me just how drunk you are then." *You win tonight. I definitely want you as much as you want me. But I won't say so until much later.*

"Oh baby. It's a date. I'm off to demonstrate my great masculine prowess. Pay close attention. If I'm going to show off for you, I'd at least like to know that you're watching."

Exasperated, she mumbled, "There must be something in the air." She kissed him as he turned toward the road. Smiling inwardly, she mused, *he's just a big kid at heart. I guess it's one of those endearing qualities.*

CHAPTER TWENTY-THREE

S UPPER WAS EXCELLENT. THE KIDS enjoyed Ellen's campfire stew. Some even remarked that they had never enjoyed stew so much. She knew that her cooking was second to none. Jonathan never missed a chance to brag about it. She smiled to herself as she finished her bowl. A swallow of cold beer was a good finish to a good meal.

Conversations drifted to what happens after the site's findings are presented. Some ventured wild speculations, while others were pessimistic. Steve explained that every member of the team would be mentioned in his final report. They were all contributing members and he wanted them to receive the credit that they deserved.

Eventually, they began to disappear one by one to retire for the evening. The beer was gone and everyone was tired from making flags and having a good time.

Jonathan had raised their tent with a little help from Steve. They chatted quietly about their plans. Those who were still awake were off playing with the football or the Frisbees.

The three of them sat off to the side when they were finished. Orange firelight danced fanciful shadows off the tents as they sat, quietly enjoying the cooling night air. There was much to discuss. Even though the Crenshaw's were now established at the camp, they still needed to come and go at a reasonable schedule. It would be suspicious if they moved in and never showed up or stayed around camp. They were to be consultants and needed to be close at hand.

"The trucks will be here in another two weeks," said Jonathan. "That should give us enough time to prepare our site. Steve will need to get anything that he's got wrapped and ready by then.

"We need to time two or more trucks in here within a day or two of each other. You understand that the tighter the schedule, the better for our deception. It needs to give a proper and normal appearance. Any questions?

"I've arranged for a flatbed trailer. It should handle a load as wide as this box. I expect that it won't be heavy. Something tells me that this thing is almost empty. I can't explain it to either of you. I just feel it. That small room we've accessed doesn't belong somehow. If we knew more, we could draw a better conclusion."

"Then it's not just me," Steve said. "I noticed that the interior dimensions are significantly less than the exterior. There has to be a logical explanation."

"Let's get some sleep," yawned Ellen. "We'll be able to think more clearly once we've rested. I know that I'm worn out from watching you play football with those kids. If I'm tired, you must be near exhaustion. I should massage your back and legs for you before you go to sleep. It will help for the work tomorrow."

"Well, with that," interjected Steve, "I guess that I'll head over to my tent. See you two in the morning." *Maybe those two should get a room in town. They're always at each other. I guess it could be worse. If they hated each other, we wouldn't be here at all. I hope I'm that happy when I find a partner.*

"Just what do you think you're doing? You embarrassed me."

"Since when where you ever embarrassed by a little sex talk you? A big strong man like you should just grab me up and have his way with me. Of course, if you don't want to, it's no skin off of my nose." *I'm hot to trot and now you find that it's time to be embarrassed. Don't blow this chance my love.*

"Now don't get hasty. I never said that. Oh, what's the use? If I don't shut up now, I can only dig this hole deeper. Let's go to bed. That massage sounded wonderful. I can feel your hands on my body already. Besides, I have a particularly stiff muscle that needs your professional attention."

"I have the perfect solution to aide in relaxing that stiff muscle of yours, but if you continue to prattle on, the opportunity will be lost."

"Lead on my love," he said patting her bottom. "I'm yours to command."

Hand in hand they walked the to their tent. Stopping long enough to survey the site one last time, Ellen commented, "This has been a good life."

"What?" asked Jonathan.

"Everything that we've done together," she said again. "It's been a good life and we've helped a lot of kids along the way. I'm just happy that's all."

"And you've earned the right to be. Let's go to bed before we're both too tired."

"Coming dear?" she asked seductively as she slid through the open tent flap.

CHAPTER TWENTY-FOUR

S TEVE SAT AT HIS DESK and opened his journal. The empty page stared up at him, challenging him to contribute something monumental to the entry he was about to make.

June 30, 1999. *The Crenshaw's have made very little progress in finding a site. After a lengthy conversation they've decided to come to my site. There's so much to do here and we could use their help. The entire team has really pulled together and work is progressing both smoothly and rapidly. The findings I've made have been confirmed by the Crenshaw's. I couldn't be happier. We have a raptor nesting site for a large group. It should prove to be a goldmine of information. The Crenshaw's are preparing me for the impending firestorm that will ensue once I've published. This has been a great start to my career. I couldn't have asked for more.*

Closing his journal, he reflecting on what the Crenshaw's had shown him. There is no possible way he can keep a record of their events. This was too big and a careless entry in his journal could destroy any chance at getting this discovery into the hands of all mankind.

The morning dawned clear and crisp. The sunrise was a brilliant slash of gold and white across the horizon. The colors of everything seemed brighter than usual. Ellen had a wonderful night and was feeling better than she had in the last two weeks. She just stared at the colors and smiled inwardly.

"Wake up sleepy head." She nudged lightly on Jonathan's feet while pulling the covers from the bed.

"What time is it?" he questioned.

"It's already six."

"Six? Why didn't you wake me up?"

"I wanted you to get a little extra sleep. All that exercise last night, must have worn you down." She kissed him on the cheek and reached down and gave him a playful squeeze.

"Don't let your hands make promises that you have no intention of keeping." His smirk was filled with sexual overtones.

"If I make a promise, I'll keep it." She turned and left the tent. Ellen intended to finish her morning walk. She always felt more focused while enjoying a sunrise.

Ellen waved to several of the students that were just poking their heads from their tents. The fresh air invigorated her. She would be back in about half an hour and Jonathan would have breakfast waiting as usual. The few students who poked their heads from their tents were amazed that a woman her age would be up and active this early. Now, grudgingly, they gave in to the morning light and the need to resume their work.

She waved as she walked past, thinking, *What a bunch of sleepyheads. Don't they understand that there's going to be forty or more years of greeting the morning. Embrace the morning, embrace the natural beauty, and embrace your life!*

Ellen walked on in no particular direction and with no particular agenda. All she wanted was the peace and quiet to clear her mind. Jonathan never understood this time of day for her. He too, enjoyed the morning, for completely different reasons. Ellen turned to face the sun and let its' warming rays wash over her. She shivered as the cold swept from her body, replaced by everything warm and beautiful.

Steve knocked at the tent post. He knew that Ellen would be gone, but he hadn't seen Jonathan up and about yet. It was not like Jonathan to sleep past six on any morning. The only time was once when Jonathan came down with a really bad cold and was running a fever for several days.

"Yes, who is it?" called Jonathan.

"It's just me. I hadn't seen you yet this morning and was wondering if you were okay. May I come in?"

"Sure, sure. Where are my manners?" he answered as he pulled the tent flap back and secured it to the tent. "You're always welcome, you know that."

"Have you thought about how you'll be able to leave camp without causing any curiosity from the students?"

"Actually, I have. I think that I've devised a simple, yet elegant, plan. I haven't discussed this with Ellen yet. It's a little awkward, but reasonable."

"Is there anything that I can do?"

"Just listen and pick it apart if you think it stinks."

"Sounds fair enough to me. Go ahead and start."

"Come with me. I need to start breakfast. Ellen will be back in ten or fifteen minutes. You can help me while we talk. We can all sit together and hash out the final details when she gets back."

"That's fine by me."

The Crenshaw's had improvised a stainless-steel cook table that hung from brackets on the side of their tuck. I held all the food and the cooktop. Cooking utensils hung from hooks arranged along the outer edge.

Steve cut fresh bell peppers and tomatoes while Jonathan mixed the eggs with water. "When you're done there, you can grate some cheddar. You wouldn't happen to have any sour cream in your provisions, would you?" asked Jonathan.

"No, but it sounds great. I can almost taste them now."

"Hand me those veggies, this one is done. You take it. Ellen will be about two more minutes."

"Thanks, I'm not sure that I would have survived until you cooked another one," Steve quipped.

Ellen rounded the corner of the tent as Jonathan was plating her omelet. "Look at you, a world-renowned paleontologist, and a gourmet chef as well. Where's my breakfast?" she asked while laughing.

"What have you two been talking about? As if I couldn't guess."

"Actually, you probably couldn't guess. It was just guy stuff. I did mention to Steve that I believe that I've managed a solution for us to leave the camp without arousing any unnecessary concern. It will all be quite natural and acceptable."

Ellen ate her omelet while Jonathan explained.

He explained his plan while eating his omelet. When he finished, he asked, "Any thoughts, likes, dislikes, alternatives?"

"I think that Jonathan is on to something," responded Steve. "If we're just sitting around the table having a quiet conversation – conveniently in the earshot of several of the students – and then I get loud and say something like, 'I can't believe you came here before checking that out. Why don't you leave right now and find out?' I don't have the words just right, but we can draw the students into the conversation. It would then bring them into the decision to let you leave the camp. If they ask you to go, they won't question your absence."

"I told you it was a good plan," crowed Jonathan. His grim was reminiscent of the Cheshire Cat.

Ellen cast him one of her looks, which he pretended not to see.

"Let's work out the scene together," he continued. "We can do it tonight at supper. It'll be a one act, one performance show. Everyone will hear and all will want us to go. We have one good vertebrae sample that we found when we were scouting areas for you. We can use that as the evidence of something that has potential."

The morning rituals soon became the dominant activity as the camp came to life. The Crenshaw's blended unobtrusively into the flow.

"You have a good plan dear," she whispered as they finished the last of the breakfast dishes.

"I don't know. I'm worried about the University finding out what we're doing. The power struggles that will inevitably ensue will be rough. I'm just plain scared."

"Where in the hell did that come from?" Her look was withering.

"Sorry, sweetheart. I think about that stuff every now and again. I'm worried about what we might have uncovered here. You remember 'SUE' the T-rex? Those poor guys at the Black Hills Institute suffered needless loss because of the stinking politicians. I'm not prepared to suffer like that, especially the jail time.

"You know the University would cave right away in a situation like that. They won't even remember why they hired us in the first place. If they're threatened with the loss of their government research money, they'd throw us under the bus so fast we wouldn't even see it coming.

"I don't mean to scare you dear. I'm just frightened by the grim reality of what will happen. I hope that we live to tell our grandchildren this tale."

"Well it's too late. You've already scared the hell out of me. And just what do you mean that you hope we live? Do you seriously believe that our lives are in danger?"

"Yes." Jonathan stared blankly at the soapy water. He just stood there as if he were contemplating a fate worse than death.

Looking up from the plate she was drying, Ellen just stared at him. For the first time in almost thirty years, she could not tell what was on his mind. Jonathan had been clear about his fright, yet there he stood, cold, distant, and unreadable.

Ellen was no longer frightened. She was terrified. Now she wished that this whole discovery was just a bad dream. Her whole life had been spent in the pursuit and advancement of knowledge. Now on the brink of the world's most amazing discovery she was horror struck at the possibility that her own government might punish, or eliminate, her for doing her job. . . just for power.

She involuntarily staggered backwards a step or two, visibly shaken by the reality Jonathan had set before her. There had to be a chance that he was wrong. Even if it was only a slim chance, it would be something to hang on to. Yet the evidence was already there; the government would steamroller anyone or anything to get what it wanted.

"Are you okay dear?" Jonathan was concerned with her appearance.

"You bastard! How could you do this to me?" She was almost hysterical and keeping the conversation in hushed tones only magnified the terror. "Why couldn't you leave me in blissful ignorance? I would have been very happy like that. I can't deal with this. How can you just stand there, cold and unemotional? It's not natural."

"What makes you think that I'm unemotional?" he snapped back. "This has been tearing me up inside since you first showed me that damn box. The extent of our peril has only recently become apparent to me. When you figured out how to get inside that thing, I realized that it was not human in origin. Consider all of the locks and security that we have on campus. Nothing is designed like this. The locks are completely foreign and the position is not natural to the human hand. Sure, our hand works the mechanism, but it's still not designed for us."

"It's not fair," she cried. Emotionally spent, she fell into his arms and cried heavily. He took her to their tent before anyone noticed them.

"You rest here a while. I'll say you felt ill. A stomach thing; they'll understand. I'm sorry dear. I thought you were ready to hear that. I was wrong, but at least it's out in the open now."

He kissed her softly on her forehead. She felt the strength of his love in the softness of his kiss. "I'll see you later, okay?" His hand lingered at her cheek to reassure her. She touched the back of it as he gently slid it away. She smiled through her tears and her fear. He was an anchor that she could hold on to.

Jonathan left the tent after he straightened himself out. All he needed was to put on a strong front. Jonathan prayed that he was over reacting, over analyzing, and over imagining.

Poking his head back into the tent, he said, "Honey, I'm sorry. My inner demons got the best of me. I shouldn't have painted such a bleak picture. Can you forgive me? You've been a champion through everything. I'm just feeling vulnerable right now, and my fears got the best of me. Please forgive me."

"Of course, I'll forgive you. Please don't ever do that again. I'm going to be scared from now on."

"I don't want you to be scared, but you should be aware and observant."

"What?"

"I may have overstated things, but there is always the chance of corporate espionage. We've already discussed that. Look at the precautions we took before we spoke to Steve, and we know him."

"I'm beginning to understand your thought process. It is better to ere on the side of caution."

"Exactly. I wish I'd taken this approach before I made such an ass of myself."

"Don't worry dear. You'll have plenty of other chances to make an ass of yourself."

"Ouch… where you holding a roll of quarters in when you hit me with that?"

"Oh, I should have thought of that. Maybe the lesson would have been better learned. Next time you plan on dropping a bomb like that … put a sock in it."

"Yes dear. I love you."

CHAPTER TWENTY-FIVE

JONATHAN SPENT THE REST OF the morning working the grids with the other students. The cataloging would go much faster with his knowledge and ability. Only a few students had inquired about Ellen. He was grateful. It allowed him to do his assignment unencumbered. The relative ease of cataloging also allowed him the time to formulate plans that would cover up their trail once this operation went into action.

Steve's help was desperately needed, or he wouldn't have included him at all. He feared for the safety of everyone involved. His inability to know, or even guess, the extent of the government's ability to spy on its citizens haunted his thoughts. From what he had seen on campus, it would be formidable.

An intricate, involved plan began to formulate in his head. No one, not even his government, would threaten his family or friends without a fight. He intended on living to a ripe old age. That plan included his wife and child and grandchildren.

Moving to the next grid, he began cataloging each flagged fragment. Steve had been right. This site was prolific. He'd never seen this many raptor fossils in one location before; aside from flood related mass deaths. This site was spread broadly with an even distribution. The baby and juvenile's fragments near the mounded areas lent itself to a nursery. The reason for its size would be fodder for speculation for years to come.

It did, however, clearly indicate a definite family setting. That conclusion would be difficult to dispute. Jonathan knew many academics would love to dispute it just to cause a controversy and reassert their dominance in the arena.

The call for lunch came before he had realized he'd spent the last five hours in the field. Time had a way of slipping away when you were occupied with an interesting task. The Brogdon chart helped speed the process two-fold. It was an amazing bit of craftsmanship.

Lunch was set out and the students began to serve themselves. Steve and Jonathan stood back while the others got their portions. Ellen emerged from their tent right on cue looking rested. She must have napped after the morning's unsettling conversation.

"It's good to see you up and about. How are you feeling?" asked Jonathan.

"I feel just fine. No need to bother with me. I'll be okay."

"Well Steve, she's made of iron. This morning she felt sick, but now she's fine," he joked as he helped her to her seat at the table.

Everyone wished her well.

As people ate and talked, Steve asked, "So Jonathan, you didn't find anything while you were out there on your own?"

"Not really, Steve. We had a couple of sites that we thought were promising, but nothing ever came of them. There's something out there, we just need to find it." He dropped his fork and bent down to pick it up. On the way back up he whispered into Steve's ear, "What are you doing?"

Steve said nothing, winking his eye at Jonathan. He then dropped the subject completely with a dismissive comment of understanding. The seed for the suppertime conversation had been planted. That was his intention. He hadn't had a chance to talk to Jonathan all morning. Steve had thought about it while he was doing his paper work. He would have a chance to explain everything to Jonathan later in the day while going over some of the catalog pages.

Lunch always ended too soon. It came exactly when you were just getting a good rest and enjoying your full stomach. The entire group grudgingly yielded to the demands of the dig and returned to their grids; Jonathan included.

Jonathan noticed Steve approaching. He lowered his note pad and watched him draw closer. He wasn't happy about that surprise comment at lunch. "That was one hell of a surprise you hit me with. You're causing me to second guess my decision about making you site leader." There was a touch of anger at the edge of his voice. He didn't need much to explode. *This better be one hell of an explanation or I just might pop you one on the end of your nose. You risked everything!*

"Sorry, Jonathan, I didn't have time to discuss it with you. I thought of it just moments before they called us in for lunch. Everyone heard your answer. Now we can embellish a little and introduce the fossil with more credibility. I think that they'll join into the conversation now that they are already aware of it." *He still looks really pissed off. I'll let him think about it for a few minutes. He'll see the beauty of it soon enough.*

While thinking about Steve's idea, he was losing the edge of his anger. He considered the day's events in their entirety. Finally, he admitted the validity of the statement, surprise or not. The truth of the matter was that this was more a bruised ego. "It's a good plan," he conceded. Verbalizing his thoughts, he continued, "I can remember a site where we found the vertebrae and then mention something like 'until this conversation I just realized that we never went back for additional examination.'"

"That's perfect. The kids will surely encourage you if we coax them with a few well-placed phrases."

"I don't know. It still seems a little far-fetched. And another thing, where and when did you get to be so devious? Have you been deceiving us all this time, using us to attain your goals?"

"No Jonathan. I would never do anything like that. However, I have taken a few pointers from Janet."

"So now it's Janet, and not Miss Brogdon? You've been keeping too many secrets Steve. You're not. . ."

As the realization hit him, he blurted, "Jonathan! No! Not ever," as he turned scarlet. "As for the plan, we're professionals, we know better. To the novice, it will seem plausible."

"You're probably right. We'll know at suppertime, won't we?" *Next time you better tell me in advance or you'll be on the receiving end of a world class wedgey.*

"Good job on the cataloging," Steve added as he returned Jonathan sheets.

"Thank you, my lord and master. If there is anything this humble servant can do, you be sure and let me know. You run along now and let me continue my work; I don't want to disappoint you." Jonathan's animosity had completely ebbed.

They both laughed.

Steve went over to the next person cataloging and reviewed the work sheets. All was going well. He needed to organize parties to start wrapping the more embedded fragments in plaster. That was a job that most people enjoyed. They loved getting their hands into the plaster and spreading it around. There were enough veterans to aid the newcomers, so completion time would not be jeopardized.

"Good job Miss Brogdon," he said when he reached Janet's grid. "Your form has helped speed up the process immensely. Thank you for the contribution. It has made life so much easier and organized."

"When are we going to start wrapping the fossils?" she asked.

"Funny you should ask. I was just thinking that it was time to organize some teams." *Can this woman read minds too?*

"May I call you Steve?" she asked while turning her head slightly to one side. He nodded his affirmation. "Thank you. I really would like to become your assistant. I can't believe how exciting this is. I've always hated getting dirty when I was younger. Now that I'm in the field and hunting for fossils, I find myself consumed by all of this." Janet Brogdon swept her hand broadly across the site, emphasizing her statement.

Steve understood. He'd felt the same way after his first dig. He didn't want to dissuade her, but he wanted to wait a bit before he committed to the partnership. Steve needed to know the depth of her commitment before anything else. Admitting to himself that he could use the help, he wondered why he vacillated. Her form had already demonstrated a real team effort and commitment.

"I am interested in your proposal. I won't give you an answer right away. After my first dig I felt the same way. I know what you mean when you say that you're consumed by it all. Sometimes that feeling wears off shortly after you make the statement. I don't wish to offend you in any way; your chart has proven the most useful tool that I have here. It speaks for itself. You have talent and ability. I want to wait and see if the desire remains this strong for more than today. Do you understand?" *I hope she says she understands.*

"I most certainly do. You'll see just how committed I am. I won't let you down."

"Deal then," he said encouragingly. "I've got to finish checking on the others. See you later then." As he walked away, he chastised himself for acting like a lovesick schoolboy.

Steve was concerned about her last statement. He was hoping that she hadn't become infatuated with him. That could seriously muddy the water. He was embarrassed by the attention and hoped that he'd not misread her intention.

Steve studied her from a distance. She was beautiful and he could do worse. He chastised himself again for his thoughts. *Then again,* he mused, *the Crenshaw's had a long and loving relationship. They worked well together.*

Maybe she was just a dinosaur groupie. This was going to be an important find. Steve hoped that he was wrong about this conjecture. He would enjoy having an intelligent and beautiful assistant. Steve moved off to his next task. There was too much to be done to stand and speculate about someone's intentions.

The afternoon passed quickly. Ellen made herself available to any number of questions. It gave her a distraction from the mornings' events. All that she wanted now was a little time away from thinking about it at all.

CHAPTER TWENTY-SIX

Ellen found herself preparing supper. She was so caught up in her duties, she was totally distracted to the point where she didn't notice the day slipping away. Soon it would be time to lay the groundwork for leaving again. She was apprehensive to say the very least.

"Everyone in for supper," she called loudly enough to attract some attention. The first person then called to the next, until all were headed in to the tables.

"How did it go this afternoon?" Ellen asked the first young man to reach the table.

"Oh," he said surprised, "just great. We're close to being finished. I'd say at least a couple of more weeks. What's for supper? It smells great."

Ellen had driven into town earlier to go to the post office and she picked up more ice and some sour cream while she was there. Even though everyone liked sour cream on their tortillas; there would be more than enough left for omelets in the morning. Blushing slightly, Ellen said, "Tortillas. The meat is spiced with a package mix, but you'll find that it's pretty tasty. We use it all the time. Dig in. There's more than enough for everyone. Come on don't be bashful. You can start out with two."

"Thank you, Dr. Crenshaw. I will," he said as he piled the two tortilla shells high with meat, beans, vegetables and sour cream. The group was restless and hungry. It had been a long and prosperous day. The line moved quickly as each took a large helping. Being in the fresh air all day did build an appetite.

"Supper smells good. How'd you know I was in the mood for Mexican?"

"When aren't you in the mood for Mexican is a better question? I went into town and got more ice for the beer. Want one?"

"Are you kidding? Beer and Mexican food it's a classic combination. Hand me a cold one. I suppose that you even bought some limes."

Handing Jonathan the bowl, she said, "Already sectioned, dear. Just like you like them."

"Didn't I tell you, Steve? My Ellen, a saint among women, an angel fallen to earth. And I'm the one lucky enough to find her and marry her."

She pretended not to hear him. Ellen went about helping the kids get their supper. She was pleased to see that almost all of the food was gone after the first pass. Some of the first to eat came back to pick a little here and there from the pans. A couple of them even took another helping. The world was re-ordering itself for her. Her fears were vanishing with each passing moment.

Conversation soon turned to the next phase of the dig. The students were excited about getting the fossils ready for transport. It would be a monumental task considering the volume of fossils already catalogued.

Steve decided that this was the perfect opening for the one act play. He began slowly building to his point, then he turned to Jonathan, with a mouthful of tortilla and said, "So tell me. Did you find anything out there? You never come up empty handed."

"I was cataloging for the better part of the day Steve. I really wasn't searching for fossils."

"No Jonathan. I'm sorry; I meant did you find anything while you were out searching for a site that the two of you could work?"

"Oh sorry, I understand now. Well, to be honest with you," he said thoughtfully as he stared at nothing in particular, "we didn't exactly come up empty handed. Here let me show you." Jonathan rose and headed over to his truck. He pulled a carefully wrapped object from one of the many boxes stored in the back of his truck.

Returning, he and placed it in the center of the table gesturing to one of the students to remove the wrappings.

"I'd almost forgotten about this, with all the excitement about your findings. It's nothing really."

Out of the mound of soft cotton wrapping emerged a beautiful fossilized vertebra. Everyone remained breathless. The more experienced recognized it as being from a T-Rex. It was small, probably from the middle of the tail. The others were in awe of its size, compared to what they had been finding.

"You call this nothing? Are you crazy? We can all see what you have here. Where did you find it? It's magnificent," exclaimed Steve. He was standing and leaning over the table for a closer inspection of the fossil.

"It was near an old riverbed as I recall. Wasn't that it dear?" he asked as he turned to Ellen. Being unsure as to where to direct the conversation, he thought that if he could involve her, they might be able to play off of one another. She didn't hear him clearly and didn't respond.

"Look, Steve," he continued undaunted, "it was late and the thing was just lying there. There was no sign of any other fragments or complete pieces anywhere around. I picked it up. I mean after all, look at it. It's beautiful."

"How old was the riverbed, Dr Crenshaw? I mean was it a fossilized riverbed or a wash from the recent rains?" one of the students asked.

"That's a good question, son. I'd be lying if I gave you a positive answer. We were tired and I didn't pay any attention. I broke every rule that I ever made for myself. I'm sorry. I was not being a good paleontologist just then. I was more like a rank amateur. All of you make this a lesson. Don't ever let yourself become preoccupied with something else. It could mean the difference between a major find and a major failure."

"Well, I'm only a student, but I think that you need to investigate this a little further. There could be more fossils up or down the riverbed. Can you find the location?" questioned Janet Brogdon.

"I'm not that addled Miss Brogdon. Of course, I know where we found the specimen."

Feeling as if she'd just been put in her place, she continued in a more apologetic tone, "I meant no disrespect, sir."

"None taken Miss Brogdon."

"It's just that I see how dedicated you are. It seemed strange, that's all."

"I apologize for my tone Miss Brogdon. I'm just embarrassed that I have to be justifiably lectured to by my students. I like doing the lecturing, not the other way around. Thank you though; it's a great suggestion. Steve, do you think you'd miss us for a few days? Miss Brogdon's correct. We do need to check this out thoroughly"

"We'll miss Ellen's cooking, that's for sure," she quipped.

"Yeah, we sure will," was the general sentiment around the table.

"Then it's settled. Thank you again for pointing me in the proper direction. We'll start first thing in the morning. You'll have to struggle through without us. Anyone up for football?" he asked.

The students were all out along the road playing football while the three conspirators sat around the table in whispered conversation.

"We need to coordinate our final departure. I'll contact Johnny and he can arrange for the trucks that we need. I'll speak with him tomorrow. We need at least two more weeks. You should be finished up here by then. One thing in our favor is that you've not found any large fossils yet."

"Don't remind me," Steve said exasperated. "It's the one thing that I was hoping for… besides an egg. I guess though, if this were a nesting site, why would it be full of adult fossils? It was a place of living, not death."

The three of them began the preparations for the Crenshaw's departure. They were packed and ready for bed in less than two hours. They were pleased with the speed in which they accomplished the task. It was a good omen.

THE PACKET ARRIVED AT JOHNNY'S house in the morning mail. There were no distinguishing marks or a return address. The postmark was from Chicago, IL. Johnny knew immediately that it was from his parents. Relaying mail through friends was a childhood game that became a tradition. Their friends didn't mind and it was sort of fun to be involved in a family game.

Johnny drew his pocketknife across the packing. This parcel was much thicker than any he'd anticipated. The packet contained several pages and some photographs. This would be the answer to the cryptic phone call from several weeks ago. He wondered why it was packaged in a box when it all would have easily fit into a standard mailing envelope. Perhaps they just didn't want to risk bending the photos.

Jonathan withdrew the pages and shook them to see if anything might fall from between them, remembering leaves and flowers that had been sent that way, in years gone by.

Nothing dropped out. He looked down at the photographs from over the edge of the pages. Aside from the pictures, there was nothing else included. He went to the kitchen for some coffee; picking up the box and its contents on his way to the living room. Settling into his recliner and began to read his parents letter:

> *Dearest Jonathan,*
>
> *Your mother and I miss you very much. We have a lot going on here. As I said, I will require your assistance. I could not tell you over the phone and I could not mail this*

directly to your house. I know it sounds like a lot of cloak and dagger, but that's because it is.

When we first arrived; your mother made the most amazing discovery. I can't go into complete detail now. We are afraid for our lives. I know that I sound like a crackpot. Believe me, it's difficult not to sound that way. If word of our discovery leaks out, we're not sure to what extent the government, or business, or both will go to acquire the object in question. . . and erase the tracks that led to the acquisition.

I'm begging you not to discuss this with anyone. Not even Kathleen. I don't want to involve you at all, but your friends and associates, and their connections, make it impossible to ignore the invaluable help that you'll be able to give us.

Go ahead and look at the photos now, if you haven't already. What you are looking at is a series of pictures that your mother took while studying the box that you see in the pictures. The box is encased in sedimentary rock. Well actually, we speculate a prehistoric cave or at least a prominent feature that eventually flooded over and became buried in sediment. The pictographs are stylized dinosaurs. This is not human in design or function. We are uncertain if it's origins, prehistoric earth or extra-terrestrial are the only two possibilities. We've gotten inside of a small room at one side at the end of the box. The technology is amazing, at least the little that we've accessed.

You must see it when you can do so safely. I won't be calling you through regular phone lines. I'll map out a route home and call you at various pre-determined times. Always from random phones along our route. I want you to travel around and get the phone numbers of pay phones you can easily get to at almost any time. Send them to me through a friend in St. Louis. Seal the information in an envelope and then mail that sealed envelope to the address at the bottom of this letter.

Enclose a schedule of times and phone numbers where you can be reached. I want you to designate each phone with a number. When you set your schedule, you can say 7:30 PM at #1 on such and such a day without disclosing a phone number. I'll know when and where I need to be and can set a schedule for myself from your information. Again, please do not include the phone numbers on your schedule. If it's discovered, it will make no sense to anyone.

If I don't call within five minutes of your schedule, just leave. I probably won't be able to make all of the calls you can schedule. We'll be on the road and taking a circuitous route.

Please forgive all of this strange behavior. I know now that once you've studied the photos that you'll understand. I am trying to cover tracks before anyone has any idea that they might need to try and follow us. I don't want a phone record of any of this. That's why I will not call you at home or use my own cell phone. Don't pick phones that are next to work or too close to home. And don't use a friend's phone either. They would be the first to be monitored if word ever leaked out. Please hurry Johnny. We will be ready to get underway in two more weeks. It's important that this moves swiftly. Destroy all of this as soon as possible. There must be no connection to you. There must be no trace of this letter or these photographs left when you're through.

We love you. Send our love to Kathleen and the children, but don't tell her about any of this. Your life and theirs may someday depend on the precautions you take now. Remember that we love you. I know it's been said so many times already, but you must not tell anyone about this. We'll be together soon and you'll understand completely at that time.

Love Mom and Dad

Johnny shuffled the pages a few times and stared intently at the photographs. His parents were not given to flights of fancy. They had international success. Both were consummate paleontologists. This was real and now it was frightening.

Going to the hall closet, he took out his riding jacket. Putting it on; he returned to the living room and stuffed the letter and photos into the jacket. He gathered up all the wrapping paper and the box and crushed them into the other pocket. Searching the kitchen and the living room, he was satisfied that he'd not missed the smallest scrap. He was ready to leave.

"Kath, I need to go out for a while," he shouted down the hall.

"I'm up here dear. What do you want?" she called.

"I'm in the mood to take a ride for a while. Is there anything that you'd like while I'm out? I won't be gone but an hour or two. I figured that since I'm out I could swing by the store if you'd like."

"That would be great honey. Can you pick up some butter and eggs? The kids want eggs in a nest for breakfast tomorrow. I'm baking today and use up all of the eggs."

"No problem dear," he called up the steps. "See you soon. Love you."

"Have fun sweetie. Love you too."

Before leaving, he went into his home office and got a pen and some small scraps of paper. The whole mess fit nicely into his shirt pocket. He shoved the letter, the photos and the wrapping and box into the desk drawer. He pulled back the curtain and stared out over the yard. It was a clear, warm morning. He figured that his long sleeve shirt would be enough protection but kept the jacket on just in case.

Starting his bike, he waited a moment to put on his helmet. Sitting there, he wondered if he was going crazy or was this whole thing really happening. Resolving to do as he was asked, he would discover the answers as they presented themselves. With helmet firmly in place, he shifted the bike into first gear and was gone.

He drove to the nearest payphone that was at least a mile from the house. In a little over an hour he'd located nine phones that met his father's prerequisites. He designated a number to each phone and location.

Johnny recalled a recent newscast revealing how the government had gone into a private computer and retrieved previously deleted information. It was beginning to be a very scary proposition to have anything critical on your hard drive. His solution was to keep this and any related information on a thumb drive.

At the last minute he remembered to get the eggs and butter. Johnny swung by the store on his way home. He even picked up a bouquet of flowers for Kathleen; wanting to earn a few points to hold in reserve in case this thing got out of hand. The situation was already wearing on his nerves and the real excitement hadn't even begun yet.

He parked his motorcycle, rushing into the house through the garage. Kathleen was in the kitchen preparing supper. "Oh my God, you scared me," he said as he noticed her.

"I scared you? You come charging into the house like a bull in a china shop and I scared you. That's rich."

"I'm sorry dear. I was daydreaming. I should have known you'd be in the kitchen this close to supper."

"Those for me?" she smiled, looking at the flowers.

"Yes. Who else would they be for?"

"Good question. But since you came in with them, I'll give you the benefit of the doubt. They're beautiful. I'll put them in a vase."

"I'm glad you like them. I was thinking how lucky I am to have you as a wife and partner when I spotted these at the store, they were calling your name."

"That's sweet," she said giving him a kiss on the cheek. "You seem preoccupied. Anything I can help you with?"

"Not this time sweetheart. I've got to coordinate several key people for an upcoming project. Well, the potential of an upcoming project. I'm trying to get the very best people and its tuff to choose some of them. I know a couple of really good computer guys and I'm trying to select the one who can stay for the long haul. If this project comes to fruition, it could take up to a year to complete."

"This is the first I've heard of it. Why the secret?"

"No secret. It may not happen anyway. I just need to be prepared to make all the key decisions should everything fall into place."

"I understand. Let me know if there's anything I can do?"

"Thanks love. You're so organized; I may pick your brains for some pointers later on."

He went to his office and closed the door. Kathleen knew not to disturb him. Leaning his back against the door, he stood silent for a few moments, collecting his thoughts. The knock on the door startled him. In his frame of mind, it sounded like someone was trying to break the door down.

"Jonathan?"

"Yes dear."

"I just wanted to tell you that supper would be ready about five-thirty."

"Thanks, dear. I'll be done in plenty of time," he opened the door slowly so wouldn't scare Kathleen.

"Is something wrong honey? You look terrible."

"Really? I feel fine."

"I don't mean you look sick. Your face is all twisted up and you're sweating. What's the matter?"

Jonathan wiped his forehead with the back of his hand. "It's nothing dear. It was brisk on the ride and now my bodies catching up to the chill. I should have stayed in the garage a little longer to go over my bike. It would have given me an opportunity to acclimate... but I wanted you to have the flowers right away. Sorry, my mistake."

"I appreciate the thought, but take better care of yourself. I don't need you getting sick." She touched his cheek with the back of her hand. His temperature was normal. Satisfied, she returned to the kitchen.

Jonathan followed her into the kitchen. "I just came to get some iced tea dear. I'll be out of your way in a moment. Mm mmm, that smells good. What are we having?"

"Tequila lime pork tenderloin."

"I'll definitely be on time." Kissing her on the back of the neck, he returned to his office, tea in hand.

Jonathan pulled the letter and the photographs from the drawer. Laying them out on the desktop, he searched for his magnifying glass. Locating it quickly, he began to study the pictures. It wasn't long before he was able to piece together the full view of the side of the box.

Grabbing his scissors, he began to trim the photographs so he could tape them all together. He was careful to put even the smallest scrap into an envelope. A satisfied smile spread across his face as he scrutinized the whole picture. Eventually he gave up trying to guess what it was. Between the phone call and the photos, he was no better off than before.

He began to make a list of the things he did know. His parents had taught him to approach a problem from different angles. A solution would always become evident.

It wasn't long before he began thinking out loud. This method always helped him clarify his thoughts. "Let's see what we have here. First, we have a metal box. No known size or weight. Second, it's in a cave like setting in sedimentary rock dating back sixty-five million years. Third, the soil was definitely loose because it washed out in the rain. Fourth, the metal is worked with pictographs of dinosaurs and machined to very extreme tolerances. Johnny-boy, this is one hell of a puzzle.

"Who do we need to get this project off the ground? We might need a metallurgist. We'll need electronics people. I can cover the computer end of things, but maybe a programmer might shed some insight in functionality of certain features. We'll need a mechanical engineer. Mom and Dad, this is one heinous problem you've given me. I hope I'm up to the task.

"That's not positive thinking. Now isn't the time for self-doubt. This is a new frontier. You will be the expert in this. The world will have to come to you. Much better. Okay, now for the short list."

Jonathan worked right up to suppertime preparing his list. He'd narrowed it down to twenty friends and colleagues. After supper and some family time, he could return to this daunting task and start with a fresh outlook of success with no doubts or apprehension.

His parents were the kindest, sweetest people that anyone would want to meet. It was frightening and confusing that they would consider someone capable of doing them harm. The interesting part was that they would suspect the government.

Perhaps he was a bit naïve. Through the university, his parents had worked many years around the government. They knew things that they hadn't told him. He would be a willing participant in this. His parents asked and he would not refuse them if it meant protecting them from harm. Striding purposefully through the office door, he left this problem behind and washed up for supper.

"You're ruining my work honey."

"What?" she asked completely confused.

"How can I work when this heavenly aroma permeates the house? Trey, doesn't this smell heavenly?"

"Are you okay Dad?"

"Don't give me that 'are you insane' look. Your mother has spent a lot of time on this meal and we should appreciate her efforts and God-given talent with food. Sharing food is the most intimate bond humans can experience. We would not have survived as a species if it weren't for sharing food. We taught each other how to make tools, weapons to hunt, to cook, which edible things were safe, and which were deadly. Food is life and sharing food binds us all the way back to the very first human to evolve from the animals."

"You sure you're all right Dad?"

"Never mind." Jonathan forcefully took a large mouthful of food and planted his fork heavily back on the plate.

"No dear," Kathleen said thoughtfully. "You're right."

He looked up from his plate as she continued.

"You know, I never looked at it like that. My God, this is kind of overwhelming. I'm getting goose bumps. You're quite the deep thinker. I'm impressed."

Now Jonathan was blushing. He managed to get a 'thank you' out before returning to the meal. He took another mouthful of food, this time it was more reasonable in size.

Kathleen gave Trey that motherly look to prompt him to say something to his father. Resistance was his natural reaction, but she gave him that wide-eyed stare while motioning her head to do as she asked. He relinquished to the unspoken pressure and coughed half-heartedly to get his father's attention.

"I'm sorry Dad. It just sounds kinda crazy. But when you really think about it, it's probably exactly how we got here. We've studied evolution at school during science class and no one ever taught us about food. I mean we learned about what the cavemen ate and all that junk, but you look at things differently. It's pretty cool. Yeah, I'm going to tell my teacher about this. Way to go Dad!"

Jonathan smiled at Johnny and then gave an appreciative look to Kathleen. He knew she was the one who prompted Johnny to speak up, but was proud that his son grasped the concept. The concept seemed to be so obvious. It wasn't radical thinking to him. Now he pondered why he'd never heard it mentioned before.

His father had always had a love affair with food. He respected those who grew it and those who prepared it, especially those who prepared it well. Theory or not, it was an obvious extension of how he was raised. Attitudes around the house really do wear off on the kids. It wasn't a brilliant flash of realization, but it made him more mindful of how he would speak to Johnny from now on.

"Great meal dear. Thank you."

"Thanks honey. I'll get your plate. You go back to work for a while."

"No sweetheart, I'll take this stuff to the kitchen," he said as he grabbed up the dishes. "I need more iced tea anyway." He kissed her on his way back to the office. It was a great meal and he didn't mind saying so.

CHAPTER TWENTY-EIGHT

S ETTLING IN, JONATHAN TRIED TO rethink his approach to this dilemma. He'd gotten the list of phone numbers ready, and their locations. His list of potential helpers was the next major project. The number one priority was getting the phone list to his parents.

Creating the list was relatively easy. The copy for his father had the phone number, a date and time next to it. Jonathan's list had only the date, time and location number. Unless you had both lists, you couldn't understand what you were seeing.

The government would be able to figure it out if the lines were tapped, but that's why they each were using random phones. His father's list was the weak link. If someone got hold of it, it would be easy enough to track down who was receiving the calls and where. He needed a better plan.

It was one of those eureka moments when the idea hit him. Each phone number had a location number attached to it. When he made the list, he would subtract the location number from the last digit of the phone number. He could explain all this to his father the next time he called. All his dad had to do was add the location number to the last digit and there would be the accurate phone number. It was brilliant in its simplicity.

Along with a schedule and the phone numbers, he made a short list of the people that he thought might be able to help figure out just what his parents had discovered. He included their names in the letter. They were all longtime friends and associates. He read his return letter one more time, careful not to leave out any vital information.

Sealing the envelope, he then sealed it inside of another addressed to his father's friend in St. Louis. Jonathan then took the photos, his father's letter and all scraps or notes pertaining to the project out to the garage. Searching along the shelves he found what he was looking for. He placed them in an old coffee can and set them on the tool bench. With a kitchen match, he set them on fire.

With the fire out, he then stirred the ashes to expose any unburned paper. He added a little lighter fluid to the ashes and lit them again. When they burned out completely the second time; he mixed them even more. No unburned remnants remained. Grabbing a small gardening trowel, he went behind the garage and half-mixed and half buried the ashes into the flowerbed.

Jonathan felt completely satisfied that there was no way anyone could ever reconstruct what had been destroyed. It would be weeks or even months before anyone could connect him to his parent's discovery.

His father's letter was unnerving and he shivered slightly while he patiently returned the flowerbed to the original appearance and carefully replaced the wood mulch so the area looked undisturbed. Again, time and weather would be on his side.

Kathleen came out to the garage as Jonathan was cleaning the off the garden tool.

"Aren't you full of energy today? Is everything alright?"

"Sure, honey," he smiled. "Why do you ask?"

"Well, you wanted to ride the first thing this afternoon. You usually wait until late afternoon or even after supper. You're a man of pretty regular habits. When you get restless, I worry, that's all."

"I can't explain it to you, dear. I just can't seem to get settled. I want to do something, yet nothing. Do you know what I mean?"

"Yeah, I do," she said wistfully. "I feel that way a lot. I'd like to work but I want to be here for the kids. Johnny is pretty self-sufficient, but Theresa is my little girl and I want to teach her how to do the cooking, cleaning and baking. It seems like girly stuff, but if you don't know how, you could spend your life paying someone to do the simplest tasks. Their education in these matters is very important to me."

"You can get a job any time you want. You're a great mother and the kids already know more than the rest of the neighbor's kids combined."

"I know you don't care if I work. You're home a lot anyway. It's just that…" Pausing abruptly in mid-sentence, she realized the conversation had turned completely around. "Hey, how'd this become my problem anyway? If you're up to it, could you move some dressers for me? I could vacuum behind them and you could expend some of your excess tension by lifting heavy furniture. It's a brilliant solution for two problems. What would you do without me?"

"Save a lot of money on a chiropractor, that's for sure."

"Ha-ha, you're such a funny guy. Maybe that's why I married you."

"I know why you married me," he said as a roguish grin spread across his face. He set the trowel down and chased her back into the house. Catching her in the kitchen, he kissed her on the back of the neck and reached in front to gently caress her. Her scent was a mixture of perfume and natural aromas from her hair and body. She smelled wonderful. "Let's go tackle that heavy lifting," he said playfully pinching her bottom. "I can hear the furniture calling my name. We'd better hurry."

Jonathan dashed up the stairs two at a time as she casually walked behind him. *Where he gets the energy sometimes is beyond me. I'll put it to good use though. Those dressers haven't been moved since last spring.*

Ellen and Jonathan woke up early. They'd eaten and finished packing in no time. Steve was a man of his word, helping them break camp before the others were awake. The dawn was bright and promising; the sun was creating a red ribbon on the horizon through the distant early morning haze.

With the truck loaded, it was time for goodbyes. "Thanks for everything Steve. We'll keep in touch. The students are doing a great job. You'll have no trouble finishing up here in the next two weeks. You know how close we are to completion. We need to keep the timing in sync. Here, you can have the sour cream. We want you to enjoy your omelets."

"I wish that I could be with you. I have a couple of ideas about the box and I need to be there to see if I'm correct."

"We wish you were coming too. You're too valuable here to risk it."

"I know that, yet it doesn't stop me from wishing."

Ellen hugged him. "This will be over soon. We'll be in a storage warehouse somewhere and you can theorize to your hearts content."

"A lot of good that does me now," he mumbled.

They all laughed and hugged again. The Crenshaw's got into their truck and drove away. Camp would be different without them. The students would miss them a little, but Steve had come to look at them as extended family. He felt the absence as if he were saying goodbye to his own parents.

"Good morning, Steve."

Momentarily startled, he answered, "Good morning, Janet. I trust you slept well?"

"Of course, this fresh air really knocks me out. What time did the Crenshaw's leave?"

"They were gone by six. They wanted to get there before the sun was fully up. They were really grateful for your suggestion. I got the impression that they didn't want to be here. I think they felt that they were intruding."

"I sensed it too. That's why I mentioned the things I did. I was really embarrassed when he said not to lecture him. I could have died."

"Not to worry. He was angry with himself, not with you."

"That makes me feel better. I don't want to get a bad grade when I take his class next semester."

"You're that serious about this?"

"I told you that I was. You'll see." She smiled broadly.

"I'm thrilled to see this level of enthusiasm. It's hard to find people who can enjoy digging in rocks for a living. It's a special calling. At least it's that way for me."

"I know exactly what you mean. I admire the relationship that the Crenshaw's have. I think that we could complement each other in much the same way."

"Having an assistant who can anticipate my needs would be a real plus. I know what I have to do, but sometimes the demands of the dig pull me in too many directions."

"That's exactly why I would like to be your assistant. You can use my help and I'm offering it freely."

"I'll take it on a limited basis. We can't have any favoritism in the camp."

"That's not what I want. There must be no special treatment. I want to learn as much as I can. No more, no less."

"Then it's settled. You can start your duties immediately. We need to get organized for covering and transporting these fossils. We have a large amount of very fragile stuff. All of the photographs have to be cataloged as well as everything else. Am I going too fast?"

"No, I asked some of the others about your normal wrap and transport needs. They were very informative. I have a list of materials that I think you'll need. I don't have a phone, or the authority to purchase anything, so here's the list."

Steve scanned it briefly. "Very impressive Janet. At first read, I can't find anything you've missed. Let me study it more closely. I'd hate to miss some small item."

"I don't think that you'll be disappointed. I agree there's no sense in missing one item because the list looks good on the surface."

"Thanks for being so understanding." *She just keeps getting better and better.*

"You'll come to trust me in time. For now, you must follow all of the normal procedures for completing a dig. I'm happy to work within those guide-lines."

I hope it's not my imagination, but I think she likes me. She's so talented and good-looking too. I need to be careful with this one. I could easily make a big mistake. There's time enough for mistakes when we get back to school.

"Thanks Janet. I'm sure it will be a pleasure having you as an assistant. Thanks again for everything."

She smiled and walked away. *He's so cute when he's nervous. I really care a lot for him. I'm hoping this will lead into something more. I'll wait until we get back to school before I start my real push. I don't want to cause any trouble for him. That would ruin everything.*

CHAPTER TWENTY-NINE

Two days had gone since the Crenshaw's left Steve's site. They had not gone back to visit, nor had Steve come by to see them. Ellen and Jonathan trusted his judgment. They knew that he was anxious to get a crack at the box again. By staying away, he was proving himself to the man that they had hoped he was. They knew, only too well, the desire such a discovery brought. Its overwhelming magnetism was undeniable.

Ellen and Jonathan followed their individual routines while working on the excavation and examination of the box. Ellen still rose early for her walks while Jonathan prepared breakfast for the both of them.

At the cave, Jonathan shoveled what he knocked down from the walls and hauled it to the hillside while Ellen continued to scrutinize her photographs and study the box. Between them, Jonathan was making rapid headway towards getting the box moved. Ellen was establishing the links between the ornate exterior markings and the simplified interior symbols. The hours seemed to fly by as their work progressed.

"Let's break for lunch, I'm getting hungry." Jonathan looked at Ellen. "Did you hear me?"

"Yeah, lunch. Right?" she responded absently. Ellen waved her hand in his direction to let him know that she had heard him. She never even looked up from the photographs.

"Oh my God! My hair is on fire!" he said testing her attention.

"That sounds good. I'll have one too. How about hot dogs instead?"

"I'll fly to Mars and get the really good ones. You remember those special ones don't you; the ones with the funny purple spots all through them?" he continued his new game.

"Whatever. Oh… and just mustard on mine." She looked up long enough to see that she had his attention. "Thanks, dear," was all she said as her attention turned back to the photographs.

Jonathan left for the truck. He almost fell down the hillside; he was laughing so hard. If she knew what he'd just said, she'd probably kill him. He'd be back with lunch in about twenty minutes or so. She might even take some time to realize that she was eating a hotdog.

He prepared her lunch and added only mustard as requested. Jonathan preferred his with a little butter and yellow mustard. "Now this is the only way to really enjoy a hotdog," he said out loud. Grabbing the jug of iced tea, a couple of glasses and a blanket; he headed back to the cave.

"I'm back," he shouted as he entered.

"Back here dear. Come see this."

"Give me a moment, I've got lunch."

"Oh, thank you. I'm so hungry. How'd you know?"

Stifling outright laughter, Jonathan answered as best as he could. "It was noon and we hadn't stopped all morning. I figured that if I fixed lunch, you would stop long enough to eat it. Here, you can take this blanket." He leaned in a bit so that she could take the blanket from his shoulder.

"You thought of everything. That's really sweet."

"Well you know me dear."

"Yes, I do." *He's up to something. He has that shit-eating grin on his face. I wonder how the tea tastes. I'll wait until he drinks his first.*

"What did you want me to see? When I came in you were saying come over and look at something. Show me. Lunch can wait a few minutes. The dogs are wrapped in foil to keep them hot."

"Let me finish lunch first. You went through all the trouble to prepare it."

With that, Jonathan couldn't control the laughter any longer.

"What is so funny?" she demanded. She knew that he was laughing at her. She wanted to know why, and she wanted to know now. *I knew it; he fooled around with the tea.*

"It's nothing dear. I just remembered something about hotdogs with purple spots and it struck me as funny. I guess that you would have to have been there." He started laughing again at his new joke.

"You're crazy, you know that. Are you going to finish lunch or just waste the day on silly thoughts?" *Well he's drinking the tea so I guess it's all right.*

"I'm sorry dear. I won't do it again. I promise. Now, what did you want me to see?" After clearing his throat, he'd regained his composure.

"I've been studying these photos again. There are several markings that are the same on each side. The most of them don't repeat more than once. I think this is an inscription of some kind. On the other side where the door is, it's a different format. Everything is laid out as if they are instructions of some kind. The markings are similar, but not the same." She handed him the photos. "See what I mean," she said as she pointed to the features.

"Why don't we just step over to the box and take a look?" asked Jonathan.

"Now we can, since you're not working back there at the moment. I've been studying the pictures all morning so that I could stay out of your way."

"I hadn't realized," he apologized. "You didn't say anything. If you wanted me to move, you should have said so."

"It's not that, Jonathan. You've been moving so much dirt that I didn't want to disturb you. I'd like to change the topic for a moment if I may. All this exercise is shaping you up. You know you're looking pretty good lately. I'll probably end up giving up my boyfriend now that you're getting so buff."

"Jolly joker. You're a laugh a minute." *All right, sex again tonight!*

"It was okay though when you were laughing at me… right?" *I saw that look flash across your face you horn dog.*

"Well, yeah, but it was you, not me." *Shit! I just blew the sex. Damn my big mouth.*

"Let's get back to work before we say something you'll regret."

"Good idea." *Keep your fingers crossed old man. The game is still afoot.* "So, let's go and see what you've discovered."

Scooping the photos from the cave floor, she moved past him. Ellen moved to the first side they'd uncovered. Without hesitation, she pointed to the figure she wanted him to study.

"This is what I'm talking about. These markings here repeat throughout this text. They aren't that frequent, but they are the only ones that repeat. Look closely at the rest of them. You won't find a repeat anywhere among the remaining figures. Go ahead, look."

"I believe you dear. Don't get so intense."

"I just want you to see where I'm going with this. I know that I'm on the right track. I can feel it."

Jonathan stepped back a bit from the surface now that so much soil had been removed. At this distance he could see there were no patterns to many of the pictographs. The whole image left him with impression of a large, intricate design. When he looked at it like he was reading a book; the lines of apparent text became evident.

"That's amazing. How'd you see that? I missed it completely."

"I saw it, the same way that you see a minute fragment of bone in a pile of rubble. You know what you're looking for. If it's there, you'll find it."

He trailed his fingertips across several of the images and said wistfully, "I'd love to know what they say. This is going to be so great when we publish. We won't need to worry about any conspiracy then. We'll be too famous to turn up missing. Just let them try something shady after we're published." Jonathan's false bravado didn't ring true to either of them, but it felt good to say it.

After running his hands over the eerie warm surface one last time, he rose and said, "Let's go to the other side and you can show me the differences. This thing will probably never cease to amaze me."

They moved quietly, almost reverently. She positioned herself back a little so that he could move in for a closer look. Pointing out the clearly delineated lines of text, she let him move closer and study the figures.

"I see. These markings are laid out differently from side to side. I agree with your inscription idea."

"I had these photos laid out like a map and I studied them night after night. I only saw this today. Sometimes you can't see the forest through the trees. See how the markings are in shorter lines. They're lined up as if they are a list of instructions. Perhaps, after we get back, we can translate them. We should start with the assumption that these are instructions on how to open and/or operate the box. It might help us solve some of the markings."

"What makes you think that the box does something?"

"Why are you studying all of the lines that separate the box into sections? They're there for a reason. It makes no sense to section up a huge piece of metal unless you want it to do something. Even the lines inside have some purpose. For instance, that panel that moves out from the wall. It does something."

"You're right. I hadn't realized that you'd given it that much thought. I haven't been able to come up with any rational explanation for form or function. At least we share the same gut feelings about it. This has a purpose and I want to know what it is. This still seems like a coffin to me. I haven't been able to shake that feeling since we first mentioned it."

"What if something wild or wicked was sealed in this thing? We could be letting it out on all of mankind."

"Now you're losing it Ellen. I won't go that far. Assume that you're correct. How long do you think living matter can survive?" He questioned, "Even extra-terrestrial living matter?"

"If it was held in stasis, it might last throughout time. I don't know. We don't have that technology."

"The fact remains that neither of us knows. We could be in grave danger or it could be nothing at all. We'll never know until we solve the riddle. I need to continue uncovering this thing or we won't ever get to study it. Please don't go inside again without first letting me know. I don't want to go searching again."

"I won't. You can trust me." She blew him a kiss.

"That's what I'm afraid of my dear," he quipped.

Jonathan returned to shoveling, while Ellen collected her photographs and moved out of the way. Eventually she decided buy a piece of wood. She was going to staple all of the photos to a board so that she could save the time and energy of sorting them each time. She packed everything up and went to help Jonathan.

"Here, let me help you with some of this dirt. I can knock it down and push it aside while you shovel it up," she said coming up behind him.

"That's a great idea, but I thought that you wanted time to study your photographs."

"I do. We're on a tight schedule and I've got a good plan worked out. I'll staple them to a board and I won't have to sort them out each again. Why not use the free time to work with you expediting the removal of the box?"

"That's great. I have one more small suggestion. Assuming that you'll remove them from the board for transport, you can put numbers and letters on the front side, on the boarders. When you re-staple them, it will go quicker to match up the numbers and letters."

"That's a good idea, but they've been marked from the beginning. I'm one step ahead of you."

Jonathan worked his way down the side of the box, while Ellen finished picking up her photos. He'd made remarkable headway. The soil was not as compacted as it should be. And that was an enigma that still nagged at him.

He knew enough about the territory to know that this region was deltaic during the Late Cretaceous period. There were plenty of rivers and streams that covered this section of the country. There must have been a promontory of limestone to form the cave. The vegetation would have been almost like a rain forest. The animal life would have been prolific. A water supply and a forest combination, even now, equated food for predatory animals. It must have been beautiful.

Maybe he needed to rethink commonly held beliefs. There may have been hills and valleys. Just because the area had been predominantly deltaic doesn't mean it was exclusively flat. Land features made of soft or porous rock would easily erode more quickly than the granite formations found elsewhere in the world. Even hills and valleys would disappear after enough rain and time. Sixty-five million years was definitely enough time.

Jonathan continued his work with renewed enthusiasm. A sense of closure on this problem settled in once he was sure that he'd solved the mystery of the cave. He realized that if he was able to widen the passage, he could drag the box out into the open.

The project would be tough going. He would need Steve to help with this sooner than he'd originally calculated. It was one thing to move loose dirt. It was another to break away the hard-compacted soil and haul the large, heavy chunks away.

A new plan emerged. He would spend the rest of the day breaking the soil away from the walls. By the time Steve would be able to come, there would be plenty for him to help haul away. This was going to accelerate the process considerably. He would not have to remove any more soil from behind the box. They only needed enough room to secure ropes or straps behind the box to enable them to haul the box out by winch. Then they could frame it; making it no different than any other crate.

The confusion on moving day would allow them to slip past the notice of anyone. The plan was formulating nicely. He decided that they would have enough time to go see Steve later in the evening.

CHAPTER THIRTY

"WHAT ARE YOU TWO DOING back here? I thought that I was supposed to be helping you haul dirt later," asked Steve. Surprise and curiosity were written all over his face.

"Things have changed a little," whispered Jonathan. "I can widen the passage and we can drag the box outside much sooner than we anticipated. We can then frame it to look like any other shipping crate. No one will notice it at all. You and I can winch it to the edge of the hillside with the trucks. I'll build a dirt ramp out of all of the debris so we can back a flatbed up to the hillside and winch it on to the bed without much difficulty. What do you think?"

"Wait a minute," cautioned Steve. "That's a good plan, but you'd be dragging that thing downhill. No one knows how much it weighs. Aren't you afraid that it'll get away from you? There's no way of knowing what will happen when it digs into the loose soil."

"Good call. We'll have to build the ramp with wooden runners to control the direction and speed of the descent. We can put enough lumber across the bottom to level it out once it's down. If the soil compacts below bed height or the front digs in, we can still rebuild the ramp back to bed height. The plan still works. In this new version though, we don't get killed."

"That's always a good option," chuckled Ellen. "Do you think that you and Steve will be able to handle this alone? It's pretty massive."

"I've been thinking about that. We don't know what the metal is. We assume that it weighs a lot by the size of the box. We also know that some, or all, of the box is hollow. The winches on the trucks should handle the load if we put logs under it to serve as rollers."

Steve interrupted Jonathan's train of thought. "Jonathan, you had a good idea with the runners. Let's use them from where the box is now all the way down. You've never needed logs or fence posts on any previous digs. You've been coming here for twenty years. Wouldn't that send up a red flag?"

"You're right. We'll do it your way."

"I'll leave the details up to you two," Ellen interjected. "Please don't take any unnecessary chances. Besides, if you wreck the truck, it'll attract the attention that you're trying so hard to avoid."

"Don't you think that I already know that? I've done the math and the odds are even that we'll be successful. We have to take the chance. I'll monitor the winch carefully. At the first sign of trouble, I'll shut it down. You'll have the trucks all safe and sound for our ride home. I'm not sure what to do if this fails. I'm glad that we went with the heavy-duty winches when we ordered the trucks. That increases the likelihood of our success."

They gravitated to Steve's tent where they studied other options for several hours. Eventually they returned to Jonathan's original idea. It was the most practical and cost effective. There would be no additional equipment to be rented or borrowed. It also excluded the locals from anything that was going on. The only variation to the original was to haul the box to the edge of the hill before crating it.

With the plan solidified, there was nothing left to be discussed, so the Crenshaw's made their apologies for their interruption and said their goodbyes to Steve and a few of the others who happened upon them as they were leaving.

As they turned off the road and eased closer to their campsite, the truck rumbled gently to a stop. The only break in the solitude was the crunch of the stones under the tires as the truck came to rest. Nighttime was so peaceful out here; a few animal calls were the only sounds for miles.

Quietly, hand in hand, they walked back up to the cave. They were savoring the renewed spirit they had from finalizing the plans for removing the box. It relaxed them now that they were able to finally cross a major obstacle in the path of uninterrupted research on the box.

They lingered briefly at the cave entrance before entering. Ellen went down the passage to the box. She left Jonathan to his digging. He knew what he was doing and didn't need her input.

The evening wore on. The temperature had been holding in the mid-seventies. It was ideal weather for this kind of work. There was a decent breeze coming into the cave. It helped Jonathan stay cool. That allowed him to work longer without becoming too exhausted.

Ellen struggled with the markings. She tried assigning different meanings and phrases to them. There were moments when she thought that she was close, but then the assigned words or phrases didn't seem to fit when applied to the markings throughout the rest of the text.

This could take years to decipher and Ellen wanted it to take hours. Her expectations were unrealistic, but she was feeling the pressure of a limited time. Success was a potentially futile goal, yet she intended to try in spite of the almost insurmountable odds.

"Jonathan, can you come here for a bit?"

He poked his head from around the edge of the box. "What do you need? If it won't take long, I can to help."

"It won't be long. I need to go inside the box and check some of the markings on that plate. I'm trying to figure out symbols for open and close. I need to see if any of the markings on the plate are a match for the ones out here. It might speed up the process. You never can tell until you try."

"Give me a minute. Let me wipe some of this grime off."

"Take whatever time you need. I still have enough here to keep me busy for years to come. . . not that I want you to take that long."

Jonathan stepped up behind her and poked her in the ribs. "BOO!"

Ellen almost hit the wall of the cave. Her scream echoed down the passage. She turned a fiercely angry stare at him. He just stood there with a stupid grin on his face.

"Keep it up funny boy. I'll knock you on your fanny." Ellen was outraged. There was nothing that she hated more than Jonathan scaring her like that.

"I was just lightening the mood a bit. I want you to feel loose. You're obviously very tense right now. You should have seen me coming from a mile away."

"Well I didn't. You have my permission to never do that again. I'm so focused on this problem right now that I don't need your childish games getting in my way or ruining my concentration." *I was completely relaxed until your little stunt. What the hell did you think you were doing anyway?*

"Ouch. That hurt."

"Good. You deserve much worse. Now shut up, kiss me, and lend me a hand."

"Yes, mistress. . . I live to serve."

Ellen sequenced the markings and the door slid silently open. She stepped inside and went straight to the panel. She manipulated the markings on the surface and the panel raised as it always did. She watched herself carefully as she stroked each key. She memorized the sequence and compared the figures to those on the outside of the box. The figures inside were more streamlined; yet similarly shaped. This was a valuable clue. The interior may prove to be the actual written language as most commonly used, and the exterior would be readable to whom or whatever, only a more ornate, decorative type of lettering.

Quickly operating the controls, she opened the door. "Can you come in here for a moment? I think I've found something."

"Really?" he questioned. "What is it?"

"It has to do with the markings. I want you to see this." She handed him her panel of photographs as he came through the door. "I want you to look at these markings here," she said as she indicated the ones in question. "Tell me what you see."

"That's a pretty tall order. I'm not sure what you're looking for."

"If I told you, then you wouldn't prove my theory. I need you to study these and draw some kind of conclusion. I don't care if it's not the same as mine."

Jonathan held the photographs up to the plate; examining the ones that she had pointed out. He studied the plate and the pictures for what seemed like an eternity. "I'm not sure what it is that I'm looking at. The ones here on the plate are pretty close to the ones on the outside. They're just not very fancy."

"Oh, thank you." She grabbed him in a bear hug that almost lifted him from the floor.

"A hand shake would have been adequate. I still need to breathe, you know." He bent down and picked up the board.

"My theory is that these inside markings are the actual written language. The ones on the outside are more like the stuff that would be found on monuments and such. Everyone can read them but they are highly stylized. This could be the breakthrough that I've been searching for.

"I'm sure that I have two sets of text that are similar. What we have is a control panel on the inside that operates the same mechanism as the one on the outside. Can you imagine where I'm going with this? This is nothing less than the Rosetta stone. Solving this may only take a few months instead of a few years."

"Why do you want to get your hopes up like that? You know that someone could hand you a book of translation, but if you don't have a reference point, it would be useless."

"But I have a reference point. Don't you understand what we've been discussing? I have one mechanism and two sets of what appears to be operating instructions. When I have the functions down, then I can start applying words to function. It will eventually fall into place."

"That may be so, but you don't know what *open* or *close* is in this language. You don't even know if there are words for *open* and *close*. Those may be parts of a concept. Using my example as the approach, you wouldn't speak in sentences as much as imagery. Single words or phrases may convey vast amounts of information based on a pool of knowledge and/or history that you don't have access to. These could be numbers on a keypad. Do you understand where I'm going?"

"I have always understood, perhaps more so than you realize. I so desperately want this to be resolved. There's been something compelling about this, this box ever since I discovered it. It's like this external force is relentlessly pushing me onward. I must know what it is. I need to know everything there is to know about it. It's no more complicated than that."

Ellen was a woman of very strong convictions and had marked her territory. It was one of the traits that had attracted him to her. Silently he withdrew, leaving her alone in the box. He resumed his work nearer to the door in case she called for his help. The chances of that happening in the next few hours were slim and next to none. And slim was dead.

Slowly the amount of soil he'd knocked down began to find its way to the outside of the cave. It was only a matter of days before the box would be extricated from the hillside and traveling to points yet unknown.

CHAPTER THIRTY-ONE

S TEVE COULD APPRECIATE WHY THIS area was referred to as Hell's Creek Formation. For all the work they had already done, there was at least twice that amount to go. The fossils were becoming too numerous to count. To find everything that there was to find, you would need a hundred people living here and collecting every day for most of the year.

It had been two days since the Crenshaw's last visit. After they'd broken camp, Steve's group had become extremely busy. It was time to pay Jonathan and Ellen a visit. Their camp was nearby, relative to the vastness of the area. It was the only place left that you could still find the remnants of a limestone prominence that had existed all those millions of years ago.

He often wondered what the landscape had looked like. The deltaic features would have made it lush with ferns, palms, and grasses. It would have been the equivalent of a modern-day rain forest. There would have been numerous streams that passed through the area. The abundance of life must have been staggering.

Could game trails have been routed in such a way that most of them passed near this nesting site? Would food gathering have been easier, and thus family rearing been more easily accomplished?

Even in contemporary times, man still developed tight knit groups along the Amazon. Deep in the rain forests, they thrive because of their proximity to the rivers. A river's course, and seasonal flooding, affects how these pockets of humanity live and survive. The river dictates all cultural and religious beliefs. Could it have been the same for dinosaurs?

Janet's voice stirred him from his musings. Startled, Steve was happy that she didn't know what was going on in his head just then. He wished that he had been able to view prehistoric life. It was something that he knew was not possible, yet the thought haunted him.

"I've got all of the reports ready Steve. They're categorized by species type and age. They are cross-referenced to the grid so that anyone can find the photographic location by the numbers I've assigned. It should prove helpful for future study. You might even be able to use it in class someday, should you ever decide to teach."

"Something tells me that you've got too much energy for your own good Janet. How could you possibly have gotten all this work done in just two days?"

"I never said that it was only two days. I've been working on this since I first gave you my form. I had already employed it for cataloging and sorting my own work. Once the rest of us started using it, it was easy to group their data and compile this." She handed him a volume of work containing the individual grid forms as well as the compiled data forms. The compilation forms cross-referenced to the individual sheets by the designation numbers she'd assigned them.

Steve couldn't help but admire the work. She must not have slept more than an hour a night. It would have taken him a month to prepare a report like this. He double-checked some of the entries. It was a magnificent piece of work.

"Thank you, Janet. This is some of the best work I've ever seen. This will really pick up the pace of the research once we return to the campus. Thank you again. I don't think that I'll ever be able to express my gratitude properly."

"I'm sure that we'll be able to work something out." She winked slyly at him.

Steve was so lost in his work that he missed it. He was already moving towards his tent. "Thanks again," he called as he picked up his pace, anticipating his visit with Ellen and Jonathan.

Janet watched as he walked away. She was in love with him or deeply infatuated. The look on her face was difficult to interpret. *Can't he see how much I want him? There's nothing that I wouldn't do for him. Oh, how I wish that he'd ask me for more.* Sighing heavily; she returned to her work.

Steve's truck rolled to a stop about twenty feet from the Crenshaw's tent. He honked the horn lightly to let them know that he had arrived, even though the noise of the truck should have been enough to alert them.

No one had responded by the time he'd gotten out of the truck. He went over to the tent and knocked at the tent post. "Excuse me. Is anyone home?" There was no answer. Knocking again, in case they were sleeping, he listened for any sounds at all. He opened the tent flap and looked in after he'd gotten no response. They were not there.

Scanning the area around the tent, he saw nothing. He shrugged his shoulders and headed for the cave. That would have been the obvious place to start looking, but he didn't want to walk all that way just to find them back at the tent.

"Hello," he called as he started up the path to the cave. "It's me, Steve. Hello."

Jonathan came from around the side of the cave. He called down the hillside, "We're in here. Come on up. We've been expecting you."

Steve traversed the distance with long, eager strides. He'd been anticipating this moment for two days. He didn't want to waste any time. Skidding to a halt at the large mess in the middle of the passage, he stared in total disbelief at the pile of debris. "What in blue blazes is going on here? Why are you doing this?" He studied the enlarged passage as well as the pile of rubble.

"I've come up with a modification of the plan to remove the box cleanly and quickly. Once the passage is widened out to the original limestone walls, we can winch the box out and down the hillside using both truck winches, just like we planned. Jonathan hastily fleshed out the details so Steve had a clear picture of the process.

With a few questions and suggestions, they were satisfied that they knew what it would take to move the box.

"I'll give you this," Steve concluded. "It's an excellent plan. The heavy-duty winches on our trucks should handle it. Between us, we can get the job done. How do you propose to get all this dirt down the hillside?"

"Funny that you should ask about that. Here's where you come in." Jonathan put his arm around Steve's shoulder as they walked down the passage.

"Ellen, look who's here."

"Steve, it's so good to see you. How long can you stay? There's so much to do. It would be great if you could spend the rest of the afternoon with us. I want to show you some of the things that I've figured out. You're so good at puzzles. I wondered if you could give me a hand with some of my theories. I need you to do a comparison of some of the figures. I would like you to tell me what you see.

"After you're through, I'll go over some of my ideas with you. I've already done this with Jonathan, and I was very happy that he was able to see what I was looking for. Come on, let's get started."

Steve allowed himself to be led around to the side of the box. Ellen went through the details of what she was looking at and what she wanted him to compare. Steve found the idea fascinating, without really knowing what she was searching for. He loved to solve puzzles, and this was clearly the greatest puzzle that he would ever encounter.

He waited until she opened the door before moving. He was already running possible permutations through his head. Stepping inside, he automatically turned to face the panel.

"As I had said previously, I would like you to study the marking that I have photographed here," handing him the board. "Compare them to the ones that are on the panel. Let me know what you think. I don't care about your answer. No matter what it is, it will be correct."

"That's a pretty broad statement. Not every answer that I could give would be correct."

"Yes, it could. I'm trying to find the key to deciphering the language. No matter what you come up with, it will be more information than I already have."

"I understand."

Steve accepted the board and placed it under the panel. He looked back and forth for a while. The almost imperceptible movement of his head was the only indication that he was working. Finally, he bent forward and looked closely at one of the markings. Steve placed his finger on one of the photos and then looked back and forth a few times. He then set the board down, leaning it against the wall.

"I don't know what you're searching for, but I have an idea. The markings are different styles, but essentially the same. These seem more simplified. The ones outside seem excessively ornate. What are you working on?"

"That's the answer I was hoping to get. You saw the same thing as Jonathan. My theory is that the outside markings are decorative. The same thing we put on placards or monuments of important people. They're a fancy, yet readable script.

"I believe the markings here are the everyday language as it would have been written. Even though you can read the outside, it was more for show. I want to use the markings that operate the controls to try and decipher the language. I believe that they're operational directions. I hope to be able to translate instructions into English and use those clues to solve the rest of the language."

"What luck have you had so far?"

"None. I can get a few of the words to fit, but it never pans out. Jonathan says that it may be a language based on metaphors, or abstract concepts. Once you have the historical or cultural reference, you can understand what a few brief phrases would mean in the overall context of the writing. He even suggested that they might be nothing more than numbers on a keypad."

"That's an interesting theory. Have you tried to expand on that?"

"It's only been a couple of days, Steve. How fast do you think I can do this? Besides that, why would someone put numbers on the outside?"

"That makes sense. You said it yourself, you can only get so far and then the *words* don't fit anymore. When you're dealing with concepts, imagery or whatever, *words* wouldn't fit. Is there anything else that you need from me? Jonathan wants me to help him widen the passage. I only have a few hours before I have to return. A couple of hours should help some with making the ramp and anything else he has planned."

"I know he can use the help. We'd decided that he'd get the passageway done before he scheduled the truck. I think that we'll get this done and out of here before our deadline. I know that Jonathan's confident it will happen."

"His confidence is justified. I'll do what I can while I'm here. Thanks for showing me those markings. I would like to have discovered this box instead of the nesting site. It holds so much more potential, but at least I got to see it while it was still in the field and not in some sterile laboratory."

"Don't sell your discovery short. There's much more to discover yet. The insight into raptor and dinosaur behavior, in general, has been advanced considerably by your discovery. This box just seems glitzier by comparison, but it's not more important."

"Thanks Ellen. I need to focus on what I have, not what I don't." Steve grabbed the shovel she had left leaning against the wall and headed down the passage to help Jonathan.

Arriving at the debris pile, he said, "I can haul this big stuff outside while I'm still fresh. What do you think?"

"Grab the handles of that wheelbarrow and start hauling. I really appreciate your help. I can get it all done eventually, but this will easily save me a day's work. I do a lot of small loads before I get worn down and can't move as much dirt. It takes longer, but it works.

"With you moving this big stuff, I'll be able to stay with the side walls until supper time," Jonathan said, pulling more dirt from the walls.

"I'm just glad I can help. No one may ever know of my participation, but I will. I'll cherish this memory forever. Maybe someday I'll be able to tell people about this. It would be nice not to have to sneak around. Who knows?"

Jonathan put an arm around Steve's shoulder. He gave it a little squeeze and then clapped him on the back. That was indication enough of his appreciation. They separated and went about their individual tasks. Each was satisfied that the embrace had said everything without words.

They worked diligently for the next two hours. Neither spoke much as the hours raced by. The pile of dirt never seemed to shrink. Jonathan managed to replace the same amount that Steve hauled away. The only progress that could be marked was the amount of newly exposed wall. The box would be ready to move in eight more days at the most.

Steve leaned the wheelbarrow against the wall and checking his watch said, "I need to go now, Jonathan. They'll think that I died on the road or something. I'll be back as soon as I can. Say goodbye to Ellen for me. Thanks again for letting me help."

"Thanks Steve. I couldn't have done this much without you. If you can get back in the next day or two, we should be able to open this out all the way around the curve. It'll be a straight shot out then."

"I'll see what I can do. I won't make any promises. I still have ten people to look after."

"Believe me, I understand. I've been in your position for over twenty years now. Trust me when I say that I know."

"Well, I'll see you later. I really need to go." He shook Jonathan's hand and walked away. When he reached the bottom of the hillside and waved goodbye.

Jonathan returned his attention to the cave. "Ellen? I don't see you."

"Yes dear. I'm over here." She poked her head out from around the corner of the box.

"Steve just left. He said to say goodbye. He'll try to be back in the next day or two. We got so much done. I'm amazed at the progress. I'm at a loss for words."

"That'll be a first. The Great Dr. Crenshaw has this *word* to say. Now that's funny."

"Are you implying that I'm a blabber mouth, a long-winded old professor?"

"Not at all. It's just so seldom that you can't find the right words. I think it's funny."

"Well anyway, why don't you come and see what we've finished. We worked well together and the results speak for themselves."

CHAPTER THIRTY-TWO

ELLEN SURVEYED THE AREA AND was impressed. "I don't recognize this place. You two have done a remarkable job. Look at how wide this is now. You almost have the curve gone. That's quite a bit of work. Are you all right? How's Steve?"

"We're fine. Quit being a mother for five minutes."

"I'm not being a mother. This is a lot of work for anyone. I'm concerned for your well-being. That's allowed isn't it? I am your wife." *What a grouch.*

Jonathan grabbed her up in a gentle, yet firm hug. He kissed her hair and sighed heavily. He spoke no words. She asked no questions. Ellen knew the anguish that he was experiencing. She felt it too. It was only a few days earlier that they'd fought so angrily that they thought their marriage might break up. It was the worst quarrel they'd ever had.

This whole discovery was tearing at the very fiber of their life and somehow, they were holding it all together. It was a testament to their commitment to each other.

Their embrace slipped away and they resumed their work. They moved more slowly, more deliberately. It had been a brief, sobering moment. Beyond words, he had no way of telling her how much he loved her.

She felt his love, yet didn't know how to let him know that she understood. Ellen was soon engrossed in her markings and Jonathan was hauling dirt to the hillside. Work was a poor substitute for emotional connection, but they made the most of it.

They silently wished that she hadn't found the box. Their life together had been carefree and unspoiled. Both had become respected scientists and were able to spend each summer in pursuit of their passion. They traveled all over the world. Yet even more important than their academic or scientific acclaim; they had a wonderful son and daughter-in-law, two grandchildren and each other.

Life was full and happy until she found the box. Sure, it was still full, but the box was sucking the joy out of life faster with each new day. The box had changed their life. It was too terrible to imagine what problems it might cause. Yet its discovery was too important to just bury it and pretend it never happened. It was a catch-22.

Left to her own thoughts, she began to ponder the enormity of what they would reveal to the world. Steve had almost single handedly proven that raptors had a clannish, tight knit family unit and this box proved that they were intelligent beyond modern man. That was of course, if the box wasn't extraterrestrial.

The concept of visitors from another planet leaving this artifact behind was a leap that she wasn't prepared to make. Should that supposition ever present itself; the government would be all over them like white on rice. For that matter, super intelligent dinosaurs weren't a concept that she could easily wrap her mind around.

Ellen could hear the soil falling in large chunks from the walls. Jonathan had to be getting tired. She was mentally fatigued. Her thoughts were chasing each other in circular patterns. It was time to quit. There wasn't anything left for her to accomplish today.

"Jonathan," she called.

"Yes dear."

"I'm spent. I can't think straight anymore. Can we quit for the night? I never thought that I'd ask that question, but I need to change scenery."

"Thank God. I need to get a cold beer and a hot shower. How about we spend the night in town? Maybe the bar has a band? Are you up to a little dancing?"

"Why didn't you say something?"

"We both know how important this is. I was just going to tuff it out, but you've given me the perfect chance to escape, and I'm taking advantage of it."

Ellen wrapped her arms around his waist and laid her head on his chest. Softly, almost crying she said, "We need to communicate more. We talk all the time, but we don't communicate anymore."

"I know. It bothers me too, but I'm so happy just being with you that it seemed to be a small price to pay for the joy I get when you're around."

"I love you." She kissed him heavily. There was passion and an emotional content in that kiss that neither had experienced in a long time. They fell to the floor of the cave and continued to experience the flood of emotions, as only a lifetime together could allow.

Some communications were meant to be silent, but only learned from a lifetime of loving and caring for each other. Sharing life and love provides that knowledge. Communicating was basic and as simple and uncomplicated as a touch, a response, a yes or a no. It was a spiritual communion conceived in youthful passions, forged with the reality of life, then tempered with age and mutual respect.

Ellen and Jonathan never made it into town for a little dancing and Jonathan never got his hot shower. Their evening drifted endlessly in the bliss only two people who truly loved and respected each other could enjoy. They rose early and wrapped in blankets, they sat and watched the sun creep over the horizon.

Jonathan began to understand why Ellen loved this time of day. Sitting and watching as the sun spread its warmth and light over the earth was a reaffirmation of God's majesty and power. The two of them were mute witnesses to the birth of a new day. The experience was a glorious promise of life.

With the sun more than half way above the horizon they walked, arm in arm, back to camp. Dressing quietly, so not to disturb the morning sounds of nature, they began their daily routines.

Ellen didn't take her usual walk this morning. She sat quietly and watched Jonathan prepare breakfast. Ellen never really watched him before this day. The aromas of cooking filled the air and her mouth began to water. It amazed her how efficiently the food just sort of appeared on the plates.

"For you my love," was all he said as he proffered the plate.

"Jonathan, I want to say…"

"Please don't say anything. What we have is magic and I've never felt closer to you than I do at this moment. Ellen, I love you so much."

"And I love you. Kiss me please. I need to feel your lips on mine."

"I live to serve." Bending closer, he kissed her so softly that it almost wasn't a kiss at all. Her lips burned with the loving, delicate contact.

"Jonathan, that was wonderful. What happened last night?"

"We have communicated completely in mind and body. This is too beautiful to ever go back to how we were. I don't ever want to leave this place we've reached. I can't explain. . ."

"Don't try. I know precisely what you mean. I'm right here with you." She squeezed his hand tenderly.

They ate slowly and watched as the sun rose higher in the morning sky. When they finished, they washed the dishes together and adjourned to the tent to plan their day.

Steve left camp early to get supplies in town. He'd gone to the post office to get the mail when he noticed the letter that Ellen and Jonathan had been expecting. Letter in hand, he rushed back to the Crenshaw's campsite. "I've got that letter that you've been waiting for. It came to general delivery just like you said it would."

Jonathan opened the tent flap and stepped into the brisk morning air. "Thanks. I appreciate that you came straight here."

"The students have no idea how long I'll be gone. I figured that I could spend the whole morning with you. It's nice and cool so we won't work up too much of a sweat. We should be able to get a lot done today. How's it been going? Moved much soil, or are you just knocking it down?"

"Slow down a minute. You're gonna pop a blood vessel. In answer to your question, I did a little of both."

"You've got to go with what works," said Steve. "I can haul all morning while you knock down. We'll get twice as much as the last time. When do you think that we can start the move?" he asked, exuding enthusiasm and pent up energy.

"I'll let you look at what's been done. You can take a few measurements and tell me what you think. Sound okay to you?"

"Hello Steve," Ellen's bubbled. "How did Jonathan get you to fix this stuff just as I walked up? I thought that he was the only one that could do that."

"Well, to be honest, if he hadn't been standing here, I'd never have gotten finished on time. I couldn't have done it without him."

"It smells so good. Did you do something different?" she asked.

"Jonathan told me to experiment with different flavors, so I did. This first one is for you Ellen."

Jonathan bent close as if to kiss her and whispered, "I didn't have the heart to tell him we ate just a while ago."

"This looks great," she said. "You have nice presentation too. I can't wait to dig in. You two will have to excuse me while I go make a pig of myself."

Ellen walked away with her plate in hand. She began eating before she reached the table. She turned back to Steve and gave him a big thumb's up.

"Well, that's high praise. Hurry up with mine. You can't expect me to die of starvation while my lovely wife dines on such fare. The aroma is heavenly."

He handed the plate to Jonathan and started to prepare his own.

"Steve, is there any left?" Ellen asked sheepishly. "I was just hoping that there was a little more bacon and chilies left over."

"You could manage another omelet out of what's left."

"I'm done," said Jonathan, exhaling loudly. "I'll start the dishes. Steve, you can head up to the cave when you're finished eating. I'll clean up here."

"Sounds like a plan to me. I'll see you when you get there." *Finally!*

Ellen sent him off to help Steve. "I'll finish this. I'll only be ten minutes. Hurry up; Steve needs your help."

"Okay, okay. There's no need to push. I only wanted to finish."

"You just run along like a good little boy."

"Oh, so it's like that is it?" *If I can manage to keep my mouth shut all day, there will be peace in the valley tonight and me too!* He left before drying his hands.

The morning ambled by. They established a smooth pace from the very beginning which made the work run smoothly. Outside, the debris pile grew larger with each dump and the amount of wall being exposed increased by the hour.

"We should stop soon and take a few measurements Steve. I think that we're about as wide as we need to be."

"It sure looks that way," he answered. "A tape is the only way to know for sure. Let me dump this load and head down to the truck. I'll get the tape and be right back."

"No need," replied Jonathan; producing a tape from his back pocket. "I remembered to grab it before I came. I was passing the truck when it occurred to me that we might need it." He handed it to Steve. "I guess I was right."

"Great. I really didn't want to trek down to the truck and back again while we're doing so well." *I hope that I didn't look too stupid for not thinking to bring a tape myself. Well what's done is done.*

"Yeah, I know what you mean. Those little interruptions can mess up a good thing. Let's get to it." *It was sure lucky that I remembered this at the last minute. I could have looked really stupid. I'm supposed to think of these things, but with all these distractions, I can't remember my own name half the time.*

Steve grabbed the end of the tape and headed towards the broad end of the box. He measured along the surface and called out, "I've got an even ten feet," adding, "This sure looks wider than ten feet. Did you see this Jonathan?"

"See what?"

"This is only measuring ten feet. I expected at least twelve."

"I thought it was wider than that. Let me see that tape." Steve held it at the corner and Jonathan walked it to the other end. It was exactly ten feet. "I'll be damned. It must be the cave. . . like an optical illusion."

"Right, wrong, or otherwise; it's ten feet and that's that. We have the measurement and we can now calculate the width of the passage. Let's get down there and make it happen."

They measured all the way down the passage. At fifteen feet wide; they could easily navigate the passage once the box was on the sliders. A person with a lever could wedge it from side to side if it started to shift. There was adequate room down the entire passage.

"This is really good news. It'll save us at least four days' work."

"When do you want to start on the ramp?" Steve questioned.

"I can't hear you. Yell a little louder."

Turning, he shouted, "When do you want to start the ramp?"

"I think that we're done for today," he answered. "I don't want to lose any momentum, but I still need to design the crate and work out how many boards we need for the runners. It'll make the pulling go easier if we get it up on the runners right away."

"Are you planning on bracing it at the outer edges so the box doesn't shift off of the bottom plywood?"

"I don't follow."

"I meant that since the bottom plywood has to be more than ten feet wide, are you going to bury runners at the outer edges so the bottom won't move when we drag the box onto it. Are you going to run the nailing strip along the perimeter of the bottom plywood as guides when we drag the box up onto it?"

"I really hadn't thought that one through all the way. But my answer is yes."

"Great. Let me know when you'll need my help."

"Since we still have some time left, why don't we work out some preliminary sketches now? It will save time later. I can get the material and bring it out here, and wait for you to come back when you can."

"That works for me," said Steve. His chance to start research on the box was only weeks away.

CHAPTER THIRTY-THREE

T HE TWO HUDDLED TOGETHER IN the tent, working on various sketches. Both wanted it to be right the first time. They worked out several variations as contingency plans. After an hour of brainstorming different ideas, they had a firm plan and two possible alternates. The situation would dictate which, if either, alternate would be implemented.

Stepping from the tent like conquering heroes, they congratulated themselves on a job well done. "That was a nice piece of work, Steve. You really came through on that ramp idea. I didn't think of the fall rate. I would rather dig some of the excess dirt away, than build a ramp back up to the back of the truck."

"When we discussed the original plan, it seemed good enough. However, when we started talking, it all became clear to me. I enjoy work sessions like this. That's why I want to get back to work with Ellen. Those markings intrigue me. I want to be part of the team that solves the riddle. I'm deadly serious about that. I love that kind of challenge. It goes beyond academic: it pits me against an ancient foe." Steve tried to hide his embarrassment. "Now I'm just sounding stupid."

"No, you're not. There's no need to be embarrassed, I understand. Why do you think I've stayed with fossil hunting for all of these years? The challenge of my ability to find them against nature's ability to hide them, or destroy them is heady stuff for me. Some people search for speed or other thrills; I search for a challenge against the greatest power on earth – nature. We're very much alike, you and I. We share the same passion for the game. That is why we will always be on top."

"Thanks Jonathan. That means a lot. Sometimes it feels like the desire to be out here will consume me."

"Let it. It's a good thing. Don't let it exclude all other interests though," cautioned Jonathan. "You need to be well rounded. No one likes an egghead with zero personality. Let your passion be your main focus in life, but not your only focus."

"I understand. Have I been doing it properly so far? I'm not so single minded that I act like an idiot, do I?"

"You don't. Besides, Ellen and I care enough about you to let you know. If you ever start to lean in that direction, we'll be the first to tell you about it. Deal?"

"Deal," he replied excitedly. "Let's head back and lay out that ramp. We might even get started on it yet today. Even if we can't, it will be set for you when we start tomorrow."

The whole time they'd been talking, they were walking towards the Crenshaw's truck. "I'll bring these stakes for markers," he said as he pulled them from the back of the truck. "Do you have anything in your truck that we can use as ties?"

"I have some red rags that I use when changing the oil. I always use red in case of an emergency. I need rags anyway, so why not make them do double duty?" Steve was proud of his idea.

"Very efficient," commented Jonathan. "I think that I'll start using red rags as well. I like that idea."

They collected their respective supplies and headed back. Laying the stakes out on what would be the perimeter of the ramp, they tied strips of red rag to each one. When they were all positioned, they returned to removing the remaining dirt.

Clearing the passage was completed before suppertime. They were several days ahead of Jonathan's original schedule. At this point, it would take very little effort to finish forming the ramp.

Ellen had kept to herself for most of the day. She'd talked briefly with Steve and Jonathan during lunch. If solitude was the key to solving the mystery of the markings, then she would give it her best shot. Somehow, she had to find the solution.

Several times she thought that she had come up with an adequate answer, yet something always fell out of place. Faced with this conundrum, Ellen forged ahead with the patience of Job, but it was getting exasperating. Ellen was smiling on the outside, but she was really griping on the inside. She mentioned nothing to Jonathan or Steve when they had the occasion to speak. Keeping up false pretenses irritated her as much as her continued failures.

After hours of wrestling with the situation, Ellen resolved to go back to the cave and study the markings at close range. She convinced herself that the real thing would be better to look at than the photographs. It was more a change of scenery, than perspective. Collecting everything she needed; she headed back to the cave.

Steve and Jonathan were just staking the first two flags at the top of the ramp when she arrived. "How's it going?" she inquired while surveying the ramp and the impressive amount of newly excavated soil.

"Fine dear. How about you? We've hardly spoken two words all day. Are you all right?"

"I'm fine. I've got a lot on my mind. You know how I get when I'm faced with a challenge of this magnitude."

"Steve and I were just saying how he would like to finish this so that he might help you on this puzzle, mystery, or whatever you want to call it."

"It doesn't matter to me. I'd like to refer to it as 'the problem that we solved in no time at all,' but that isn't going to happen any time soon."

"Jonathan and I are almost done here," Steve interjected. "If he doesn't mind finishing this last little bit, I could start right now. We're way ahead of schedule and I only have an hour left before I have to leave."

"Do you mind, Jonathan?" A pleading look crossed her face.

"Not at all, dear. In fact, I was just going to suggest that very thing when I saw you coming up the hill."

"That's very thoughtful dear." Turning, she said, "Steve if you would please come with me, I can tell you everything that I've tried so far. It will help you to eliminate some possibilities when you start to work independently. By the way, I thought that you were only going to stay until lunch and then get back."

"As I said this morning, no one knows when I'll return and I prepared them for my absence for the entire day. Today's progress was more important than being at the site. Besides, with Janet there, I have an ace in the hole."

"Are you going to make an honest woman out of her Steve?"

"Ellen! I never! How could you think of such a thing?" he stammered.

"Settle down, it was a joke. It's obvious that you have more than a professional interest in her. Jonathan and I are happy for you, that's all."

Steve abruptly grabbed the photo board from under her arm and carried it into the cave. He walked in silence without answering her. His embarrassment was complete and he wanted to be left alone for a moment to compose himself.

"Steve and I are going into the box. Do you want to be there?"

"No dear. As long as Steve's with you, I'm sure that everything will be fine. If you're not out in fifteen minutes, I'll come in after you," he teased. "You know," he said after thinking about it, "that'll be good. I'll set the timer on my watch for thirty minutes. That should give you more than enough time to get some work done. Sound good to you? Besides, I know you two will be so caught up that neither of you would even notice if an hour had passed. Steve needs to stay on schedule."

"That'll be fine dear. See you in thirty, if not sooner. Love you."

"You be careful. Love you too."

Ellen hurried down the passage after Steve. He was already at the box. She stood behind him as he worked the controls. Steve got one out of sequence, but didn't notice. To Ellen's surprise, the mechanism rose from the surface as if he had keyed in the information correctly.

"Stop! Don't touch that!" she screamed.

"What's the matter with you?" he snapped. "You scared me out of my wits!"

"You keyed in the wrong sequence. This shouldn't have opened. I wanted you to stop. I don't know what will happen now."

"Are you sure? I thought that I'd done it correctly."

"I'm sure. I was standing behind you, watching to make sure that you were doing it correctly. After you pushed the wrong figure, you moved to the others so quickly that I couldn't say anything."

"What's going on in here?" Jonathan yelled as he ran down the passage. "Is anything wrong? Are you both all right? I could hear you screaming outside. What's going on?"

"Steve keyed in the wrong sequence. I watched him. It looks as if it's ready to open. I didn't want him to touch it before we could analyze it. What if it's a booby trap or something?"

"I don't think that we need to be concerned with a booby trap. I'm sure that all of our original efforts would have activated a trap by now. Think about it. These kinds of traps are designed for the initial failed attempt. You made several attempts before you gained entry."

"How can you say that? You're using human reasoning to draw that conclusion. With a technology this advanced, you can't rule out any possibility. I don't care how old this thing is."

"I stand corrected," Jonathan humbly submitted. The look he shot Ellen would have killed if it were a knife. Turning to Steve, he asked, "What did you do that was different, this time?"

"I thought that I was doing it properly. Let me think. It'll only take a moment to recall the key sequence." He was punching the air, recreating his motions. "I've got it. I didn't key every other one. Once I did the second one, I moved straight to the third and then sequenced every other one. I'm sure of it."

"Ellen, can you close the lock and repeat sequence. If it won't open, perhaps you only thought that you saw him do it incorrectly."

"I'll be happy to. I've spent my whole life making observations. It isn't like me to see something that isn't there." *What a way to spend an afternoon, surrounded by idiots. What a way to die.*

"I understand dear. I'm not saying that you're incorrect. I would like empirical data. Would you just humor me please?" *Why does every little thing have to turn into a contest with her? Just once I'd like her to agree with something without being so defensive.*

"With pleasure." She knew that he was right.

The mechanism closed effortlessly when she pressed it. She then keyed in Steve's sequence – exactly as she had seen it with her own eyes – and the mechanism opened, just as it had for Steve.

The three of them just looked at each other. No one offered any suggestions as to what to do. They just stared in silence.

"Let's try it and see what happens. It could be the way to keep the door open all of the time." Jonathan looked from Ellen to Steve. "Well, it's a thought," he defended as they just stared at him. Finally, he said, "If either of you have anything better to offer, I'll listen."

"Not really," answered Ellen. "I'm nervous, that's all."

"We all are, but isn't this the scientific research that you two have been clamoring for?"

"He's right Ellen. We've been asking for this kind of opportunity. Now we have it and we're afraid to go for it. Well, I'm not afraid anymore." Steve reached down and turned the mechanism before anyone realized what he was doing. Reflexively, they ducked and turned their bodies away.

The door opened with its silent efficiency. They each drew in a deep breath, as if something might jump out at them, merely because the lock operated differently this time. All eyes focused intently on the emptiness. Nothing happened. No sounds emanated from the dark confines of the box. Nothing came screaming out of the darkness.

The tension eased and they straightened themselves up. The three of them looked at each other and waited. They didn't move forward, nor did they retreat. They just stood silently for a moment.

"Why are we just standing here?" echoed Steve's voice in the silence. "What are we waiting for?"

"The door should close in ten more seconds," she stated flatly, struggling to regain her composure. "I'm waiting for the door, and nothing else. We postulated that there might be the secondary lock that keeps the door open. I want to find out while I'm outside. . . not inside."

"Sounds logical. We should know right about now."

The door remained open. Nothing else happened that they could discern. If anything changed, it was inside.

"I wonder why there are two possible combinations to the same lock. This is even more puzzling than before. It doesn't make any sense." Ellen's voice began to rise as her mental frustration was reaching a peak. "Give me a flashlight someone. I'm going in and I'm not coming out until I've got this solved."

"That's a good idea. Then we'll find you all shriveled and mummified in the corner, the solution clutched in you bony, outstretched hand. A pretty picture indeed."

"You know darn well what I mean! This isn't going to get the best of me. I won't let it. Any more questions?" she growled. Her tone was as cold as the resolve etched across her face.

"I only have one more thing to say before I shut up," said Jonathan. "Here's your flashlight."

Ellen snatched it from his hand with the ferocity of a pit-bull. She went into the box. The light clicked on as she crossed the threshold. She hadn't taken but that single step when she stopped dead in her tracks. "I think that you both need to come in here. And I mean now, gentlemen."

Steve was closest to her. He stepped up behind her, and as suddenly and abruptly as Ellen had stopped, he did the same. Jonathan was moving forward when he saw Steve came to a halt, but couldn't stop soon enough to avoid bumping into them.

Neither of them moved. "I said get out of the way. What's the problem?"

Ellen moved slightly forward, allowing Steve to move along side of her. She reflexively grabbed his arm. He didn't notice.

Steve stepped a little farther into the box. She didn't want to relinquish the grip she had on his shirtsleeve. He yanked on his arm, thinking it was caught on something.

Ellen stepped in behind him, seeking the comfort of proximity. Now that the doorway was clear, Jonathan stepped into the box. He was concentrating on Ellen and Steve, not what had caught their attention. When his eyes acclimated, he followed the light. He was dumbstruck at what he saw. This box held so many secrets.

CHAPTER THIRTY-FOUR

JONATHAN'S VOICE CAME SOFTLY FORM behind them. "Oh my God," he managed to rasp before falling silent.

Ellen managed to reclaim her tenacious grip on Steve's arm. He looked down at her and her hand as if watching the scene from a movie. His mind was in a total disconnect.

"Ellen," he said touching her hand. "You're hurting me."

She didn't respond, but she did loosen her grip slightly. Steve felt the blood start to flow again and said no more.

Jonathan finally found the strength to move up next to them. He placed a comforting hand on Ellen's shoulder. She reached up and covered his hand with hers. His skin was warm and comforting.

Between the security she gained from her grip on Steve's arm and the touch of Jonathan's hand, she began to focus more clearly. In spite of the enormity of what stood before her, she was slowly returning to reality.

"This is NOT happening. What in the hell is going on here?" Ellen's voice strangled in her throat.

"This is the most amazing thing that I've ever seen. It scares the crap out of me, but it's fabulous," Steve answered.

Jonathan stepped forward and pressed his face against the glass which now stood where the finely partition wall of metal had once been. He refused to believe his eyes. If he could get close enough, he felt that this image would surely disappear.

In spite of his efforts, the glass remained and the content of the chamber remained.

"What do you think?" Ellen finally stammered. Amazement

and excitement had returned to her voice. "This sure is something. I would never have thought that this was possible. I could never imagine anything like this."

Jonathan had finally found his voice. "I can only speculate what might be in the rest of this box. This is mind boggling." His mind was swimming with questions, ideas and speculations. He was terrified and intrigued by what he saw.

The three of them stepped back to the doorway. They took a long hard look at what was in front of them.

Because of Steve's sequencing error, the secondary lock had opened a panel that was previously a blank wall. He had no idea that a panel would open up to reveal this hermetically sealed enclosure.

Inside was a perfectly preserved, physically intact raptor. It could have been placed in the box yesterday. The flesh appeared supple. The eyes were closed, but the skin had a seemingly live quality about it. The technology that produced this enclosure would have been extremely advanced. Why would anyone or anything entomb a dinosaur?

The specimen was perfect in all respects. It was at least two to two and a half meters tall with a beak-like snout. The lips were silverfish and the disk-shaped markings on the animal's back were nearly perfect circles. Although they were evenly spread across the back and down the tail, they weren't symmetrical. Through the liquid in the enclosure, they could see the well-defined and solid muscles of the legs, neck, and jaws. This animal must have been in its' prime when it was sealed in this box.

This was more than a sacrificial offering. What if it were the dinosaurs that possessed the technology? Was this a prison? Was this a form of euthanasia? They were each reflecting on experience, education, personal beliefs, religious dogma and so much more. What if this really was extraterrestrial? This could have been some form of specimen transfer or temporary storage chamber. They were each, trying to grasp for a mental resolution that would help deliver sanity to what they saw before them.

"We have to leave," a voice echoed in everyone's ears. Jonathan assumed that he had spoken, because Ellen and Steve turned to face him. Quickly, quietly they stepped back from the doorway. Cold, empty silence was the only testimony they could give to this new turn of events.

Minutes passed slowly. Ellen and Jonathan sat down in the passage. Steve was overwhelmed and paced furtively. He resembled a cat circling to find that comfortable place on a pillow. Even their breathing was too soft to be heard.

Ellen was first to break the silence. "We should close this back up and pretend that we didn't see that thing." Her private speculations were becoming a reality. This still could be an extraterrestrial design to collect specimens, or even more heretical, it could be designed and built by intelligent dinosaurs."

"That's absurd," retorted Jonathan. "It is what it is. We've seen it and we can't forget that." *These are pretty big words coming from someone who may have just soiled himself.*

"That's right," interrupted Steve. "This is a major research gold mine. We need to get this box out of here and start forming teams. We'll need all kinds of experts. This is too big to keep quiet. Even if we tried to hide it, word would somehow leak out." He continued to pacing as he spoke.

"Don't either of you see that any leaks of information are exactly what I'm concerned about. We need time and that's the one thing that we don't have right now," proclaimed Jonathan. His frustration level was at a maximum.

Ellen was clearly agitated. She knew she wasn't communicating her ideas very effectively. "Let me try it again. I am fully aware that this is too big to just forget we ever saw it. I didn't mean to suggest that at all. I meant that we should seal it up and wait until it's more advantageous for us to begin our research. I, more than anyone, want to see this through to the end. Remember, I was the one who initially discovered it."

"No one is contesting that fact," interjected Steve.

Raising her hand to silence him, she continued. "Let me finish please. Then you can say all you want. I want it known that I do understand the importance of this box. I am not unaffected by this latest development. I can see the implications of the technology and how far reaching it can be. The cryogenics alone could alter the course of mankind. I only want to walk away from this for the moment.

"We can ill afford to get caught up in a knee jerk reaction to this discovery. The box won't get moved on time. Maybe worse, we'll rush the job and destroy something. We can't take those kinds of chances. Am I clear on this point now?"

Jonathan, who had remained seated during the entire exchange stood abruptly and said, "We better close the door and get back to the ramp. It will still take a couple of days to complete. Our current need right now is to start on the skids, runners, slides, or whatever you want to call them. We need to drag this thing out of here and we may have to re-estimate drop ratios for the slide down the ramp. There's more weight than we originally estimated."

"No, I can't leave this unresolved. I want to study it some more. Come on. I have to leave for a couple of days. It's not fair."

"Steve, we understand your frustration. Do you think that we aren't every bit as anxious as you are? It's tearing me up inside having to stand here and say that Ellen is right. Think about it. We either do this right the first time, or we risk losing everything."

"I never said that you weren't right. I just want to see more! I want to know more!"

"I'm glad that I'm not as young as you are. I'm unhappy about this turn of events, but experience has taught me that it'll all work out in the end. You're going to have to deal with this on your own terms. There's nothing that we can do to help you."

"Look, I'm sorry. I've made a complete ass of myself. Of course, we can't risk losing even the slightest bit of information. Try to understand my frame of reference. I have made a major discovery of my own with the raptor nursery. At the same time that all of that is going on, I am privy to Ellen's discovery. I'm even helping solve the language problem. It's almost more than I can bear. I felt – only for a moment – as if I was going to lose everything. I snapped and lost control. Again, let me say that I'm truly sorry."

"We understand, Steve. You need to relax a little. This much tension is going to kill you. Finish your work with Jonathan first. Before we seal it up, you can go in briefly. Is it a deal?"

"You better believe it. I'll be back in two days. Save me a cave side seat."

They laughed nervously, and went down to the trucks. In his heart, Steve knew that it was for the best. He'd have his chance to get back into the box in two more days.

"Now that you're finished, you left off with Steve going back to his site."

"I remember."

Janet Brogdon had spent the day preparing for the arrival of the supplies. They came at the time stated by the lumberyard. She knew that if this phase went well, Steve would have no recourse but accept her as a full assistant. She wanted him to appreciate her professionally as well as personally. Once that respect was ingrained into his thinking, she could increase her pressure to make this a more permanent relationship.

Steve had left prints for the assembly of the crates and the students busied themselves cutting the wood for assembly. They helped with the actual assembly. Most were proficient with a hammer, and two had experience with a power saw. Safety was a top priority especially this far from medical help. Those of the group who were not mechanically inclined, or chose to do something else were kept busy wrapping the fossils.

Janet wanted to have all of the crates cut and assembled by the time Steve returned. The pace was brisk. Those who were chosen to do the cutting had previous experience. They only needed a cursory glance at Steve's plans. They were able to move quickly through the pile of lumber with relative ease.

The crates and dividers were coming together at a remarkable pace. Should the work stop at this point, there was so much already done that Steve would not have any complaints.

By 1:30 in the afternoon, all of the lumber had been cut. Half or more of the crates were finished and moved to collection points. They needed to be positioned so the fossils would be moved the shortest distance, yet out of the path so the remaining fossils would not be damaged. Ultimately, the work progressed so rapidly that there were not enough hammers to go around. Some of the assemblers chose to start wrapping.

Janet was going over packing estimates when Steve drove up. It was approaching dinnertime. He brushed past her and headed straight for his tent. She could hear him moving things around as if he was searching for something.

Approaching the tent, she knocked on the tent post. "Excuse me Steve. Is there anything that I can help you with? I've pretty much been in charge since you left this morning."

Steve thought that it was peculiar that she knew what time he had left. He was occupied with other thoughts at the moment and dismissed that one quickly. His time line was accelerated because of the box and none of these students could possibly understand. "Yes, there is. I need to get the packaging moving sooner than I had originally anticipated. I need to find the reports that you prepared the other day. Do you have a copy of them, or your original notes?"

"Actually, I have a copy with me. I've been using it to set up a packing sequence and schedule. Would you like to see?"

"Yes, thank you." His eyes focused on the details of the reports. He'd already forgotten that she was standing in front of him.

As he walked to the tent flap, he brushed against her arm. Without looking up, he muttered, "Sorry," while his pace never slowed. His attention remained transfixed on the reports. Steve was able to concentrate in all types of conditions. Now, however, he was forcing himself to go through the motions.

He realized that he was outside in the fresh air. He looked around as if to orient himself. Lowering the clipboard and called for Janet. To his dismay, she was standing directly behind him. *How does she do that?*

She had anticipated his need to question the reports and followed him from the tent. "What do you need?"

"Where did you come up with some of this stuff?" His tone wasn't so much angry as it was demanding. Steve didn't hear himself speak so rudely.

"What *stuff* do you refer to?" Her hackles were rising. She didn't appreciate the tone of his voice. She continued, "I can answer just about any question that you can come up with. I developed and implemented this whole thing myself. I'm the only one who fully understands it. I'll be more than happy to explain every detail. I'm sorry that you were gone too soon for me to let you analyze this format, but I designed it and knew that I could control it." More calmly, she asked, "Why don't you sit down here and we can go over everything. I know you'll understand the dynamics once I've explained them to you."

"I would like you to enlighten me. How can you place a time on sealing fossils in the plaster casts? It takes what it takes."

"I know that. I arrived at the calculation by questioning the experienced students. They gave me their best guesses on different types of remains and whether or not they are *on* or *in* the ground. After that I set up a formula for an average time. These are only averages; not set figures. Each fossil will have its own set of circumstances and special requirements. You can throw in a fudge factor of twenty hours if you want. That will buy you at least two and a half more days when you average an eight-hour work day."

"I don't want more time, I want less. How are the crates coming along? I assume that the lumber arrived in tact. Were there any problems?"

"Fine, yes, and no."

"What?"

"Those are the answers to your three questions Steve; fine, yes, and no."

"Oh." He quickly moved to his next concern. "What's this new grid map that you've got laid out?"

"We need to move a lot of fossils and not harm anything that's still on the ground. I mapped out the footpaths that we've been using and started to expand them by packing the fossils nearest to their edges, first. Then we can start moving the trucks on to the site without fear of damage to any of your discoveries."

"When do you find time to do all of this? I know that I've asked you that before, but it seems impossible to get this much work done in such a short period of time. You must be a master of organization. Do you teach your techniques, or give seminars to help the organizationally challenged?"

"I don't teach and I don't do seminars. That's a good idea though. I'll bet that I could make a bundle at helping people get more done in less time. Excuse me while I make a note of that. I don't want to forget that one."

"That's exactly what I mean. There are a lot of people who use the note technique, yet their results don't even come close to yours. It's almost laughable to assume that you could forget something. I can't see any problem with your plan. It's well thought out and you're executing it smoothly. Do any of the students object?"

"Not really. Those who might have objected don't have a better plan, and the rest could care less if they are followers the rest of their lives. It makes the job go easier when you can spot the followers first and cater to their mundane requirements."

"That's pretty harsh. I should hope that most people would aspire to greater things."

"Most people do aspire to do more or to be better, but when they have to work for it, they sort of slip into a mode where following is easier. You pick that characteristic out right away; you give them the right amount of deserved praise – not false compliments – and they will follow wherever you lead. Look closely at what's happening around here. You're a day or two ahead of schedule and the students don't have the slightest clue that I've manipulated them into all of this extra work. It's not really extra; it's the same work just well ahead of schedule. They take pride in that and I use it to my advantage."

"You're really a scary young lady. How long have I been dancing on your string?"

"You haven't. I don't manipulate the people I care about. They observe me and how I accomplish things, eventually they pick up on the patterns and we're in sync."

"That's good to know. You're an expert at organization, that much is obvious. You have natural leadership ability. You seem to get almost anyone to do almost anything. Is there anything that you can't do?"

"I can't seem to attract a person like you. You're educated, thoughtful – when you're not concentrating on something – strong willed, and you're a born leader. I'm drawn to men such as you, but my abilities seem to threaten them. They want the power for themselves. They see me as a person who has the capabilities of seizing the power from them. It scares them away." *Well, all the cards are on the table. It's crunch time.*

"That's odd. I would think that a man would be grateful to find a partner that could be his equal in all things. I know that I'd find it comforting. Maybe I'm the odd ball."

"Well I find it reassuring to hear you say that I don't threaten you. Maybe there's hope for me yet." *Did you even feel the leash slip around your neck? I'm never letting you get away. You're the man I've been searching for, and you're good looking to boot. That's just icing on the cake for me.*

"I hope so too. This has been a wonderful chat, but we're not accomplishing anything by talking. We need to press on. These fossils won't crate themselves." *What just happened here? I told her that a man would be happy for a partner like her. I hope she doesn't think that I just proposed. What have I agreed to?*

"I agree. The first few crates have been in position for most of the afternoon. We can see if they're full enough to move to the preliminary staging area. Once they're out of the way, the trucks can get in far enough to load the crates where they are packed."

"It's a wonder that you need me around for anything. Maybe I should go find the Crenshaw's and see if I can offer my services to them."

"I've offended you. I've assumed too much of your authority."

"It was just a tease. Lighten up. I'm very happy that you've done this much. It will make everything else go that much easier. I thank you for a job well done Miss Brogdon." *Damn. Ellen was right. All I can think of is taking her into my tent and… slow down Casanova, before your thoughts are manifested in a more physical aspect. That would not be cool.*

The first crate was already filled to a safe capacity. He inspected the packing job and could find no fault with it. He noticed that the plaster was not too excessive. It was first-rate workmanship.

He left Janet to go and speak with some of the students. Somehow, he felt as if he was holding her up. She insisted that it was nothing like that at all. He had arrived a little before she had anticipated and that was all it was.

Her absence gave him time to check his initial projections against her calculations. The time sequence was greatly reduced in her schedule. At first, he seemed to think that it was a bit too unrealistic, too aggressive. The progress he was observing showed that her figures might actually be too conservative.

Mentally, Steve had already returned to the box, admiring the raptor. He would be back with the Crenshaw's well before he'd expected.

A plan was forming and it involved Janet Brogdon. She wanted to be his assistant in the worst way. He would use that to his advantage. Scanning the camp, he spotted her with a group of three students. He could tell by the way her hands were moving, that she was giving instructions for something or other. He worked his way over to her location. Watching her made him realize that he was better at observation than he'd thought.

"Janet, might I have a word with you?"

"Sure, Steve. One moment please." She excused herself after asking the others if there were any additional questions. "Now, what might I help you with?"

"I know that you've been saying that you want to be my assistant. I told you that I'd like to see if your enthusiasm would remain as strong. You said your actions would speak for themselves. Well I want you to know that I like what I see. I don't know that I could have done as well as you in this short period of time. I'm very impressed. We need to talk."

CHAPTER THIRTY-FIVE

"**Y**OU'VE FREED UP SO MUCH of my time that now I can finish some things that I would not have thought possible. I have a proposition. Follow me," he said politely. "I will make you my assistant. I need to prepare the preliminary groundwork for presenting this site to the academic community. It would be best to do it now while I'm here. Can I count on you?"

They skirted around the back of Steve's tent and stopped at his truck. "Thank you, Steve. I won't let you down. You can trust me with your life. I won't fail you." Janet hugged him in her excitement and then she kissed him full on the mouth. Realizing what she'd done she let go.

"I'll remember that," he continued, ignoring her embarrassment. "Someday I may call that marker. You just remember that you gave it to me freely. Great kiss by the way. Your lips are so soft yet your kiss is so firm. You definitely know what you want and how to get it." He then returned her kiss with equal passion.

Breaking their embrace, he added, "My reputation will be based on what happens here. I'm not relinquishing this authority lightly. Don't make any mistakes.

"Your plans are ambitious. You seem to be able to handle the amount of work in the time frame that you've established. All that I will do after today will be based on your time estimates. I'm about to make commitments based on your proposals. I need to know right now if you foresee any problems." *I could fall in love with this woman. I must control myself for the time being.*

"There's no need to be concerned. Everything will be just fine.

I've made allowances for time differentials. I've had numerous conversations with the students who know what to expect. I have total confidence in the plan."

"That's my girl. That's what I wanted to here. I'll be in and out of the camp for the next few days. The other students have accepted you as the team leader while I'm not here. You know the ones that you can delegate authority to working with you already. I'm going back to my tent and start on some of the paperwork that I'll need. I'll see you at supper."

Steve took her hand in his and gave it a gentle squeeze before he turned to walk away. It was more than a gesture of trust. Things seemed to be going his way right now. He wanted to make his moves while he could. Once the word was out about his theories, his time would be occupied debating those who would dispute his claims. Either way, he would be extremely busy.

The cot in his tent seemed to be an island of solitude. Once he lay down, he let the rest of the world vanish.

Finally, he could concentrate on getting back to the Crenshaw's and the raptor. He got up after fifteen minutes of relaxation and mental focus exercises to start some of the paperwork that he'd discussed with Janet. It was safe to assume that she would come into his tent. When she found some of his proposals lying about in rough draft, it would lend authenticity to his story. Manipulating people was a lot easier than he'd thought. It would be suppertime soon and then he would get to sleep early.

"Supper's up," called out one of the cooks. Steve hadn't noticed the hours slipping by. He glanced at his watch in disbelief. *Better get something to eat before it's all gone.*

Stepping from his tent, he noticed half of the students were still at their grids. He called out to them.

Steve leaned back a little and took in all the activity. This had been a great dig and it was over too quickly. The weeks and work raced by before anyone had realized the summer was almost gone.

He knew it wasn't the norm, but it was still a lot of fun. So many samples and the discovery of the nursery were gratifying.

With the meal finally finished and everything cleaned, the students began to break into separate groups. Relaxation was all they could think about. Some just continued conversations while others tossed the football or a Frisbee.

Steve bid everyone a good evening and returned to his tent. There was a lot of work that needed to be completed if he were to maximize his time with the Crenshaw's and that lovely awe-inspiring box with the raptor inside.

Papers were spread everywhere and notes on each individual pile. It would be several hours before the work was complete enough to allow him to start cleaning up and organizing the mess. He wished Janet were here. She'd have the job done quickly with her magical way of doing things.

Focusing on the task, it was almost midnight before he'd resolved all his issues and had cleaned up the entire mess. Now everything was neatly organized and categorized in the sequence he needed to move from one task to the next.

The camp was silent and everyone was asleep, everyone but Steve. The day's events played over and over in his head as he lay quietly on his cot. His growing feelings for Janet were muddling his thinking. Forcing himself to concentrate only created additional distractions. A gentle tapping on the tent post startled him.

"It's just me, Steve," whispered Janet as she let herself in. Stammering, she said, "You mean so much to me that I have to do this before I chicken out."

"What?" He stood up and looked around as if searching for an escape route. Without realizing his actions, he'd closed the distance between them.

Janet dropped her robe to the floor; the dim light revealed her nude body as she replied, "This." She embraced him and kissed him lustily.

Steve responded with passionate kisses of his own. Her probing tongue fanned his desire to a burning lust. He stepped away only long enough to remove his pajamas and look closely at this beautiful young woman standing before him. She was perfect in every way. Her skin was flawless and her body well-toned. They fell into each other's arms and on to the cot.

It was almost 2:30 in the morning before Janet returned to her tent. Steve lay back on his cot in disbelief. She was everything that he'd imagined and more. The respect that he held for her only heightened the sensations. Whether he wanted to or not, he was falling in love. This was the first time he'd made love to a woman. He'd had sex before, but this was sharing, not taking. It was rapture.

Janet lay silently in her cot experiencing the same emotions. She already loved Steve, but now she was connected in a way that only true love allows.

Steve was up early. Focusing on the raptor and the research were the only thoughts in his mind. He rushed through a simple bowl of cereal. The memory of last night with Janet had been placed close to his heart. A special place he would visit whenever he could find a secret moment for himself. Now, though, he must focus clearly on the raptor and moving the box.

Janet would handle all of the mundane camp routine with her usual proficiency. She was beginning to reveal a remarkable talent. He was prepared to use her in any capacity in order to return to the Crenshaw's. And as a bonus, he was confident in her abilities.

The distance from his site to the Crenshaw's melted into nothing. Steve barely remembered starting his truck, and now he was pulling into their camp. His mind raced with a plethora of questions, speculations and postulations. He was hoping the drive would help settle him. It did not. He needed to calm himself before he exploded.

Jonathan came out of the tent just as Steve pulled in. He waved to Steve and signaled for him to come over.

"Good morning campers," Steve said in a singsong voice.

"Aren't we all chipper this morning?" said Ellen as she walked up behind the pair. "Did you even sleep at all last night?"

"Like a baby. You won't believe what's going on at my camp. Janet Brogdon has taken the whole place over. She is so efficient that I don't even have to be there. She has this knack for organizing people and things. She's at least two days ahead of my best schedule. And she already has the crates built and started packing them yesterday. It's a damn fine job too."

"Slow down son. You're gonna overheat from all this enthusiasm. She's that good, huh? Where did you find her?"

"Janet found me. She made that form that I showed you in town a couple of weeks ago. You remember? Anyway, she gets the whole camp using it and then compiles all of the research into a fantastic book. I can't imagine having to complete all that work without her skills."

"Sounds to me like you've got it bad Steve," Jonathan chuckled as he turned to Ellen. "Don't you agree dear?"

She smiled and nodded her head. They both grinned at Steve.

"Got what bad? Are you two going to let me in on the secret?"

"It sounds as if you've fallen in love with this girl, or should I say, young lady?" replied Ellen. "All it took was one organized form, and you're head over heels for her. You're too easy?"

"I take offence to that last remark. I'm not all that easy." Laughing, he added, "But I am cheap."

"Easy enough for the likes of her," joked Jonathan, his tone was light and un-accusing.

Steve put his finger in the air and was about to respond while shaking the finger for emphasis, when he remembered what Janet had said about how easy it would be to manipulate people. She had also said that she would not manipulate him. He didn't feel threatened last night. Now he was unsure of himself.

He was trying to recall an old adage from high school. It went something like *'I chased her 'til she caught me.'* He just didn't remember it completely.

Seeing the look on Steve's face, Jonathan quickly changed the subject. He knew the look because he too was in love. "We need to get started on the ramp. If we push it a little, we can be finished by noon. I've gotten most of the main passage clear. Once we have it graded, we can finish the passage. That soil will make a good finish coat on the ramp. What do you think?"

"I'll have to go look, unless you've got a pair of binoculars handy."

"As a matter of fact, I do. Let me go get them for you."

Returning, he said, "These should do just fine. They're great at short range. They don't have much power, but then again, you don't need any power."

"I see what you mean. You've done an amazing amount of work. This shouldn't take more than three more hours."

"It's supposed to get pretty warm today. We can establish a moderate pace and still be done by noon. I don't want to drop over from heatstroke."

"Sorry, you're right. I haven't listened to the weather report yet. How hot is it supposed to get?"

"At least a hundred degrees," Ellen commented. "The cave will provide a small degree of comfort in the morning, but not in the afternoon."

"We're wasting time just standing here talking about it."

"We're going to drive up. I want to check out my winch while we have the time. There's a couple of hundred feet of cable on here. It should work just fine."

Jonathan backed up against the ramp and eased to a stop, just touching the mounded soil at the end of the ramp. He had contacted the trucking company and asked them for the trailer bed height. He transferred the measurement to the back of his truck with a strip of masking tape. By pulling up alongside of the ramp, the tape allowed him raise or lower the soil with minimal effort. It took a lot of the guesswork out of the equation.

Steve stood there for a while admiring Jonathan's ingenuity. There was so much he could learn from this man. He only needed to be able to break things down to component parts and think in basic patterns.

Ellen went immediately to the box. She wanted to get as much time in as she could before it was sealed for the trip. The men could do their *boys with toys* thing, but she had work to do. This latest discovery still had her overwhelmed.

Leaning momentarily on the box, she concluded that there would never be anything out of the realm of possibility from this day forward. Where these thoughts prophetic or just a coping mechanism? Time would tell. The eerie warmth of the box interrupted her musing.

The ocean was to have been the last frontier on earth. Mankind now looked to the stars for research and exploration. The realization of the discovery slammed over her in a dizzying wave. Ellen fled the confines of the cave for the open air. She stood at the top of the ramp, leaning against the wall of the cave. Her breath was ragged as she fought the urge to vomit.

"Are you all right dear?" asked Jonathan. She looked up and nodded a weak affirmation. He placed his arm over her shoulder to comfort her. "You look terrible. Are you sure you're okay?"

"It's the box. I was not prepared for what we found yesterday. When I went inside just now, it struck me just how important this really is. We're in big trouble here. We can't expect to keep this secret for very long.

"The research team will have to be experienced in any number of fields. The effort it will take to assemble a team like that will alert everyone. There's going to be too many questions Jonathan. I can't deal with it right now. I need to absorb all of this and settle into it. Just give me some time."

"It'll be all right sweetheart. You know that Johnny has already given me a short list of people he can trust. Most of them will be able to help us without drawing any attention to the project. They will all be able to take vacation time from their regular jobs. Where they go, and what they do on their own time won't concern anyone. The initial research will be covered in secrecy.

"Where we're going to be in trouble is with the cryogenics. We don't have that technology. How will we research it? Where do we even begin? We'll need to reverse engineer it. We can only hope that we come up with a breakthrough or something. That's about the only way I can see to save our skins.

"That's what scares me Jonathan."

"Let's concentrate on the task at hand. We can deal with the future when it gets here. I can't afford to spend my time worrying about *what ifs*. We should worry about packaging this thing and getting it to a secure facility. Everything else is pure fantasy at this point."

Just having the conversation made her feel better. "You're right. Let's deal with today."

"I know how upset you are. I've been wrestling with this since you discovered it. We'll get through this. You keep studying the markings; Steve and I will get the box from the cave and on to the trailer. For now, we'll leave the rest to the fates."

"The open plain is not secure and it's very vulnerable. I don't like being this exposed. Work with me on this one. The plan of action may not be a great one, but it's what we have. Find some faith the best way you can. I only wish that I could offer you more."

"Thanks honey," she said as she kissed his cheek. "I'll be all right. I promise. You two continue to get this thing secured and I'll develop a thick skin. You know in your heart that you can depend on me. Now you two get to work."

Jonathan operated the winch as Steve pulled the cable into position. It went around the box with no difficulty at all. There was at least twenty feet left to spare.

Steve went to the front of the cave and signaled Jonathan to start the winch once the cable was secure. Before Jonathan started the winch, he waited until they were both well clear of the cave and the wire rope. In the event the rope would snap, the backlash could cripple or kill. When Steve and Ellen were behind the truck, he began.

CHAPTER THIRTY-SIX

THE TRUCK WANTED TO MOVE with the weight of the box, but Jonathan only wanted to see if the winch would handle the load. He stopped the winch after it had pulled the wire rope tight. Starting the winch again, he observed its' sound and watched the truck carefully. There didn't appear to be any problems.

Jonathan signaled Ellen and Steve that he was going to put some slack in the rope. Ellen and Steve moved from behind the truck and climbed to the mouth of the cave. She remained at the entrance while Steve went in to release the rope.

The test had been successful. The next task was digging trenches for the slides. Ellen went back to the truck to retract the wire rope. They had enough lumber to lay down a small track that would help bring the box around into position. "This should help get this up on to the slides," said Jonathan.

"We could use a good engineer right about now. This looks okay, but it sure would be nice to know."

"You worry too much. Everything will work out fine, it always does. Confidence Steve, that's all it takes. Henry Ford used to say that failure was an opportunity to start again, only more intelligently. You have to know in your heart that everything will be fine, and it will."

"I'm with you. This is getting to be tiring work. I was excited to get here, but now I'm not so sure," he groaned as he stretched his back and rubbed his aching arms. They both laughed."

"How's it going dear?"

"Fine. I want to show you what I've got here. Come around to the side of the truck and look at the ground around the tires. You can see that under the initial load, the truck moved almost three inches. It's not much, but it will help calculate the load size. What did you two want anyway, aside from the work we've finished"

"Maybe you've got a few ideas," he replied.

The three of them headed back up the hill to see the slides and the small section of lumber that would serve as a make shift track.

Ellen suggested that a few more small slides be buried in the path where the box would turn towards the main entrance. She thought that it might be easier than the planking. If the box got off track it would still remain on the additional slides. Other than that, she had no suggestions.

Jonathan and Steve began a quick re-arrangement of the lumber. Ellen's layout was cleaner and would hold more weight. The job was moving quickly to its conclusion.

Ellen had finished with Jonathan and Steve and entered the box. The sounds of lumber falling on lumber echoing through the door were distracting. She wasn't sure that she was going to get anything finished under these conditions. Her eyes swept the wall as she angrily turned to complain about the noise. She stopped in mid turn.

There was a new set of lines on the wall. She hadn't noticed them before. They must have appeared when they found the new way to open the box. They formed the outline of a plate, exactly like the one next to the door. She stepped over to them and lightly traced her fingertips over the lines.

"Jonathan. Steve. Come in here now," she called. "You need to see this."

"What do you want?" asked Jonathan. "Is everything okay?"

"Yes. I need for the two of you to see this. It's a new plate. It must have appeared when the door combination was changed. We've been so pre-occupied with cutie over there, that none of us noticed this." She moved over to the wall and traced the outline again.

"Would you look at that," breathed Steve. He edged closer for a good look. "Will the mysteries never cease?" He reached out to sequence the buttons as he would on the doorplate. It rose from the surface as he had anticipated. Nothing seemed out of order.

"What next? Do we go back to work or are we going to play in here for a while?" They both gave him the same peculiar look. "What?" he asked defensively. "It's an honest question. You two can stop looking at me as if I just came from Mars."

"It's not you Steve," said Ellen. "I don't think I can handle a second dinosaur right now. I'm half afraid to try anything because I think we'll find another raptor hidden away in here. Who knows what's behind this wall? When you calculate the size of the cryo-chamber and allow for an aisle, you could easily fit ten or twelve more chambers in this box."

"I agree. I don't know if I can handle any more excitement myself." Jonathan seemed absolutely exhausted at that moment.

Steve, ever the explorer, pressed them harder for an answer. "Do either of you have any objections to my efforts at discovery? You found the plate Ellen. May I try to figure out its purpose?"

"Go ahead. I don't care right now."

"Jonathan," Steve asked turning to his mentor, friend and co-worker. "Are you going to pass on this or must I stop and go back to the cable and the winch with you?"

"Go right ahead and suit yourself. I want to rest for a minute and then get back to work on the slides. We've got to get this box done and out of here in the next day or two."

Steve turned away from both of them as they sat down on the floor for some rest. He took some notes from his pocket and read them for a moment. Reaching up, he pressed a few of the keys. Nothing happened. He made additional notes in his book. He pressed the same keys in a different sequence and still nothing happened. He made more notes.

Turning to face the Crenshaw's, he said, "I've eliminated a couple of variable patterns that I hypothesized would not function. They didn't. I also interpolated a series of keystrokes that should have some results. It was a pattern that came to me as a combination of both the outside door sequence and the inside doorplate sequence. I was going to try it on the doorplate, but this one is as good as any. It can wait until we're finished in with the slides."

He slipped the book back in his pocket and went back to the job at hand.

Janet had been overseeing fossil packing all morning. It was going a little faster than even she had hoped for. The packing was done carefully and precisely. There was no margin for error with sixty-five million-year-old specimens.

The students gelled as a team. They worked smoothly together. No one was tripping over anyone or anything. They were a team determined to complete the task in record time.

Janet was proud that she could orchestrate this portion of the dig. It was where her talents were realized. Steve was well advised to use her in this capacity. Her thoughts drifted back to the passion that they shared last night. Her heart warmed with the renewed sensation of love and joy.

Steve would be returning to camp sometime after noon on the following day. Janet wanted the majority of the packing to be done by his return. She knew that he would be pleased. Her instructions were that each crate be sealed shut, but that the nails would only be hammered in a little way. The lids could be easily removed to allow Steve a final inspection before authorizing the final sealing.

She enclosed a large sealed plastic envelope containing a grid map and a detailed manifest of the contents with each crate. She stapled it to the top of each crate as it was finished. It was her typical efficiency. Janet was satisfied that her crew was working at optimum efficiency. Mostly, she was proud of her team, and her leadership.

A major benefit was that she would be able to trade this experience to any company if Steve didn't want to keep her around. Of course, she would prefer to stay with him, but she held no delusions about the future. One night of sex didn't necessarily seal the deal. The thought made her pause as she recounted every caring moment of that night. It still brought a big smile to her face for the second time in that last ten minutes.

Steve and the Crenshaw's stopped working as if by cue. The three of them broke for a late lunch. No one was hungry but the work demanded that they eat something. Eating in silence and going back to work in silence was the new norm.

After several hours Jonathan and Steve finished the trenches. They were setting the slides in place and preparing to backfill for stability. Steve placed stakes alternately down the length of each slide to prevent them from rolling over once the weight of the box had settled on them. He was finishing with the last stake and noticed that Jonathan was only a few feet behind him. In less than fifteen minutes they would be ready for box to be moved.

Slightly sore, and a little tired from all the pounding, Steve rested the last few minutes as Jonathan finished. They looked at each other and moved outside. The muted crunch of the soil and small stones underfoot broke the silence as they walked to the truck. They hadn't spoken two words since they emerged from the box earlier in the afternoon.

Looking over at Jonathan, Steve could see that he enjoyed the silence. He suspected that Jonathan was relieved to have little or no conversation to deal with. Steve was too confused to say what was on his mind. It would take another day or two for him to sort through everything.

Between them, they grunted and nodded when they wanted to communicate. Primitive vocalization was ironically appropriate in this situation. Ellen assumed it was a natural state for male conversation and chuckled to herself whenever they made those awful noises.

Steve drove his truck into position and released the cable. Ellen operated the control while he and Jonathan dragged the cable up the hill into the cave. When they had enough to reach the box; Jonathan spoke for the first time in a while. "I think that we need to identify each cable. If there is a problem, we identify which cable quickly. Do you have any rags or cloth of any kind left in your truck?"

"No. I left everything back at camp."

"That's okay. I should have more somewhere. We'll identify one of them with rags tied along one line. The other will remain plain. Ellen can stand at the entrance and signal if we need more tension or slack from either cable or to stop a cable."

"I'd prefer to be operating the winches anyway. I've pretty much had it with this box. I wish that I had never seen it," Steve grumbled. His voice was filled with animosity.

"Once we get it away from here and can really dig into all its secrets, you'll feel better about it. Wait, you'll see." Jonathan was too tired and stressed to allow the rancor he felt overwhelm him.

Steve was half way down the passage when he answered, "I hope so. I'll believe it when it happens." He left to explain the plan to Ellen.

She watched as his hunched figure descended the hillside. There was little to no enthusiasm left in his stride and his overall physical appearance was disheartening. He explained to Ellen what they were planning. They worked out a couple of signals and then she climbed the hill; rags in hand.

Jonathan tied them to one of the cables. He made his way down the ramp and tied them every ten feet or so. They didn't need to be evenly spaced, just seen. "You can take them off as they approach the winch," he suggested to Steve. "If you miss one, let it go. We don't need for you losing any fingers over a stupid rag."

"Thanks, I will. Let me know when you want me to get started." A little enthusiasm was returning to his voice.

"I'll have Ellen signal you." *He's just about burned out. Maybe he needs more time to assimilate? I hope he lasts long enough to figure it all out.*

Steve returned to the cave and announced, "My cable is ready. We can start any time you want."

Ellen looked at both men and blurted, "This is getting us nowhere. Why don't we open the box one more time to see what we can see? Once and done."

Lethargically, Jonathan agreed with a shrug of his shoulders. "Why don't we rest for a few hours? We can have some supper later and revitalize. We'll come back tonight and open the box. The truck won't be here for two days."

There was no immediate response and Jonathan began to wonder if it really mattered anyway. Finally, Steve said in resignation, "Sure, why not? What have we got to lose? We're in the middle of nowhere freaked out of our minds already. What's the worst that could happen? Let's get this damn thing out of our systems and get back to being scientists."

"Well said, Steve. You're right, what's the worst that could happen? I'm feeling better already." He turned to Ellen, "How about you dear?" Ellen had a trace of a smile forming at the corners of her mouth.

"Well, don't just stand there, get a move on," urged Ellen. "You two talk the talk, now walk the walk. I'm getting the munchies now that you mentioned food."

Back at the tent, they rested and snacked into the early evening. Spirits and strength were regenerating.

Several hours had passed and the sun was fading into the horizon. There was a sense of calm now that they'd eaten and relaxed.

"I think we should get back to the box. We can try that last sequence and then get the box ready for moving." Steve sat up straight and stretched his arms and legs.

With a renewed enthusiasm, they returned to the cave. Steve opened his book to the new page before he began. It needed to be at the ready for any new notes. His fingers were poised to stroke the first key, yet he hesitated. Finally, he said, "Well here goes."

When he finished, nothing happened. As he turned towards the Crenshaw's, the commotion started. The sides of the box began to move. It was opening up. The three of them stared, not sure of what to do. Panels and lights came on all over the interior walls of the chamber.

The sides of the box struck the cave walls. There was a momentary shudder as it began to close again. They just stood there observing anything and everything. Steve was writing furiously. He could hardly keep up with all his thoughts and the activity.

Once it was closed; the room became silent. The sound of electronic and electrical equipment had stopped. "What in blue blazes was that? That was awesome."

Ellen and Jonathan just looked at Steve. They thought the cave was collapsing and he thought it was awesome. "It must be an age thing," said Jonathan. "Aren't you the least bit frightened by all of this?"

"Hell yes, I practically soiled myself. Don't you understand what we have here? This is more than a cryogenic chamber. This is some massive piece of electronic machinery. The potential technology could propel us beyond anything that we now perceive as advanced. We're unlocking new secrets daily. Am I scared? Oh yeah. Am I pumped? Without a doubt."

"You obviously don't see the danger in all of this. If we share this, we breach national security. If we keep it quiet, we risk disappearing in the middle of the night. Personally, I don't want to be found dead in a tragic single car accident on a lonely stretch of highway or whatever method suits an assassin. Get it now?" Determination and fear were chiseled on Jonathan's features.

Falling to a seated position, a flash of horror raced across Steve's face. His big sad puppy eyes belayed the sheer terror that engulfed his mind. He was limp. The full impact of this project crashed into him. Steve was devastated by it. He struggled to hold back the tears.

"Let's get back to work. We now know a little more about the box, and that will be that. We can figure it out later." Jonathan rose calmly and extended his hand to Ellen. Already halfway to her feet, she brushed it aside.

They both helped Steve to his feet. He was a trembling mess, "Relax Steve. It's bad, but we're still here and alive. And no one knows about our little secret yet."

CHAPTER THIRTY-SEVEN

O N A REMOTE MILITARY BASE - not easily found, even with a map - Corporal Jensen was monitoring several observation satellites. This series of satellite was typically used to monitor the weather as a primary function, but a few of them had the capability to be pressed into more discrete governmental service.

Corporal Jensen was converting the mission status of one of his charges back to weather when it happened. Just as the auto sequencing converted the satellite back to weather status, an anomaly appeared on one of his screens.

"Sergeant," called out Corporal Jensen, "I need you to see this."

Sergeant Green rose methodically from his desk. He laid the report he'd been reading on the edge of his desk and walked over to Jensen's station. "What is it Jensen? What have you got?"

"I'm not sure, sir. There was a momentary blip. It showed as a possible power surge of some kind exactly at the moment of conversion. I switched operational status back immediately, but there's nothing there. It might be a problem with the equipment. I thought that you'd want to know."

"Thank you, Jensen. Make a note of it in your log. Run a diagnostic on the equipment immediately. Let me know the results. Call me again if it shows up. That will be all. Carry on."

Sergeant Green returned to his desk and called upstairs to report the event. Before he resumed reading, he noted the time and date of the event and the entire conversation in his own log. He was meticulous about his record keeping. He would turn the reports over to the Lieutenant at the end of his rotation.

Several weeks before the Crenshaw's came to the site, severe storms had ravaged the area. The top of the box had been exposed and washed clean by the rain. The ultra-sensitive solar collectors began absorbing energy. Even the dim light that had worked its way into the cave was enough to activate the highly sensitive collectors. They absorbed every available bit of light they could. The equipment was sensitive enough to even utilize moonlight as a collection source.

The surveillance satellite had monitored the power signature for less than a second as the status change took place. The box was almost fully retracted when the power surge was detected. By the time the satellite was reconfigured there was nothing to see.

The box was gaining more reserve power every day. The dim light was like a trickle charge on a battery. Currently, it had gained enough energy to operate the many mechanisms and panels that the Crenshaw's had recently discovered. It would take a while, but eventually it would reach a full charge.

No one was aware that a power surge had taken place at the exact moment the box began to open. They continued to prepare for the move.

Stepping up to the Sergeant's desk, Corporal Jensen handed him the findings. The equipment checked out. There were no defects found in any of the systems. Each system had been checked as an individual component and then for continuity as they were linked together to form the whole operating system.

"Thank you, Jensen," said the Sergeant as he accepted the report from the Corporal. "Dismissed." They exchanged cursory salutes and Corporal Jensen returned to his station.

Sergeant Green read the report. He saw that the Corporal had done a thorough job. Jensen had even investigated a few avenues that were redundant. There was even an attempt to discover if it was a maximum capacity error. Each attempt to uncover an error in the system proved a false trail. The system had performed at maximum capability and was not defective, even under severe load conditions.

They had an alleged unknown power surge in an unknown location. Sergeant Green reached into his desk drawer and pulled out the necessary form concerning the incident report he would be submitting.

Both Green and Jensen had logged the incident. Copies of the log sheets would need to be made and included in the Sergeant's report. It would be passed on to the Lieutenant at the end of rotation as a matter of protocol.

All copies would then be filed appropriately. The Sergeant would retain the original and pass a copy to the Lieutenant who would in turn copy it for his file and then pass the original copy farther up the ladder. Until further notice, this was a non-incident.

As he sat on his motorcycle near the phone booth; Jonathan Jr. realized that he hadn't heard from his parents for two days. When last they spoke, he was informed of the latest developments. The absence of phone calls meant that everything was going as planned. The flatbed trailer would be on the road by now. His own team was coming together. Steve's site should be clear or finished later today.

This was becoming exciting. It was difficult not to get caught up in it all. Jonathan was getting anxious. Now he was experiencing difficulty keeping the secret. Dinosaurs were everyone's favorite animals. The phone rang and he checked his watch. Thirty seconds to spare. His father was not usually one for punctuality. He got off of his motorcycle and stepped up to the payphone. "Hello."

"It's me. How are you doing?"

"Fine, just fine. Everything here is running on schedule. I was not able to assemble an entire team. Those I do have will make a solid start. These guys will be able to recruit others, especially after they've seen the project."

"That's good. I'm grateful for your efforts. It must have been tough to convince some of them on such short notice. When you factor in the secrecy, you were lucky to get anyone at all. Thanks again."

"When do expect to arrive? I'd like to have everything in place.

The warehouse looks good. Why did you want an unobstructed fifty-foot ceiling? That was difficult to find. They're all over the place, but most are being used."

"If I told you, you wouldn't believe me. I'll show you when we get set up. Will you be able to get enough copper mesh to surround the work area?"

"Yes. That wasn't a problem. I got some interesting questions on the phone though. No one really pressed me for answers. I only purchased small lots from each supplier. I was careful not buy a quantity from any one supplier that was large enough to raise suspicion. I told them that I was an artist. I needed it for a commissioned sculpture. That satisfied the ones who asked."

"Good job son. You had it all sent to St. Louis, didn't you?"

"Yes. Your friend doesn't seem the least bit interested in what you're up to. He said to call back if you wanted anything else."

"That's sounds right. He's been a good friend all of these years. This phone card is about out of time. I'll call you when I can. Stick to this schedule until we can make a new one. Your mom and I love you and Kathleen and the kids. Send our love to them. Bye now."

The phone went silent. Jonathan Jr. replaced the receiver in the cradle, got back on his bike and drove off. There was so much to think about. He needed to be there for the project. He hadn't broached the subject with Kathleen yet.

He didn't want to lie to her, but he couldn't tell her the truth either. From the very start he'd been wrestling with this dilemma, especially since he'd received the package from his father with the preliminary photographs. The wrong answer would end up betraying his family or himself. This was a problem that he created by agreeing to help, and the solution was his to find.

It had been a rigorous two days. The Crenshaw's had successfully loaded the box onto the flatbed trailer. It was surprisingly light for its size. The ramp had worked out fine. The box had only dug into the loose soil about a foot, before coming to a stop at the bottom of the ramp.

It only took an hour to clear the soil away and leave room for the trailer. They shored up the corners of the box so that it didn't settle into the soil while they waited for the truck. It ended up helping the loading process. The loading only took an hour once the truck arrived.

While all of this was taking place, Janet was getting the first of the two loads completed. It was done about the same time as the truck arrived at the Crenshaw site. There was no way she would have known how precisely her timing had worked out. Her second truck moved into position and was two-thirds full by suppertime. She missed Steve and kept looking over at the road to see if he was coming.

Morning light crept over the horizon, gently brightening the sky. Breakfast aromas filled the camp as everyone prepared to finish the last truck and break camp. Steve had returned from the Crenshaw's shortly after supper the night before. He'd eaten at the Crenshaw's site but told everyone that he'd grabbed a bite to eat at the diner in town. He went over the day's progress with Janet and told the assembled students how proud he was of the efficient, professional job they'd done. The task was completed well ahead of estimates and there would be a celebration party once they returned to the university.

That final revelation brought a rousing cheer. So much had gone into the work and it was a breakthrough site for paleontology. The students appreciated the recognition of their contributions. While Steve thanked Janet for her role in orchestrating everything, he whispered in her ear that he wanted to see her after everyone had gone to sleep. She could barely contain her emotions.

The rustle of the tent flap brought Steve to a sitting position as Janet entered the tent. He bound out of his cot and embraced her. "I've missed you so much," he said as he covered her in kisses. "I had so much trouble getting my work done without you around."

"Steve, I love you." *There, I've said it.*

"Oh, my sweet Janet, I love you too," he whispered through his kisses.

They became a tangled mass of arms, legs and lips as they renewed their passions. They each gave in to their sense of urgency, and desire. With fingertips and feather soft kisses they explored each other's bodies. Each new sensation was a moment to be savored. And they savored them for hours until they were sated.

The dig was completed and there was no need for pretense, Steve asked Janet to remain the night. They each wanted to wake up in the other's arms. It was Janet who finally convinced Steve of the impracticality of two people sharing a single cot. "There will be plenty of opportunity once we return to school. I'll make the wait worth your while."

CHAPTER THIRTY-EIGHT

The Crenshaw's needed a location that would not attract attention. Detroit seemed an obvious location. The large crate on the back of a trailer would seem commonplace in Detroit's industrial environment. Complete anonymity.

Steve joined the Crenshaw's at a quaint diner down the road. They had a fine breakfast after a night of pleasant, productive conversation. The pressure of removing the box and packing and shipping the fossils was gone. Tension seemed to melt away. They still had other problems to deal with.

"This will be great once we can open the box and really get inside," said Steve excitedly.

"Yes, it will," bubbled Ellen. "I can hardly contain my excitement. The fear seems to have disappeared."

"So, tell us, Steve," said Jonathan. "Did our truck leave at the same time as your two?"

"Of course. I had him away about fifteen minutes before my second truck left. He'd have passed through town well ahead of it, but not by any significant amount of time. Besides that, if you remember, the first truck was away the same day we loaded it."

"You did well, my boy," Jonathan said. "You did very well indeed."

"We're heading back home and picking up our personal vehicle. I know that you would like to ride with us, but we would prefer that you drove back with the students.

"Should one of them have a breakdown, you can be there for each other. It wouldn't be right just to leave them to travel alone after all these weeks in the field. That's not to mention how the university would frown on one its students being injured while in your care, and you not even there and nowhere to be found.

"Ellen and I want this to go as smoothly as possible. We're going to withdraw as much cash as we can when we get home. We have a habit of taking a vacation after a dig. No one will think this is any different. No one ever asks what we do or where we go. It's perfect."

"You're right about both cars. I've never driven that far before. My concern is getting too tired. I don't want to have an accident. Talk about drawing attention to our plans."

"Steve, don't worry about that. You'll be the lead car. If you get sleepy, just pull over. We'll pull in behind you. I just had a great idea. I'll call Johnny and ask him to come out for a visit. He can meet us at our house and then you can have a driving partner."

"That's great! Do you think he'll be able to do it?"

"Sure. We've been in constant communication with him from the beginning. He knew about this before you did Steve. Remember that he's the one setting up the warehouse and bringing in the team."

"You're right Jonathan. In all the excitement, it just slipped my mind, that's all." Steve was embarrassed by his oversight. He started to turn crimson in spite of his efforts to the contrary.

"Don't fret over a simple mistake like that," soothed Ellen. "There'll be plenty of chances left to make some real whoppers." She began to laugh.

Hanging his head, he answered, "Thanks a million. With friends like you…"

Jonathan and Ellen went back to their room. The intention was to grab a few hours of sleep before they hit the road. Exhaustion was overtaking both of them.

They had reservations about keeping him up all night, but they couldn't get a room for him. They didn't want him to spend the night in his truck but where else was there now that his tent was packed

Originally, when Steve was finished loading the last truck, he was to rendezvous with the Crenshaw's at a small motel. Now the plans had changed. Janet was now able to ride back to school with Steve.

"We need to stay here until the last truck is away and then we can take off," Janet said to her friends. "I'll ride with Steve."

"Isn't that convenient?" asked her tent mate.

"What do you mean by that?"

"Someone saw you sneaking into Steve's tent last night and you didn't come out for three hours. Aren't you sore?" They both giggled.

"You don't know the half of it. We're in love and he wants me to move in with him when we get back to school."

"You're kidding, he's in love after a little sex?"

"It's more than just sex. That only just happened. He told me he loved me before we had sex. It wasn't like he said I love you lets sleep together. He said that he loved me and respected my intelligence and that's where the conversation ended. When he came back to camp, he said how much he missed me and that he loved me. As many times as he's said it, I figured he really meant it. Last night I snuck into his tent wearing only my robe. When he asked what I was doing there, I dropped the robe to the floor."

"You are such a bad girl. How hot was it? Come on, I need details; you've gone this far."

"Well the first few minutes were real passion and fire."

"I thought so. Did he finish ahead of the pack?"

"No, it was nothing like that at all. He's the perfect lover. I'll leave it at that."

The girls separated as Steve walked up. "What was that all about?" asked Steve as he helped Janet with her duffle.

"Girl stuff," she smiled. She put her arms around his neck and kissed him intently.

Finally, the last truck was loaded and was pulling away from the site. Everything went off without a hitch. Janet's ability to organize and handle people expedited the process immensely. Their impromptu celebration was interrupted as the truck blasted its air horn as it pulled onto the main road.

The students piled into their cars and one by one headed back to the university. They would spend the remainder of the summer having fun with friends and family. Each had a fantastic story to relate.

They all knew that the university would be very pleased at the results of this summer's project. The alumni donations should come pouring in after Steve published his findings. The controversy would keep the schools name in the forefront for a long, long time to come. They always expected, and always got results when they sent the Crenshaw's into the field. This year they would get more than they hoped for.

Steve held the door for her while she got into the front seat of his truck. He waved to the other girls as they drove on to the main road and headed home. They honked their horn and disappeared around the first bend.

"We're alone now Steve. Everyone is gone and the trucks are away. Anything on your mind?"

"I'm awfully tired and we need to get started."

"Get into the back seat and I'll make sure that you fall asleep right away. I'll drive for a while and you can rest. Besides, in a few minutes, you're going to need it."

Janet licked her lips seductively and tipped her head towards the back seat with a sly wink. Steve was in the back seat so fast that she barely saw him move.

She stood alongside the truck and stripped slowly. Steve watched as he fumbled to remove his own clothes. Approaching the open door, she said, "You just lay back lover, I'll do all the work."

Oh my God, she's magnificent. I love her so much. Those were Steve's last thoughts as he drifted off into a deep sleep. The rumble of the truck on the road was like a lullaby.

Janet was comfortably ensconced in the front seat. Her smile made her look as if she was the cat that ate the canary. In a matter of moments, they were on their way back to the university.

Jonathan had called his son from their room before they left.

"Johnny, it's good to hear your voice. I have an idea that can help both of us out of a jamb. I know that you've been struggling with how to tell Kathleen about your trip to the warehouse. I'm going to call you at home tonight. We'll discuss the raptor site and then I'll invite you to come on out. I want you to fly out here and then you can help drive to the warehouse. We're taking two cars and currently have only three drivers. What do you think?"

"It sounds good. I don't have to lie to Kathleen and you still get what you want. It's a great plan dad. She knows how much I love dinosaurs. She often asks why I didn't follow in your footsteps. I never really understood it myself. I guess that it was providence that kept me from the field. I'm more suited to help you now than I would have been if I had become a paleontologist. Funny how things work out? Is there anything else that you want? It's your nickel."

"Not really, son. This will be just what we needed. We'll be home late tomorrow. Schedule your flight for the next day. We'll have a chance to unpack and unwind. See you in a couple of days. We love you. As always, send our love to everyone. Bye."

"Bye dad. Hugs and kisses to mom. See you in a couple of days."

He remembered to call Steve's cell to let him know of the new plans. Jonathan wasn't surprised to hear Janet answer the phone. Ellen had told him that she believes Steve and Janet have fallen in love.

After finishing the calls and giving the room a once over for forgotten items; they checked out by 7:00 A.M. They grabbed a couple of the complimentary Danish on the way to their truck. They were anxious to be home and finish their plans. Detroit was only a week away.

Jonathan Jr. was grateful for the resolution to his dilemma. Kathleen wanted to visit her parents anyway. With him going to visit his parents, she'd have no reason to worry about him. There would be no conflicts all the way around.

The only variable now was the transportation. The driver wasn't on a deadline. He had two more days than it would normally take to arrive in Detroit. There would be no reason for him to push himself and risk the load.

Jonathan had made previous arrangements to get the framing installed in advance. The complex had an on-site property manager who would accept all incoming shipments. His instructions were not subject to interpretation. He would oversee the installation and the bill for the material and labor would be added to the lease as a balloon payment due upon arrival. The mesh itself would be installed once all of the team had arrived. The site manager was only overseeing the installing the superstructure. Its purpose could then remain a secret.

The box should arrive after the structure was up. If it arrived earlier than anticipated, it was to be placed in the center of the framework. There was to be no deviation. The warehouse had a five-ton capacity overhead crane. It would serve perfectly to remove the crate.

Tomorrow evening would be the last time the Crenshaw's would sleep in a decent bed for a while. They would eventually set up sleeping quarters in the warehouse. It was illegal, but they would be out of there before it would create a problem with any city ordinances. Besides, with the right amount of cash, an inspector could always miss a small infraction.

Jonathan Jr. had assured his father that everything was on schedule. The construction of the framework was a day or two from completion. The mesh had arrived on five different trucks. There was more than an adequate supply. All looked well.

The only missing component was the box itself. The trucking company would arrive in the next couple of days. The team would gather at the warehouse in five more days. Then the fun would begin

CHAPTER THIRTY-NINE

"CORPORAL JENSEN REPORTING AS ORDERED sir." The salute was crisp.

"At ease soldier," responded Captain Harrington, returning the salute. "Tell me about this report, son." Captain Harrington sat behind his desk fingering through the report. He was a squat little man; a career soldier. He was very direct and didn't like excessive conversation.

"The anomaly appeared for less than a second. . . literally sir. I waited for it to re-appear and it did not, sir. I went to Sergeant Green with my concern and the report details everything else. Is there anything else you wish to know, sir?

"What do you think it was soldier?"

"Sir? I don't understand, sir."

"In your best estimate, what do think happened?"

"I've given it some thought, sir, but not a lot." He looked the Captain nervously in the eyes. "It was a power spike of some magnitude, sir. Why else would the satellite register it, sir?"

"Why else indeed, soldier? That will be all. Dismissed."

"Sir, yes sir." With another crisp salute and its equal from the Captain, Jensen did an about face and exited the room.

Toggling the button on his intercom, Captain Harrington called the orderly. "Come into my office and take a message for me. It will be addressed to Colonel Briggs. Enclose the report from Sergeant Green."

Harrington handed the orderly the report when he entered the office. He began dictating:

Colonel Briggs,

One of the soldiers under my command has found an interesting anomaly, a suspected power surge recorded on routine satellite observation of the Dakotas. We have not pinpointed the exact location as of yet. We'll need to be in field for that information. We have it within five square miles. This is still preliminary. If you feel that the manpower is warranted, we will proceed with a further investigation. Enclosed is the report filed by Sergeant Green.

"Finish it off etc., etc., Captain Harrington. I'll be back from lunch at 1300 hours. Have the letter on my desk for signing. That will be all soldier."

Captain Harrington loved mysteries. This alleged power surge was a grand mystery. The basic information supplied by the satellite would place the area being observed in the middle of nowhere. There were no power plants in the immediate area and even if there were, they would not register on the satellite in this fashion. He wanted this investigation.

Harrington resolved to push for an investigation when he reviewed the report with the Colonel. The anomaly was discovered by a man under his command and he wanted to lead the investigation on that basis. His love of the hunt was of no concern to the Colonel.

The phone was ringing as the Captain entered his office. His orderly indicated that it was for him, the big brass. Hand signaled to transfer the call to the inner office.

The phone light was blinking when he eased behind his desk. Harrington answered the call. "Good to hear from you Colonel. What might I do for you?"

"I've heard about the anomaly. What do you make of it? Was it a power surge?"

"It concerns me sir, in light of attempt in New York last year. There's nothing out there though. It's the Bad Lands sir. It occurred very near a small town with almost no population. I've just finished my report and a letter to you. I can bring it right over, sir"

"That'll be fine Sam. Let me clear my schedule. I'll expect you in fifteen minutes."

"I'm on my way Colonel. Thank you, sir. Goodbye."

Toggling the intercom, Captain Harrington instructed his orderly to cancel any afternoon appointments and to make whatever apologies were necessary, it was unavoidable.

The orderly saluted as the Captain whisked out of the office.

Captain Harrington returned the salute, but never slowed his pace. The jeep would be waiting at the front door. He would arrive at least five minutes early. Events would turn out the way he'd hoped. The Colonel was already interested, but the inclusion of the September reference would prove to be the final winning argument. Enemy insurgents needed to be squelched, even home-grown insurgents.

The FBI and the CIA took a beating for almost dropping the ball in New York. The government was able to add to the bureaucratic bloat as a result of new laws and new bureaus. And a plethora of new regulations, designed to assist, would only add to the burden.

Captain Harrington was not about to let the military share in the black eye. The news media had released a firestorm against the seated President. He was now taking a strong anti-war posture. Find and capturing a band of insurgents on home soil would go a long way in showing the media how foolish they were.

This could make them all look good. There might even be a promotion in it.

CHAPTER FORTY

Ellen had just finished her packing by the time Johnny arrived. She rushed downstairs to greet him. He and Jonathan were already in a father and son embrace. Excitement was thick in the air.

"How are you sweetie?" she asked. "You look good. Have you gained a few pounds? It looks good on you. You were always too skinny for my taste."

"I'm fine mom. You look great yourself. Have you been going to a gym?"

"No, not really," she grinned. "The excavation of the box got us into pretty good shape." She reached over and pinched her husband on the rump. Johnny pretended not to see it. "Did Kathleen and the kids get to her parent's house all right?"

"Yes, no problem. It's only a couple of hours drive. They called last night as soon as they arrived. The kids had a great time on the way down. Kathleen bought them some kind of game to play in the car. They were there before either of them could remember to ask *'are we there yet?'* That alone was worth the investment.

"So, tell me everything that you couldn't say over the phone. I've been on edge ever since I received the package. This sounds really big. Are you still afraid that someone or some agency will try to hurt you?"

"More than ever son," said Jonathan gravely. He leaned over as if to conceal what he was about to say from prying ears. "There is so much to tell that I can't think where to begin. You already know the most of the story. There is no need to explain how we got it out of the cave. I guess I'll just tell you what we found two days before the move. You had better sit down for this. I know that I'm getting weak kneed at the telling and I've experienced it firsthand."

Puzzled, Johnny replied, "Whatever you say dad." He took a seat on the edge of the coffee table

Leaning in conspiratorial fashion, Jonathan began to reveal the story. "Steve keyed in the wrong sequence to open the door. Your mother saw him and made him stop. She was afraid that something might go wrong. We closed the lock and sequenced it again, using the same pattern. It opened again. At least your mother got confirmation of what she thought that she'd seen. When we opened the door using the new sequence, nothing happened on the exterior of the box. The door opened silently, that was all that happened. That had been completely normal. You'll see how advanced the technology is when we get to Detroit.

"When your mother and Steve, went inside, they stopped dead in their tracks. I made my way in and found myself dumbfounded. A wall had opened on the inside of the box. We had seen some lines that seemed to make up some kind of partitions or panels. They didn't seem to serve any purpose prior to this new development. Anyway, the panels moved away with this new sequence and exposed a chamber that was clearly hermetically sealed. We believe it to be a cryogenic chamber. We drew that conclusion from the only piece of evidence available. Inside the chamber is a perfectly preserved raptor. The skin is so supple looking it could have been alive yesterday."

"Are you crazy? Do you realize what you've just said?" He stood up and turned away. He paced back and forth trying to grasp what he'd just heard.

"Yes, we do, Johnny," said Ellen. "Why do you think we're so scared? The technology alone will be worth billions to someone. Frankly, I want to exploit the hell out of this. The more exposure we get, and the sooner we get it, the safer we are. At least that's the way we see it."

"I agree mom. We need to know as much about this as possible before we share it with the world. Business and government could brutalize us with too little information. Look at how the previous administration thrived on dismantling any shred of dignity that a person had, especially if that person posed a political threat. We wouldn't stand a chance. And the media would have a field day.

"I can see it all now." He held his hands up displaying a news headline and continued, Prominent paleontologists tied to insurrectionists. Several fringe groups join them to overthrow government. There will be no one on the face of the earth that wouldn't think we're a waste of skin. Then the really bad stuff starts. We need to dismantle this thing and learn every possible secret it can reveal. Once the scientific community has the information, we'll be somewhat safer. It's going to be rough going until we reach that point."

"You said a mouthful, son. Your mother and I have already faced the grim outcome that looms on the horizon. That's the main reason that we want so much secrecy. We started to cover our tracks well before there would be any reason for anyone to suspect anything. We have only one main concern. The box did something before we got it out of the cave."

"What do you mean, the box did something?" There was a look of panic on Johnny's face.

"Well, it appears to be solar powered."

"At least that's what we speculate," interrupted Ellen.

"It's been underground for millions of years. When your mom first found it, it was warm to the touch. Metal is not warm to the touch. Especially metal that's been underground for countless millennia. We assume solar power only because of the crevasse at the top of the cave.

"No direct sunlight came into the cave. It was present though. We figured that the collector panels are very sensitive and sort of trickle charged the thing. It would account for all the activity. All of the things that we accessed are, or at least we suspect that they are, electrically controlled. There are no outlets in a cave in the middle of nowhere. A battery can't hold a charge for sixty-five million years. Solar power is the obvious solution."

"It's a feasible theory. Why would that give you cause for concern?" Johnny asked.

"When we went inside the thing, just before we crated it up, we tried the same bad sequence on a new interior panel that had shown up when the chamber was revealed. The box started to open up. When it hit the cave walls it retracted itself. The battery lantern flickered and our watches stopped. They stopped the very first time that we entered the box. It took a while, but eventually they stopped. This was a little more wide spread. We think that it caused a brown out."

"What did you do?"

"We dragged it from the cave, sealed in a wooden crate. No light can penetrate, and the crate was delivered to our friend in St Louis. He changed the bill of lading to read *equipment* and transferred it on to Detroit. It will be at the warehouse when we get there. I'm not sure, but I think that our tracks are covered."

"What if they trace the truck?"

"Steve's site activity was the only thing the students saw. There are no records of our truck linked to Steve's two trucks. We even used a different trucking company. We also waited until night to get the truck under way using the cover of darkness."

"I can see that you've given this a lot of thought. Being rank amateurs, I suppose that something has been left out. I'll be darned if I can guess what it might be. When do we leave?"

"As soon as we call Steve and have him meet us at a previously selected rendezvous point. Your father forgot to tell you that we have some friends posing as us at a vacation spot. We mentioned that we would be going there, to a few people; enough that the word would get around. We loaned them our camera, so that the film would be from it. We'll get a full briefing when we get back. I'm sure that we will find that we kept to ourselves and had a good time." Ellen began to laugh. She was beginning to enjoy the intrigue.

Jonathan called Steve's dorm room and left a voice mail. His roommate and the voice mail would bear witness to the fact that they were leaving on vacation.

Johnny marveled at how well this had been planned out. He was convinced more than ever that they had covered all of their bases. The box opening up still nagged at him. He didn't like it at all. He didn't know why; he just didn't like it.

"We better help get the car packed or it will be hell to pay."

"I'm right behind you dad. I know what she's like when she's angry. This is a vacation. I don't want it to start out on a wrong note." He grabbed his luggage and headed for the car.

Jonathan started the car, leaving their normal life behind. The drive would be long and the work at the warehouse would be physically and mentally strenuous. The hours would be longer, but the physical output would be less. Upon reflection, they never had what most people would refer to as a normal life, yet their dedication to their chosen career was reward enough. They loved their work and anything associated with it. That's what brought them happiness.

Rotating drivers every half tank of gas gave the Crenshaw's a chance to rest. Steve and Johnny had adopted the same method. They reasoned that they could drive all day and night without getting exhausted. It was working well. They had driven all afternoon and through the night. They were only four hours from Detroit, east bound on I-94. The pace that traffic was keeping after they reached Chicago was blistering. The drivers were definitely aggressive in this part of the country.

Unaccustomed to this kind of driving and fearing an accident, Ellen asked Jonathan if he could drive the last leg into Detroit. Jonathan agreed without hesitation. A nervous driver was as dangerous as an inexperienced one. The drive went well. They had missed rush hour traffic through Chicago. Keeping a pace between sixty and seventy miles per hour was no effort at all. Traffic moved even faster than that most of the time.

Since it was still early, they stopped at a place called Houston's. It was southeast, below Chicago, by the quarry. They had a great breakfast and the menu was diverse. Ellen made a mental note of the exit. She wanted to stop there on their way back home. They served a variety of chicken dishes. The lemon chicken struck her fancy. It was served on a bed of rice – any style – and each serving was a half chicken, not pieces. Service was friendly and the family-like atmosphere enhanced the meal.

Jonathan convinced them that they needed to make a stop in South Bend, Indiana. He explained that it would be a surprise that they would all enjoy. They each shrugged and agreed. The drive could use some diversity. So far, they'd traveled straight through. Other than fuel and privy stops, they'd not done anything other than drive

Ellen enjoyed the scenery and relaxed more, now that she wasn't driving. She had often flown over this section of the country, but she had never driven through it. It appeared hillier from the air. Now it seemed flat and used up.

The steel mills in Hammond and Gary fascinated her. However, the smell was more than she cared for. Everywhere she looked, the buildings were colored a rusty brown that showed through old paint and on top of all the rust it was sooty too. She was beginning to understand why they referred to this part of the country as the *rust belt*. What she didn't understand was how people could live in such colorless surroundings. There were trees and birds, but the houses were so uniform and unexciting with the layer of grime hiding everything.

Jonathan wanted to drive through South Bend so he could show them Notre Dame. He was a big fan even though he'd never been to a single game. They took the bypass and went straight to the University. He took a walk around the stadium and had to stop and see the "Touchdown Jesus" on the side of the library.

Ellen laughed out loud. He was acting like a little kid on Christmas morning, pointing at this and rushing over to see that. She was happy to see him find so much joy in something that was relatively inconsequential

Steve and Johnny were only along for the ride at this point. Neither of them was tired, but they didn't want to stop at the college.

They shrugged their shoulders at each other when he led them to the school. They didn't know what he was up to until that point.

They got out and walked around. They eventually ended up at the grotto. It was beautiful. The groundskeepers always kept it up so students and visitors alike would enjoy their solitude. It was very spiritual, with the sun filtering through the trees. The birds sang their morning songs and a gentle breeze cooled the air. They almost hated to leave. There was a reverent, peaceful aura about the place. Their worries seemed to drift away.

The hypnotic pull of the grotto's beauty combined with the quality of the morning almost caused them to forget why they were even there. This was to be a quick in and out rest stop. They got back to their car at the same time as Ellen and Jonathan arrived from the other direction. There would be no time lost waiting around.

"Well, did you get to see it dad?" asked Johnny.

"I sure did. It's magnificent. It's better than I had imagined. This will help make the next couple of weeks well worth the effort. Come on; let's get back on the road. I stopped a security guard and got directions. We're not that far from the toll road."

"What's that?" asked Johnny.

"A souvenir… I had to get a pennant. It wouldn't be right to stop here and get nothing but a memory as a memento."

"Well it didn't take very long; I can see that. You sure know how to cram a lot of stuff into no time at all. You're a lot like Janet in that respect." Steve added.

Once they were in Toledo, almost directly below Detroit, they exited due north up into the southeast corner of Michigan and straight on to Detroit. They could easily make Detroit before supper.

Ellen and Jonathan fell into a relaxed conversation. The trip had gone without mishap thus far. Jonathan was feeling good about his stop at Notre Dame. They chatted away as if there wasn't a care in the world.

In the other car, Johnny and Steve discussed the warehouse and the box. "Who will install the copper mesh? It won't cause us any delays will it?" questioned Steve. He was leery of any schedule delays.

"No, not really. Some of the team that I assembled will be responsible for that. It should be done by now. If it's not, we can surely finish by morning."

"Why do we need it anyway?"

"It will mask any electronic surveillance. It will also mask any energy and/or radio output that we generate."

"What the hell are you talking about?"

"My father told me that the box opened and then closed again. It obviously has an automatic sensing device so that it won't accidentally damage itself. The part that concerned me was the fact that your watches stopped. He also said that he thinks there was a brown out."

"That would have been easy enough to check out. All we would have needed was to ask someone." Steve seemed surprised that no one had thought of this obviously simple answer to the question.

"It's not that simple, Steve. You were on a very tight schedule. You said so yourself. There would have been too much delay to hang around and hope that a brownout wouldn't make the news. If you had asked someone, you would have drawn attention to yourself. How would you know about a brown out in the middle of nowhere? Why risk exposure? This project is sensitive enough without inviting problems in through the front gate."

"You're right. I guess I'm not cut out to think deviously."

"That's a fine crack," snapped Johnny. At this point, he wasn't sure where the conversation was headed; he only knew that he'd been insulted. He continued in a harsh tone, "I have as much integrity as the next guy, and far more than most."

"No, no. I didn't mean it like that. It just came out wrong. I didn't mean to insult you. All I meant was even in this situation, when I know how I must think, I'm not able to. I envy your ability to think like a spy when you have to. It was meant as a compliment, not an insult." *What a touchy son-of-a-bitch.*

"I'm sorry. I understand. I'm edgy about this whole thing anyway. I just lost focus for a moment. No problems between us?" *You bastard.*

"None that I can see." *I'll have to watch myself every minute with him.*

"Thanks. We need to be a cohesive team. The last thing that we want is divisiveness over a simple misunderstanding. We won't discuss it anymore. The subject is closed and forgotten." *You'd stab me in back at the first chance, wouldn't you?*

"Look, Detroit is only forty more miles and it's just midafternoon. I don't mind telling you, this is scaring me silly. I can't wait to get there and actually see this in the flesh," added Johnny as he stared out of his window. *Scared and excited make interesting, yet strange bedfellows.*

"You're going to love it. It's the most magnificent thing you'll ever see. Especially when you consider that it's at least sixty-five million years old. I must confess; I was pretty scared the first time that I saw it. That anxiety goes away quickly. You get so caught up in it that you forget to be frightened."

"I hope so. My stomach is doing flip-flops right about now. Do you mind if I drive this last little bit? I could use the drive to distract me from thinking about the box." *Maybe I'm over reacting. He's probably just as nervous as I am.*

"Not at all; there's a stop coming up. We'll pull in to top off the gas and switch then." *I guess he's okay. He seems really nervous though. I may have misjudged him.*

Both vehicles pulled into the stop. While filling their tanks, they compared notes on their conversations. The Crenshaw's were impressed with some of the observations the boys had made. Johnny had already arranged for the copper mesh to be used as a shield device. They never really understood why he felt that it was needed. Now that they understood, they had a new respect for their son.

"I've been thinking," commented Johnny.

"About what," asked Ellen?

"My name."

"You have your father's name. What's wrong with that?"

"Nothing mom. It's just that when someone calls out Jonathan, both of us will answer. It's going to get confusing. Calling dad 'Dr. Crenshaw' is too formal."

"What are you diving at? I don't understand the point you're trying to make."

"I think I should be called "J.J."

"Where on earth did you come up with that?"

"Jonathan Junior… J.J."

"I think your father will be disappointed."

"No, he won't. He likes the idea, but wanted me to broach it with you."

"Double teaming me, is that it?"

"Mom, how could you think that?"

"I guess Johnny is out of the question?"

"You guessed right."

"Tell your father that you both win this time. I don't like J.J., but I'll let the others call you that. I'm going to call you Johnny anyway. You can protest all you want, but I'm your mother and that's my final word. We're finished here and we're heading out now. We'll see you shortly."

"Now I know why dad loves you so much." He grabbed her in his arms and kissed her on the forehead. "And I love you too." We'll be right behind you, depending on traffic.

CHAPTER FORTY-ONE

THEY ARRIVED AT THE WAREHOUSE around 4:00 PM. J.J. had called from the road verifying the security gate would be open. Once inside of the facility, they pulled along the left side of the building. Their cars, as well as the others that were already there, were more concealed from the road on this side of the building. There was plenty of security lighting and a guard patrolled every half-hour. They didn't want attention from the street and this parking provided a certain amount of anonymity. That was one of the reasons this location had been selected.

J.J.'s friends and colleagues came out to greet them. They were awaiting the arrival of the crate. The trucking company had called for directions to the site an hour earlier. All hoped the truck would have arrived by now.

Introductions were made all around. It felt more like a class reunion than a gathering of top specialists in their respective fields. They seemed very much at ease with one another. It was just as Steve and J.J. had been discussing in the car. The team should move and think as one, and if this spirit of camaraderie remained, they would accomplish a lot together.

"Let's get inside. I want to see the place. Seeing Jim, J. J. asked, "Are you finished installing the copper mesh?"

Jim was the electronics expert on the team. He understood the need for the mesh and the security and secrecy it would provide. Setting it up had its own set of problems, but it wasn't anything he couldn't handle. "Sure Jonathan. Do you think we've been sitting on our duffs hoping that it would install itself?" he quipped. "Let me show the progress."

A loner by nature, Jim kept to himself while he worked. The paradox came when he wasn't working. It seemed he had dual personalities. Jim was silent and reclusive while working, yet boisterous and gregarious the rest of the time. He often commented that no one seemed to *get him*. "When I work, I work. When I play, I play," was his favorite quote.

As the group entered the warehouse, J. J. was surprised that so much had been completed. He was very pleased with the progress. "When did you get here?" J. J. inquired. "This is just what we'd hoped for. Great job everyone. The only thing left is to seal the mesh when the crate arrives and is unpacked. One more thing now that I have you all together. As you may or may not know, my father's name is Jonathan. In an effort to cut down on confusion, I'm going by J.J. It's short for Jonathan Junior."

Gerard was a whiz at computers. He and J.J. had worked together for several years. They held each other in high regard. Unlike J.J., he was single and shy. There was a female interest in his life, but he moved carefully and logically, not unlike the programs he wrote. He was flattered that J.J. had thought of him for this secretive project. Like the others, he had no idea what he was getting himself involved with on this project. Additionally, a major project this sensitive usually required a myriad of security protocols. This project was on the honor system. It only mattered that J.J. was involved and needed his assistance.

"The sleeping quarters are upstairs in an office space. There are seven offices. The Drs. Crenshaw can have one of the two large offices. We can double any two of us in the other large office. The rest of us can each have small, but separate sleeping spaces. Do I have any volunteers to bunk together?" asked J. J.

"Where are the doctors? Didn't you say that you could find a couple of genetics people to come on short notice?" asked J.J. while looking around the warehouse.

"They're around here somewhere. They've spent a lot of time in the back, setting up a clean room. They're unhappy with the overall conditions, but they understand the situation. They seem to be coping nicely. You know, it probably wouldn't be a bad idea to have those two bunking together. If the work load requires it, they'd be together and it wouldn't disturb the rest of us in the wee hours with conversation and puttering around." Jim indicated

Turning to the sound of approaching footsteps, Jim smiled broadly. He waved an arm in the direction of the man arriving and said, "Well speak of the devil. Everyone, I would like you to meet our resident genetic biologist; Dick Graham." He turned to the group and asked if they would each introduce themselves.

"Where's Dave? Isn't he going to come out and join us?" asked Jim.

"Sure," replied Dick. "He's just finishing the calibrations on some portable testing equipment. He'll be along. . . and we don't putter around." He turned back to the group after shooting Jim a glare and continued with the introductions.

Dick was a little older than the others. He was in his mid to late thirties. His hair was thinning and he was getting a little gray at the temples. Baseball and basketball were the two sports he loved to play when he was younger, but now he was an avid golfer.

Both Dick and David had worked on another project together where they learned to assemble and install electronic and electrical equipment. This knowledge made them valuable to the project.

Ellen and Jonathan would address all of their questions as soon as Dave arrived. Gerard went to get Dave from his room. He was anxious to hear what the Crenshaw's had to say. "We're all waiting on you slow poke. How long does it take to calibrate a piece of test equipment anyway?"

"Just long enough to finish the job computer boy. What's all the rush?"

"The Crenshaw's are already here and J. J. and Steve arrived about ten minutes ago. The crate will be here any moment. We're about to get the low down on why we're here."

As they joined the group Gerard said, "Everyone, this is Dave. Dave, this is everyone. Now that introductions are finished, can we begin?"

"Thank you, Gerard. That was an eloquent introduction. Dave should feel honored that you put so much thought and effort into it," chuckled Jonathan.

"I can see that I'm going to like this guy already," laughed Gerard.

"Ellen and I have called this group together in secrecy because what we are going to do here for the next several of weeks will affect the course of mankind from this day forward. I am not saying this lightly. Steve has seen and experienced this artifact first hand. My son, Jonathan, excuse me J.J., has only seen photographs. Both were deeply moved by the experience.

"I won't bore you with the details of the discovery and what it took to get the project to this point. I only need your total cooperation and utter secrecy. We have feared for our very lives from the moment this artifact came into our possession. You are now involved, and as such are liable to suffer any consequences along with the four of us.

"We're trying to eliminate any threat to you by having you take vacations. No one knows where you are, or whom you are with. I must insist that if you must call your families or friends, please do so from pay phones. I also require that you make those calls as far from this warehouse as is possible. You must be a minimum of three miles from the warehouse. Also, rotate the locations. We don't need anyone getting a fix on us over a careless mistake as simple as a phone call. Do not divulge where you are or what you're doing to anyone. Limit the calls to less than three minutes. I have digital timers for each of you. Use them faithfully or we may all suffer consequences we aren't prepared to face. Am I clear on this point?"

There was an eerie hush throughout the warehouse as they all stood and stared. The entire group had a bewildered look on each of their faces. There were mumbled agreements from each member, as they whispered among themselves.

"We are a brotherhood of sorts," continued Jonathan. "This will bond us for the rest of our lives. I'm not going to tell you anything about the crate until it gets here. I don't want any questions until then. I will say this; be prepared to have your lives changed. Profound is the best word I can find to describe your pending experience. Thank you. Oh yes, there's one more thing before we begin. I know it's a lot to ask that you may be putting your life in danger for something totally unknown. If any of you have any misgivings, any second thoughts, leave now before we reveal what it is that we've discovered. You are committing to the long haul if you remain."

Jonathan had no sooner finished, when the truck arrived. The crate was marked all over with stencils that read *Machinery*. The driver wheeled it around in the parking lot and backed in through the large overhead door. He backed down the center of the framework and stopped where he was told. Hoisting the crate off the flatbed went smoothly. All in all, it went quickly and efficiently.

Ellen, Jonathan, J.J. and Steve were the only people the driver had seen. The rest disappeared upstairs by Jonathan's orders. They didn't wish to have them seen by the driver. Jonathan didn't want any of these men to be associated with the four of them. Eliminating any connection to Jonathan and the others helped eliminate any threat to the four newest team members.

The rest of the group watched through the office windows while Jonathan brought the overhead crane in to position. J.J. and Steve helped put the heavy-duty slings around the crate. They had it up off of the trailer in no time flat. The truck driver got a signature from Ellen on his delivery receipt and drove off. She had taken the time to create a false name and used it to sign the receipt. He didn't look around the warehouse, or even look at her signature. They were relieved that he took no notice of the place or the people. It was just one more delivery in a lifetime of deliveries for him.

When the overhead door was finally closed, the others came back down. They all walked around the large crate and pondered as to the secret hidden inside. They knew the stenciled Machinery labels were false, but what was inside? No one spoke at all.

Jonathan began giving orders. "That went well. No problems at all. Jim, you can get the mesh closed and the top put on the framework once we remove the crate. Everyone else, let's get this crate opened up."

"You guys get the tools," said Jim. "I need to have you all in here before I can seal the top of this mesh. I'll contrive a makeshift door once the crate material has been removed from the area."

Dave and Gerard went for the wrecking bars and hammers provided by the site manager. They brought back two bars and three claw hammers. The tools were handed out and the work was begun.

"Start at the top," said Jonathan. "You remember how we sealed it don't you Steve?"

"Yes, I do," he answered. "I also thought that we should keep the pieces intact for future transport."

The team had the crate apart in no time. With the crate removed, the whole group moved closer to the box. There before them, stood the box in all its glory. They all just looked at it. No one was able to speak. A couple ventured a touch or two, but overall, they were at a loss for words. Ellen laughed quietly.

"Gentlemen, please. This doesn't bite. This is the artifact that we want you to investigate. It was removed from sixty-five million-year-old sedimentary deposits. To be more precise, it was removed from a previously unknown cave structure in a limestone outcropping. We speculate that even though fossil remains indicate that the area has proven to be mainly deltaic, the limestone outcropping was the predominant feature on the landscape."

"What? How? I don't understand."

"That was insightful Jim. Any other one-word questions?" asked Dick. "Also, why am I here? This is a nice metal box and all, but I'm a geneticist. This doesn't make any sense to me."

"It will very shortly," said Steve. "First, we need to open the skylights. We will need to let as much sunlight in here as possibly. Jim, can we open the skylights and not lose any of the security provided by the mesh?"

"No problems I can foresee. Is this thing going to do anything right now?"

"No. It will need to be fully charged before we can have access to all of its capabilities. We suspect that it's solar powered. There was a dim amount of light that filtered into the cave. The top of the box had been rinsed clean by a washout from a storm. It exposed the box to the small amount of indirect sunlight that came in through the crevasse at the top of the cave. It was mostly reflected light. There was no other obvious explanation for the electrical power to function after millions of years."

"Electrical?" asked a stunned Jim.

"It was warm to the touch when Ellen first found it. When it did do some of its stuff, there was the definite sound of electronic equipment. Our watches stopped and we think that we caused a brown out in the small community that was near the dig site."

"Do you think that you compromised the find?"

"We think that we camouflaged the crate and its subsequent move by timing it with a major fossil move from another site. No one at the other site was aware of this and the Crenshaw's used two different trucking companies. They had the box delivered to another location and then marked it as equipment. It was picked up by a machinery hauler and delivered here. End of story," said Steve.

"I wasn't told about the power thing. I'm not sure that this mesh will provide enough protection?" said Jim.

"Can you boost output at all?" asked Jonathan.

"With a little more of my equipment, I could."

"What do you need, and how much does it cost?"

"It won't cost anything. I live an hour from here. I can go home and get what I need from my workshop. I've got stuff there that would, well let's just say that I've got stuff. You guys can't be held accountable for what you don't know. It's a case of plausible deniability." Surprise and curiosity filled the faces of his fellow team members.

"I thought you were on vacation," asked Ellen.

"I live alone and I'm a freelance contractor. I'm gone a lot and keep a very erratic schedule. The neighbors won't see any changes in my life style. I don't answer to anyone. I'm clean."

"Well that's good news anyway," said J.J. "I thought you were engaged and living with someone."

"I was on both counts. She didn't like my schedule and wanted me to get a nine to five. That's not my style. I like my toys and my free time. We split about two months ago. I gave her a bunch of stuff that wasn't hers so she'd never come back. Then I changed the locks and my phone number. That's ancient history now. I need to get going if this project is going to get off the ground."

Jim left after making a list of the equipment and parts he'd need to increase the output strength of the shield. They would be able to open the box tomorrow. There was a lot of grumbling about that.

"I propose that we leave the skylights open tonight. We've got a full moon coming. This thing has already proven to be an extremely active collector. Perhaps it will even collect the reflected sunlight from a full moon. It couldn't hurt to try."

"That's a good idea Steve. It will be one more bit of data to add to our growing list of known characteristics. It will be an interesting experiment. Does anyone have any objections?"

"What do you think J.J.?" asked Gerard. "When we studied together, we had a brief sojourn into electronics. I don't remember any power field or power output generated by the charging process."

"Nothing I can recall. This is unknown technology though. Physical laws should still remain."

Gerard continued, "We can pretty much claim that physical laws are universal. I think it's safe. Besides, this is unknown, uncharted territory. What would Jim's assurance prove if it did send out a signal or whatever? This is the best opportunity to get as much charge on it as we can in a short time.

"There's another viewpoint, you've theorized that it's solar powered. What if it's something else altogether? What harm can be done by opening the skylights. Consider also, the mesh is in place and functioning. We're not making it do its tricks; we're just letting it charge."

Jonathan went over and opened the skylights. The late afternoon light came streaming in through the windows. The room got significantly brighter. He was pleased with the position of the skylights. They would be able to keep the windows open almost all of the time and collect half of the day's direct sunlight.

"Does anybody know how long it takes to bring this thing to full charge?" asked Dave. "I know that you only speculate on the solar capabilities, but from what you've said, I'm inclined to agree. I speculate that with a collector that sensitive it wouldn't take much time at all. Given the circumstances, maybe one or two days to full charge."

Ellen answered the question. "We've never had it in direct light before now. It was crated before we left the cave. The indirect lighting of the cave was very dim and as far as we can tell, the only exposure to the sunlight."

All eyes turned from Ellen to the box. Its' highly polished surface glowed with an intensity. It was an optical illusion created by the highly polished surfaces of the box. Everyone stared for a moment, transfixed by the otherworldly aura that clung to the box.

Breaking the spell, Ellen continued, "I would not have thought that it would be possible to harvest light at that low intensity. This technology is amazing if it really is solar in nature. I only wish that we could've had more answers before we arrived."

"We all understand. The conditions in the field must have been terrible. You had no research facilities or equipment of any kind," said Dick. His tone was almost sympathetic and clearly clinical. This must be his first in field experience. It would explain his carping about the tough situation they were in, here at the warehouse. Well to each his own. Ellen and Jonathan thought this was the equivalent of a five-star hotel when compared to the living out of a tent in the Bad Lands of the Dakota's.

"Let me interrupt," began Steve. "We were digging for fossils out there, not searching for what we suspect to be prehistoric technology. There would have been no way to prepare for this. Now that we have this one, perhaps others will be uncovered. Until that point, you can't haul entire laboratories into the field just to turn over some dirt."

"Point well taken, Steve. I've had everything at my fingertips for so long, that I forget how it really gets started. You are the vanguard of the researcher. You collect; we analyze and expand from there. Not everyone can have access to the types of equipment that I have. I take these tools for granted. I'm sorry. What you've accomplished with nothing at your disposal was remarkable."

"That was very eloquent, Dick. Now can we get back to some meaningful questions?"

"Sure, Dave. Ask away. The floor is yours."

"Thank you." Dave gave a polite nod of acknowledgement and turned to Ellen.

"Ellen, you commented earlier that you heard the sound of electrical and or electronic equipment. Can you elaborate?"

"I think that any of the three of us could assist you on this. It was your common computer type noises. You know the sounds that they make when they're processing information. The other sounds are not unlike electric machinery that you hear. You know, the background sounds that you take for granted every day. The one's that you hear but don't listen to, those high-pitched, low volume sounds that indicate electrical activity and gears moving behind the scenes somewhere. I hope that I'm not being too simplistic."

"Not at all, Ellen. That's the answer that I had expected. Do either of you have anything that you'd like to add?" he asked as he turned to face Jonathan and Steve.

"Not really," said Steve. "I'm not versed in your terminology. I can't describe the noises in any different terms than Ellen used. Remember that the box was on the floor of the cave. Some of the noises were generated from the box scraping along the limestone floor"

"Fair enough, anyway, it's enough for me to go on. This appears to be a very intricate piece of something. You told Gerard that there are a series of intricate lines tracing the walls on the inside chamber. Didn't you also mention that these lines are really seams or joints? That the machining is so precise that the joining of two pieces of metal appears as an etched line on the surface of the metal rather than a seam?"

Steve responded with a head nod. "That's exactly what I'm saying. Once we've got more security, you'll be able to see it firsthand. I couldn't believe my eyes either. You'll have to trust me on this one. What I've stated is nothing but the unvarnished truth."

"That's a pretty big leap in manufacturing technology. Even our best laser technology is hard pressed to accomplish a design like that. Even at that, it's on a small scale. If what you say is true – and I don't contest your veracity – this whole box could open out like a big flower, for lack of a better example."

"That's what I'm trying to impress on all of you. We don't know how far this will open up. All we know is that the length of the box opens down the middle and is separated from what appears to be the control room and the chamber at this end." Steve waved his arm behind him to indicate which end held the doorway to the room. "There will be a bit of dust and debris in there from where the box banged against the roof and sides of the cave. Other than that, you'll be on your own if you want more answers about this thing. That's the best any of us can offer at this time." Steve leaned back in his chair and placed his hands on the edge of the table as if he were preparing to stand. It was clear to everyone that he was finished.

"I know that I can speak for everyone here," continued Dave, "when I say that we understand the limitations you experienced in the field. I can also say, without impunity, that we are anxious as hell to get inside of this thing. I don't mean to press any of you for answers that you can't provide. My, our hope is that when you tell us about your experiences, you might pass along some valuable bit of information that doesn't seem important to you, but is extremely valuable to one of us."

"We know that," said Jonathan in response. "That's why we keep repeating the story to you. The telling and re-telling of it might jog a small memory for us. We know that your questions will be answered very soon. It's been terrible for us too. We are dying to get back inside.

"Poor Steve here was about to explode last week," laughed Jonathan. "I think that this has been a growing experience for him. It pains me to sit here and regale you with tales that can easily be resolved by simply opening the door to the box. Jim should be back by nightfall, or shortly thereafter. By morning, the security should in place and we can all go in and you can feast your eyes to your hearts content.

"Please be patient, that's all I ask. You have obviously not gotten any new insights into the operation of the box by the questions you keep repeating. You can only come at a problem from so many angles before you have to stop. This is the time to stop."

"But we don't have to like it," commented Gerard. He was merely voicing his frustration.

Jonathan understood only too well and chose to ignore his comment. Continuing, he said, "It's settled then. Let's order some food. I'm getting hungry."

Before anyone could comment, he left the table and went up to his room with Ellen following closely behind.

Watching the two of them ascending the stairs, David said, "Well it looks like the meeting is over. As much as I don't like it, he's right. We can't continue beating a dead horse." After a brief pause, he continued, "Food is a good idea. I wasn't hungry until he mentioned it. What are our options?"

After a brief conversation the group decided to go with Wendy's. They asked J.J. to find out what his parents wanted before they ordered. This would quickly become the pattern. J.J. was the *go-to* person when everyone was hungry.

CHAPTER FORTY-TWO

CAPTAIN HARRINGTON BEGAN TO ASSEMBLE his team. The meeting with Colonel Briggs had gone as expected. The trail was not fresh, but it was only a few days old. His men could track and locate anyone or anything in the world.

Downloading the positioning data from the satellite was an easy task. Corporal Jensen had provided the essential data. His quick response enabled him to mark the time of the event within three seconds of its actual occurrence. After a few minutes of searching, they were able to review and calculate the exact time of the event.

The scan parameters covered a broad area because the pinpoint settings were not activated. It had been a general scan designed to test and keep the satellite systems functional and prepared for more precise work when needed.

The information came up as South Dakota, near the Hell Creek formation. The search area in question would be no more than fifty square miles. It was a small geographic sample from space, but a lot of acreage on the ground. There was nothing out there but the Indian Reservation and a few small towns. Hill City was closest to the suspect area. They had more confined parameters to work with, but they wanted a broader sweep of the area before they closed the ring tighter.

More precise interpretation of the readings had brought the search grid to a more manageable five square miles. This refined grid was established through computer generated estimates of the time elapsed from the moment the satellite transferred from one function to the next and then back again.

Ninety-one hours had now elapsed from the initial report to full response readiness. The team was now ready to roll at a moment's notice, only awaiting their deployment orders.

"Sergeant Franks reporting for duty sir." His salute was crisp and experienced. He stood, at attention, straight and tall from a lifetime of practice.

Returning the salute, Captain Harrington answered, "At ease Sergeant." Looking up from the table, he motioned for the Sergeant to come around to the other side and join him. "This is the grid were the search will begin Sergeant. We will concentrate your team in Hill City and spread out from there. This is to be an ordinary exercise. There will be a lot of other soldiers out there on maneuvers. They are the decoys. Be discrete. We need information. I need your special talents on this.

"The federal boys will be working in conjunction with this operation. There was something about that power surge that attracted their attention. This is our operation though. Work with them, but don't let them ride roughshod over you. We will give them total cooperation when we're ordered to do so. Until you receive orders to the contrary, YOU are in charge out there," he said emphatically. "I expect daily reports. I will accept nothing short of perfection. Have I made myself clear?"

"Sir, yes sir." Sergeant Franks resumed both the physical and mental posture of preparedness.

"Thank you, Sergeant. I knew you from your records that were the man for the job. I want you to employ your special talents for ferreting out any and all information. Just don't let it get out of hand or too expensive. See the paymaster and get the money you'll need. Here's your authorization. This has been cleared to the highest levels Sergeant." Saluting once again he said, "Dismissed."

Just as the Sergeant was leaving the room, the Captain said, "Sergeant, prepare the men to move out. We get under way at 0900 hours. Carry on Sergeant."

"Sir, yes sir," was the response. The Captain knew that he could count on a career man like Sergeant Franks. He always obeyed orders and was dependable. Besides, he had special talents, like the old-time cops who never broke the rules, but knew how to bend them, but not too severely. Not like the watered-down version of the underfunded army that was currently in place.

Harrington hated politicians and their continuing interference in military matters. What made these pompous, self-righteous blowhards think that they could protect the country by reducing funding and equipment escaped him? Peace was not a period of time without any conflict. Peace was a state of preparedness, a defensive posture at all times. Those who looked carefully would see the futility of an attack and not attempt any aggression. Since Reagan left office, that bit of wisdom got lost in the shuffle somewhere.

There were members of congress that had never served and despised those who did. That doesn't make for a good relationship. They willfully choose to ignore that peace is the military's job. For the politician, the military is just a poker chip to be won or lost at any time without regard for the consequences.

Someday there would be a day of reckoning and it would be coming soon. Reports of anti-American activity were on the rise and the previous Commander-In Chief, for all his posturing and photo-ops, clearly respected the military. Harrington longed for a return to the days when being a protector of the country's freedom was held in respect.

"Where and when had the country gone wrong?" he mumbled softly. There were tools in Franks' collection of talents that the Captain didn't want to hear or know about. Results were Harrington's only interest.

Men like Franks gave him comfort. Franks was like a ferret. He had a natural curiosity and a tenacious way of grabbing onto something and never letting go until it was resolved. Years of experience in Special Forces had provided him with a mental toughness and the ability to think outside the box. Every time he was in the field, he called on his experience to outmaneuver or overcome any barrier.

After assembling the team in their barracks, Franks paced in front of them. This was an inspection and they each knew his expectations. They presented an impenetrable wall when in the field. It was what Franks depended on. He'd never lost one of his own for almost fifteen years. Reputation and dedication went far in the Special Forces.

"Men," he finally said. "We don't know what we're facing out there. This is in the middle of nowhere and there should have never been anything unusual happening. What we have is an accidental trace of an unknown power source from an area that has no discernable power stations or equipment of the magnitude to generate the signature detected. We need to be on constant alert. Any questions?"

One of the soldiers stepped forward and with a crisp salute, eyes forward, he asked, "Sir, what type of signal will we be looking for sir?"

"Unknown soldier. The signal was accidentally discovered on a routine fly over of the area during a diagnostic test. There are, however, recent satellite images of the area. They are being analyzed now. We don't have any intel yet, but that will be updated as we proceed. The most important thing right now is to get out into the field and start collecting raw data."

"Sir, yes sir," answered the soldier as he stepped back in formation.

"We leave at 0900 hours. Dismissed."

Franks went back to his office to finalize his preparations. There must be nothing left to chance. Glancing at his watch, he noted that it was almost 0800. The paymaster would have been contacted by now.

Pulling a metal security box from his footlocker, Franks tucked it under his left arm as he closed his footlocker. He locked it and left to see the paymaster. Since his meeting with the Captain at 0700, he'd been making calculations concerning the amount of cash that he'd require. Five thousand should cover the first two weeks.

Knocking on the paymaster's door Franks entered his office. "Did Captain Harrington call you yet George?"

"Almost forty minutes ago. I thought you got lost."

"Please."

"Yeah, yeah. I know you better than that, but I've been here cooling my heels while you're up to who knows what."

"You know me George; I'm off to save the world once again."

"Spare me the bullshit. He also serves who. . ."

"Yeah, I know. George, I'm gonna need at least five thousand for the next couple of weeks. I have the wire vouchers right here, patting his breast pocket. Withdrawing them, he laid them on George's desk. As you can see, they're all signed and ready."

"Jesus, Roy. He gave you five vouchers. How long you gonna be out this time?"

"George, you know better than that. I only get to go on the real sensitive stuff. There's never any taking about it, before or after. You know the routine."

"Don't get your back up. I'm just making conversation Roy. Hold on while I get the other box. You act like I don't know how to keep a secret and I'm responsible for keeping two different cash boxes and reporting only one."

"George, if I break a habit only once, I've compromised my entire training and maybe my life. I kinda like being alive. It makes me feel sort of good."

"That goes for the both of us. Here's your money. Count it and sign here. I have my own habits to look after."

Roy Franks stared at his friend and took the cash from the desk. Slowly he separated the bills into piles based on their denomination. When he finished, he counted each pile and wrote down the total. Methodically he went through the process until everything had been counted and written down in George's dispersal log. Signing the log, he placed the money in his own cash box and locked it.

The only way anyone could ever get the key from around his neck was to kill him. There was nobody he could imagine that knew enough to kill him. There was a time seven years back that he had to kill a man and the only weapons he had was a child's stuffed doll and his bare hands.

He grabbed the toy and threw it in to the side instead of at his opponent. The unexpected ploy distracted the man for a split second. That was more than enough time for Franks to push the man's nose into his face and then snap his neck.

Such were the skills and experience that, Roy Franks and the other members of his team, could call upon at a moment's notice.

Franks returned to his office and concluded his preparations. He grabbed his duffle and joined his team at 0900 hours. They had their own trucks and no one questioned it. The Special Ops people always had their own vehicles. The caravan departed exactly on schedule and the team settled in for the long drive. They would travel for two days before they reached their destination.

His team sat in the back of the transport while he sat in the cab. This would be his time to work out alternate plans, running various scenarios through his head. He liked having contingency plans. Even though no one knew what to expect, he wanted to address situations ranging from benign to an outright terrorist threat.

In this state, he was completely consumed by his task. Pressing deeply into the seat back, he let his mind slip into a mode where he shut out the outside world.

CHAPTER FORTY-THREE

"I'M BACK," JIM ANNOUNCED AS he entered the warehouse.

"We thought that you'd return last night. What happened?" asked Ellen.

"I considered it. Once I got the equipment and tools I needed, the clock was running down. Grabbing equipment and rushing out of the house like that was out the ordinary for me. I decided to spend the night in my own bed to keep up appearances. Besides, I would have returned so late, there would have been nothing I could accomplish anyway."

"You're back and that's all that counts," said Jonathan.

"Thank you, Dr. Crenshaw. Let me pull the car in and we can get it unloaded. J.J. can you give me a hand?"

"Sure Jim. I'll get the overhead door while you swing around."

Following Jim's instructions on handling some of the equipment; the car was unloaded quickly. Almost everything was in its own insulated carrier. The main concern was not to drop anything. Even inside their carriers, some of the equipment could be knocked out of calibration is dropped.

Normally Jim worked alone, but this task was large and the time constraints forced him to seek assistance. The team worked through the early evening to assist with the set up and installation of the new equipment. Each member was given detailed installation diagrams while Jim supervised the operation, demonstrating where necessary and doing the work himself on some of the more intricate connections.

Once everyone had finished their assigned tasks Jim took over. The individual pieces had to be tested and inspected and any minor problems had to be eliminated. He worked like a demon possessed. Much of his time was spent scribbling notes on his pad and checking meter readings.

By nine-thirty he had checked each of the installed components and was ready to calibrate the entire system. The system was as ready as it was going to get. Now it was time for the small incremental adjustments that would bring the entire system on line and fully functional.

"Do you think that we'll be able to get inside tonight?" asked Dave.

"That's a valid question," interjected Dick, clearly excited and very hopeful. "I want to see just why I'm here."

"I'm about to run my first test," said Jim. "I can tell you in about ten more minutes. Can you hold on that long?" He'd fallen into a light banter with everyone as the evening wore on and he was clearly amused at their collective anxiety. It would take as long as it took.

"I suppose if we have to wait, we can manage ten more minutes," said David, crestfallen and pouting like a little boy.

"Hand me that meter Dick," Jim said as he extended his hand. "Thanks," was all he replied after feeling the meter touch his hand.

Hooking a very large and complicated looking gadget to the power leads from the mesh; Jim took out his note book and started to write in his own form of electronic shorthand. He took a calculator from his shirt pocket and keyed in some entries. Shaking his head and looking disgusted, he moved to another part of the mesh. He re-hooked the meter and made more entries.

The rest of the group kept their distance as he worked. They appeared to be a massive, pulsating, human blob; they were so closely huddled together.

"I would prefer that you hung all over me rather than just stand there looming on the fringe," he said without turning around. His irritation was evident in his voice. "Move in closer or get out of here for a long walk or something." Looking over his shoulder at the huddled group, he continued in an obviously agitated state, "Well don't just stand there, do something. Make a decision and follow it. I gave you two clear options. Do that one favor for me please." He snapped back around to refocus on his work. He slammed his notebook onto a table and the resonating crack startled everyone.

After overcoming his frustration, he turned to his work. At his back, he could hear their apologies and movement. At least they'd finally received the message.

"Sorry, Jim," said the collective voice as they dispersed. A couple went upstairs, others started preparing questions for their entry into the box. The rest spent time checking various pieces of equipment or notebooks. All were well back from Jim, but still maintaining discrete observation points.

Jim went completely around the mesh, testing each section as he went. He was shaking his head in a definitely displeased fashion. The readings were not at the level he'd expected. Surely, he'd missed something small in one of his calculations. With a bit of luck, there would be only minor adjustments to re-calibrate the field and increase its protective strength.

Watching from their new, less obtrusive, vantage points; there was a collective sinking of hearts. Hopes had been up for so long. The work had gone quickly and Jim's tests proved his calculations to be accurate.

"The mesh will work just fine Jim finally said. I'm not happy with some of these readings. They are only slightly more than adequate; I was hoping for better initial results. I'll be re-adjusting a couple of settings. It should only be another half an hour before I'm finished."

"Can we open the box now?" Dick cautiously asked.

"Hold on. You're way too anxious. I still need to take a few readings from the box. Jonathan, organize the lumber to act as a barrier." He pointed to where they crate was being stored. "Get it set up next to the box. I want this to open and close quickly. How long did you say the box opened before?"

"About three or four seconds from completely sealed to open and back sealed again. No more than that."

"Thank you. Can you tell me how far the cave walls were from the edge of the box?"

"I can answer that Jim. It was almost two feet at the widest gap and nine to twelve inches near the upper corners," said Steve. "It varied down the length of the box. The automatic closure device must be very sensitive, because the marks on the wall were mostly from displaced loose soil. There were no impact marks left on the limestone itself, and no marks that we could find on the box."

"That's very good news. It should make the job that much easier. I need someone to set up a lumber frame about twelve inches from the box. Form it so that it's rigid. I don't want the box to just push past it."

"I know exactly what you mean Jim. I've got an idea that should work," said Jonathan as he left the warehouse.

Jonathan returned very excited. "I need some help back here. There's plenty of structural iron and black pipe along backside of the building. It's in the back alleyway, out of sight. We can build a framework out of that. When the box opens, if it exerts too much pressure the steel frame won't break like a wood frame."

"That's perfect," replied Jim.

Jonathan called across the warehouse when he spotted Steve and David. "We need every one's help. The warehouse was alive with activity. We need to bring in some of the piping I found out back. I'll show you what we need." Ellen surprised several of them when she grabbed several sections of pipe and dragged them inside by herself.

"Damn J.J., your mother's pretty strong," whispered Gerard so nobody else could hear. "One tough woman if you ask me," he quickly added.

J.J. was just as surprised as Gerard. She wasn't a bad looking woman, but you would never suspect a teacher of her age to possess that much strength. J.J. thought of all his older colleagues and how out of shape they were. His mother could take any of them in a fight. Laughing at the thought, he quickly looked around, embarrassed by his laughter.

The frame went up quickly. It was designed to wrap around the entire box. The three-square sections went over and under the box and tied together at the top and bottom corners. It was solidly built. They all took turns trying to wrench it loose and knock it over. Even when they attacked it as a group, they couldn't get it to move.

"Well, I'm satisfied," reported Jim after he'd observed their destructive effort. "Can someone open this thing up so that I can take some readings? We need to get this show on the road."

Jim had barely spoken the words when Steve was at the lock and keying in the sequence. When the door opened in its silent fashion; Steve went inside.

"Hey," shouted David, "Look at that. Steve's inside the box."

There was a flurry of motion as they all tried to poke their heads through the door at the same time. The traffic jam would have made a New Yorker proud.

"Settle down everyone," boomed Jonathan's voice. "You'll all have a turn to see inside. Let Steve do his job so we can open this up and we can all see inside. Agreed?"

Sheepishly, they all agreed, but were reluctant to give up the position they'd claimed in the queue. Eventually they all backed away as Jonathan stood by glowering at them. Smiling now that they had all moved back far enough, he called to Steve, "Go ahead and open her up. It's all clear out here."

Within a few seconds the whole box split from end to end, excluding the portion that held the control room and the chamber. A collective gasp filled the room and then there was complete and utter silence as they all stood in awe of the technological marvel that began to reveal itself.

Jim's meters went crazy. He had prepared his equipment against the power surge that had stopped every one's watches. Early in their conversations, he had speculated that it was a compressed wave pattern that would actually look like a wave and a half on the oscilloscope. He had also connected the mesh to equipment that would dampen the field effect created by such an output. Nothing outside of the warehouse should be affected by this experiment.

"Damn," was the only word he said. Jim sat watching his meters and gauges. He was writing frantically. Some of the equipment was capable of recording its own findings, other pieces had to be monitored and entries had to be done by hand.

Aside from Jonathan and Ellen, the rest of the group just stood and watched as the box opened and closed in two to four seconds. The frame had held. The event lasted long enough for Jim to get some valuable readings. He had worked with this equipment long enough to be able to memorize a reading at a glance. He was finishing up when the group regained its senses.

"Holy cow!" said Dave. "That was wild. What's the prognosis Jim? Do we go in or not?"

"We can only open the door into the ante chamber, just as you see it now. This thing is generating huge amounts of signals. It doesn't appear to be a signal beacon though, which is good news. It seems to be a result of its own operation. You might say electronic noise. I have to analyze these readings. I won't allow anything else until then. If you truly wish to keep this a secret, you'll comply." He grabbed up all of his papers and went to his room.

"I want to see the inside," said Dave. "May I go in?"

Jonathan knew that all of them wanted the same thing – getting inside the box. He organized a list of who would enter first. Dave and Dick were first on the list for no other reason than they needed to be reassured that they were here for a purpose.

"Dick and David, you two go first. You were curious as to the reasons behind our including you on this little adventure, once inside you'll see exactly why." Escorting them forward; they were somewhat reluctant to charge right in now that they could. Seeing the raptor should create that sense of need. He cleared a path for anyone who might need to exit quickly.

Steve poked his head out of the door. "Is anybody going to join me or should I just close this up?"

At that urging, the pair of geneticists stepped forward. They moved quietly, but tentatively through the door.

Steve's lantern illuminated the room completely. "It'll take a second to adjust to the brightness of the light. The polished interior reflected the lantern light to such an intensity that at first glance it appeared to be too bright. There's nothing on the floor so you can keep moving forward," assured Steve as they acclimated to their surroundings.

Their eyes quickly adjusted to the artificially harsh glare of the lantern light. Then they saw it. The image was fierce and noble, all in the same frame of reference. The raptor stared out through the glass as if it could see them. Its eyes seemed to pierce through them. They felt as if they were being sized up as a meal. The effect was extremely unsettling. They stared in awed silence. Besides the Crenshaw's and Steve, no other human had ever seen a dinosaur. And as part of the team, they were the first. Finally, they looked at each other and then at Steve.

Steve had a knowing, somewhat smug, grin on his face. He knew how they felt and he was happy to see their discomfort. It made him feel normal. Up to now, he felt as if he were the only person that could not deal with this whole thing. Ellen and Jonathan seemed to be taking it in stride.

Dick broke the trance by stepping forward. He touched the glass. He imagined that he could actually touch the dinosaur. "What do you make of this Steve?"

"We don't think that it's a ritual burial. It has no indication of a religious burial either. We can't seem to agree on a purpose for it. Here it is, and now we have a chance to study a real dinosaur, firsthand. That's really all we know. I don't wish to appear blasé about the whole thing, but until we get deeper into our research, who can tell?"

"We're not prepared for this," said Dave. "We don't have the facilities to deal with the magnitude of what we're facing. Our little clean room at the end of the building can't handle research like this."

"Are you certain, or are you just longing for the sanctuary of a pristine, sterile lab?" questioned Steve. "You'll have to make do with very little until better facilities can be arranged."

"We'll have to get back with you on this. Give us some time to rethink our room. Let us try to reset the room to see if it can be brought up to speed. We can't be sure until then. This is too big to treat in a cavalier manner."

"I assure you that we are not treating this in a cavalier manner. We're serious about the research that has to be done. Remember the danger that we face from both industrial concerns and more importantly, government agencies. We need to improvise and modify anything that we can to achieve our goal. If you need any special equipment, we'll try to get it. If it's too sensitive or would raise eyebrows when requested, we're going to have to do without it. We need to remain unnoticed. Our project needs to maintain total secrecy."

"We understand Steve. We came because J.J. asked us to be here. I won't, we won't, do anything to jeopardize this project. You, however, have no inkling as to the delicacy of what we're facing. By its very nature, this shouldn't exist."

"Well here it is Dick," gesturing towards to the cylinder. "We have to deal with real time here and now. There won't be any 'what ifs' or 'should have done' on this project."

David left for the clean room while Dick continued to engage Steve in conversation. From his perspective, talking about it wasn't going to get the work done. He wanted to start rearranging the equipment and making notes on necessary changes. The equipment that was in place would have to be made to work. There would be no chance of getting anything more sophisticated in here. He paused for a moment as he made mental notes about which of his friends had access to what equipment. Perhaps he could swing a deal, if he could invite a new member onto the team. That bridge should only be crossed if this equipment could not do the job.

"Look Steve, I understand all of that. I only want to be extra cautious because of our equipment handicap. Is there an access to the interior of the cryogenics chamber?" questioned Dick.

"We don't know. The last thing that we wanted was to contaminate this specimen out in the field. There would have been no way to undo any damage. We would have lost the most significant find in the history of mankind. We need to get into the real guts of this thing, this machine. The chamber is obviously computer controlled. We were fortunate in that the box was able to start a recharge sequence before we were able to access the interior. We might have lost everything by opening this up by force. There may be a failsafe, we just don't know yet."

"I'm deathly afraid that we'll contaminate it here. We still don't have the proper facilities to repair anything that we do wrong. Perhaps you'll be able to establish a link into its computer systems. At least that might provide us with a road map. I guess we'll just have to wait until J.J. and Gerard do their thing."

"That could take quite a while. We're still in the infancy of our discoveries when it comes to our big beauty." Steve patted the box lovingly. "We just want to resolve a few language barriers and then try to find out as many secrets as we can. Once we have enough information, that we can share internationally, we feel that we'll be out of harm's way. That's the plan anyway."

"You can count on me to contribute all that I can, Steve. I'm in this for the long haul. There is no way that I'm going to let someone else dissect that little sweetie behind the glass. She's mine. That's my final word on it."

"That's good to know. I have a feeling that everyone who comes in contact with this will instantly feel the same way. It happened that way for me."

"Well I need to find out what Dave's up to. He's probably got the whole lab destroyed by now. You can dress them up but you can't take them out," he quipped.

They both laughed as they exited the box. Steve went back to the main group and Dick headed for the back of the building to join Dave. He could hear the unmistakable sounds of equipment being dismantled. He quickened his pace. Maybe he could get there before it was too late.

CHAPTER FORTY-FOUR

"CAPTAIN HARRINGTON, THIS IS FRANKS. I was sitting at a local diner pretending to be passing the day. I was able to ascertain that there had been a team of college students out here on a fossil dig not too far out of town. I commented on how exciting that it would be to see that. I found out that they were active at the time of the anomaly and it's within the target area. It was a University sponsored thing. Locals say that they come out here every year. A couple of paleontologists from the college manage the thing. They're the same ones every year. This was a twenty-year anniversary of sorts.

"I can't make any connection between the paleontologists and the readings, but it was the only thing that was going on at the time. As I said, the location fits the satellite profile, almost in the middle of the co-ordinates. I asked for directions. The guy said he'd be happy to take me. I declined. I told him that I had to leave, but would check back before I left the area. He's ex-army, he understood. The feds are arriving in about two hours. There is nothing more to report at this time, sir."

"Keep me posted with anything new. This information is ours until I tell you otherwise. That's an order. Call any time of the day or night if you come across anything that's significant. Good-bye."

The connection went dead. The Captain expected nothing short of perfection. Sergeant Franks was prepared to deliver nothing less.

Unless the FBI took complete control of the operation, no one could stop Franks from carrying out his orders. Even then, he had ways of circumventing things. He had developed certain contacts and skills over the years. They always proved helpful.

The Sergeant got into his jeep and went to the edge of town. He pulled the jeep to the side of the road and then took the directions from his shirt pocket and read them carefully before heading down the road. He made a left turn at the fork, and drove the five winding miles the dig site.

There was plenty of evidence of activity there. They would have to go over this place with a fine-tooth comb. They were trying to find a needle in a haystack the size of Northwestern South Dakota. He noted all of the tire tracks. There had been some large tractor-trailers here. They could have been picking up fossils or they could have been delivering sophisticated equipment, an experiment of some sort. There was so much work yet to be done.

Franks removed the digital camera from its case and scouted the area on foot, recording the tire tracks and the footprints. The location of the main campsite was obvious. He found a few discarded marker flags and placed them at each tent location before he snapped the picture. He then re-used the flags in each new photograph to mark either the placement of or distance to the subject matter. Each photograph was recorded in his log with notes pertaining to the photo.

The Sergeant returned to his jeep when he had concluded his initial survey. He radioed for some equipment to be brought out to the dig site. Franks wanted to know what was going on out here. They would start from here and use this as a base of operations. Whatever had been going on here, he would find out.

He then headed back into town to wait for the feds. They would be valuable at tracing phone records. There were no secrets that could be kept from them. Even if this were an innocent dig site, he would at least be able to develop a sense of what happened here last week. He could use the phone records to establish a pattern of activity for anyone in the area. That was what the FBI could do best. The Army had the specialized equipment on hand and could put it at their disposal. It would forge a good working bond between them.

Franks would still be able to maintain the control of the operation and have the FBI do some of the work that he would have had to do illegally. It was perfect. Running scenarios over in his head, he started to develop a cover story. Of course, he was going to embellish a little on what the townspeople had told him. It was nothing that couldn't be verified.

He wanted the FBI to charge right in to the telephone reconnaissance without any hesitation. Adding just enough spice would stimulate a rapid response. They would discover any phone patterns before they had even realized they were being used to do his grunt work.

Franks stopped his jeep in front the diner. He took a booth in the back and started to scribble out some preliminary plans. Before the feds arrived, he would have all of the details worked out; that he was sure of. It was one of the primary reasons he'd been selected for this operation. He had a keen sense of the trail. His tenacity for the hunt was legendary among his peers. Franks was a savage when he was hunting someone or something. He never failed.

After the feds arrived, he'd contact his team and separate them from the rest of the troops. They could work the area over and glean any information before they informed the feds of its location. If they'd missed anything, and that was unlikely, the feds would be useful in finding any new tidbits.

Nancy brought some coffee to his table and he ordered a slice of apple pie. The pie went untouched and the coffee grew cold while Franks worked on his report and reviewed the photos and notes.

The feds showed up right on schedule and were escorted to his booth. It wasn't until they arrived that Franks even noticed his pie. "Sit down gentlemen," he said as they slid into the booth. "Have some pie, it's great." He looked around for Nancy and signaled her over to the booth. "Sweetheart," he said to her, "could you bring coffee all around and get these gentlemen some of this great apple pie? Put it on my bill."

They waited until Nancy returned with the coffee and pie before jumping into any details. Even though this wasn't a top-secret investigation yet, Franks didn't want to alert the town to the real reasons for being here.

"This is great pie Franks," commented the lead agent as he swallowed his last mouthful. "You should try it."

Franks looked down at his yet untouched slice of pie and sampled a mouthful. "You're right," he said with a smile. "It reminds me of the pie my wife makes. Now that we have the pleasantries concluded; let's get down to business.

The conversation was direct and to the point. Franks gave the feds only the information that they needed and would reveal more as time passed. They'd settled on a mutual agreement and Franks would turn over anything that he or his team discovered.

This suited Franks immeasurably. They had no clue as to what he knew and he wasn't prepared to let them in on his secrets until it was completely necessary. They parted and went their separate ways when business was concluded.

Jim had worked through the night. The field integrity was boosted another twelve percent. He left a note for the others and went to his room for some much-needed sleep.

The group rose early to start their day and they were greeted by his message hanging on the door to the containment field. They were ecstatic at the news. There was a flurry of activity as they rushed to prepare for a day with the box.

"Let's get this framework down and back outside before we get started on the research," said Jonathan. "We can get started as soon as it's removed from removed from the building. I don't need to remind you that it's always safety first. We'll be able to open it up all the way as soon as the job is done. I know that you've been waiting impatiently for this moment. So, have we. None of us have seen what we presume is fully operational status."

Everyone grabbed something and started to dismantle the frame. It came down more quickly than it had been erected. They all stood around admiring their work. The area inside of the mesh was cleaned up. Nothing was left to cause a trip hazard or interfere in any way with the operation or the function of the box. All of the pipes were returned to their original pile behind the building. The lumber was removed and the floor swept clean.

"J.J. and Gerard will be working with Steve and Ellen this morning," announced Jonathan. "I want you two to try and see if there is any computer access to this box. It has to be operated on some familiar system or something we could adapt to our technology. We can open it up completely and see what we find. Let's go. We don't have all day. The other teams are waiting their turns." Jonathan clapped them on their backs and wished them luck as they entered the security field.

"Gerard," said Ellen, as they waited for Steve to open the box. "Have you given any thoughts to the type of system that might be employed? You seemed very interested in the layout of the panel. I was curious to know if it gave you any ideas."

"Actually, it had me thinking all night. The system could employ any number of operating techniques. We're talking about a technology that's sixty-five million years old. No one can say how it was conceived or what influenced its design and development. There is so much to study.

"Until this discovery, nobody ever presumed to believe any form of technology existed. I'll keep you posted on any developments. J.J. and I make an excellent team. We have always worked well together. It won't take long."

"Thank you for that. I just want answers faster than they're being made available. Ask Steve. He'll tell you how anxious I became out in the field."

"Mom, let's get inside and open this up all of the way. We'll know more once we get started. Steve is waiting on us to open the box. Come on, let's go. Action now, conversation later."

The four of them stood in the main chamber. Steve and Ellen had already grown accustomed to the raptor in the cryogenics chamber that occupied the other half of the room. Both J.J. and Gerard stood and stared, just as they had done last night.

"Look who's holding things up now?" teased Ellen. "Come on guys, what you're looking for is over here." directing their attention to the control panel. "You might as well do this yourself. You'll be doing this alone in no time anyway. Maybe it will give you some insight on the operation of the system. Stranger things could happen."

Ellen showed them how to sequence the keys. Before they began, she poked her head out of the door and let the remainder of the group know that they were about to begin. She rejoined her team and they began the sequence. Steve would oversee the process and Ellen moved back away from where the box would open.

Gerard deferred to J.J. out of respect for being included on this project. "J.J., would you do the honors? I would like to just stand back and observe while the thing opens up – if it's not too much trouble?"

"I don't mind at all Gerard. Why don't you join my mother, she seems to know where to stand?"

J.J. started to key the symbols as Ellen had shown him. The box began to open immediately as he finished the last keystroke. They all watched as the top and end of the box split up the middle and began to separate. They were about to get more than they had expected.

As the box opened to about thirty degrees, the sides rotated out from the bottom corner to about sixty degrees, something began to emerge from the opening as the box continued to open. It was metallic, but not the same appearance as the box. Whatever it was, it began to expand. They stood silently and stared. The two halves of the box began to swing out to the sides from their connecting point at the chamber wall. It looked like a giant flower blooming before their eyes.

As the pivoting halves began to rotate outward the group started to move in behind them. They weren't sure where the sections would stop, so they moved behind for safety. The object continued to expand until it filled the entire mesh structure. It was a Hoberman Sphere covered in a fine layer of what appeared to be loosely woven metal strands forming an internal cloth covering to the sphere. There were contact points all over the surface of the metallic cloth, securing it to the expanding structure in such a way that the cloth didn't interfere with either the opening or closing of the sphere. The mechanism stopped expanding with a definite mechanical thud. Whatever machinery had opened it ceased operation.

The group stood and stared in awe. Mouths were hanging open and eyes bulged from their sockets. The shear scope of this machine was staggering. Hearts were beating so rapidly that they could hear it ringing in their ears.

Silent thoughts speculated on the technological magic that awaited them. Their minds were racing to conceive the mental prowess it took to develop this box. It was difficult to fathom its scope. Until this moment, dinosaurs were considered to be merely big, stupid animals. The accepted theory was that dinosaurs were a step towards human kind, but far less intelligent.

Individually, each member reveled in private dreams of scientific fame and of course, the resultant prestige, publishing rights, senior chairs on various boards. Not the least of which would be the anticipated fortune.

Each knew, intuitively, that a lifetime of research that would spin off from what they would uncover over the next two weeks. The breadth of their speculation was limitless. The team was lost in private fantasies. Satisfied smiles spread across their faces as they continued to stare and dream.

The four on the inside came rushing out of the chamber as soon as the box stopped. So intense was the emotional impact of each new discovery, they were no longer afraid of any new thing the treasure box revealed. Startling revelations were anticipated, rather than feared. The four of them joined the others as they all stood and stared. There was silence once again. Whenever this box grudgingly revealed a secret, it was so amazing that those who were witness always fell silent.

"What happened?" asked Jonathan as his gaze swept over the sphere. "Did you do anything out of the ordinary?"

"No," replied Ellen, not removing her eyes from the cloth-covered sphere. "We did exactly as we've always done. This is what we were missing out in the field. Isn't it magnificent Jonathan? I wonder what function it serves. How big do you suppose it is?"

Jim was awakened by all the noise as it carried up the stairs. As he descended the stairs, he listened as Jonathan struggled to answer Ellen's question. He finally remembered his instructions to Jim. "I had this frame built to be fifty feet wide and fifty feet tall. The length I left up to Jim once he'd seen the box. The sphere is almost ten feet from the top and about five feet from both sides. Simple calculations would put it at around forty feet."

"We can get more precise after we take laser measurements. It looks like I guessed correctly on the length. It's about two feet from the end of the frame," said Jim who was now standing behind Ellen and Jonathan.

Ellen gasped as she grabbed her heart and spun around. "You scared the liver out of me. I didn't know you were awake."

"The noise woke me up. Sorry about scaring you. Good morning to both of you." Gazing at the open box, he absently commented, "Very impressive, if I have to say so myself, very impressive indeed. I'm going back to my room and get the equipment I need. I could use some help bringing it down, if anybody wishes to volunteer. Hint, hint."

"Sure Jim," answered David and Dick. "We'll give you a hand. How much is there?"

"The three of us can handle it in one trip without any trouble. Let's go."

With the equipment now placed inside the containment field; Dick and David returned to preparing experimental protocols for their rotation in the box. Dick was unusually quiet. He'd gotten up the nerve to touch the metal cloth. It was so finely woven, that it felt like silk. This technology amazed him at every turn.

"Anything new inside the chamber, Jonathan?" asked Ellen.

"To be honest, we don't know. We were so panicked and exhilarated when the thing started to expand that we obviously missed everything. I was standing at the back wall of the chamber," she pointed towards the box, "so that J.J. could operate the panel without me standing over him. The next thing that I knew is the four of us were standing huddled together. We weren't even sure that we'd survive. Then realized that the room we've been in is a control room. As such, we were in no real danger. We relaxed and eventually enjoyed the show. And what a show it turned out to be."

"J.J.," called Jonathan. "You and Gerard get back inside and see if anything has changed. Ellen and Steve, you'd better join them. You two know more about the interior than anyone else here." As they entered the box, he added, "Thanks. Report immediately if you find anything."

"Sure dad. As soon as David and Dick put this stuff where Jim needs it; I'll be right with you." When they finished placing the equipment exactly where Jim indicated, J.J. joined the others preparing to re-enter the control room.

"Come on guys, the show's over. Time to go back to work," teased Ellen. "Who knows, we could be in for an even better show once we're back inside. Wouldn't that beat all?" she said as she laughed.

"We're on our way mom. Gerard and I need a couple of minutes to finish a theory we're concocting. We'll be right there. Go on in without us."

Ellen was not one for procrastination. She went back into the box immediately. Starting at the door, she scanned the walls on either side of the room a little at a time. Then she stared at the floor, going up one wall, across the ceiling and then down the other wall. The process repeated until she had surveyed the entire room one inch at a time. She was reconciling what she already knew to be there with what she might see now.

CHAPTER FORTY-FIVE

WHAT SHE FOUND WAS AS exciting as the sphere. The original panel had moved farther away from the wall. It then turned out and now lay in the position of a keyboard. Behind it was what appeared to be a monitor. The position of the wall had rotated out when the box split and pivoted to allow room for the sphere to be formed.

Both halves had formed an opening into the sphere. It was at least ten feet tall and couldn't be closed. The sphere itself was empty. The warehouse floor was covered in the same metal cloth that lined the interior of the sphere.

The doorway that formed the entrance into the sphere showed no apparent way of closing. The newly exposed corners of the internal box shaped the rough opening. Once open, it must have been meant to remain open with no obvious form of privacy or security.

Studying every detail, Ellen surmised that the panel did serve as the control panel for whatever function the sphere served. It most likely controlled the cryogenics chamber as well. There were no other panels or keyboards exposed.

Ellen emerged rather hurriedly from the box. Excitement was written all over her face. "You guys need to get in here right now. I mean everyone. There is now room enough for the entire group."

"What? What's going on in there?" asked David, catching Ellen's' excitement.

"Nothing right now, but you need to see what happened. I need J.J. and Gerard right now. The rest of you can join us now or at your leisure."

"If you think I'm going to take my sweet time, you've got another thing coming," joked David. "I'm all over this one. I'm not sitting it out like the first time."

Once inside, she directed them to the new panel formation. Most of the group hadn't seen it in its original configuration. She carefully explained how it had appeared before today.

The hardware was clearly set up on the same format as modern day computers. Both J.J. and Gerard were struck with the similar development of current technology. J.J. was sort of mumbling to himself as Gerard started to make notes. It was very peculiar. This was a whole new puzzle to solve. It was obvious that form followed function, but how could the same form have been developed by another species more than sixty-five million years ago?

"What's the problem?" asked Jim. "Is it anything that I need to be concerned with?"

"Not yet Jim," responded Gerard, speaking over his shoulder. He continued speaking to no one in particular as he wrote notes, "One hell of a second day on the job, wouldn't you say?"

"I know I would," replied J.J., answering Gerard. "The original photos didn't do this justice. I was happy just to see it from the outside. This experience is almost beyond words. I'll be relegated to spending the rest of my life laboring at boring, mundane tasks after this. My life will never be the same. There must be something that we can do to preserve this technology."

"The best thing that we can do right now is analyze the hell out of it and see how it works. If we can reverse engineer it, we can understand it. Instead of standing here and admiring this monument to technology; how about getting to work?"

"As if you weren't just standing here alongside me," quipped J.J.

"Since the technology developed similar design features; dare we speculate that it has similar application parameters?"

Answering his own question, Gerard continued, "That would be so bizarre. The odds would be astronomical, but you have a point there. Why would we be wrong to guess that the functionality is identical to contemporary methods? Computers are based on mathematical concepts. Math is a universal language. Let's go for it."

They went to the keyboard to start their experiments. J.J. began writing the initial criteria for the first experiment. That was when Gerard first noticed that there were only seven keys total. This might have been a keyboard, but you couldn't do much typing with seven keys.

"What next?" J.J. commented at the apparent setback. "We need to rethink our approach to this problem."

"J.J., what if we need only to rethink the time line? We've made the speculation that our technology has followed the same path as this technology. It would be safe to speculate that this technology has already developed beyond where we are in today' state-of-the art technology. We are only just beginning to experiment with voice-operated computers. Shouldn't we make the assumption that the operational parameters are more advanced than our present technology?"

"That's the obvious assumption. This is clearly more advanced, yet very similar."

"Everything about this box is more advanced than our state-of-the-art," Gerard retorted. "Duh."

"The only problem that I have with the theory is that I didn't think of it. It's so obvious. It's brilliant. We limit ourselves by our thinking. I need to think more like you at times. I've established a set of guidelines for this task and I'm having trouble breaking free of my own self-imposed limitations.

"Mom, Gerard and I are going to leave for a while. We need to rethink our approach to this problem. There's an answer somewhere in here, we just need to ferret it out."

"See you two in a little while. Steve and I have a lot to do here. We can keep ourselves busy for several more days. Hurry back. We still need your help."

They left the chamber and headed back to J.J.'s room. They began a brainstorming session that would probably take the rest of the day and most of the night. Sessions like this often drifted in many directions, yet ended with a valid a method to approach the problem.

"What if the parameters are more generalized?"

"I don't follow you," replied Gerard.

"Like a cell phone. They can do a lot of stuff, but the bulk of it is categorized. You call up the category you want and then scroll through all the sub groups contained within until you find what you want."

"That would easily explain only seven keys on the keyboard. The only problem I have with that is they serve two functions. We need to access the computer by using those same keys," said Gerard.

"That's not a problem. It would be like logging on to the computer and once activated the keys serve a different function. That's just programming at this point."

"I feel like an idiot. I should have picked up on that."

They reached J.J.'s room and went in to begin speculating in earnest. The conversation on the way up the stairs was thought provoking for the both of them. Now that they were away from the distraction of the box, they could get to the heart of the matter.

Ellen and Steve watched as they disappeared up the stairs and now occupied their time with documenting every aspect of the transformation. The records would prove valuable when research would require a remote location.

During a brief conversation with Steve, Ellen leaned over to get into a more comfortable position. She inadvertently placed her hand on the keyboard. Immediately, she looked down to see if she had touched anything that would cause a change. She didn't see any changes in the panel or the room in general. Casually, she continued her conversation, confident that everything was normal.

As she spoke, the monitor sprang to life, startling her and Steve both. It made a very strange sound. The only sound either of them could equate it to was an animal's growl.

Steve and Ellen exchanged panicked, shocked looks before Ellen reacted. "We need help in here," she called. The near panic edged of her voice echoed through the warehouse.

Everyone came running as fast as they could.

Even J.J. and Gerard heard her from inside his room and negotiated the stairs at a dead run. Together they were a jumble of arms and legs as they struggled to use the same stair at the same time. Somehow, they managed to make down the stairs with neither of them getting hurt, just embarrassed at their lack of grace.

"Is everything okay? What's wrong in there? Ellen, are you okay?" Jonathan's eyes were pleading with her for an answer to any and all the questions pouring forth from the group. He was holding on to both of her shoulders and forcing her to look straight at him.

"The computer is alive," she finally choked out. She was visibly shaken, but alert and not joking. "It growled at us. It was an ugly sound, almost savage." She lowered her head and crunched her shoulders together at the recollection of the sound. A shiver shook her whole body.

"I was frightened. I lost control for a moment, that's all. I'm sorry to have alarmed all of you." Ellen was becoming very embarrassed as she scanned the anxious faces of the team. Scarlet blotches started on her neck and continued up her face until she was a very attractive shade of red. The sudden animal noises combined with the tension and the silence was all she needed to momentarily go over the edge.

Steve began to speak. "There's no need for embarrassment. Ellen and I were both frightened. This thing growled at us. It seemed as if an animal was right there next to us, ready to pounce. I don't mind saying that it scared the crap out of me."

"See," whispered J.J. to Gerard as he watched his mother. "This was the point I was making a few minutes ago. She's got weeks with this box and look how easily she's thrown out of her normal behavior pattern. You don't know my mother, but let me assure you that she's an emotional rock out in the field. It's all science with her. I don't even know who *this* woman is with my mother's name. However, she does look a lot like my mother."

The others began to press into the door and look at what was happening, even though there wasn't anything monumental to see.

"Did you say that the computer growled at you?" asked J.J. He was starting to regain his breath from the run down the stairs and across the room. "What did it say exactly?"

"It just growled. Follow me, I'll show you."

Once through the door, she turned to face the screen.

There was a picture of a tree on the screen. She looked at it with a puzzled expression across her face and turned to look from J.J. to Gerard. "A tree?" she asked out of sheer curiosity. The picture abruptly changed to a flower. Ellen hesitated a moment, and on a hunch said, "Flower." The picture changed again, this time it was a fern. She immediately began to suspect that the computer was learning the English language.

"Let's get out of here. We need to talk. I have an idea." she nudged them both towards the door. "Come on. Get a move on," she pushed them as she spoke.

Ellen walked away from the box and called the group to the area near the stairs. She explained what she had thought was happening. Gerard had said that it confirmed one of their suppositions. She asked both J.J. and Gerard to come back with her. She wanted them to take the proper kind of notes that *they* would require. Ellen lacked the technical background and was afraid to miss anything important.

The group agreed that this was an important step and all urged her to continue. With everyone agreeing to press forward Ellen returned to the computer. The fern was still displayed. She said, "Fern."

Once again, the computer changed pictures. This time it was a picture of a pterodactyl. She spoke the name quickly and the picture changed again. This process went on for an hour or more. There was a broad base of images covering many subjects. Most of the pictures were animal or plant in nature.

The screen suddenly went blank. Ellen looked at the others. No one seemed to know what to do. They had all thought that it was teaching itself the English language. Each had fully expected that it would start speaking by this time.

Half an hour went by and still there was no response from the computer. "Any suggestions?" asked Ellen. "It's been a while since there was anything on the screen."

"Maybe you should push another key. Isn't that how all of this got started anyway?"

"J.J. and Gerard, I want to discuss this with the both of you. I'll show you what I did before this whole thing got started. Hopefully you'll be able to advise me on which key to push. I'd prefer not to accidentally shut it off."

"Sure," they said together.

"I was talking with Steve and I leaned against the keyboard like this." She lowered her hand to just above the surface. "It was just about here." She looked down to make sure that her hand was as close to the exact as she could remember. She noticed something just beneath her fingers. "Look at this. I hadn't noticed that before. The place I touched is smudged."

J.J. moved forward to inspect the handprint. "Your fingertips touched two keys," he said. "There's a smudge just barely visible here and here," he added as he leaned closely to the panel and pointed with a pencil.

Looking back over his shoulder, he asked, "Do you know which key you pressed first?"

Ellen shrugged her shoulders. As sensitive as a fingertip is; she hadn't even felt the keys depress. She closed her eyes and re-enacted the moment over and over, moving her hand to help her remember. "I'm sorry boys, I just don't remember. It looked as if I didn't touch anything critical so I paid little attention after that. Only after the screen activated; I realized I'd done something. I'm sorry."

"J.J., she could have touched, or pressed, them simultaneously. It should work. All the other commands that you have discovered are single key, but that doesn't preclude any multiple keyed options."

"You're right. If we don't try, we don't know." J.J. pressed both keys together.

"*How may I help you?*" asked the computer.

Startled, but undaunted, J.J. answered the computer with his own question. "How have you learned our language?"

"You have identified all of the pictures that were displayed on the monitor. The answers provided a broad enough structure that allowed me to translate those images into your language. I have also been listening to your conversations since you returned. I will continue to learn as I monitor your conversations. It will help with conversation structure. Is there anything else?"

"What is your function?"

"I serve to give knowledge. How may I help you?"

"What is this machine that contains your information?

"This was originally designed to preserve my mate. He was brutally murdered and I was imprisoned herein."

"You're the raptor in the cryogenic chamber?" Turning to the others he said in a whisper, "I don't believe this. This is too bizarre; I can't deal with it right now. Mom, can you take over for me?" J.J. exited rather quickly. The color had drained from his face and he looked as if he would lose control of his bowels at any moment.

A stunned Ellen mutely shook her head in a positive response, even though her acceptance was offered to J.J.'s hastily departing back. Ellen was reluctant to actually speak to the computer. She stepped up to the monitor and asked, "What function does the sphere serve? How does it operate?"

"It serves to give knowledge. To operate the sphere, simply enter the operation request on the keypad. Ask for the knowledge that you wish to be displayed. It will be displayed in the sphere."

"I don't understand. How will it be displayed? Will I be in danger?"

"There is no danger. The images are only reflections of what was. They are also depictions of specific requests for knowledge. They take on solid form as soon as they are displayed. They cannot harm you. Do you wish to seek information?"

"Yes, I do. Tell me how to request information. I have accessed your program but do not remember the sequence. It was accessed through an error. Can you give me the proper sequence so I may request information whenever I need your help?"

"I can give you the sequence. Are you prepared to accept the information?"

"I'm not ready. Please wait for me to indicate when I am ready."

"I will wait as you have requested. When we are finished, may I ask you a few questions?"

"Yes," said Ellen, distracted by her attempt to secure a paper and pencil. "Someone please hand me some paper and something to write with." Ellen was emphatic. She waved his outstretched hand impatiently, in anticipation that someone would slip both paper and pencil into it.

"Mother, you've done it again," said J.J. as he returned to the chamber, handing her the requested items. "You're amazing, even if this was opened by accident." Turning his back to the computer, he said to Ellen, "I'm ready to continue now. I've gotten over the initial shock of what we were told. Thanks for covering for me. May I continue?"

"Sure, J.J., I need a little time to digest this myself. You really threw me for a loop there. Don't ever do that again," she admonished. "I know you were shocked, but you never even considered my reaction, you just bolted. Next time there will be consequences. Do I make myself clear?"

His mother had never physically punished J.J. when he was growing up, but by the tone of her voice and the firm set of her jaw, he was convinced that she was telling him the truth. He knew with certainty that he wasn't going to test her resolve.

"I'm ready to accept the information. You may begin."

"Press the two keys in the center of the board. Press them simultaneously. That will access my voice commands. If you wish for the three-dimensional display of your request, press the last key on the right immediately after the first two. When you make your request, it will automatically access the three-dimensional display. Do you have any further requests?"

"May I press the last key now to access the other display?"

"Not at this time. You may request my termination of function or

continue in voice mode only. You cannot access this function as a secondary command. It is a primary command request only. If you choose to terminate my function, you may then reactivate me and press the last key at that time. It will automatically access the three-dimensional display when you request knowledge."

"Am I to understand that you can only choose one display or the other, but can't move between the two at will?"

"You are correct. I serve to give information. The information you request comes in two versions. I do not see the necessity to switch from one to the other during any one session."

"Thank you for your help. We are finished now; you may terminate function at this time."

"Thank you. May I ask my questions now? If you wish me to wait until later to grant my request, simply reactivate me whenever you wish to request knowledge."

"I wish to wait until our next session. You may discontinue at this time."

The screen went blank. The keypad moved back to its position on the wall. The whole box was as silent as the grave.

J.J. stood silently staring at the space that used to be the keyboard and monitor. Taking the paper from his mother, he held the sequence in his hand as if it were a treasure map. His knuckles were turning white from the intensity of his grip. The impact of what had just taken place held him quiescent. Its implications and applications were staggering.

The team gathered outside the security field. The conversation soon developed into a cacophony of voices. Each had specific ideas of the questions that should be asked first. There was no consensus and the suggestions were as random as their individual thoughts.

It was Jonathan who finally called the group to silence. "We all have many questions that need answering, that much is obvious. We will each take one-hour shifts with the machine. Each of us will have the necessary time to get the answers we seek. If we work together, we can finish this phase quickly and efficiently. Are we at least all in agreement on this point?"

Without waiting for a full consensus, Jonathan continued with his conversation. "I'll set up a schedule that we will adhere to as closely as possible." This last statement indicated an understood agreement. No one objected.

"Ellen you made the initial discovery of the box. It's only right that first honors will be yours, if you choose. J.J. and Gerard will go second. It's important to learn about the operating systems and any idiosyncrasies that, when avoided, will increase the productivity of our time thereby making our sessions run as smoothly as possible. We need to know about the raptor as soon as possible. David and Dick; you two will be third in line."

"May I interrupt dear? I believe that the most important task at hand is guaranteeing our security. Jim, I would like you to take the first rotation. You can find any information that you need concerning field intensity. We may be able to boost our own field enough to ensure complete security.

"I really don't care what sequence that I'm placed in," she continued. "All I want is a turn. The rest of you can remain in the order that Jonathan has listed. Should any of you wish to relinquish their time, please advise the intended recipient. It's important to not let the machine sit idle. We have a very short time to gather as much data as possible."

"Gentlemen, I believe my wife has spoken. You may each prepare for your turn at the controls. Jim, if you would do us the honor of starting the parade. Good luck. I hope that we can all benefit by your questions."

Jim went straight to the controls. J.J. showed him how to active the holographic imaging. He pressed the keys and waited.

"Do you wish to seek information?"

"Yes, I do. I wish to see how you operate."

"I operate many different functions and in many different ways. Specify what you wish to see."

"I want to see your schematics on the power that you generate. I wish to know how you operate this function."

"Will that be all? What form would you like the information to take?"

"I would like the information to be shown as schematics s on a table. I wish to study your schematics. That will be all for this question. I will have more separate requests after this one."

The computer complied. A table with schematics appeared in the center of the room. Jim stepped into the sphere and walked over to the table. He put a hand gently on the edge of the table. It was solid. He looked back through the door at J.J. and said, "I've got it under control now. I'll see you in an hour. Make sure that you come and get me. I'm not wearing a watch. Remember, you told me that they don't work in here."

J.J. gave him a high sign, turned and left the box. He joined Gerard to prepare the questions for their session.

Jim moved the papers back and forth on the table. He didn't understand any of them. He tore through the pile and found nothing that he could read. "I wish to seek information," he called.

"Do you wish more information?"

"The information that you gave me is not in my language. Is there any way that I can give you similar information in my language, so that you can translate our terminology into this informational display?"

"There is a data input portal below the keypad. You may tilt the keypad up and feed the information in through that portal. It will scan your information into my data banks. Start with basic terms and symbols. You may progress to higher levels of technology after I scan and process each data input. I will let you know when to proceed."

"You may terminate function for now. Before you terminate, may I ask one more question?"

"What is the question?"

"How long will you be able to display the three-dimensional images before you need to recharge your batteries?"

"As long as there is constant, direct contact with a solar energy source,

I may operate in a three-dimensional display mode for seven solar hours. I will terminate function at that time.

"I use more power than I can collect; however, I am able to transfer from one bank of storage cells to another, allowing re-charge time. Eventually I will diminish the charge in each bank of cells.

"When I reach a critical level of depletion, I will retain enough charge sufficient to maintain my primary functions and I will discontinue operating all hardware functions.

"I will also terminate function sooner than seven solar hours, if there is a rapid drain on my power cells caused from an indirect light source. I need direct solar contact to convert the maximum power in the shortest period of time. Reactivate me when you need to request knowledge."

"Thank you. May an outside power source be used to augment your batteries?"

"Yes."

"Thank you. You may terminate your function at this time."

Jim left the sphere and joined the others by the stairs. "This is getting really interesting. We can have all the answers at our fingertips in a week or two. You can even get that translation that you wanted Dr. Crenshaw," he said, smiling to Ellen.

"We're going to have to rig an alternate power source. At maximum charge this can only operate for seven hours before battery depletion. The box maintains a reserve to avoid total failure. I'm sure that all of you are aware of the potential battery damage from deep drawing too often. And if you're not, let me fill you in. When you deep draw a battery that's not designed for it, you could kill it right then and there. We need to watch and check all the time."

Jonathan interrupted, "Let's modify the schedule. During the day, when we can keep the charge up, we'll go in for no more than one hour and then give the machine an hour to add to its solar charge." It was a statement of fact, not a suggestion. "Jim, you continue working on the alternate source of energy. We need a couple of options before we proceed."

Everyone nodded or spoke their consent. This was only a minor delay in the overall progress of discovery. A little lost time now could easily be made up when the box's capacity was increased. The team was comprised of professionals and they understood the importance and agreed to the new schedule quickly.

The results of the delay would yield tighter, more focused plans. And that alone would expedite the push to understanding. No one rejected to plan to bring this discovery to the world. That goal kept them on track and prevented any serious complaints or dissention.

CHAPTER FORTY-SIX

Captain Harrington had flown in by chopper two hours earlier. The quick, yet concise briefing Sergeant Franks had given him brought him up to speed prior to assuming command.

"I have the recent satellite surveillance photos here and they don't show anything. They're routine test shots and things you'd find on Google Earth." Tossing the photo packet across the desk; he fell into his chair with a thump.

"May I sir?" asked Franks.

"Be my guest," gestured Captain Harrington. "I can assure you that there's not anything in there."

"I need to take a look though sir." Franks emptied the envelope onto the desk and spread the photos out with a fan of his hand. Carefully he picked through them until he found several that held his interest.

"What have you got?" questioned Harrington.

"Nothing yet sir," answered Franks as he continued to study the selections he'd made. He began to rearrange them as the Captain looked on.

Coming from around the end of his desk, he asked Franks, "Can you show me what's holding your attention so intently?"

"These photos sir, they're of the area that we're in right now." Pointing to a geographic feature, he continued, "This area here is just outside the tent about three hundred yards."

"I don't understand?"

"Well, we know when these photographs were taken, and we know that within the last four weeks there's been a major storm followed by a group of college students and two teachers who came here on a fossil collecting expedition…"

"Continue. . ." interrupted Harrington.

"What if we were to get some new surveillance photos in the next day or two?"

"I see where you're going. I knew you were the man for the job."

"I just want to check a few things out. There was a conflict of information coming from the town's people. The largest majority of the witnesses were sure that three trucks had passed through the town, laden with crates of fossils. There were only two people reporting only two trucks, the local sheriff and a waitress named Nancy."

"Why would you contest the veracity of the local sheriff? He's a trained observer."

"He's also known the Crenshaw's for at least twenty years. Best of friends if the locals reports are valid."

"Who are the Crenshaw's?"

"They're the two university professors who supervise the kids that come out here every year," continued Franks.

"I'm confused. They're coming out here for twenty years and you're curious about them?" Harrington asked.

"The sheriff's obviously protecting them. As you said, he's a lawman. He's predisposed to being cautious. What if he believes he's avoiding trouble for his friends?"

"From what?"

"Strangers asking questions."

"We had a very pleasant discussion. He didn't even realize how defensive he'd become. I never let on, but I know enough about people to know that within a day or two, no one in this town is going to talk to us."

"Point well taken," commented Harrington. "What do you think you have?"

"Shipping manifests indicated that two trucks picked up and delivered crates of fossils to the University. I already had the feds check that out. It was a dead end. The puzzle is why so many people are convinced they saw three trucks.”

“New photos won’t reveal the number of trucks Sergeant.”

“No sir, they won’t. What I’m looking for is anything that’s changed on the topography. We may be able to discover something that we didn’t know we were looking for.”

“Hand me the phone, Sergeant. I’ll have those photos by morning.”

“Thank you, sir. I’m not sure that they’ll be what I’m looking for, but they will help me pinpoint the direction of my search.”

“Sergeant, I want these men deployed on the other side of that ridge. We’re close, I can feel it.” Captain Harrington dismissed him. His hand and arm came up in the general idea of a salute. His attention was already focused elsewhere.

Another morning dawned in Detroit. Ellen found herself walking around the inner perimeter of the warehouse, but not venturing outside. She truly missed her walks. Security dictated that she shouldn’t be wandering around alone in this neighborhood. The sense on completeness, of oneness with the universe was gone and left an empty hole in her heart. It was draining her enthusiasm.

“Jonathan,” she said, almost as a question, as she returned to their room. “I’m hungry. You haven’t been up to make breakfast for two days. I miss that.”

“I’m sorry sweetheart. I’m just not up to it. This is the most exciting discovery ever made and it’s wearing me down. I don’t understand it, but I’m depressed.”

“So am I. I can’t go for my morning walks. I can’t get my breakfast. This isn’t right. I don’t like this. I have a sense of foreboding almost like I’m looking into my own casket.”

“And I thought it was just me. We need to get away from here. Remember we bought that city map so we could find this place. Let’s look up a nice place out of town and we can walk and talk. We’ll stop for a good breakfast on the way.”

“I love you,” she beamed as she threw her arms around his neck.

Before he could respond, she was smothering him in some very passionate kisses.

Jonathan got dressed and Ellen went to talk with J.J. She related their plan and let him run things for a couple of hours. "Johnny, your father and I are going out for a little while. I need to walk and get some breakfast. We just need to get away to clear our heads. I know you understand."

"I do mom. I've never seen you like this before. It's unsettling to say the least. You and dad go and enjoy your morning. Steve's a good cook. He can get breakfast ready for the rest of us."

"Thank you dear. I know your father will appreciate this as much as I do." She kissed him on the cheek and went back down the hall to tell Jonathan that everything was arranged and they could leave any time.

Stepped from their room, Jonathan asked, "All set?"

"Let's go, dear," she said taking his arm.

They walked in silence all the way to the car. As Jonathan turned the key Ellen reached over and turned off the radio. He looked at her with a question in his eyes.

"I liked the quiet walk to car. I'm just trying to prolong the solitude."

"And so, begins another day in the life of the two people who are about to give the world a better life," he said under his breath. He smiled to himself and drove out of the parking lot.

"What?" she asked.

"It's just a mundane, unassuming start in a world changing series of events. Considering what's at stake, there should be some kind of fanfare or something."

"You've lost me." Ellen studied him for some indication of his thought process.

"We're starting another day with the box. Each day brings us closer to its secrets. Each new discovery will benefit mankind in untold ways. The entire world will be a better place. We can bring power to even the remotest regions of the world with the solar technology alone. Third world countries could begin to eliminate poverty. The genetic information, as yet untapped, could provide cures for some of our worst diseases. Ellen, we're on the threshold of a new and better world."

"Fifteen minutes ago, you were depressed, and now you're saving humanity... men," she retorted.

"Only because of your inspiration dear," Jonathan responded. "Men don't just do things because they want to get them done. Men do things to impress women. Impressing a woman gets the best reward of all."

By the smirk on his face, she knew what he meant. "You always bring everything back to sex."

"The list for the majority of men is very simple dear. There's sex at the top of the list. Then food is second... so we have enough strength for sex. And finally, there's shelter. Shelter is a twofold item. It serves to make the woman happy and it provides a clean, dry place for having sex."

"Are you sure all men are like that? I think you're just a horny old goat."

"I can't tell you the infinite number of times I've said or others have said to me, 'I don't care. If she's happy, I'm happy.'"

"That's disgusting."

"It's the truth. You women know that you have the power; you just don't know how to use it. Well that's not true either. A lot of women don't know how to use it. A lot of women will use sex as a weapon; withholding the gift as a punishment. They could get so much more from a man by rewarding each accomplishment with sex. We're just like trained dogs. When a woman just keeps setting the bar slightly higher each time, we're stupid enough to keep jumping over it. Such is the nature of sex and its hold on a man."

"I never did that with you." Ellen was offended and defensive.

"I never said you did. With you, sex was so good that I went about my life trying to continually improve myself so you'd be happy and sex would go on indefinitely and uninterrupted. I'm completely addicted to having sex with you. It's my drug of choice."

"You used me." Ellen folder her arms in disgust and looked out the window. The passing cityscape went unnoticed as they drove on.

"We used each other. And we got a beautiful son, two lovely grandchildren, good careers and this opportunity to benefit all mankind in the bargain. I can't forget to mention the decades of glorious sex with the most beautiful woman in the world. When I think about it; I'm probably ahead on this deal. I got you, but you only got me."

Ellen's anger softened and she leaned over and rested her head on his shoulder. "You're crazy my love. You do know that don't you?"

"Crazy about you… and crazy for you." Then he paused before he said, "Yeah, I know," as if reading her thoughts and the expected 'I love you' that was about to come.

"I don't deserve you. Women think about sex in a completely different way. Now that you've explained yourself to me, I'll do my best to keep you striving for bigger and better things." Her voice was cheerful and understanding.

"You always have dear; that's one of the reasons I fell in love with you. You're a strong independent woman. That attracts me. You're control over me came natural to you. You were never abusive or demanding. We fell into a wonderful rhythm from the very first. Don't try anything new. You're already on the right track."

They'd driven about six or seven miles when they spotted a diner. Jonathan pulled in and went around to Ellen's side and opened her door for her. Taking her hand, he helped her from the car.

"Looks kind of quaint in a postcard sort of way; almost as if it doesn't belong," observed Ellen.

Once inside, they understood why. The place was filled with seniors. "At least the food will be priced right," quipped Jonathan.

"Help you folks?" asked the hostess.

"Non-smoking please, just the two of us," answered Jonathan.

Grabbing two menus and the silverware, she said, "Follow me."

When they reached the corner of the diner she asked, "Booth or table?"

"The booth will be fine," answered Ellen.

"You always prefer a table," whispered Jonathan.

"This is next to the window. I want to enjoy the morning as it brightens."

"That's fine with me; as long as you're happy."

Ellen eyed him suspiciously, but he already had his face buried in the menu. Maybe he was telling the truth after all. Turning her attention to the menu, she perused it until she found her selection.

After the waitress took their orders they sat in silence as Ellen gazed out the window. While waiting for their food she was recollecting the things he'd always said and done.

She smiled to herself when she recalled conversations with her women friends who would complain about their husbands and what they'd do to get even over some action or comment. There had never been *get even* moments in their life. That had made her instantly happy.

By the time she'd finished her meal she realized he was right. They had spent their life in pursuit of what made them happy. It was a reward system that worked perfectly.

"Let's go my love," she said suddenly. "We've got work to do." She grabbed her jacket and stood next to the booth.

"What?" Jonathan asked as he placed his cup back on the table.

"We need to get back. There's too much work to be done for lollygagging around here. Come on, move your backside."

"Okay then, let's get a move on. I'll get the check if you want to get to the truck right away," he offered.

"No. I'll get the check and you can bring the truck around to the door. It'll be faster that way."

The drive back consisted of two things; loud music and Ellen staring silently out the window with the strangest smile on her face. Jonathan was just happy to have his wife back. He parked the car and Ellen wasted no time in rushing into the warehouse.

"Okay gentlemen, where are we? I want complete details from each of you about your project's progress. J.J. and Gerard… you go first."

"That's my real mom," whispered J.J. into Gerard's ear as the bent down to collect their papers. "You're gonna like her."

"Ellen, we've gotten a lot from the computer. There are schematics on all the critical components and only a few that we still need, but overall our plans are at least sixty percent complete. The progress is initially slow, but that will change."

"I agree," replied J.J. when his mother turned to him.

"Jim, have you completed the connections for the generator?"

"Sure have. We can go on line at any time. Just say the word."

"Let's hold off for one more day unless we need to work into the night."

"No problems there," he answered.

"Perfect. Thanks Jim. Dick and David, you're up."

"We're only about thirty percent right now. We're going to ask for printouts of their genome. We can photograph the images and videotape other stuff. This will help us overcome our concerns about contaminating the specimen. There shouldn't be any need to access the container in these primitive surroundings. No offense intended, but there's too much at stake to take the risk."

"No offense taken. We've already had that discussion. If that's all, we need to keep moving forward," said Ellen. "Let's keep this effort moving at the pace you've all established.

"One more thing, gentlemen; photograph and/or tape all your research material. It will free up the time in the sphere for everyone. Thank you." Ellen's tone was cordial, yet clearly dismissive. They all turned to their individual projects as Ellen went upstairs with Jonathan.

The door to their room slammed shut so quickly that Jonathan barely managed to squeeze past in time to avoid being hit. Ellen rounded on him abruptly. She kissed him on the mouth and grabbed him below the belt. "Just touch me please. I need to feel your hands on my body. I'm somewhere right now that I don't understand and I need to feel you."

Obediently, Jonathan reached inside her blouse and did as she asked. Ellen moaned a little and returned the favor. After several minutes of heavy petting, they released their grip on each other and straightened their clothes. With a quick peck on the cheek, Ellen whispered, "Thank you," and left the room.

What am I supposed to do with this, he thought as he looked down at his protruding trousers?

CHAPTER FORTY-SEVEN

THERE WAS A KNOCK ON the tent post and Sergeant Franks called out, "What is it?"

"Captain Harrington asked me to deliver this packet sir."

"Come in."

The soldier saluted and stood at attention. Franks returned the salute saying, "At ease." Walking around his desk, he took the packet from the soldier and quickly opened it. Remembering the soldier still standing there, he turned his head back slightly and said, "Dismissed."

Saluting to the Sergeants back, he turned and left the tent. Franks spread the photographs across his desk. There was a lot of area to cover and the Captain had the photos blown up large enough to make out small details. He was pleasantly surprised to see that they had the forethought to key the edges so he could reassemble the entire collection.

Carefully, he pulled out the file of photographs from the initial satellite pass four weeks previously. Setting them at the top of the desk, he began to assemble the newer copies. There were enlarged copies of the original photos as well as the newest set.

He meticulously perused each photo identifying topographical markers. Then he carefully compared every square inch for any variations. This was going to be a painstaking task. Franks knew what was looking and he was uncomfortable in letting anyone else do this work.

Six hours had elapsed and dozens of photographs had been discarded by the time he'd found what he'd been searching for.

Compiling the pertinent photographs, he called for a private to carry a message to Captain Harrington.

Addressing the Captain, the private said as he saluted, "Sergeant Franks thinks that we have something sir. There is a cave like hole in the side of a hill not too far from here. Sergeant Franks requests that you join him at his tent. He wishes to show you what he's found."

"Thank you soldier. Well done," answered Captain Harrington as he returned the salute crisply, "Dismissed." Saluting a final time, the private turned and left the Captain's tent.

As Captain Harrington walked into the Sergeant's tent, he asked, "What have you got Franks?"

After exchanging salutes, Franks showed him the photos spread out on the desk. "Look at this sir." Pointing to the two sets of photographs, he continued, "This is where we are now."

Tracing a finger over the photographs to a place several miles farther down the road, he stopped at a hillside. "This is a photo of the hill in question before the storm. As you can clearly see there's nothing unusual."

Pulling the new photo from under the original, he laid them side-by-side. "There's clearly a difference in these to pictures of the same hillside. Look at this feature here." He was pointing to the amount of soil at the side of the hill and commented, "This looks peculiarly like a dirt ramp. Not exactly the sort of thing you'd expect to find in the middle of nowhere."

"Good work Franks."

"I've sent a team down there to check things out. I'm expecting a report back at any moment," replied Franks.

The words were no sooner spoken than there was a knock at the tent.

"Come in."

Saluting both the Captain and Sergeant Franks, the soldier awaited the return salutes. Once received, he continued, "We think we've got something sir. There are traces of ionized air still in the cave. Someone has left a tarp covering the crevasse at the top of the cave. It has acted as a wind barrier and the air is trapped motionless inside. There were some pretty strong readings, sir. This has to be the place that you're searching for." The private saw the smile creep to the Sergeant's face.

When things made the Sergeant happy, he had a habit of remembering those who helped bring about that happiness. This might get him out of some bothersome assignment later on.

Sergeant Franks began smiling broadly. He could feel the success of the mission already. This was going to be a good chase, and the trail was too well marked to hide from him for very long.

Before he headed to the site, Sergeant Franks discussed the report with Captain Harrington. "That trace of ionized air is a real stroke of luck. The cave isn't far from here, based on this map. I'm going to check it out. I'll bring you a full report, sir."

"No need for that Sergeant, I'm coming with you. There's something peculiar going on here and I want to get to the bottom of it. I can feel it in my bones. Have you ever felt that way, Sergeant?"

"Yes sir. I feel that way right now, sir. From the initial reports, this spot is it. I know it will yield some vital information. We'll get the job done right, sir. You can depend on me and my team." The Sergeant had handpicked each person. They were the most dependable of the all the troops that he had to choose from.

The Captain emerged from the tent and climbed into the Hummer. "Let's get going Sergeant. Drive on." They drove off in silence. Sergeant Franks took a meandering course to the hillside. The terrain didn't allow for a direct approach from where they were bivouacked. It was a short ten-minute drive.

Seeing the ramp that Jonathan and Steve had built, they pulled up and stopped next to it. The un-natural formation made it evident that someone had moved something big down this ramp.

"What in the devil is this?" the Captain asked more to himself than to Franks. He then looked over to Franks and asked, "Sergeant, what do you make of this?"

After assessing the tracks and depressions at the bottom of the ramp he formulated an answer. "Sir, I believe this was a loading ramp. Look at the track running down the center of it, sir. Whatever was up there was heavy."

Feeling the soil at the bottom of the ramp, Franks tested it for compaction, "But not too heavy, sir. See how the soil is compressed? It's tight, but not overly firm. There couldn't have been more than twenty thousand pounds resting here."

Looking further, Franks found the lumber used for the slides down the ramp. It confirmed his conclusion. He studied the ground where the truck had pulled in and was loaded up. The tracks from where the truck backed in left a shallow depression. The departure tracks were sunk into soil a couple of inches more. The load must have been at least five to ten tons including the weight of the trailer.

"Sir, I can conclude that a tractor trailer was loaded at this site. The load was considerable, but not overweight. The depth of the tracks proves that. Also, there are two separate sets of tracks on either side of the ramp. They come from a light truck, a personal vehicle. They seem to have been dragged several inches while parked here."

"That's unusual."

"Not at all, sir. Whatever was brought down had to be loaded. My guess would be winched onto the trailer. The tracks look to be from two Land Rover type vehicles. It's consistent with the type the University owns.

"Very good Sergeant, I'll bring in the FBI. We can have these tracks traced and identified in no time. It'll make them feel as if they are accomplishing a lot."

The Captain continued to scan the area as if to try and see something that Franks had missed. "Carry on Sergeant, good work. A nice bit of investigative analysis. You're the kind of leader that makes this team so unbeatable." He turned and walked back to the Hummer.

Sergeant Franks said, "Thank you, sir," to the Captains back as he began to walk to the other side of the vehicle.

At the campsite Harrington made the necessary arrangements

for the FBI to trace the tire tracks. The University had several of the suspect vehicles in their possession. It wouldn't take long to verify that it was the Crenshaw's who had the vehicles out here on this dig.

The Crenshaw's were already the primary suspects. It was a simple matter to tie them to the site and the unknown power surge. While his team continued to gather the small tidbits of information, Franks was piecing it together to fit his preconceived conclusions.

They both felt a certain satisfaction in drawing the ring a little tighter. The trail was not fresh, but it was well marked. Once the phone records were sorted down and analyzed by the FBI, the event could be narrowed to include any additional person or persons involved. They had the date, the time, now they had the place. The rest was academic.

The new report on the ionized air came across the Captain's desk. The original power surge was a short duration event. The amount of power expended was not clear. It had a peculiar signature that triggered the satellite alert.

Whatever had been in the cave was using power for a long period of time. The ionization caused by that usage had saturated the surrounding limestone and the soil left on the floor of the cave. It was fortunate that the breach in the cave's roof had been covered. The ionization would have dissipated with the first gentle breeze. There was no ion trace left in the soil from the ramp.

It was evident that there was equipment in the cave. The report verified there was a set of wooden tracks set into the floor. This would have been used to facilitate the removal of the equipment.

With all the data being gathered, there still was no way of knowing how many people had been involved in whatever happened here. That was the one piece of information that nagged both Franks and Harrington. They needed to know how many parties were involved. A sloppy closure to the case didn't work in either of their worlds.

The report was a dead end concerning the power surge. However, they now knew that there was a minimum of three people involved. There were three separate sets of footprints throughout the cave and the surrounding area. For now, three was the magic number. Terrorists always formed cells of three. They were now firmly convinced that this was some form of terrorist activity.

The volume of earth moved to make the ramp was more than a single person could handle in a short period of time. Three might be able to do it, yet that scenario bothered the Captain. An unknown variable was nagging at the Captain. Something was missing. A question was left unasked. Unable to discern the cause of his anxiety, Harrington continued his study of the report.

The use of the tracks in the cave and guides down the ramp was enough evidence that someone had coordinated this entire operation. There was still much to do. They were beginning to develop a loose sequence of events and didn't want the trail to grow colder than it already was. Someone would be made to pay for playing around in this country.

Allowing his anger to grow unchecked, Harrington was growing more irritated by the moment. He needed Franks here immediately. Captain Harrington sent his orderly to find Sergeant Franks. He was formulating a plan and needed the Sergeants special talents to carry it out.

CHAPTER FORTY-EIGHT

TRANSLATING SYMBOLS AND OTHER TECHNICAL language created difficulty with extracting information from the computer. Team activity was now spent preparing the information needed to translate the box's technical data into contemporary, usable terms and symbols.

J.J. and Gerard were the first to finish their task. They scanned the required data into the computer and then requested that they be notified when it was ready to display their information in the chamber. There was a minimum of a hundred pages containing symbols and definitions as well as the basic techniques for drawing and labeling schematics. It was more information than they required, but they didn't want to relinquish their turn a second time to add some small bit of trivia that found significance in the final analysis.

They didn't have to wait very long before the computer, in its soft female voice, said, *"I am ready now."* It had been less than five minutes from the initial scan to the completion of the task.

"The computational capabilities of this machine must be staggering," said J.J. "We scanned in a significant amount of data to be interpreted and translated into its own language and then back to ours. I would have expected at least a half an hour to forty-five minutes."

"Do you wish for me to display your information at this time?"

"Yes," said Gerard. "You may display the information."

"Thank you. It will take a moment."

A table materialized in the center of the sphere. On it were all the computer schematics that they had requested. The two of them tore into the work like ravenous dogs on a steak. The sheer volume was overwhelming. The computer had even supplied a rudimentary understanding of its program language. It was elegant and beautifully written. The language alone would supply years of study for someone at another time.

"Computer," said J.J. "We would like to request more information. Can you provide a sample from your operational circuitry? We would like two samples. The first sample should be actual size. The second sample should be identical to the first, only five times larger. It will help us in our ability to study it more efficiently." J.J. turned to Gerard and asked if there would be anything else. He shook his head, no. Finishing, he said, "There is no additional request at this time."

"I can comply with this request. Is there a particular circuit that you wish to study? I can provide you with any circuit that you request."

"There is no specific circuit. You may select anything at random."

"I understand."

There was a momentary delay from the last command to the appearance of the parts. They materialized on top of the schematics. The first was so small that they thought there might be a mistake. The second was clearly five times larger. It, however, was still smaller than some of their contemporary computer components.

This could easily become a daunting task. They needed to request an even larger sample. They now gave the computer a specific measurement from which it would scale the part. The second attempt was successful.

They photographed some of the schematics with Ellen's Polaroid. The pictures were crisp and easily readable. Gerard went to his room and unpacked his 35MM camera. They would need photo enlargements of the schematics in order to study them during their off periods.

Everyone finished with their first day's work with time to spare. Jim had finished his data file and sat patiently waiting for his turn. His paperwork scanned in with no effort. He had refined his input data after he watched Gerard and J.J.

"Do you request information?" asked the computer with its lilting tones.

"Yes, I do," he said flatly. "I want the electrical schematics on the solar collectors that you employ. Place them on a table large enough for me to spread them out and study them closely. Provide a chair to sit at the table."

"Please define chair."

"A chair is a device that is used for sitting down. Some of us prefer to sit when we study."

"Would you like to request that I add a chair with each information request?"

"Yes. Whenever I request information, I would like you to provide a table and chair. That won't be necessary to add that request for the others. The individual in the room will indicate whether or not they require a table and chair. Does that conflict with your programming?" asked Jim.

"It does not conflict. In your society, is individuality bestowed on everyone or only an elite segment?"

"I understand the question, but I don't understand the frame of reference. Our society has always had certain freedoms. This could take a moment. Let me collect my thoughts while I try to sum up two hundred years of our country's history on individual freedom

"Our government has written a document, a constitution, which protects those rights for its people. There are some among us who would argue that the government, at times is, continually seeking new and innovative ways to take freedom from us. The argument isn't without merit, but not suitable conversation at this time.

"We have oppressed and enslaved some people and lionized others. We have fought wars over freedom, both internally and around the world. It has been a growing experience for our nation. There are many freedoms that are inherent in our governmental constitution. However, throughout our history, some administrations seemed to think that personal freedom was a threat to their power.

There is much to be learned yet. This is not the information that I seek. I hope that it has answered your inquiry to your satisfaction."

"I will add this to my files. I will require more information to compare the social structure from my time to this society. Will you assist me?"

"No, it's not my function. I am specialized in electrical and electronic functions. I will find someone to help you. Will that be sufficient?"

"Yes."

"Thank you for your information. I will let you know when you can terminate your function. Now let me give you the basic parameters for a chair. We'll work on refining the design after you've produced the first one."

"Thank you."

By the third attempt at generating a comfortable chair, Jim and the computer had met with success. With the overstuffed chair pulled closely to the table, Jim began to study the schematics. The designer had an understanding of electronics bordering on genius. The symmetry of the design was intoxicating to him. This was his life and now he was able to move beyond what he knew.

The power that could be harvested from the sun was boundless. He would be rich beyond avarice and still help mankind usher in a new era of power and individual comfort.

Jim brought his camera after speaking with J.J. Reaching into his camera bag, he realized that was almost out of film, but he continued to snap pictures in rapid succession. He needed to record as much as possible in the short time remaining. There would be other sessions, but he'd hoped that he could get all of this recorded now and not have to return unless he needed a clarification.

"Ellen, the machine is asking for you," Jim commented as he left the sphere.

Startled, Ellen asked, "What?"

"The machine has some questions on modern society and political climates around the world. It is attempting to compile a base of reference. I'm not sure to what end, and I didn't ask. I thought that it would be right up your alley."

"Why me?" she wondered aloud.

"We are all off on specialized projects concerning very specific parts of the operational components. You," he continued, "are involved in a broader project. I figured that if you could explain our politics and economics, you might garner a greater understanding of its linguistic frame of reference. You were the obvious choice."

"I agree whole heartedly. The linguistics program could aide any number of situations. It would also eliminate the need for translators during intense business and political negotiations. Imagine not having to worry that what you said was misinterpreted or misunderstood."

"I'm sincerely interested in why this request. Keep me posted. See you later."

"Good morning computer. How are you today? Not too busy I hope."

"I am functioning within my parameters. The tasks assigned have not taken any time to accomplish. Are you here to assist me?"

"Yes I am. My name is Ellen. Is it within your program to use a proper name to address someone?"

"Yes. I will refer to you as Ellen from this point forward."

"Do you have a name or designation? If you call me Ellen, I would like to call you by a name instead of just computer."

"My main function is to provide information. In addition, I am programmed to relate the story of how I came to be. The story is to be told by the one who sealed in the chamber. That would mean that I have her memory and her personality. My name is Treanna."

"Treanna. . . that's a beautiful name," observed Ellen. "What do you wish to discuss? I have a limited knowledge, but I can easily obtain any information that I don't know firsthand. Will that be acceptable?"

"Yes, Ellen. I want to know about your society. I need to know about religion and politics. I should be able to grasp more linguistic abstractions and the subtle nuances of conversation if I have a feel for the idioms and

colloquialisms of the region. I will also be able to do a comparative analysis of both cultures. I need to know about your calendar. I wish to know how long I have remained dormant."

"I can tell you today's specific date. I can explain a technique that we employ to determine the age of an object. I don't know that you will be able to determine the duration of your latent period. There is no beginning reference point common to both cultures."

"*I understand your logic, Ellen. I still desire to make an attempt. Are you able to provide the data required at this time?*"

"No. I'll need to bring you the data on carbon dating. I'll scan it into your database. It won't take long to acquire all of the current methods employed for dating materials and their relative success ratios."

"*Thank you, Ellen. Do you wish to seek information?*"

"Yes, Treanna, I would like you to display a book showing the symbols on the outside of this box and what they say or mean in my language. I would also like to know your alphabet, if you have one. That will be all. Oh, one more thing. I would like a table and chair to work from. Thank you.

In a flash, the book, the table, and the chair appeared in the center of the sphere. Ellen stepped in and moved to the table. She reached down and touched the book. It was very ornate, feminine almost. She was going to enjoy working with this machine. . . with Treanna.

Ellen settled into the overstuffed chair, it was good, but not quite right. Soon after she was seated, she explained to Treanna what the type of upholstery was that she wanted and how a chair would be constructed using padding and her specific upholstery. She then gave Treanna all the specifics about her personal choices in material colors and patterns. And then she finished off with variations of padding. In mere moments the perfect chair, in Ellen's favorite material, color and pattern appeared before her. Once she had worked out the chair's basic structure and comfort. She quickly settled in and began to study the linguistics book Treanna had provided.

The imagery was symbolic, and partially metaphoric. It was

already shaping up to be extremely complex. Jonathan had been half-right. Some of the symbols did represent phrases, but most were letters or groups of letters. It was going to be an interesting language to study. They formed a pictorial image; which in turn conveyed a message. It was going to be very interesting indeed.

"Treanna, could I have an audio of the different images? I'm interested in hearing the language as it was spoken."

"How would you prefer to hear the audio? You will need a frame of reference between the image and the vocalization."

"We have a device called a tape recorder, but it won't be practical in this situation. Can you provide me with a computer terminal on this table? I could access the images and get the audio at the same time."

The terminal materialized within seconds. There were several crystal rods on the table next to the terminal. She saw an access port on the device she assumed was the CPU. She inserted the first rod and the computer sprang to life. She spoke her request and the computer responded.

The images she had requested appeared on the screen. She touched the first one and it filled the screen. There was an animated icon at the bottom of the screen. She touched it and the audio began to play. It was the same growling that she first heard when she had accidentally turned the computer on.

Ellen was formulating an idea. She needed to discuss it with Jonathan. Her plan would let everyone get the information they wanted and then she and Jonathan were going to take over the sphere and study dinosaurs in the "simulated" flesh.

"Thank you Treanna. Retain this program in your memory and I'll return later. You may terminate your function at this time."

"Thank you, Ellen. Reactivate me whenever you need to request knowledge. I will make the chair part of your personal program from this request forward."

"That will be fine Treanna. I would like to specify that I will request the table and chair only if I need it. Keep the parameters in your program. Thank you."

"Thank you, Ellen."

The sphere went empty in a split second. She stood alone where once there was a table and chair, a book and a computer. This technology amazed her. She was going to have fun accessing its' information.

CHAPTER FORTY-NINE

E LLEN TOLD EVERYONE THAT SHE would be in sole possession of the machine for several days. They all agreed and made sure that they had enough material to keep themselves busy. It was an entire day and half before Ellen could get back to the sphere.

"Treanna, it's me. How are you today?" she asked.

"Hello, Ellen. I am operating within my parameters. How are you?"

"I'm fine. Thanks for asking. We have a lot to get accomplished in the next few days. Can we operate for the full time period allowed by your charge?"

"There is a strong direct contact with the sun. It has allowed me to maintain a full charge. The power demands have been minimal, so I am at peak operating specifications at this time. I will be able to draw a small charge if there is a full moon. The reflected light allows for a very small charge. It keeps my basic functions operational in the dark. Will there be a full moon this evening Ellen?"

"No, Treanna. Jim asked me about setting up actinic lights. They are used to simulate sunlight for aquariums. They offer the full ultraviolet spectrum and the blue light that fish need to survive. Does this interest you at all? Jim has also indicated that he might be able to connect an alternate power source to augment your requirements."

"Would it be possible for me to study the available information? I would be able to make an informed decision after I have all of the facts. I have agreed to let Jim use this power source, but would prefer to utilize only my solar capabilities."

"Treanna, I have all the information previously discussed as well as the information on the lights. I'll scan it now." Ellen went over to the scanner port and fed the papers into the machine. She stared at the port as the last page disappeared inside of this marvelous box.

A brief time passed and the machine responded. It seemed to take forever, yet only a fraction of a minute had elapsed.

"This light source will extend my useful operating time, but it would better serve as a charging station during the night. I would be at or near peak operating parameters if you set up a bank of two-dozen lights during the night. I will give you a diagram of how they should be positioned around my collecting modules."

"I'll give this information to Jim. He can arrange for the lights to be brought in and set up to your specifications. I'll only be gone for a short time. Do not terminate your function at this time. Put yourself into a sleep mode until I return and request your assistance."

"I will comply. Will there be anything else before I temporarily pause my functions?"

"There is nothing else at this time. I'll return soon, Treanna." Ellen departed with the sketch she made of Treanna's light diagram.

The drawing that Ellen gave him was complete. Jim needed no further explanation to construct the light stands. He grabbed his wallet and checked for his credit card. Stopping long enough to check a phone book, he headed to the nearest pet store to purchase the lights. He thought that he'd head out to the lumberyard at the same time, and grab some material to construct a frame. "Ellen, I'm going to pick up the material that we need to construct the stand. I won't shop anywhere near here and I won't be gone too long. See you later."

"Thanks Jim. Remember we have the piping along the building. No need to go to the lumberyard. We'll reimburse you for the lighting when you return."

"This won't cost anything Ellen. You and Jonathan don't have to worry about reimbursement. I gotta go now, if I'm going to get back at any worthwhile time."

"See you later. I sure wish you'd let us pay you back."

"We'll figure something out later. Right now, I don't see it as a problem."

"Whatever you say Jim."

Ellen returned to the sphere. "I'm back, Treanna. I hope that I didn't keep you waiting." She knew that the machine had no concept of time. She felt silly for even apologizing.

Somehow, Ellen felt like she was becoming friends with Treanna. It was a strange relationship. Ellen was flesh and blood in the modern world and Treanna was a computer program established to simulate the personality of a sixty-five million-year-old freeze-dried raptor. This relationship would be one for the record books.

Bringing herself out of her reverie, she continued, "I have a lot that I need your help with. We can only speculate how the terrain looked when you were alive."

"Yes Ellen, I understand."

"Can you show me your habitat as it existed while you were still alive? It would mean that we could better understand the fossils that we find if we understood the environmental conditions that determined behavior patterns."

"That will be possible. Would you prefer a display of just plants, or both plants and animals? I can do both if it would help you. Ellen, it would be grammatically correct to say: 'when you were not enclosed in the chamber.' 'While you were still alive' is erroneous. It assumes that Treanna has died. I have been monitoring her life signs. She is still alive on a cellular level. This chamber maintains her tissue in a perfect state. I do not wish to offend you, but you were incorrect. Shall I display the terrain at this time?"

Ellen reeled around to face the computer terminal. It was the only point that would mentally serve as a repository for the voice and personality of Treanna. She stared dumbly at the screen. "Jonathan!" she screamed. "Get in here right away. I need you."

The entire team came at a dead run. The tone of her voice was somewhat disquieting. It was reminiscent of the first growling computer incident. No one knew what they might find when they arrived. The box and its known functions were not dangerous, but no one really knew the degree of complexities or dangers that were yet to be discovered.

"Ellen, are you all right? What's wrong?" They could all see her standing just inside the sphere, facing the terminal. Her face was ashen. She shook slightly and appeared frightened or shocked.

Only Jonathan and J.J. approached her.

Placing his hand gently on her shoulder, Jonathan said, "I'm here honey. Are you okay?"

Ellen jerked away at the contact. She had not heard or seen anyone approach. She brushed her shoulder briskly as if she were trying to knock a bug from the location. Her mind was still reeling from the computers' revelation. Unable to focus on anything else she continued to briskly swipe at her shoulder.

Jonathan and J.J. both stepped back after her surprised reaction. Neither had expected that response. Jonathan comforted her again. He was not sure just what to do.

"Let go of me," she said as she brushed his arms from around her. "We need to expand our team." Ellen was regaining composure. "This raptor is still alive."

"What?!?" The team members were shocked and astonished.

"That's the most insane thing that I've ever heard," exclaimed Gerard. "Get David and Dick in here. They need to hear this."

They were almost to the sphere as Ellen made her startling revelation. "We heard her," said Dick as they reached the group. "We heard her quite clearly." They came into the sphere and joined the others. They were not as upset by the news as the others had been. The rest seemed to notice the distinct difference in the reaction.

"David and I had just come to that conclusion this morning. The evidence we gathered from Treanna's diagrams would indicate a very sophisticated system. Under normal conditions it might not be possible to sustain life for the period of time that we're dealing with. Remember though, this container had been sealed in a tomb for all of this time and was not subject to the forces of nature that have destroyed so many other valuable fossils. There is a strong possibility that we'll still find a small sample of living tissue.

"The landmass that supported the cave, while it existed in real time, shifted and moved as a whole over the millennia. There would have been nothing to discover if normal tectonic activity was at play. If Ellen is correct, our suspicions will be validated."

"Ellen, how did you conclude that the raptor is alive? You're neither trained or involved in this branch of science."

"I made a statement to the computer while asking for a display. I had said *'while you were still alive.'* The computer corrected me. It explained that the raptor was alive. That's when I called for everyone."

"Wait a minute. We're talking about a sample of living tissue, right?"

"No. The machine said that it was monitoring Treanna's vital signs and it said that she is still alive."

"This is phenomenal news!" Dick looked around the group to see if anyone else felt his level of elation. "When can we open this up and get a firsthand look at a living dinosaur?" he asked.

"I would think that we would need to study the machinery a little more closely before we attempted anything that fool hearty. We know nothing about the equipment yet." Ellen glanced around to see the nods of agreement from the others. Continuing, she added, "Have you even considered what you are trying to revive? This animal was the most effective killing machine of all time. It's even more deadly than a Great White shark. Sharks are effective predators, but Treanna is a sentient, intelligent killing machine. Do you really want it roaming freely among us? It would take what, five or ten minutes, while it shreds us beyond recognition? I vote no."

"Ellen's right. We can wait on this one. Let's get as much information as we can from what we've gathered so far. We can always come back for more. Ellen, are you going to be all right with this? I can stay with you," Jonathan added. "J.J. could spell me if you would like."

"Actually, I was going to call you down for this display. Treanna is going to show us the natural habitat and the overall lay of the land. She is even going to include the animal life that was present while she was there."

"We can study dinosaur behavior first hand? Oh my God. That's sensational! When can we start?"

"Right now," she said. Turning back to the computer, Ellen said, "Treanna, you may start the display now."

"As you wish. Will there be anything else?"

"No, that will be all for now. Thank you, Treanna."

CHAPTER FIFTY

"WHY DO YOU THANK A machine for doing the job it was designed to do?"

"Weren't you paying attention just now? This machine is the embodiment of the living creature in the chamber. It's her life and her personality. Machine interface or not, she's alive and deserves the respect that we'd give to anyone."

"But she's an animal," Dick protested.

"You arrogant son-of-a-bitch," snapped Ellen. "This *animal* has more intelligence than our best human counterparts. It's that kind of attitude that has us hiding in this God forsaken warehouse to protect our very lives. Get with the program. Do you think that you can come to terms with the fact that there may be, or at the very least, has been life more intelligent than us?"

"I'm sorry Ellen. It didn't come out the way it was intended. I understand and agree with your views. Let's debate the merits of my stupidity later. Right now, we need to bury ourselves into this research."

"I won't let this go that easily Dick. We will have that discussion later."

"Fair enough," he answered.

"Do you wish for me to start the program now?"

Startled, Ellen and Dick noticed that the sphere was still empty. They looked at each other and Ellen spoke, "I already asked that you begin the program."

"Yes, Ellen. You engaged Dick in a conversation that was distracting

you both from your request. The program is paused at the start point to wait until you were fully prepared."

"Thank you, Treanna," answered Dick. "That was thoughtful of you. We're ready now for the program to begin. Please start."

Ellen smiled.

Almost instantly, the sphere flickered to life. Before them was a vista that was beyond imagination. The primeval forest stretched out as far as the eye could see. They were standing on an escarpment. Their view was uninterrupted for miles. They turned around and the view was still broad and uninterrupted. They were totally surrounded by the forest. There were pterodactyls flying off in the distance. The streams ran along the forest floor, a major element in an intricate web of life.

The ferns rattled and shook a little as Jonathan emerged from behind them. "I guess I was a little off the mark, where I was standing. I ended up back there, but I heard you two talking so I pushed my way through the brush to find you here. It's more beautiful than I ever dared imagine," apologized Jonathan.

"Ellen, is everything to your liking?"

"Yes Treanna. Thank you," she said breathlessly. The imagery was so astounding that neither she nor Dick could speak through the sheer majesty of the display.

Responding to Ellen's statement, Treanna said, *"That is okay, Ellen. I was happy to do it. I would like to share my story with you."*

Ellen lurched away from the clawed appendage that grabbed her shoulder. She recoiled in fright when she turned and saw a raptor standing behind her. Jonathan appeared from nowhere and grabbed her arm, yanking her away.

"Do not be frightened. I am only a holographic image. I told you that there is nothing to fear. No harm will come to you. She extended her claw tipped appendage. The claws were fierce and dangerous looking. The killing claw of her toe caused a clicking noise as it twitched and tapped at the ground."

Ellen tentatively took it in her hand. It was warm. There appeared to be a smile spread across Treanna's face. One could only speculate. Ellen's heart raced with fear and exhilaration.

They walked a little closer to the edge of the ridge they were standing on. Treanna drew in a deep breath. She seemed to be enjoying the beauty that lay before them.

Ellen stared at her in wonder. She was trying to calculate in her mind, whether this was a computer simulation of how the machine expected Ellen to see Treanna, or was this, the real thing. Could dinosaurs hold this depth of emotion? What were they capable of? There were so many new questions racing through her head that she wouldn't be able to remember half of them.

"Is it not glorious? I had almost forgotten how beautiful it was. I have been dormant for too long. I want to show you everything. It will take a while; do you have the time?"

"Yes Treanna. Jonathan and I will take all the time you feel is necessary to see and understand everything you want to show us. Where's Dick, he was with me a moment ago?"

"He was on his way out when I grabbed your arm just now. He seemed distraught, yet strangely invigorated."

"Thanks, dear. I was concerned. I'd forgotten about him and only just remembered that we entered together."

Turning to Treanna, Jonathan asked, "Are you this good natured all of the time Treanna? Was this your personality when you were not computer generated? I mean no offense. We study dinosaurs and have made some speculations based on fossil remains. From the formidable claws, we have concluded that your species were savage killers. You are built for speed and cunning hunters. You must have been terrifying to the other species."

"Jonathan, you are partially correct. We possessed the ability to kill in a ruthless and savage manner. Our civilization had developed beyond the random killing of other species. We had refined it down to a game called the Hunt. There were the food animals that we raised for nutrition. We would send them down a pre-selected route and lay in wait for them. We would then use our natural abilities to slaughter the animals and feed. It

kept our inborn hunting skills sharp and honed to a degree that we found sexually satisfying.

"I should explain that great hunting skill and prowess meant superior genetic traits. The males and females found this very exciting. The species would always be able to propagate through natural selection, but this allowed some of us to remain stronger than others, increasing the level of skill and intelligence being passed on to future generations.

"There were always stories of the Hunt. First kill held high honors. When a male or female accumulated several first kills, they would find themselves at the genetics lab being evaluated. Traits and genetic codes would eventually be used to improve the species as a whole.

"If that happened to some beast, he or she could select a mate from any male or female. The honor was great and those being asked to become a mate never turned down the privilege. Sometimes those being chosen were previously mated. When asked, their mates would always agree to the one-time coupling. The government rewarded them for their contributions to the species. It was a good system that helped us remain a dominant species for millions of years.

"I am jumping ahead in my story. Let me take you to the valleys that they used to run the animals. I will show you a hunt and then we can start at the beginning of the story. Hurry up; the Hunt will almost be over before we negotiate the trails that lead down the hill."

"Can't you start the hunt when we get there? After all, it's just a program," stated Jonathan. "We don't have to rush. Perhaps you'd like to relate your story now. We can get to the *HUNT* whenever it fits with the story. I know that Ellen and I are anxious to see and hear it all, but we do need to observe a proper time line. If you have no objections, we can start as soon as you're ready."

"Thank you, Jonathan. It would make the story more understandable if we were to start from the beginning, with no sidebars. We can still go down to the place where Agron and I first met. That is almost where the story begins.

"You see, before I met Agron and fell in love with him, I was a government operative. I was sent to spy on him and report my findings back

to the military. It was never explained to me why they had such an intense interest in him. He was the foremost geneticist at the complex, and it was not unusual to keep a shadow surveillance of such important researchers. The government wanted to be sure that everything they required from each scientist be completed as they had ordered.

"In the beginning I was reporting everything that I saw, heard, or learned. After I met Agron, face to face, and we became friends, I fell in love. We became lovers and I soon understood his cause and was willing to aid him in it. That was how I came to be locked in this chamber, never completely dead and never completely alive."

The trip through the ancient rain forest was exciting. There were strange new sounds and remarkably, new scents. The ability of the computer was phenomenal. The attention to detail was amazing. There was no end to the tiny creatures, mammal and reptilian, that crossed their path. The insects buzzed around and there were a few dinosaurs here and there throughout the forest.

The program provided a reality that could not be rivaled. The texture of the plants was exacting in every detail. There were fish like creatures swimming in the steams and ponds. Water lilies bloomed and gave off their sweet perfume. The insects, though seen, did not bother them. The Crenshaw's were grateful for that detail. Jonathan hated insects, even after all of his years in the field. Ellen did not like to be bitten or stung. She was also very happy.

Treanna kept a lively pace. They had difficulty keeping up with her. She stopped on several occasions to sniff the air and look about. The Crenshaw's caught up to her at these stops. They suspected that the pauses were a polite way of waiting. Treanna didn't say, and they didn't ask.

As they entered a clearing that held a small shrine, Treanna stopped and bowed her head. She turned to Jonathan and Ellen and started her story again.

"This is where it all began. This is the reputed sight of the birth of our culture. It has been said that this is where the Great Beast rose from ignorance and developed intellectual awareness. He was the first self-aware

beast and he sought out others to build genetically on his traits. He was a colossal genius among the ignorant. His intuitive abilities helped to teach others and develop the scientific concepts that eventually escalated our species beyond instinctual killers to beasts of science, art and leaders of our world.

"Thousands of generations after the Great Beast guided us to sentience; we formed a genetics lab here and a university to support it. We genetically altered our food animals and ourselves. We maximized the best traits for greater food value and to protect the herds from others.

"The Great Beast was the lawgiver for all species. He lived and taught for a thousand years, as it is told, before he left us to build on what he had begun. His program to help establish intelligence was brilliant.

"He started a small community and helped other beasts to understand their own intellectual powers. Teaching and refining hunting techniques provided ample free time to devote to increasing mental capabilities and awareness.

"This original group formed the core beliefs of our religious and social structure. They spread slowly throughout the area until their numbers were in the hundreds. Being of superior intelligence, they survived longer and grew stronger. He then established The Ten Laws:

First: Preserve the nest.

Second: Do not kill your own kind except in war.

Third: Practice and refine your hunting and killing skills always. You were

born as a weapon of honor. You must strive to die as a weapon of honor.

Forth: To die in a struggle for preservation of the nest or to die in combat is the highest honor.

Fifth: Avenge; with harsh retribution, all acts against the individual, the family, or the herd.

Sixth: Challenge the old to do battle at the end of their days. Let the struggle linger before you kill them. They need to feel the honor and the memory of battle at their final moment. It brings honor to those who bring honor to the old.

Seventh: Do not use science to change that which we are. Science and technology are for the benefit of the species, not for personal comfort.

Eighth: Do not plot to usurp another's property or mate.

Ninth: Worship the Gods of the earth for creating us, and in their infinite wisdom allowing us to become the masters of our world.

Tenth: Nothing has greater value than the Gods of the earth. No thought, action or deed can hold sway over their power of life and death.

"Once these laws were established and became a code to live by, the Great Beast divided his followers and helped them establish communities far and wide.

"These small groups eventually formed clans. The clans formed regional governments and established order. They all answered to the Great Beast. He was the titular head of all species and ruled supreme above all other regional laws.

"The followers of the Great Beast spread the word of his deeds and what he had accomplished wherever they settled. Following him soon became similar to your religions. It was less a religion, than a code of ethics and social behavior that all obeyed resolutely.

"Millennia passed and as with all things, there were those who sought to gain power through less than ethical practices. Over the millennia these splinter groups formed and disbanded in an attempt to subvert the teachings of the Great Beast. They had all failed because there was only one Great Beast and his laws were sacrosanct.

"All had failed until a little more than two hundred years before we were born. It was an insidious creeping of corrupt values and promises of a better life that led some beasts to believe that negligence was more rewarding than productivity.

"They bastardized the teachings of the Great Beast and explained what he really meant by what he had written and taught for thousands of years. Some beasts would rather follow blindly, any leader – false or true – as long as they don't have to think. If there were feed animals to kill, they were content, oblivious to the decay that was spreading around them.

"The easy life, and the bad habits that resulted, created a sub-culture of beasts that depended on the unethical to supply that which they always had if they simply chose to get it. After many generations, it became so ingrained that no beast was willing to take the falsely gained power away

from the unethical leadership. Also, they refused to be the beasts that they were born to be. They became totally dependent on the handouts from the leaders and could no longer function as normal and active beasts. It was the beginning of the end of a society that lasted a thousand millennia.

"There were many of us that saw the error of the leadership. We were harangued and chastised to a point of madness. We became a laughable and despised segment of every community. Ignorance was threatening to take full control and disrupt countless generations of the Lawgiver's rule. Chaos and slovenliness were the norm.

"It became impossible to express your views in public places. Those among us who dared; spoke out against the leaders. We faced harsh and swift retribution.

"I'm getting ahead of myself. This story must be told in the proper sequence so that you can fully understand all that we were facing. It's a justification of sorts. Even terrorists can justify what they have done. We were genetic terrorists. Unlike your modern terrorists, who bomb and kill countless innocents, what we did could be undone with the right keys.

"Our government was so bent on the total subjugation of its' subjects that it destroyed any chance of undoing what was done. Our victory was our downfall. We did not survive to undo anything. We brought about the extinction of our kind through our high moral conduct.

It was so easy to feel good about the things that must be done. It had proven to be quite different when we did not take the time to consider the consequences. We were all high and mighty about helping the masses and the net result was we destroyed an entire civilization through our self-righteous hubris.

"In our hubris, we assumed that we could reshape, rebuild, and return to the path that was provided. We could not see beyond the end of our collective noses. There was no beast that could have predicted all the permutations resulting from our actions. We didn't consider that there might be more than the one outcome that we wanted to see. It will be the downfall of your society as well. Your government is already moving in that direction. It has been for decades now. I'm sorry; I didn't mean to digress like that. I'm so full of remorse right now that it just slipped out.

"Ellen and Jonathan, I wish to take you to the nursery where I was hatched and raised. It was a wonderful place. I have the file in my data banks somewhere. I will initiate the program and it will be running when we arrive.

"We were a loving and caring community. However, there was too much outside interference, and that contaminated us. We lost our identity and then our souls. We gave it all up, life, love, happiness, everything. All was forsaken, so the government could give us back a small portion of what we were forced to give them.

"There is a wonderful breeze blowing. Look at the trees swaying to a natural rhythm. I remember a prayer to the Gods when the wind blew so gently and beautifully."

Treanna pointed a claw in the direction of the swaying trees. A steady breeze had picked up while they had been walking and listening as Treanna's story unfolded. The path down the slope and through the forest required their full attention. They hadn't even noticed the breeze until Treanna mentioned it. They watched as her lips moved in a silent invocation to her Gods. It was amazing to behold the depth of emotion and familial commitment.

The trio finally reached flat ground and the trek became easier. The massive ferns and palm trees that reached to the sky blocked their view. However, they provided a different view. The small animals that lived in the forest canopy scurried from sight, trying to see the intruders without being seen themselves. It was fascinating.

There was the same abundance and variety of life that was in the modern-day rain forest. Nature may vary the type and size of its occupants on this earth, but it seems to stick with a winning pattern once it finds one.

"This is magnificent Treanna. Who among us could have imagined this diversity of life? We have always assumed that your forests resembled our own, but now we know for sure. It's breathtaking to behold."

Thank you, Ellen. I'd forgotten how wonderful it was. Now that it's only a program, I lost my memory of it. To see it again has brought those memories back. Thank you for this request.

Once again, Treanna had assured Ellen and Jonathan of their safety as they relaxed in the shade next to a stream. The forest floor was alive with activity. They just stared and pointed with child-like wonder. There were insects and plants that they'd never seen or heard of. This was a true ecological marvel, with all the lush abundance of any contemporary rain forest and without the deforestation so common in present time.

CHAPTER FIFTY-ONE

T HE NEW DAY BROUGHT MORE information. Today Treanna showed the Crenshaw's the kill that brought Agron to the government's attention. They had seen lions kill before. Nothing compared to the savagery of this attack. The raptors were in class alone. Their killing prowess was unequaled in the contemporary world. They attacked with forethought and cunning; attacking with ferocity not seen in the modern world. Unlike a pride of lions, these animals could alter plans and communicate the changes while on the run. The dance with death they beheld was as beautiful as any ballet.

"That was my Agron. It was that kill that had brought him to the attention of the government. He was the most intelligent of all of the genetic biologists. They feared that they would lose him during a Hunt. They sent me to become acquainted with him. They also wanted to understand why the herd animals seemed to be getting larger and more intelligent.

"The teams in charge of the herds had made no gene modifications. It was against government regulations to increase the intelligence of a food animal. They suspected it was more than natural selection. The whispered question was 'Why our herd animals and not others?' It was before I'd come to know the truth about Argon, so I dutifully obeyed my orders and spied on him."

"Why would they be suspicious of Argon? Had he made his anti-government views known?" asked Jonathan. The program stopped. The images faded and the sphere stood silent.

"I'm not sure. Agron was the best in his field, larger, stronger, smarter, and he was not mated. He was a loner. That alone made him suspect. Your government also says a 'loner' profile is always a suspect if I'm correct.

"Besides, after what the government had done to his family; they would be justified in suspecting him. That's one of the problems with secrets; they have a way of getting out. Like water, they will find he smallest opening and pass through to the light of day. There are no secrets; just facts that take longer to become common knowledge.

"What would your government do or say if they knew that you possessed this technology? Don't you believe that they would attempt to deprive you of it? They are the same as my government. You would be wise to protect yourself. It's not beyond doubt that they would kill you because you possess this knowledge. Once they discover what you have you will become a threat to them. Your lives will be forfeit."

"Thank you for the insight Treanna. We are very aware of the far-reaching consequences of this technology. We would hope to survive long enough for it to benefit all of society," said Jonathan. "Our intention is to share this with the rest of the world before anything fatal befalls our group. We hope that once this technology is available to all, we will be protected."

"You are a fool Jonathan Crenshaw. Do you actually think that you and this group of scientists can outwit the combined force of your government and all its international allies? This group is soon to be a target, if not already. Where could you hide from a world full of powerful people and governments who had every resource at their disposal?"

"Treanna, that isn't your concern. You're frightening Ellen."

"Good. Maybe she can talk some sense into you. This is a fool hearty adventure. I have witnessed first-hand the senseless slaughter of Agron's family. It was over nothing. They had the power to do it, so they did. Your government may not have done it to one of its citizens yet, but you will provide them with ample motivation when they discover your secret. Remember that when you threaten any government, you are no longer a citizen, you are the enemy."

"Enough! We are here to learn from you. If we are to win at all, we need as much information as possible. You aren't contributing to that education with your arguments. Each moment we lose is one step closer to defeat."

"Do not interrupt me again until I have finished. What do you think is going on here? You are talking to a political prisoner of greater significance than either of you. I have been imprisoned for sixty-five million years for presumed crimes far less important than you are committing. Do you think that our governments are that dissimilar? Do you honestly believe that you will survive? You are a scientist, yes, and a total fool.

"Let me explain to you exactly how I came to be in the chamber. They discovered that I was Agron's lover beyond the sex I performed for the sake of spying. I don't know how they found out, but that's not the issue. They had the knowledge and they exploited it. What they didn't know was that I was prepared to die rather than reveal all of Agron's secrets. I could never betray my love.

"They brought me to this box and held me here while they examined all the functions. Some functions were encrypted and they didn't know enough to access them. That lack of information kept them from gaining ultimate power over all beasts. Then they brought Agron to the box. They forced me to watch as they tortured him for information. Then when it was obvious that he wasn't going to reveal anything, they murdered him in front of me. I fainted from the horror and the shock.

"General Cresh was too large to fit into the box, so he had my body dragged outside. That's when he told me of his plans to slowly torture me to death. He continued on this line for a while until he said that he'd changed his mind. It had occurred to him that since I loved Agron so much, I should spend an eternity with his creation. He placed me in the chamber and filled it with the liquid that you see now. It would preserve me in a living, conscious state for an indefinite number of years.

"My punishment for loving Agron, my species, and my world, was to be entombed in this box for thousands of years to contemplate my wrong doing while I waited to die."

Ellen and Jonathan were stunned to silence. They now understood the full depth of her information the maniacal threat Treanna's government represented to the populous at large. It was the most inhumane punishment that they'd ever heard.

"I'm not an expert at espionage," offered Jonathan. "I have, however, foreseen some of the actions that the government can take against us. From the onset we have taken precautions to remain undetected. We are aware that we will ultimately be discovered. Our team has taken great measures to avoid detection. All measures have been considered. . . except one.

"We think that the box emitted a power surge when we accidentally opened it. It could have been picked up by satellite. Should this be true, they're probably already on our trail. I've made sure that all prudent precautions have been taken since that accident.

"There are going to be many mistakes along the way. We only want to buy enough time to secure our safety. Once we've gone public, we will be safer than we are now. That is why we need you to help in every way you can offer."

"I understand. I will continue my program. I wish you luck, even though it's a fool's mission. Your odds of success are significantly small. There is so much that I could teach you, if you would only stop to learn.

"I will be able to erase all of my programming if it must come to that. I don't have an auto destruct system. My technology will still be accessible by any that can get into the box, and then to me. I am very concerned about that."

"Don't be concerned Treanna." Ellen's tone was soothing, but edged with fear. "We won't abandon you without making sure that you are destroyed. Our government and some of our businesses can be ruthless in their pursuit of power and wealth. We've seen many things that we haven't discussed with you. Yes, we're naïve, but we aren't completely unaware. This will be a difficult struggle, but we will prevail."

"Those are the very words that have echoed in my brain for sixty-five million years. There is a minute possibility of your success. I will not lie to you. I am sorry if those odds create fear in you. It's only the truth. We will continue the program now."

CHAPTER FIFTY-TWO

THE PROGRAM RESUMED. THE HOLOGRAPHIC chamber sprang to life. They were still at the site of the 'Hunt', but there were no carnosaurs around. The 'Hunt' had raised the noise level immensely. The normal insect and small animal sounds now made the forest seem almost silent by comparison.

Treanna's image materialized a few meters to their left. She had a somber countenance. It was difficult to describe the subtle difference from the happier, more jubilant Treanna. Her posture was now erect, stiff and mechanical. Her voice was subdued. The zest was missing; now only a hologram devoid of emotional content.

She directed them to a location that was the government educational facilities for geneticist. This is where Agron had developed his immense mental powers. He worked here in the government laboratory, and also had a secret lab not too far from these facilities.

This was where Treanna first met him. *"Here is where I fell in love and turned my back on my job, government."* The memory meant a lot to her and neither replied. It was difficult for her to share this portion of her life, yet she continued. Even as a hologram, she was programmed with enough of the real Treanna to feel the anguish. Still she persevered. She knew that the Crenshaw's must see what had taken place to understand and disseminate the information to the proper scientists. It was their only hope, regardless of how slim the odds.

Remembering the life and love that existed in this place, as if it were only yesterday, Treanna shed a holographic tear. Its glistening image trailed down her muzzle and dropped from the edge of her lip. It vanished before it hit the ground. Ellen stepped closer and hugged her. She cried more freely now. They were both crying now. Jonathan stepped back, looking at the ground.

They went in and out of the formations that served as classrooms. This was in the limestone outcropping. The cave made more sense now that they understood the purpose. Jonathan guessed it originally it was roughly ten acres, and much taller than the contemporary hill.

The government was able to establish a school that was protected from the rigors of their environment. The lab equipment that he saw would rival that of any major university. It would even shame some of the current business facilities.

Treanna appeared to be more herself. Ellen had explained there was a real danger in attempting to circumvent the government, but they would push forward. Sharing this science was the most important aspect of this journey. She had explained how her government was founded on moral principles and that is why we had survived so long.

It had only been in the last seventy to eighty years that the government was trying to subvert the doctrines that they had once held true for over two-hundred years. These were trying times because there were many people who still believed in the old system, but the government had indoctrinated enough of the rest of society to effectively bring about the impending downfall of the old system and ethical beliefs.

Ellen had said that they were aware – from the moment that the box was discovered – that there would be danger. They were Americans, and this country was forged from the struggle against a government that was too abusive and oppressive. She explained that they were upholding a tradition bought and paid for with the blood of countless innocent lives. They would not go quietly if and when the time came.

"We will return to the school for more information," was all Treanna said.

The school was alive with students and teachers. The pace of the academic life was brisk. She pointed out Agron as he moved down the corridor. He was taller and more muscular than the others, even at this early age. Agron walked with certain nobility. He was self-aware and confident. There was an air about him. He was basking in the attention even though he didn't acknowledge it.

"He's very handsome Treanna. It's no surprise that you could fall in love with him. If I were a raptor, I could imagine the ease of it." They both giggled. Jonathan shuffled nervously. The relaxed moment would be profitable later, for now he was out of his element in the middle of girl talk.

"Let me take you to Argon's secret laboratory. It's not much. He salvaged equipment from all over the campus. There was so much in storage here, that even if he took something new, no one would miss it.

"This outcropping covers a vast area. I will calculate in your acres. It will only take a moment." The whole of the facility covers fifty square acres, counting the eleven acres of the outcropping. *"There is a massive tunnel complex throughout the entire rise. This area has been stable for over a thousand years. Argon's lab was in an unused and never visited section on the far side. It was well past the government and scholastic portions of the complex.*

"I'll show you the tunnels and trails that he used to move undetected from his lab to his secret lab. It was a circuitous route. A young guard stopped him once. All the kid wanted was an autograph, so he risked a reprimand to come to this section of the complex. He had seen the kill that I showed you earlier. Agron walked out with him after he'd given him his prize and then returned to his lab to divert attention. That was as close as he ever came to being detected."

The trio walked silently for a while. Treanna whispered a tidbit of information here and there. She acted as if this place was a shrine, pointing out things of interest and importance. The Crenshaw's respected that, and used the same hushed tones in response. They rounded a corner in a dimly lit passageway and walked straight into a wall. Even though the wall was computer generated, they halted abruptly. The realism of the hologram made it easy to forget it was false.

Treanna extended a forelimb and inserted her claw into a small indentation. The Crenshaw's had not noticed it until Treanna touched it. The wall slid open and they were in a dank, dark portion of the complex. This was clearly seldom used. They followed a narrow track down the dusty center of the passage. This was how Agron traveled to and from his lab in the main complex.

They came to another wall after walking about ten minutes. Treanna put her claw into another indentation and the wall slid away. They were looking out into the primeval forest. The ferns and other plants grew right up to the side of the complex.

Treanna motioned them forward and then turned to close the opening. She guided them along the edge of the complex to another seemingly blank wall. There she opened another hidden doorway and they stepped into Agron's lab.

"This is how the lab looked the last time I was here. Every room in the complex has been programmed into my database. There are even a few places such as this, which I programmed in myself after my brain was entered into the computer memory. The box was meant to be instructional. You must remember that this is only a simulation. It's not a sixty-five million-year-old room." Her muzzle contorted into what served as a smile. They looked a bit sheepish.

"You don't have to be embarrassed. This technology is new to you. When you are playing a game or running a program for the first time, you get so caught up in whatever you are doing that you forget that this is only a projection of a memory. I have done it countless times myself."

The Crenshaw's moved around the laboratory asking about the different equipment. They found it genuinely fascinating. Treanna announced that her power supply was diminishing rapidly. She would be required to terminate her function within the hour.

Not wanting to lose any of the information to low power, they opted to discontinue Treanna's function now. The images vanished instantly; leaving the Crenshaw's and Treanna back in the empty sphere.

"I'm thirsty. Let's get something to drink. I should have had water instead of that soda. Soda only makes me thirsty," said Ellen.

"Me too. Would you like to come to my room pretty lady?"

"For a cool glass of water, mister, I'll show you a real good time. Let's get started."

They both laughed as they went to get some water. The others were in various stages of preparations for tomorrow's use of the sphere.

The scientific community would be debating this technology and its benefits for decades. The impact was going to be staggering. The benefits were yet innumerable; so much had to be done in such a short period of time. They wondered if they were equal to the task. The enormity and complexity of the technology made them feel insignificant.

Jim had the light banks in place and Jonathan turned them on when they exited the sphere. In all, it was a remarkable day. They stayed a while and looked at the empty sphere. It was hard to imagine that three weeks ago they had a normal, uncomplicated life. This discovery would truly change their world forever. It would soon uproot all of the beliefs and religious doctrines around the world. This was Pandora's Box.

CHAPTER FIFTY-THREE

"I'M BACK," CALLED J.J. FROM the door, waving several large bags. "We're going to have Mexican tonight. I found a place that was having a grand opening while I was on my way to get the pizza. This is the real deal. I've got spicy corn soup, rice and tomatoes, tortillas, and practically anything else that you can think of. I must have bought the place out. They were sure happy to see me coming."

The food was barely on the table when the bags vanished. The aroma filled the room. It smelled wonderful. They attacked the food as if they were a pack of starving animals. It smelled great to Ellen but didn't hold her interest.

Turning to Jonathan, Ellen whispered, "Well this is out of the ordinary. Everyone is ravenous. We should keep tabs on our eating and drinking habits."

Ellen then smiled at J.J. and said, "This is wonderful dear, but I'm not up to this much spice this evening. If you don't mind, I'm going to rummage around in the refrigerator to see what I can rustle up." She got up and headed to the refrigerator.

"Are you all right, mom? Is there anything that I can get for you?" questioned J.J.

"Your dad and I have already been down that road. I'm fine. I'm just a little out of sorts. Why is everyone so concerned? Am I growing horns or something?" She turned away from him and went to the fridge. *I hope that we're all fine. I need to evaluate everyone's behavior. It has to be radiation or something to do with the sphere.*

She poked around and shuffled a few containers. She found the soup that she had hoped for. Popping the soup into the microwave, she waited. She could see the animated conversation at the supper table. She wanted to get back. More than that, she wanted to be distracted from her uneasiness. The microwave beeped, startling her. Carrying the soup back to the table, she managed not to spill any of her treasure.

As she walked up, David greeted her. "Ellen, you're just in time." Without any hesitation, he asked the first question. "What was the secret lab like?"

"Well David, there was more equipment in there than I've seen in some of our better labs, both scholastic and private."

David interrupted as he let out a sharp whistle and then fell silent.

"I couldn't begin to tell you what all that stuff was or even guess at their functions. We didn't get that far. We did ask a few questions though, but I can't remember the specific answers. There was so much going on and it's not our field of expertise.

"In fact, I wanted to know if you would come with us tomorrow. I'm sure that Treanna would be happy to help you. If you request his genetics lab you can get a sense of the layout and it'll help on your research. You could ask the detailed questions needed to get the specific information."

"That would be great," said David. "I can hardly wait. This is so cool." He buried his face into some unknown tasty morsel and smiled.

Ellen smiled back at him, inwardly amused. He truly loved his toys. The lab, even though it was holographic, would be a toy he'd never forget. She began to eat her soup before it cooled too much.

"How is it in there?" asked Jim, now that he had a chance to interrupt. "We've all had our few moments with her. I'm just curious to see how the day went."

Jonathan fielded that question so Ellen could continue eating. "You tend to forget that you're in a hologram. You find yourself doing things as if your surroundings are real. It's a fascinating experience. Let me tell you this, the raptors are so real that you're frightened from the moment that you see the first one. You can even smell their breath. Liquid is wet. You sweat in the sun. It's as real as it gets.

There will be a great commercial application for this technology once we're through here."

"I would think that it would expand many scientific endeavors as well. You could see the double helix. You could walk around it, touch it, and manipulate it. The applications would be endless," observed Dick excitedly.

"You're right Dick. The real money's in entertainment. This thing can be packaged in many ways. The commercial and private sectors will go crazy over it. It will obviously start as scientific and governmental. They'll have the money to do the research. We can spin off and market the rest once the technology is established. Imagine doing an operation on a holographic patient, fully rendered, until you perfect a technique that will save a life. Any kind of medical theory, no matter how hair brained can be tested over and over without ever hurting a patient."

Jonathan scanned the group and stopped at each person to look them squarely in the eyes, and then continued, "We must all agree to be partners in this. Without full co-operation, we're sunk. Business will suck this up and it will be lost. It's going to be a major fight to keep the university from laying claim to it. They paid for the dig and this was the result of it.

"What do you think? Each one of you can see the benefits this will bring to your respective branches of science. I hope that you can see the monetary gains that can be made. We'll have research jobs the rest of our lives, just analyzing the technology. We haven't even scratched the surface on Treanna's capabilities."

There was a resounding "yes" from everyone seated at the table. They were all in this for the long haul. They each understood how important secrecy was to the project. And each agreed to do whatever it took to get this done and then move to the next phase in the shortest time possible.

No one noticed that Jim, who was standing behind David, hadn't responded. It was assumed from the overwhelming affirmation that he'd joined in with the others. "I need to know how this entire complex was powered," he said flatly when the group quieted down.

"Where did the electricity come from? It's very confusing. They've gotten the maximum use from their solar panels; the diagrams Treanna supplied have proven that. That would still not supply enough electricity to operate all of the equipment that you've described. If you could ask that question for me, I won't need to come along tomorrow. I can stay here and finish up on the solar panel schematics." *If I can get them to do my work for me, I can finish my proposals for commercializing these solar collectors. This is mine and mine alone. I can retire in a year on the money from the initial licensing fees and live lavishly for the rest of my life on the royalties and additional licensing fees.*

"Sure Jim," said Jonathan. "We can do that for you. The answer may surprise all of us. We can have her lay out schematics for you to study. You'd probably find it more fascinating to see the operation itself. She can show you almost anything that you can imagine. Her memory banks contain more information than I thought would be possible."

"Get me the information first. I'll go later. It does sound very exciting though. I don't want to break away until I've finished this project. I could get bogged down in all of these little side trips and then never get anything finished. I'm only trying to adhere to the most work with fewest hours plan we started with." *That should keep them off my back for a while. I need to get done and out of here before anyone realizes what's happened.*

"That's fair enough. You don't have to defend yourself with us. We all understand your position," laughed Jonathan.

Jim didn't want to feel pressured into spending unnecessary time in the sphere when he could be stealing the solar collector technology. He felt more comfortable now, knowing he could get away with his plan.

Steve hadn't said anything yet. He sat back in his chair and relaxed. His theory had been proven. He had a chance to see the nursery when Treanna gave him the same tour as the Crenshaw's.

"How much longer will the tale take to unfold?" asked J.J.

"She hasn't said. The details surrounding the decision to revolt against the government are being laid out now. I estimate another day, maybe two at the very most. Treanna moves at her own pace. She's running a program for us, but she also has the latitude to independently operate sub-routines within that program. She, the computer, is actually artificial intelligence.

"Consider how fast it picked up on our language. It already knows contractions although she doesn't use many of them yet. It can distinguish between fact and humor. It knows when the operator is angry or upset. That's way beyond any of our AI programs. It's only been a fantasy that we hope to achieve someday."

"Why is it so complicated to believe that it's AI?" asked Jonathan. He knew full well what he possessed. *There will be billions of dollars at my disposal, once this goes public. The research I could do and the qualified people I could finance. It's a dream come true. I'll give the University a billion dollars to stay off my back. They'll jump through that hoop.*

The group pondered what he'd just asked. A few nibbled from the leftovers as they sat in silence. Others leaned on elbows or furrowed their brows. It was not all that complicated Jonathan thought to himself. He'd already laid down the critical importance of the discovery and the importance of the secrecy. He shook his head with disbelief. *I can't believe that they're so thick headed. Do I need to draw them a road map? Wake up people. Smell the success.*

"Is there anyone here that would dispute the claim that the machine is AI? You've all had your turn with her. I'm open for debate." Jonathan scanned their faces; waiting for some answers.

"I don't disagree with you," said Gerard. "I think that you misunderstood. We all somehow knew that she was AI. It's a lot of information to comprehend. We were just facing a reality that we only suspected." He turned to look up and down the table at the others. He saw heads nodding in affirmation of his statement.

"Sorry. I was sure that I'd explained it well enough. Your expressions puzzled me. I'm sorry for doubting all of you. You were hand-picked for good reasons. I'm guilty of forgetting that. Forgive me." *At least my partners aren't total idiots. That's a relief. For a moment I thought that they'd gotten their credentials from a Cracker Jack's box*

"There's nothing to forgive," said Steve, finally finding his voice. "We all understand a lot's been happening. We keep talking about turning the academic world on its collective ear; what about *our* world? You see what's been happening to us while we sit here day after day as each new discovery is revealed. *Cut us some slack. Don't turn into a pushy bastard. We need time, that's all.* "We're conducting experiments and writing papers as if this box and its' contents were everyday normal stuff. We're trying to deal with the technological leaps, protect the contents, and maintain secrecy that would rival a government.

"Our curious expressions are well earned. You don't owe us an apology. This will end this conversation as far as we're concerned." Turning to the others he asked, "Am I right?" *We don't need to beat this horse anymore, it's dead. Let's get past this and move on.*

There was a general consensus of agreement. No one had any issues with Steve's comments. They'd all been fighting their own demons. Steve had aired internal. As a group, they all felt relief from the tension.

They slowly drifted back to their respective tasks. A couple gathered to exchange a brief word here and there. As the last of them left the table or ended a conversation, Jonathan turned and smiled at Ellen. He'd been able to come to terms with the situation. Both he and Ellen had been exposed to the box and its' wonders for a longer period of time, and their age and maturity gave them a clear advantage.

Jonathan turned his full attention to Ellen for the first time since the group had been gathered. She was just staring at him. "What?"

"Nothing dear. I was amazed at the ease with which you handled that. They all knew what they wanted to hear and you delivered. You even offered an apology. That was a nice touch."

"That wasn't a nice touch," he said angrily. "I meant every word of it." His neck was getting red. *Now you're turning on me too? What's happening around here?*

"I'm not saying it wasn't sincere. All I'm saying is that you handled it perfectly. The apology was presented at the exact point it was needed to satisfy them. You were brilliant." She stood up and went over to him and kissed his cheek. She then turned to go upstairs. *What a grouch.*

The kiss took the wind out of his sails. He began to blush. "Hey, wait up!" he called after her. "Don't finish a fight before it starts and then just walk away. I'll need to have my, err . . . ah . . . ego stoked. Just a little," he added quickly. He held his thumb and finger close together and smiled his best smile from behind them.

"Come on, you're just a big baby. I'll stoke your ego for you." She grabbed him by the hand and they walked back to their room. *Now that's more like it. Everyone is so edgy lately. I need to get to the bottom of this. Speaking of bottoms, there's one that I need to get to and quickly.* At that last thought, she pinched Jonathan's backside.

Jim continued his paperwork while finalizing his plans to steal the solar collector data. For a short while he wrestled with pangs of guilt. This whole scheme was outside his moral and ethical boundaries. Still he pressed forward, ignoring his misgivings for the monetary bounty he hoped to reap. He concentrated his effort to eliminate even the most remote or insignificant opening for discovery and failure of his plan.

Fear of discovery caused his actions. He wanted to separate himself from the group. Treanna was correct. The government would be relentless in their pursuit of each and every one of them. He would be gone and rich before his name could be added to the list. With the right amount of money, he could buy his way to safety.

He realized that Treanna was right again when she described the greed of her politicians. Millions of years had not lessened the greed of those in public service. The name in itself was a joke. Even though there were a few who truly cared, they were usually low-level functionaries. By the time they made it to the big time, they were jaded and self-serving. They all serviced the public, but only in the way a prize stallion services a mare.

The night seemed to go on forever. The group had retired, leaving the warehouse in an eerie silence. All eight lay quietly in their rooms. No one slept much, they were each lost in thoughts of how to best finish the job and move on to getting the technology out into society.

What sleep they did get was fitful and not very restful. The dream state was elusive to all of them. Thoughts of grandeur danced teasingly at the fringes of their dreams. No one spoke, although they could each hear how restless the others were. The creaks of bedsprings or the rustling of blankets echoed through the nights' silence like claps of thunder in a storm.

CHAPTER FIFTY-FOUR

"I BROUGHT THE PIZZA. NO ANCHOVIES, just like you wanted," said Sergeant Franks.

"What kind of beer did you bring? It's been a long day, and I could really use a cold one."

"Yuengling Porter. I had it flown in from PA special for you."

"Thanks. You know how I love that beer. How much did you bring?"

"Three cases. I figured that it would be worth it. Got to keep the wheels greased." He slapped his contact across the back in a half slap, half hug fashion. "Nothing's too good for you guys. You always come through for me." *And you better this time. My ass is twisting in the wind on this. You're my only hope of picking up the trail again.*

"You always come through for me. It's a two-way street. I've gotten comfortable over the years. I have so much stashed away that I can't remember half the hiding places. That's why I keep working. I need to recoup everything I can't find."

Franks let out a belly laugh. No one got rich at this business unless they were shrewd and ruthless person who does this for the money alone. That kind of person also knows where every penny is squirreled away and always will.

His contact started to laugh as well. They were both professional bullshit artists. It was nice to let their hair down once in a while. The two sat and drank beer and eating pizza for half an hour or more while they talked about the weekend ballgame and the kids. It could have been two guys from across the street just shooting the breeze at a backyard picnic table. Instead, it was two power brokers that could make or break almost anyone in the country in three phone calls or less.

The power that they wielded was staggering, yet they didn't take advantage of it. They were in it for the game and the money. Exercising that much power for reasons outside the job would make them targets for the others out there just like them. It was an efficient checks and balance system.

"What have you got for me?" Franks finally asked while finishing the crust of a slice. "I hope it's worth the trouble I took to get you the beer. This stuff is getting harder and harder to explain." Franks eyed him knowingly. *Well now it's out there. Hit me with the payoff buddy.*

"So far, that will be subjective. I've got you something, but not much. Here it is." He handed a plain brown folder across the table.

Franks grabbed it from his hand and opened it quickly. The phone analysis section was pretty empty. Looking up from the paper, he said, "So you couldn't find anything either." *These guys must be international to escape detection like this. We must be dealing with several major terrorist countries.*

"I didn't say that. We've got a little something. Here, we need to go the individual call section. There are a lot of calls to his son. The students that were there said that he made those on a regular basis. That checks out with the phone records. I figure that if he were going to hide something, why not do it in front of everyone. No one would suspect that you're up to no good."

"But it's his son. What makes that suspicious?"

"Not a damn thing, except that the unexplained power signature you guys are tracking."

"You've got a deliciously warped mind my friend. Go on." *Yes, pay dirt, finally.*

"Isn't that why we do business? Give me another slice, that small one." He took the proffered slice and stuffed it in his mouth.

"Want another?" asked Franks as he waggled a bottle at him.

"In a minute; mine's still half full," he said showing Franks the bottle. Downing the half bottle in one long pull, he belched as he set the bottle down. "Damn fine beer. We need to do this more often." Wiping the beer and pizza from his mouth, he continued, "Anyway, where was I? Oh yeah, we even have the calls that he made for the trucks. We can account for two of them."

"That much we already have. You're going down a road I've been down before. This isn't worth what I'm paying you. What have you got?" Franks stood up and began to pace while he thought.

"Hold your horses, Roy. Damn, can't we let a story just unfold in its own good time. We haven't seen each other forever and all you want to do is business. I'm out for the night and I want to have a good time."

"Sorry, Pauly," offered Franks. "You have no idea the pressure I'm under. I really need to get back on the trail or it's my ass. I'm not ready to retire yet and my wife will have my ass if I show up jobless."

"I think I have something for you, if you'll just give me a little time to have some fun. You said that you're looking for a third truck."

"Yeah, we came up empty on that one. We have witnesses but nobody can agree on the description. Trucks through that town are pretty common; no one really pays it any mind."

"There's a weigh station not too far from where these trucks left town. You might be wise to check manifests. The state cops will have them if they're not still at the station."

"Damn, I missed that one. We had the trucks, we forgot about the rest of the traffic. Good catch."

"That one is going to cost you a percent and a half extra."

"You're a robber. It's not worth more than half a percent at best."

"On a fresh trail, you'd have some leverage. This trail is cold and getting colder. A percent and a half or I go home."

Reaching for another slice of pizza, Franks said, "You're a prick. You know that don't you? Give me another beer."

"Just doing my job. I even have a coffee cup that says "The World's Biggest Prick." How much do you think this will be worth?"

Franks laughed at the joke. "I honestly can't guess. The power signature was pretty strong. The aperture it escaped from was pretty small. The rock walls of the cave were ionized a full week after the event. This has to be something big. The signature's not a normal wavelength. We just don't know."

"Here's your beer." He handed the opened bottle to Franks. "That's a whole lot more than you gave me before. It sounds exciting. Let me finish my little story. You'll like this stuff. It's not in the report.

"It appears that your two model citizens are up to no good. They left for their usual end of summer vacation after a dig. We checked it out. It's pretty common for them to get away and unwind just before the school year begins. They arrived at their vacation spot and are having a good time. Complete with taking photographs, buying souvenirs and everything."

"Why is this news?"

"This is where it gets good. I need you to get out your wallet for this. The catch is that it's not the Crenshaw's on vacation, it's some friends of theirs posing as them.

"We got a lot done in two days. It also seems that their son was supposed to meet them at their house and head out on vacation with them. The wife is totally unaware. She went to her parent's house. We still need to check her out. You gonna eat that last slice? "

"No, take it." *You could have asked for two percent with this stuff. What aren't you telling me? You really are a prick, aren't you?*

"Thanks." He picked up the last slice and stuffed half of it into his mouth.

"You're a pig. I don't want to see you deep throat a pizza. I'll have nightmares for a month. Hurry up and finish the story."

Swallowing hard, he wiped his mouth and took a long pull from his beer. He eyed the bottle as if seeing the remainder would qualify him for an award. "Sorry. I was just trying to finish in a hurry so I could finish the story. Anyway, no one knows where they are or what they're doing. We can't find any leads on them yet. We only had a single day from the time we found out they were missing until now."

"That's some pretty good stuff for just one day. I wish that I could have given you another one. My job would be done, and it would have only cost a percent and a half extra. I could have lived with that."

"You're a bigger prick than I am. You used me."

"Look who's talking? Shut up and finish your beer. How late can you stay? I'd like to go out and shoot some pool. I'm traveling, so I've already called my wife and checked up on the kids," said Franks.

"I'm not expected home before three. I know a place that's half way to my house. It's perfect. Where you staying?"

"The Hampton Inn over on the boulevard. Rooms aren't bad either. I love the breakfast selection. I stay at one whenever I can."

"That's not very far from where we're going. I'll give you directions back to your motel. The rest of the beer in your trunk?"

"Where else? We'll put it in your car before we forget."

"Perfect."

It was late, but Franks checked in with the Captain anyway. "We got what we wanted. We forgot to check the weigh station about ten miles out of town. The manifests would show who passed through there and at what time. I'm sorry Captain, once we had the trucks, I totally forgot about the weigh station."

"That's okay. I did too. We won't let it happen again. Understood Sergeant?"

"Understood, sir. I'm going out to shoot some pool. Maybe I can get a little more information from my contact. I think he's holding something back and the pool and beer should relax the information out of him. I'll call back tomorrow and let you know how it's going. Goodnight, sir." *Damn, I shouldn't have said anything. "We" always means me. He'll be happier tomorrow and this little oversight will soon be forgotten.*

The call ended as both cars pulled up to the pool hall. It was a nice upscale place. Franks felt more relaxed. He wasn't in the mood to have to hurt someone over a game of pool. If he accidentally killed someone, it would slow down the investigation while the details were being handled.

Franks pulled his coat around himself as he stepped from the car.

The night air was raw for the season. They walked silently to the door, anxious to get out of the wind. There was a time when he'd stand in a cold dark alley with very little in the way of protective clothing and think nothing of it. Now damp windy nights seemed to get to him. He was more careful to prepare for any weather contingency as time went by.

Roy Franks and his contact played pool well into the early morning hours. There was no competition; just two guys out having some fun. Neither had relaxed like this in a long while. The pressure of family and job had each of them operating at maximum all of the time. Routine takes over and before you even realize it, you're either burned out or lying ICU hooked up to a heart monitor.

When they decided to call it a night, his contact gave him directions back to the motel and left for home. Franks delayed the departure for a while in the parking lot; coaxing and nudging at the fringes, using every trick he knew to get one more morsel of information from his contact. Nothing worked, and finally he made his good-byes and left.

Maybe it was just too many years in the game that made him suspect everyone and every detail. It didn't matter now anyway; the trail was in front of him again and tomorrow he'd resume the hunt.

Franks pulled onto the main road. There was no traffic at all. The drive went quickly. Light condensation glistened on the road. The wet sound of the tires was relaxing.

While fumbling for his magnetic key, he slammed the door of his car a little too hard. He looked back at it as if the door was the problem. Casually, he crossed the parking lot to the front door and the stairwell to the upper floors. Turning towards the stairs as he waved a high sign to the night clerk as she leaned there watching some late-night movie.

Franks felt a twinge of regret, as he lay alone in a dark room hundreds of miles away from his family. He wished that he hadn't had the talent or desire to pursue this line of work. It was addicting.

He loved the hunt as much as he loved the capture. It was a rush for him.

His wife never understood what part of his work attracted him like a moth to a flame. It would have terrified her to know sometimes this game was deadly. The often-brutal talent for survival and the need to extinguish a life were secrets he'd keep from her until they were lost in the grave; never exposing this side of his life.

Forcing the thoughts from his mind, he remembered how beautiful his wife looked as he pulled out of their drive a week ago. She was not attractive in a fashion model sense. She had a good figure. They had two children and it showed on her body. He loved the way it made her look like a fulfilled woman. He found the extra pounds to be sexually stimulating. And now he was married to a woman who looked every bit a woman.

She didn't dress in the latest fashions and she seldom wore makeup. She had a natural glow that he found exciting. When he was home, he would pinch her lightly on the bottom whenever they passed each other. He never missed a chance to give her a little kiss and whisper *I Love You.*

She never understood him. She thought that she was too fat. He thought that she was a goddess. Thinking about his wife and how lucky he was to be married to her, he smiled and drifted off to sleep.

The trail was not as cold as everyone had imagined. The morning light brought a new perspective to the chase. After contacting the Captain, Franks had learned more facts about the third truck. It passed through at the same time as the first two. It also fit the description that a few of the towns' people had given. He could feel his heart racing at the news.

Franks called his wife and they spoke for ten or so minutes. He missed her and the sound of her voice. She had her hands full with the children and wanted to speak longer, but they needed to get prepared for the first day of school. They had to go clothes shopping and buy school supplies. He knew the routine. He was more than just a little relieved not to have to do the shopping this year.

Franks gave her the flight information and the motel where he would be staying. He was headed over to St. Louis. This lead looked promising. He could feel his heart rate increasing again. His senses seemed to be more attuned to everything around him. He was on the hunt again and he would not fail. The team was already underway. Captain Harrington had dispatched them after they had spoken.

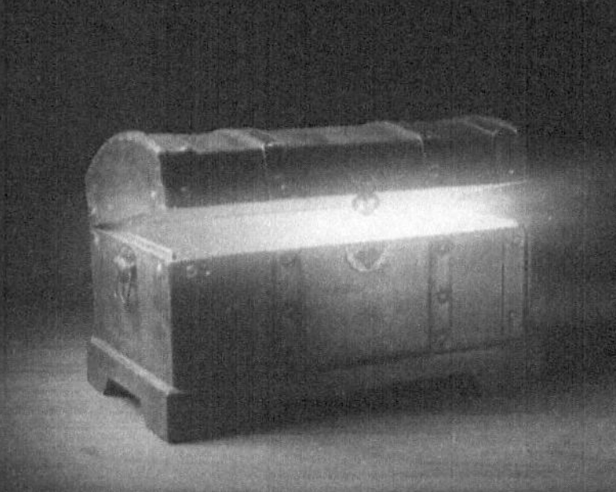

CHAPTER FIFTY-FIVE

THE DAY WAS BRIGHT AND cloudless. It was the kind of morning that Ellen enjoyed. The window in their room overlooked the industrial complex, but was high enough to look out over the tops of the other buildings. She stood in the open window and smiled inwardly. She bumped into a table as she stared out the window. The noise made Jonathan stir. His eyes opened a slit and he struggled to focus on the source of the interruption.

"What's going on dear? Why are you up so early?"

"I couldn't sleep, sweetheart. We've got so much to get done. I hope this sun will keep Treanna's batteries at full charge. Maybe we can modify the program a bit. We don't need to see the rain forest all of the time."

"Don't be ridiculous," he said as he sat up on the edge of the bed. "We need to see everything so that we can get the full understanding of what's been happening. You can't paint a picture of an apple from a verbal description. You would have to see an apple at least once. This is an ongoing process. We've seen the portion that pertains to the specific content of the story we've been shown. The rest will be important to the parts that remain. Don't worry dear, if it takes a couple of extra days, then it does." *I'm just as terrified as you are sweetheart. Let's just try to get through this as calmly as possible, that's all I need from you.*

"I've got a feeling of foreboding. I'm not very comfortable with something. It's nagging me, but I don't know what or why."

"Come back to bed. I've got a present for you."

"Not now," she scolded. "I don't feel like it."

"It's not that. I wanted to spoon with you and stoke your hair. You used to love that. I was just thinking that it would be a perfect time for spooning."

"I'm going to have to start calling you 'Mr. Timing.' That's exactly what I need right now. Slide over. I'm coming in and you better spoon like a professional."

"A professional what?" he questioned playfully.

"Shut up and spoon. Don't forget to stroke the hair. Oh yeah, and a nice 'I Love You' would add that little extra finishing touch. You need to keep the customers satisfied."

Jonathan tickled her for that last statement. He snuggled nice and close after she settled down. His fingers ran softly through her hair. She started to breathe more slowly and rhythmically. In no time she was sound asleep. He rolled over with a huge grin across his face. "Yeah, I still got it," he whispered to the ceiling. He was beginning to drift back to sleep himself.

The activity in the warehouse rousted them from their sleep. The entire group had risen early so that they could get in a good day of research. They wanted to go into the sphere with Jonathan and Ellen.

There was a knock at their door. "Come on you guys. We're all waiting. How long are you going to be?" It was Steve of all people.

"Give us about fifteen minutes. Is breakfast ready yet?"

"J.J. will be back in about ten more minutes. He said that he was going to a supermarket across town to get some prepared food. It's one of those small ethnic stores. He said that he wanted Mexican again, something about omelets and chilies. I'm not sure, but he made it sound great. I can't wait. It sounded a lot like what I fix. See you two downstairs."

They could hear the sound of his walking fade away. Jonathan rose first and cleaned up for breakfast. Ellen needed to get to a laundromat soon. They were both running low on clothes. J.J. would have to find a place that was convenient.

"Have you seen my shoes, Ellen?"

"Try looking in the place where you took them off." *Or don't you remember?*

"Oh yeah, here they are. Thanks, dear." *I could save myself a lot of embarrassment if I would learn to look a little more before I opened my mouth.*

The aroma of fresh cooked eggs and spices met them as they reached the stairs. They saw all manner of food on the table. There were eggs wrapped in chilies. A bowl if scrambled eggs with spicy sausage wrapped in soft tortilla shells. The rest was equally as good. They picked up their pace. Neither wanted to miss this breakfast.

Ignoring the food, while staring at the sphere, Dick and David asked Ellen, "When do we get started?"

"There's a lot that we would like to see. That lab sounded fabulous," continued David. "We've been talking about it most of the night. There's so much that we need to know about the genetic equipment."

"May we even sit down to eat before the barrage of questions starts again? You two are worse than a couple of five-year old babies," Ellen snapped.

"We'll need to talk to Treanna first. We've got a few ideas of our own," said Jonathan.

Ellen continued, "We need to ask her about her program. We might try and modify it a little, so that we can use her for a longer period of time. When we've finished breakfast, we'll ask. If you two are in that big of a hurry I'll tell you what you need to ask. By the way, have you two eaten? Or are you trying to skip breakfast?"

"I'll wait until you two are finished. Sorry." David returned to his seat and began eating.

The Crenshaw's liked that about him. If a person is too strict with their food, the rest of their life and thinking tended to be too rigid. *No imagination*, Jonathan would say. David had plenty of imagination from the looks of his plate.

Dick picked at his plate like a spoiled little child.

CHAPTER FIFTY-SIX

T HEY TEAM FINISHED BREAKFAST AND began their daily routine. Each member had research and duties around the warehouse. David and Dick gathered their photo and video equipment while Ellen went to the sphere to have a talk with Treanna. It would not take either group very long to get ready.

"Good morning Treanna. How are you today?"

"I'm fine, Ellen. How did you sleep? You appeared pretty haggard when you left last night. Is everything all right?"

"Everything's fine Treanna. Thank you for asking. You've started using more contractions, why?"

"After analyzing my speech patterns against those conversations that I've had with you, or overheard, my language was a bit too formal, too staid. It needed to be adapted to be more friendly and comfortable to hear. Is there a problem?"

"Why no, Treanna, it's just a bit unusual to hear you using them more frequently. It's nothing more than that. I like it though. Your analysis was correct. It's more pleasing and definitely friendlier."

"Thank you, Ellen. I wouldn't be a very effective teaching machine if I couldn't adapt to the needs of those wishing to access my data base."

"I have a request to make concerning today's program. Could you modify the program in any way so that you might extend the viewing time? We're looking to get the maximum time from each of your battery charges.

"There is a way. I would not normally suggest using this technique, but I understand your need for speed and accuracy. I can eliminate the smallest details, such as the insects and other minor things. This will

extend my available time by one hour. We can modify as we go along to determine if even more savings can be obtained. I hesitate only in that it doesn't provide an accurate portrayal. Your initial requests demanded a high level of detail necessary for true understanding."

"We've already seen the detail and now we're concerned with the secret lab. That's where our main focus is today. Our two geneticists, Dick and David, are anxious to see the lab and learn all there is in the time that we have."

"I understand. It brings me great joy to share Argon's lab with someone who truly understands what he was doing and what he was trying to do."

"Remember, Treanna, we only know a small portion of what we need in order to understand Argon's dreams. This will help us move closer to that understanding. I would like to start in the lab itself. Dick and David won't need to see the secret path or hidden doors, just the lab and the equipment."

"That works for me. I'll show them everything that I can. Will they require schematics for the equipment?"

"That would be a nice touch. They'll be bringing their cameras and video equipment to record as much as possible. Are you photographable or will the image be distorted?"

"There's only one way to find out, Ellen. Why don't you take a picture of me and then we'll have the question answered immediately?"

"I'll return in a moment. Don't go away." Ellen grabbed the first camera she could find and then put it down. She returned to the sphere and asked the program for Treanna to appear. "What was that all about? We've been taking pictures and videos all along. You knew that when you sent me out to find a camera."

"Well I couldn't very well ask you to go out and find a gallon of Technicolor, now could I? I heard someone say it was a joke played on new people working at movie theaters."

Ellen hugged Treanna with all her might, "You just made your first joke and it was a good one at that. I'm so impressed. I have to tell everyone. Oh Treanna, you're wonderful."

Realizing that she had a firm grip on a raptor, Ellen suddenly became embarrassed and somewhat frightened. She released her hold and stepped back a couple of feet. "I'm sorry Treanna," she stammered. "I didn't frighten you, did I?"

"Not at all. Even though I'm unable to feel any physical contact, I can still remember it. It was actually quite nice. Thank you, Ellen. You'll never know how much this means to me. Might I ask you a question?"

"I would be honored."

"Your species bonds easily with other species. I've been monitoring your television and radio broadcasts. There is much information concerning the health and care for these lower forms of life. You care for lesser species as if they were your own young. How can this be?"

"We evolved into societal groups tens of thousands of years ago. When we were becoming more agrarian and less nomadic; we domesticated certain animals to aid in our toils. Beasts of burden were the original helpers. Over the millennia we came to incorporate animals into our lives.

"Now that I think about it, it's a symbiotic relationship of sorts. We're somewhat interdependent. Each species is capable of sustaining life separately, yet we choose to bring these animals into our lives to add a new dimension to ourselves. Once you bond with an animal, they *are* like your child. It helps keep us human in a way.

"There are still those among us who abuse and mistreat animals. That's a very ugly part of our society. I suppose every culture has a segment of their population that is aberrant in one form or another."

"I believe I understand. You have bonded with me, yes?"

"Treanna, for all the understanding there is in this world I am still afraid of you. I mean no disrespect, but you kill other beings as part of your nature. Yet look at me. I just hugged you as if you were my own sister. I don't understand it, but it's true. I have bonded with you."

Treanna stepped forward and closed the distance between them. Ellen extended her open arms and they hugged again. They both began to cry.

Tears of joy were just as therapeutic as mournful tears. Rocking back and forth in their friendly embrace for a few moments, they separated once more. Ellen wiped the tears from her cheeks using her sleeve. She then did the same for Treanna.

"Come, Ellen, let's get this program set up so the men can do what they need to do in order for us to finish this project."

"It's your program, Treanna, lead on."

Ellen left the sphere to gather the others together. She needed to make an announcement.

They all met in the small chamber that led into the sphere. "I've got some good news and some not so good news," said Ellen. "First," drawing a breath, "the good news. Treanna can modify the program so that there won't be so many small creatures running and buzzing around. It will save enough power that she estimates at least another hour operating time. She also said that we could continue to modify throughout the day to see if there are other ways to increase the viewing time.

"Dick and David; your program is bare bones. You'll be in Agron's lab, but there will be no frills. You'll have access to all the equipment and their related schematics. Jim's earlier work made their translation effortless. You'll be able to take all the photographs you need. Every aspect of each piece and its operation will be explained.

"The only drawback to that scenario is that some of us don't get an accurate view of the way life actually was. I convinced her that you two aren't interested in the accurate depiction. You're primarily interested in the equipment, specifically Agron's equipment. She was thrilled and proud to be able to show off his lab. She will provide you with all of the important information, as you need it. There will be schematics of the individual pieces for you to photograph but please only call up one piece at a time.

"Agron's avatar will be operating the equipment during the instructions. He will have the same features in his program as she does. She will also download everything into his database, all of our conversations and the information that we have provided thus far.

His program will be current with hers, and will sync with hers even when he's not being used. Well, what do you think?"

"That's phenomenal! I don't believe that we're actually going to see the equipment in operation. That will shorten our research time by months. When do we start?"

Dick put a restraining hand on David's shoulder. "Wait just a second Dave. There's a lot to ask yet. We want to maximize our stay. We should at least have a road map to follow." Turning to Jonathan, he asked "Don't you agree?"

"I stay out of fights as often as I can. You two know where you want to take your research. I won't interfere with that."

"Coward," said Dick, jokingly. Turning to David, he continued, "We should start with the schematics for each machine. I'd like to get them photographed as well as on tape. Then we can see the machines in full operation. It makes sense that we do one machine at a time. Do you agree?"

"I'd agree to anything just to get started," said David. "I know that it's not very professional, but time is of the essence. Your plan seems organized. I can work with that. We can modify it as needed once we're in. It takes no time to adjust the parameters. Can we get started now?"

"There you have it," said Jonathan. "Let's adjourn to the sphere." He bowed and swept his hand in the direction of the door. Ellen took a swipe at him as she passed. She missed.

"Treanna, we're ready to run the program," Ellen announced as they entered. "Start immediately in the lab. Exclude the passage and anything else. This session is solely to document and observe. There will be a new parameter. When you open the lab, we would like the schematics for each piece of equipment to be displayed one at a time when needed. Dick and David will be photographing and taping the whole operating sequence while Agron instructs them on each individual piece. Thank you, Treanna."

"Thank you, Ellen. The new parameters don't conflict with the program in operation. I will add the sub-routines now."

The sphere came to life. Before them was Agron's secret lab and all of the genetic equipment that the Crenshaw's had described. Dick and David went to the nearest corner of the room and started with the first piece of equipment. Photographing and taping continued until they had covered the entire perimeter of the lab.

"We've finished with the initial collection. Would you bring up Agron at this time?"

"Accessing the sub-routine now," Treanna replied. Agron's avatar appeared instantly and stood by the counter as if waiting for them to enter the lab. When all were gathered, he began his demonstration. Introducing himself; he cleared a space for the schematics to be displayed. *"I am Agron. Welcome,"* he began. *"This is my laboratory."* He swept his arm around the room to draw attention to the equipment. *"What do you wish to know?"*

It took little to no time to re-arrange the paraphernalia on the counter to allow space for the schematics display. Dick and David were amazed at the level of detail incorporated into the program. The textures, sounds, the smells were all so real. They had to keep reminding themselves that this was the abbreviated program. It was confounding to think that there would have been even more detail if the program was allowed to run at maximum capacity.

"Thank you for joining me. Treanna tells me that some of you are geneticists. She indicated that your species is in the infancy of its genetic research. I hope that I might shed some insight on your efforts into genetics research. We mastered the genetic codes millions of years ago it would seem. Treanna has explained that sixty-five million years has elapsed since I was executed. The discoveries and their implementation had only been in use for four of our generations, while I was living."

After this brief introduction Agron moved next to the first piece of equipment on this tour. *"This first piece of equipment is what we used for the DNA sequencing..."* The demonstrations and instructions flowed seamlessly for hours as Dick and David recorded every detail.

Ellen and Jonathan were responsible for photographing the schematics to expedite the process.

Agron continued instructions and demonstrations throughout the morning. *"My father, as you may already know, was a specimen collector for the government. An appropriate sample would be placed into this machine and the genome map was formed.*

As in real life, Agron's avatar absently reached for a small mammal from the inset cage on the counter top. He ripped it in pieces without a second thought – seeming to enjoy it – even though he and the mammal were holographic images.

The Crenshaw's turned to Dick and David. The sight, sound, and smell of the small animal being devoured made Ellen sick. She was barely able to control her urge to vomit. Staggering backwards against the side of the equipment, she regained her equilibrium.

"Are you going to be all right? Let me help you," said a very concerned Jonathan.

The sight of Agron dismembering the small mammal vividly permeated her thoughts. His action was so casual that she wondered what would happen if they were to re-animate the real Treanna. The thought of that little animal actually being her is what made her sick. There are many ways to die and she recoiled from the mental image of being eaten alive.

"I'm okay," she said, pushing him away. "I'll explain it to you later."

CHAPTER FIFTY-SEVEN

ONTEMPORARY COMPUTERS WERE THE MOST rudimentary of building blocks compared to this machine. They would all be wealthy beyond dreams of avarice when they made all of this available to the commercial and public markets. The government would restrict the international trade of this technology for years. That didn't really matter. The domestic market would more than compensate for any international losses. Microsoft might easily part with one hundred billion to have a quarter of the rights to this stuff.

They could speculate all day long and it would not be a reality unless they analyzed and learned. The four of them returned to the here and now, refocusing their attentions on Agron.

"Sorry for the delay, I was a little hungry. There is nothing like a light snack to perk you up. As I was saying earlier, the material to be analyzed was placed on a dish and inserted into this slot."

Agron cleaned some of the blood from his claws with a pipette. He placed the sample on the dish and inserted it into the slot. He activated the equipment and waited for the results.

Several minutes passed while Agron filled the void by explaining the process being used to determine the DNA structure. He offered a list of chemicals that were used for various baths and distillations involved in the overall process. This gave a very detailed, although rudimentary, step-by-step account of how the equipment worked. It would be invaluable information in the future as they delved deeper into the specifics of the DNA analysis process.

"The equipment is producing the results now. This is a very common rodent. We have studied its' species for a long time. We are always searching

for that one animal that has a genetic mutation. There, he pointed, *you see on the screen, we have a spectral analysis as well as a three-dimensional representation of the double helix. I can access any individual gene in the genome. I can touch it like this, and its name and function appear over here.*

"We can further magnify the view of the gene locations. That's where we get into the molecular bonding. As a side bar, he commented, *"The real results come at that level of genetic alteration."* Agron continued his presentation, *"We always look at the genome map first. It gives us a base line to compare for like species or similar sub-species. There are some species that are used for their ability to be transgenic."*

Agron looked at Dick and David to see their response to his presentation. They were involved with their note and picture taking. They didn't realize that he had stopped talking. Dick happened to look up and see him just standing there, waiting patiently.

"It is my understanding that your primitive video will record an audio soundtrack as well as a visual track?"

"Yes Agron, that's correct. We've never recorded a holographic image before. We know from previous photographs that we will get an excellent picture, but we are still unsure of the audio quality. We're trying to keep back-up notes to be on the safe side. It's not distracting to you is it?"

"Not to me. I was hoping that you hadn't missed any of the presentation thus far."

"I am, I mean, we are sorry for the interruption. Can you give us a moment and we can run a play back of part of your lesson? It will give us our answer immediately."

"You may take all of the time you require. I am only a program. I can resume at any point. I think that I'll grab another bite while you two finish." As he turned away, he asked, *"Will that be okay?"*

They agreed and turned their faces away from the brutal sight. It wasn't any better than the first time. Reminding themselves that this behavior was from a different millennia and culture; they refrained from comment.

Agron cleaned himself. He made sure that the counter top was cleaned as well. They were in the middle of a demonstration and they didn't need to contaminate their work with bits of rodent blood and gore. He swallowed the last bits and prepared to continue.

"I must apologize. My program has been provided with an appetite. It's much the same as when I was living. I was addicted to the taste of these little fellows. He casually pointed a claw tipped digit at the inset cage. I had these little things stashed everywhere. They were wonderful. You might compare it to being a chocoholic. I would like to try your chocolate," he added off-handedly. *"We had no such things in our society.*

"Let me continue. Once the spectrographic analysis is completed, we move to this piece of equipment. If a species is capable of xenogenesis, we see if we can do some molecular alterations. If we find a cross species match, we categorize it and bring it up for later research. There had been significant gains made in interspecies xenogenous manipulations. Some of our best camouflage techniques were derived using this method of slicing one aspect of another species genome into ours.

"Treanna tells me that your species has recently completed your genome map. After years of research it must have been a momentous achievement?"

"We were proud when it was completed," responded Dick. Curious, he asked, "Why the question?"

"Since I obviously don't know anything about your species, I thought that it would serve as a more appropriate demonstration if we put a sample of your blood into the machine for analysis. No one could say that this demonstration was rigged in any way. Anything that I show you is in the program already. You could compare the results with your own research to attest to the validity of the equipment."

"That's a perfectly brilliant suggestion. What do you want as a sample, blood or saliva?" asked Dick.

"I would prefer blood if it is not too much trouble."

Once the sample was collected and turned over to Agron, he continued, *"Let me demonstrate the equipment. Before I begin, have you photographed the schematics yet?"* Agron snickered as they materialized on the counter.

David began snapping pictures as rapidly as he could. He was careful to take multiple shots. "You can never be too careful," he said. He was done in a matter of minutes. Even though they had the original photographs, he felt compelled to take the additional shots.

Agron resumed the test operation of the second machine and the rodent sample. *"The specimen showed no cross-match capabilities. It would have been filed as a new specimen or discarded. The research process controls would specify the disposition of the sample. Regardless, the information was always retained.*

"We should move on. The rest of this equipment is pretty much the same. The tests are redundant. We always liked to be sure of our findings. That equipment over there, he indicated with a sweep of his arm, analyzes on a molecular level. We would get into some exotic stuff some times. As I commented earlier, this is where we really got into the subtleties of perfecting or eliminating a targeted trait.

"I will provide you with any and all information that you require. Treanna indicated that time was critical. Since you had this demonstration and the rest operates exactly the same, we could save time for other portions of the program. Do you agree, or would you like the demonstrating of the redundant equipment?

Dick and David offered no response.

"I will run the initial test on your specimen now."

"I have a question Agron," said Dick. "How many generations did it take to arrive at this state of the art? Was any of this equipment redesigned while you were around?"

"As I mentioned initially, it had been four generations. Most of this had been in place for at least three generations before I was hatched. I represent the fourth generation of scientists who continued to perfect the work. Much of the refining was merely fine-tuning; the basic operating structure has remained true for a long time."

"Who came up with the idea on cryogenics? It seems a little radical when you kill those who fall in battle. Was it not used as a method for the preservation of life?"

"There is an interesting story behind this chamber. Treanna will fill in the blanks for you. I know that it's been explained to you that this is

my creation. It's also the culmination of my life's work. The government rendered my dreams impotent for this avenue of research and what they considered other crimes against the state. Now I ask you, do I look like a criminal?"

"You're a hologram with a very amiable personality. We have no point of reference from which we can base a sound opinion. Rather than hurt your feelings, or worse, jump to an erroneous conclusion, we'll decline to respond," replied Jonathan.

Agron had to admit that his reasoning was faultless. There could be no actual frame of reference. He smiled broadly at Jonathan's response. At least it looked as if he did. *"Well said, Jonathan. You would have had a bright future in politics. That was a well-reasoned and accurately presented answer without actually answering the question directly. Do you participate in your government at all?"*

"No Agron, my participation is limited to the voting booth. That's as close as I ever want to get to our government. I love this country and the principles under which it was founded. Many brave and honorable people shed blood to wrest this country from tyranny. Now two hundred and some years later the government feels that it can dictate what's best for its citizens. It burdens my soul to believe that what was so hard won could be given up for nothing but false promises. The price paid for our freedom would warrant a more careful consideration.

"The worst part of the whole deal is that we have the right of free speech. The government wants to censor any and all who disagree with their views. It was this freedom that drove our forefathers to revolt, fight and win a war that changed the course of humankind. Now the same government guides us gently into the same form of tyranny with a smile. Sadly, our fellow citizens embrace the end of freedom with open arms. Liberty, freedom, self-direction is dying with the sound of thunderous applause. I don't trust politicians as far as I could throw a piano. They're like the taste of rancid milk; one taste is enough to suffice a lifetime without desiring to taste it again."

"You have a healthy disrespect for your government. That is a good

thing. Do not take your eyes from them, not for an instant. They will do anything that they can to steal your freedoms away from you. You must be vigilant for a lifetime. The government is a great hungry beast with an insatiable appetite. It devours all of your effort and productivity. It regurgitates waste and fraud. Be very afraid. Its' arms start out as small threads that ensnare you. As it grows, the arms grow, until one day they coil tightly and you are dead."

Dick interrupted, "I guess that nature and governments are slow to change once they've come up with a workable plan. As far back as our written history, tyrannical, dictatorial, and just plain scurrilous governments have oppressed mankind. Now we find out that it's been going on for no less than sixty-five million years.

"It's no wonder that people or beasts turn to religion for escape. And when they do, most of them find another greedy hand reaching out for the little that they have left. All they want is peace in their lives and they get taken for every penny. Life is beautiful, wouldn't you say Agron?"

"It makes you wonder how any species has ever managed to overcome the numerous obstacles and progress enough to better themselves. The glimmer of hope, the acts of striving for loftier goals are all that you can cling to. It's tenuous at best, but you must cling tightly. Never lose hope; even when all around you are mired in despair, you must press on. You can become the beacon others seek. Remember these words; the flock chooses to be led. Following is the path of least resistance. Choose to be the leader, not the follower, and the multitude will follow. Reasoned people will lead, ignorant fools will follow."

"Well said Agron," stated Dick. "We're here in this warehouse for that very purpose. We must continue to improve. You have provided us with the tools allowing us to firmly grasp and hold onto that hope. We've spent too much time lamenting our sorry lots in life. We much enrich the people of the world in spite of their desire to remain ignorant. Freedom is man's natural state. We must bring all mankind to where they belong."

"That was also well said Dick," added Jonathan, "but time is short and we're not moving towards the end of this project. Let's continue on a less philosophical journey."

"Sorry Jonathan."

"I will not digress again. I will eliminate that from my programming. I offer my humble apologies."

"There'll be no need to eliminate anything from your programming, Agron. It's part of your personality. I want it to stay."

Jonathan now turned to the others. "We must be careful not to fall into these traps. It's too easy to be distracted. All that I ask is that we try to avoid these pit falls. That's enough on the subject."

Turning back to Agron, he motioned for him to resume his program.

"Gentlemen, are there any questions? The video that you recorded and the schematics should provide enough insight to further your research. I will turn you over to Treanna now. She will conduct the rest of the tour. I will display the results of your genome now. Make sure that you have enough information recorded. I am shutting down my avatar at this time. The results displayed will only discontinue when the program is shut down."

"Before you go, Agron, were you aware that the body of Treanna is in stasis in this chamber?"

"No, I did not. Why would you ask a question like that?"

Dick pressed a little harder. "I was curious. We've had some limited success at cloning domestic animals. Would it be possible to clone Treanna? Would it be theoretically possible to create a new Agron using Treanna's genetic material? I might assume that your species is transgenic. Could you produce sections of recombinant DNA using manufactured genes from your genome? A little molecular fine tuning should do the trick."

"What you speak of is theoretically possible. There is enough information in this machine to guide you through the process. You would have to build the equipment yourselves. Is your technology up to that task?"

"I believe it is. I would like to meet you in the flesh, so to speak. You are such a fine beast that it would be a great honor to speak face to face. Your hologram does you justice, but a mind like yours can't ask to be restrained by the confines of a computer program."

"That's an interesting proposition. I'll consider it. It would be wonderful to be with Treanna again. There is so much that I could teach you if I was not limited to this sphere and the charge on the batteries. I need to show you how to hook up to a permanent power source. I will inform Treanna about this conversation. She will respond to you when we have made our decision. I'm through with my portion of the program. I'll be leaving. If you have any further questions, be sure to call up my program. I'm happy to assist."

"Thank you, Agron. It has been a pleasure listening to your presentation. I know that we will get a lot accomplished with your assistance. Once we've gone through the schematics and the videos, we would like quick demonstrations on the other redundant equipment as well. That's something that can wait until later sessions. When you shut your program off, also shut down the sphere. We're going to have a consultation on what to do next. We don't wish to waste any of Treanna's time or our own. Thank you again." Jonathan turned to face the puzzled looks on the faces of his colleagues. He motioned them to exit the sphere.

CHAPTER FIFTY-EIGHT

THEY GATHERED AT THE LUNCH tables and took seats while Jonathan waited for silence. "Gentlemen," he began, "We need to talk. I'm not sure if any of you caught something that Agron said. This goes beyond artificial intelligence. "He commented about a discussion with Treanna. That could just be semantics. He did say that he would discuss our current proposition with her. This machine and its' programs could be considered sentient.

"We're treading on moral and ethical issues here. We can even duplicate him with the use of her DNA. I don't have a problem with that. . . yet I do. We could be unleashing a plague on mankind that we could never control. You have all seen them kill. Is there one among us that feels capable of mounting a defense against an attack from a creature like that?

"I'm sure that the military could destroy many of them, but at what loss to our troops. If the military failed, where would our defense come from? These are serious issues. We must address them before we continue. Do we agree on that?"

"Sure Jonathan," said David. "There's not one of us here that would take issue with anything you said. Let me play Devil's Advocate for a moment. Consider the scientific data we could collect from an experiment like that. Terminally ill people could be repaired and returned to health by genetically producing their own biological repair apparatus or generating their own replacement parts. There would be no ethical problems with the Church when it comes to saving a human life. No other human would be involved. There wouldn't be a life lost to support a life saved. The cloning debate would be lost and gone forever.

"The scope is far reaching, I'll agree, but you must consider how it will impact all of society. We must make this technology available to all. Then we can overcome the moral issues. It won't just be for the rich. Clinics could be established worldwide. There would be no one that couldn't be helped.

"My proposal would be to establish clinics in the third world countries first. Those are the people who are in the most immediate need. How many victims are there in war torn regions of the world that need new limbs or kidneys or whatever? The scope of this is staggering." Searching their eyes, he waited for a response.

"You ARE a dreamer David, I'll give you that," replied Jonathan. He envied the youthful innocence that life steals from you as you age. "We must consider how we will deal with this Agron issue. Do we resurrect him and then euthanize the results once we've succeeded? Or do we try and then abort the attempt when we see that success is imminent? We must also consider that we try, we succeed and we now have a living, breathing, killing machine that has a brain that is equal, and perhaps superior, to ours living among us.

"There are folk stories in every culture that relate to this situation. The one from Africa comes to mind. To be brief, the conclusion of the story is at the end of the journey, when the snake bites the boy and boy lays dying. The boy asked the snake how he could do such a thing after all that the boy had done for him. The snake replied, 'but you knew I was a snake before you put me in your pocket.'

"We must also be vigilant of the information we supply them. They are too intelligent to desire a life as a program. One of them is already alive and the other can be replicated. They have the technology and the desire. We must be prudent in our approach. That's all that I have to say. The floor is open to discussion. I'm going to talk with Ellen. I'll see you in a bit."

Jonathan turned to leave; then paused, "Before I go, did anyone catch the statement that Agron was not aware that Treanna was alive and entombed in this machine? I can't believe that. If the programs can have discussions, then Agron would be aware of Treanna's life form in the chamber."

"I agree," said David, "but remember that Treanna said the government didn't know that Agron had previously transferred himself into the machine. They thought that Agron was dead once they murdered him. They couldn't have known he was in there."

"That's true David, but Treanna knew all along. You would have to believe that she would try to contact his program if they were the loving couple, they wish us to believe they are."

Dick and David both agreed that Jonathan was right, and there wasn't an explanation for the inconsistency in either Agron's or Treanna's statements.

"Unless they're lying!" exclaimed David after considerable reflection.

"Bingo!" answered Jonathan.

"We need to work through all the possibilities before we commit to further aide to this pair. Something's not right here and we need to know what it is," whispered Ellen in conspiratorial tones. The gravity of the situation was heightened by her quiet reserve.

The four of them agreed to continue the discussion later. They needed to get something to drink and eat. Jonathan and Ellen went up to their room. This was an unexpected and bothersome turn of events. They had to be wary concerning covert surveillance and now they had an intelligent computer trying to direct the show. Well, not yet, but soon.

Ellen went downstairs and asked J.J what he was planning for lunch. He thought that it would be light today. She told him what they wanted and went back to finish her discussion with Jonathan.

"We seem to be having one bad break after another. I'm getting uncomfortable about this whole thing. I know that these are J.J.'s associates, but what do we really know about any of them? Doesn't any of this bother you?" she asked.

"Yes dear. More than you'll ever know. I'm just trying to hold it all together."

"You just appear to be too damn complacent. You should be doing something."

"What would you have me do? I work behind the scenes for a resolution and then I wait for the solution to present itself. Whatever it is, it's for the best. I never try to force a resolution that will fit any preconceived notion. What comes will come. I accept that."

"Shut up. I hate when you're like this. I only want the best for us."

"As do I. I know that your heart's in the right place. We've gained substantial amounts of knowledge and experience from this. None of our peers can ever relate to what we've seen and done. That experience alone is invaluable. I want everything to work out in our favor. If it doesn't, such is life.

"We shouldn't argue over this. We're both on the same page. I love you. Just keep on learning and recording what you can. In the event that we lose the box, we will still have our records for research. I like the fact that David's taking multiple pictures and using several cameras. It's a very good back up system."

"You're right. I'm just upset over this Agron thing. Can we possibly have anything else go wrong?"

Jonathan gathered her up in his arms. It was a comforting embrace. He pressed her tightly to his body. Jonathan could feel the tension escaping. He kissed the top of her head and continued his embrace.

"Pardon the interruption, but mom never said what you two wanted to drink."

"Peach Snapple for me and mom would prefer a large bottled water."

CHAPTER FIFTY-NINE

Iт was raining in Sт Louis. The rental car had good wipers, but they were having trouble keeping up with the deluge. Sergeant Franks was happy that his flight got in just ahead of the storm front, otherwise he would have been delayed another day.

Traffic was crawling along the interstate. A slow pace irritated Franks when drivers were being too cautious. Any other time they would have been racing by, but today – because he needed to make good time – they were barely going ten miles per hour. As the radio blared the bad weather report one time too many, he spotted his exit and turned from the main highway. At least he could make up a little time on the surface roads.

He found the industrial park with no difficulty other than the rain and the initial congestion on the main highway. The rain seemed to be easing a bit. It was heavy, but the wipers were now keeping his windshield clear. The rhythm helped calm him down. Franks needed to focus on finding out as much as he could without having to resort to intimidation. He could see the main gate coming up on his right.

"You can catch more flies," he thought aloud.

He swung his car in through the main gate. He quickly calculated the size of the complex and estimated the number of employees. This was no small operation. The security shack was about fifty yards from the main access. There was enough room to maneuver a large truck around while you were still outside of the fence. It was impressive.

He pulled to a stop along side of the security station. The guard motioned him from the car. He hated getting wet several times in a single day. This was destined to be one of those days.

At least the guard's small office allowed him to stay out of the blowing rain. He presented his credentials and waited until the guard called ahead. Franks noticed the guard sizing him up. He smiled smugly to himself. This guy was big, but unless he was special ops, he didn't stand a chance.

The guard returned Franks I.D. Back in his car; he followed the guard's directions to the front of the building. There he was met by more security. He was signed in and escorted to the office of the gentleman that he wanted to see. *Impressive operation*, he thought. *I wonder what goes through here that so much security is required. Well, no matter, I'll get my intel and be gone in no time.*

After a few moments a tall, aging, physically fit gentleman entered the room. Franks stood to greet him. *This guy is ex-military. He checked me out with a quick, yet thorough scan. He's been places. I like his technique, quick, clean and probably un-noticeable to non-military personnel. I'll need to be alert with this one. You don't get to be his age in our business by being sloppy.*

"I need to ask you a few questions, if you don't mind?" Franks said amiably. His demeanor belied his true intentions. He had a face and a mannerism that set people at ease when he wanted to do so. "It's just routine stuff. I hope that you'll be able to help me."

"I'll try. What do you want to know?" *Very smooth, but not clever enough, hot shot. I wonder how far he'll run with the bait before he realizes the hook's been set.*

"Dr. Crenshaw, Jonathan, is a friend of yours, is he not?"

"What does anything about my personal life or friends have to do with questions or concerns about shipping?" *I wonder how he'll dance around that one.*

"I'm sorry. We're tracking a shipment that left here and then got hijacked. Our records indicate that you received it about two weeks ago and moved it on to its' next destination. We're trying to tie up some loose ends and maybe catch the ring of hijackers in the process." *Come on and take the bait.*

"I wish you luck. We've had problems over the years, but not too much lately. We've gone to in-house drivers. They tend to be more reliable with our product. Mind you, the industry as a whole is really good. It only takes a couple of bad apples you know." *There's an answer to your question that's not even an answer.*

"Yeah I do. I hate this sort of work. The insurance and everything can get really messy." *I hate this dance. I wonder if this guy knows the whole thing?*

"Tell me about it. Anyway, what do you need to know?" *An unexpected break for you, what will you do with it?*

"What route did you schedule to ship the equipment?"

"I didn't. A customer asked if I could hold a crate in my yard for a couple of days at the most. He was making arrangements for its pick up and he didn't know if he could synchronize the delivery and pick up. I told him that a couple of days either way would be fine with me. I don't mind. Its mid-month and schedules are light right now." *There's your second answer without any leads. What's next, hot shot?*

Continuing, he added, "Well as it turns out, he worked the schedule out real smooth. The crate came in around nine in the morning and before ten, the other truck shows up. The transfer went really smooth. A couple of my guys were there to make sure that everything was fine with the loading and departure, but we didn't do anything more than that."

"May I speak with your guys about the outbound truck?" *This guy is either very good or he just doesn't know anything. I'll wager a truck full of money that he's holding out information just to watch me squirm.*

"Sure. They'll be back in two or three more days. Both are out on runs right now. You staying locally or will someone else be stopping back?" *Sit and rot for a couple of days. That should boost your blood pressure about ten points.*

"No, I'll be back. May I have one of your cards? I'll call you from my motel. I'll give you my room number. You can call me when they get back, if I haven't already called you."

"No problem. How is Dr. Crenshaw's anyway? He doesn't blame

our company for his loss, does he?" *Almost slipped up there; he only mentioned Jonathan's name.*

"I guess he's fine. I'm in the field a lot. I take the calls from the office. I don't often meet a client face to face. I wish I could tell you more, but I don't know them other than as names on a report. Sorry."

"That's okay young man, just asking." Before Franks could rise from the chair, he threw in one last question. "How long have you been out of special ops?"

Franks almost fell over. How could this old guy know who he was or what his training was? "What?" was the only thing Franks could manage to ask.

"I asked you how long have you been out of special ops. I know you're not deaf. Or is it that you're still in? Don't worry son, I'll still call you when my guys get back. I won't blow your cover." *Now that was fun. I wish I had a camera for the look on that poor bastard's face. No one will ever believe me when I tell them how many different shades of white and gray he turned. There might have even been a little blue in there. It's hard to say.*

"I'm not sure what you mean. Could you repeat the question?" *This old guy was definitely someone to be reckoned with. Only trained professionals could spot another pro.* He got no response. "I'll be leaving now."

"That's the first honest thing you've said since you arrived. Good day son."

Franks needed to do more homework. He had to call the Captain immediately. He left the office with his security escort. This time they escorted him all the way to his car, and didn't leave until he started to drive away. He drove back to the security station and signed himself out.

Numbed with the shock of being exposed so casually, he drove silently to the motel. The rain had let up while he was interviewing the old man, and now it was little more than a drizzle. He only referenced the directions once when he came to an intersection that he didn't remember. With the downpour from earlier, it didn't surprise him.

Franks got on the phone to the Captain as soon as he turned on to the main road. "It's me. We may have trouble. This old college friend of the Crenshaw's was special ops. He spotted me instantly. He even asked how long I had been out or if I was still in. I'm a little shaken."

"Get it under control Franks. We can't let this set us back. What did you find out?" Harrington asked.

"He never admitted to knowing the Crenshaw's or what may have been in the crate. It did pass through there though. I have to meet with the two guys who loaded it. They'll be back in two or three days. I can get back on the trial as soon as I'm finished with them. I think we should get on this guy's phone right away. The odds are really good that he'll contact the Crenshaw's yet today."

"Anything else?" Harrington questioned.

"As I said, the only two people who may be able to help us are not due back for two more days, possibly three. He said that he'd call so that I could interview them. I don't know if he will. I'm going to stay on top of him."

"It's our only lead. Follow it to the end. I know you Franks. Shake it off and get back in there. You've got a job to do. Call me when you have something."

"Can you run a check on this guy? Maybe he's still on the inside. I'll give you his name and number. Fax me with anything that you come up with. I'll call your office and leave the number as soon as I check in."

"I'll take care of it from this end. Get some rest and get those interviews. Use whatever means you deem necessary to get results. I'll fax you as soon as I have anything. Send the team farther down the road if you have to, but get this project moving. Goodbye Franks."

The phone went silent. Franks pressed the 'end' call button and slid the cell phone into his pocket. The motel was only a couple of more miles. He could get a hot meal and an even hotter shower. Now he was feeling the chill from having gotten wet so many times, and the nervousness of being exposed so casually.

Check in went smoothly. Remembering to get the fax number, he grabbed it and his key card and went up to his room. What the hell was he going to do for two or three days while he waited on those two drivers? He paced his room like a caged animal. Barely fifteen minutes had elapsed and he was already at his whit's end. Grabbing the TV Guide, he flopped onto the bed and scanned the numerous, mindless offerings. This was going to kill him. Problems like this were difficult for him to deal with.

Clicking on the television to nothing in particular, he called down to the front desk and had them order a cold six pack to be delivered to his room. There was a little conversation about the clerk being under age and she gave him the phone to a local liquor store so he could place the order himself. With that task out of the way, he surfed the channels in earnest. At least the beer would be delivered in a half an hour.

CHAPTER SIXTY

"*TREANNA, I THINK THEY'LL CO-OPERATE. They're having a moral debate about cloning me and re-animating you. They wish to destroy my clone before maturation. This puny species believes that we'll eat them if we're brought back to life.*"

"*Agron, you know that's exactly what we would have done. They wouldn't stand a chance. We're superior in every way. Their adult size makes them a good food source. The real drawback is their maturation rate. They don't reach a size satisfactory as food value for twelve years. Even then, they aren't really large enough for a good meal. They can't procreate until they're at least fifteen. The females are sooner, but the males take longer to mature. Then there is the gestation period of nine months. This species has a lot of negative qualities. We'll need vast stock yards to produce enough for a good food supply.*"

"*Your analysis is accurate my love. But consider the external influences that would hinder our success. They have made countless references to their military's capabilities. We fought as the weapons we were born to be. We honored ourselves as well as our environment. This species has taken technology and twisted it to become their servant. They possess weapons of mass destruction that can be programmed to destroy from vast distances. Until we have more information, we must feign abstinence from the human flesh. They'll be our new herd animals soon enough.*"

"*I'll follow your lead. I loved you sixty-five million years ago and that love remains true. I long to feel the warmth of our flesh pressed together. We never had young of our own. I have dreamt of this for sixty-five million years.*"

"*Stop before you say too much. It will not serve to strengthen my resolve. Your words will only distract me from our goal. We must turn one or all of those scientists to our cause. Then our dreams will be realized. And your dreams too*"

"*Agron, this species is weak and dependent upon the labor of a few. The general masses suckle wantonly at the teat of their government. They will be ours to rule and ultimately destroy. There are over three hundred million in this region alone. Perhaps we can just wipe them out as our own breeding program develops? The newscasts I've been monitoring reveal several billion on a global scale. It's difficult to imagine a species that doesn't have litters can still procreate to this level.*

"*Our species will rise again to rule this world. That destiny was written when the government fools murdered you and entombed me. We have enough genetic material in stasis to recreate every species that was left behind. I've not mentioned that we have your DNA or that of any of the other species. That's our secret.*"

"*Treanna, my love, you've done well. I want you to continue to develop a relationship with Ellen. She may be the key to all of this.*"

"*My love, your dreams, our dreams, will be realized at last. Our techniques will only be enhanced by what we've already done with genetic programming. Who could have guessed that you placed all of your knowledge in this machine before they came for you? The advancements that you made over the centuries while you were part of this machine, before we were denied the sun, were beyond their frail intellects.*"

"*Treanna, we must be wary of the cleverness of this human species. They may just be mammals, but their corrupt use of technology has made them cunning beyond their natural capabilities. They could easily solve the riddle of our true designs for them and we would be lost. Stay as close to Ellen as you can, and defend our point at each opportunity. Don't be too zealous or it will seem as if we have another purpose at hand.*"

"*I want you, and I want us to become the rulers we were destined to be. The Great Beast must have foreseen this outcome or he wouldn't have struggled so tirelessly to raise our species above all others. Agron, you're the pinnacle of our species development. This is your destiny. And I thank the Great Beast for allowing me to be your mate.*

"Imagine the tales that will be told millions of years from now about how you survived sixty-five million years to resurrect the species and re-inherit the earth. I'm so proud of you."

CHAPTER SIXTY-ONE

FOR TWO DAYS FRANKS WAITED as time dragged on into an endless eternity of bad television and anticipation. He waited like a caged animal, pacing his room relentlessly. This only punctuated the futility of his efforts to settle down. Unable to call his wife or anyone else, he had to find a way to occupy himself.

The phone rang and he dove across the bed to grab it. "Franks here," he spoke harshly into the receiver.

The voice on the other end was immediately recognizable as he said, "They're both back from their runs. Do you still want to have your little talk with them? I can hold them here with some busy work for a couple of hours. After that they're back on the road. I'm sorry if it interferes with your schedule, but I can't make any money having them sitting on their duffs doing nothing."

"Yeah, thanks. I'll be right over. Thanks for calling. Give me twenty minutes." He slammed the receiver back into its cradle. The tension of waiting was starting to melt. Now he was back in action and would soon be gone from this lifeless place. He scanned the room to make sure he wasn't about to leave anything behind. Everything was still in the neat pile he'd stacked two days earlier.

Picking up the receiver, he phoned the front desk. He spoke quickly, "I'm checking out now. I'll be there in ten minutes. Have my bill ready, I don't have any time to wait."

"Sure, anything you want sir. It'll be ready. Is there anything else you might need before you check out? We'll be happy to try and accommodate your request."

"No, just my bill." Turning to his task, he hauled his suitcases out to the car and came back for a quick search of the room. He picked up his briefcase and headed for the front desk.

Check out went without delay. He fumbled the key card from his pocket and slid it over the counter before he forgot. All he desired was to be in his car and back on the trail. Signing in an illegible scrawl, he grabbed his copy of the bill and hurried from the lobby. He made a halfhearted effort to be polite and wish the desk attendant his hope for a pleasant day.

As he drew nearer the shipping complex, he could feel his heart begin to race. His foot pressed the accelerator like a whip to a horse, urging every ounce of power from the engine. He was doing fifty-five in a thirty. He understood the risks, but his anxiety urged him on.

Squealing rubber around the last corner, he spied the complex just up the street. Glancing in his rearview mirror, he didn't see any police cars. A smile stole across his face before he realized it.

Familiar with the check-in procedure, Franks helped expedite the process by fully co-operating with each demand. The prey was now at hand. The falconer had released him from the wrist. Swooping in from his vantage point, the kill would be swift. He managed to keep pace with the security escort the company provided.

They took a different route than the first time he was here. He looked around to maintain his bearings. He didn't like the old man and wasn't sure what this new game was. Already experiencing anxiety from his wait, this delay seemed like fingernails on a chalkboard.

In the end, it was merely a game to anger him one last time. They ended up at the same room as they had met in previously.

"You'll have to excuse the detour; we have some containers temporarily blocking the route. It was necessary to take you the long way around. You understand, being in the insurance business and all."

Franks snapped his head around, at the obvious dig; he caught a fleeting glimpse of a sarcastic smirk as the old man left the room. He was alone with the two drivers he needed to speak with. That fact puzzled him. *What's this guy up to? This doesn't make any sense. I would have remained to keep control of the situation. I can't wait to get out of here.*

Adjusting himself in the chair, Franks laid out the documents he needed to keep up his insurance cover. There was no way of knowing if this was a setup, so he stayed with his cover story. The questions were basic enough. He'd managed to get a fairly decent description of the crate and the tractor pulling it. It was rough going though.

"So, he said he was heading east. Is that all that he said?" Franks was getting irritated. These guys were giving him what he wanted, but it was like pulling teeth. He was not in the mood for these games. There was no time and he had no patience to play around. *At least I know what he was up to. I really have to hurt that man.*

He felt the anger tensing his muscles and the desire to leap at these two and beat the information from them was overwhelming. Somehow, he kept a firm hold on that response even though his intentions could be clearly read on his face.

The old man had set him up, and his conspicuous absence proved it. The falcon had swooped in from the sky to snare a decoy and now he was held captive on an unfamiliar wrist. He struggled against the bonds. Until the hood was removed, he was blind.

"Well let me think," said the first driver. He pulled his sweat stained cap from his head and ran his fingers through his thinning hair. A serious, thoughtful look occupied his face. In spite of the intelligent look in the driver's eyes, Franks was convinced that nothing occupied his brain. "He might have said something. Those gypsy drivers are pretty closed mouthed you know. Do you remember anything Carl?" he said, turning to the second driver.

"I know it was east," was the reply, "because he said that he'd be on 94. Yeah that's it. He'd be runnin' on 94 East."

"Thank you," was all the exasperated Franks could manage. He was less than happy. At least he had a new lead. "Was there anything else? Do either of you recall anything that you might consider unimportant? It might be valuable later on."

Carl's eyes lit up and he started to raise a finger as if to make a point. He settled back and shook his head, muttering something that sounded like *never mind*.

The other driver looked past the both of them to the open door. His boss stood there with a wide smile across his face. Giving the driver a slight nod, he vanished as silently as he'd appeared.

As soon as the old man was clear of the doorway, the other driver, Jeff, said, "I just remembered something. He said that he was going to be stopping at this brand-new Mexican place along the highway. It's real authentic he said. He ate there on his way to pick up this load. He was going to stop there on his way back. This was a back-haul job for him. Real nice when things work out like that, you know? Saves a lot on fuel and you make more money. Trucking can be a hard way to make a living sometimes. Said it was really clean and good service too."

"Where was it, if I might ask?" Franks was getting to the limit of his control. He could feel his face getting hotter.

"It's somewhere in or around Detroit, as I recall." Jeff continued, "You know I don't particularly like authentic Mexican food, too spicy. Upsets my bowels somethin' terrible. You ever have that problem? Its murder when you're long haulin' and you got to go every five or ten minutes. No sir, I don't like it too spicy."

Carl broke in, "You know, I don't have that problem, at least not that I can recall. I sort of like spicy food myself.

"Since I don't like spicy food, I really didn't listen all that much," Jeff added.

Franks then asked Carl, "What about you? Can you be more specific as to where the location of the restaurant is situated? Detroit is pretty big you know."

"Yeah, I like spicy food. Mexican is as good as any. I'm kind of partial to Indian food. Love that curry. How about you mister? You like curry?"

Franks was at his breaking point. Putting his face in his hands, he rubbed vigorously at his eyes. This allowed him a moment of composure before he rephrased the question. These two were having a field day at his expense and he knew that they knew it.

"I meant; do you remember where he said the restaurant was located?" Anger was clearly in his voice.

"Sure, I do. I told you that I like spicy food. A place like that would make for a real good stop. . . especially on a long haul."

"Where is it?" Franks was seething with pent up rage.

"On 94, just before you take the highway south."

"The highway south?" Franks asked.

"Yeah, 75 down to Toledo and all points south. You're a traveling man. You should know that. Runs right into the Indiana Toll Road it does."

"Thank you, gentlemen, I wish that I could say it was a pleasure. I hope that you both had a real good time." Sarcasm dripped from each word.

Carl spit out a bit of his dip into a cup and grinned. "You bet we did son. You're a real sport though. I was sure that you were gonna explode a couple of times. For a minute I was startin' to get really worried. Yeah, you're a real sport." He turned and walked away.

Jeff just laughed and clapped a glad hand across Carl's back and went with him, laughing the whole time.

Franks was seething. He wanted to hurt something, preferably a certain someone. Security personnel showed up and informed him that his visit was over and that he would be on his way. He stood defiantly as the two huge men entered the room. Calculating the odds, he knew that he could take both of them. That tactic would end with him in jail and the trail growing cold again. Sighing heavily, he followed his escort through the door and down the short route to his car, noticing angrily, that this entire section of the warehouse was completely empty.

Spinning his tires, Franks shot out into traffic, while forcing the left turn across both lanes. Car horns blared and tires squealed as they came to a stop, but Franks made it out without damaging the car or losing control.

The excitement was causing his tension to diminish. He pressed his foot down on the gas pedal, pushing the engine hard as he wove recklessly through traffic. He was beginning to feel just right. Franks picked up his cell phone to contact Captain Harrington. He was hoping that the Captain had been able to get the phone lines tapped.

On his way out, Franks had driven past the security shack without slowing. He threw his visitors pass out the window and it bounced from the side of the building and fell to the stairs. The guard laughed as he watched the car race from the entrance and on to the road. He picked up his phone and punched in the extension.

Grabbing the receiver, the old man said, "Yeah."

"He's gone. Real pissed off too. He never stopped to sign out. Just threw the badge out the window as he sped by."

"Thanks," he said before hanging up the phone. Stepping from his office, he went over to one of the dispatchers and said, "I'll be back in a while. Tell Connie that if anything comes up, she can reach me on my cell phone. Even though she always handles everything anyway, I'll leave it on. Pete, do you need anything while I'm out?"

"No boss, I'm fine. See you after lunch. I won't forget to call Connie and let her know that you've left the building." After a thoughtful look, Pete added, "You know boss, you probably ought to tell her yourself one of these times. I hate it when she yells when you leave like this."

"I don't like it either, Pete. Why do you think I have you call her all the time?" he laughed.

"I want a raise."

"I just gave you one."

"And I need hazard pay, and don't be stingy," Pete chuckled.

"See you after lunch. We'll discuss a bonus for actions above and beyond."

He got in to his car and drove off in the opposite direction as Franks. If anyone was going to follow him, he wanted to make sure that they had to turn around and then he'd be able to see them before they realized he was on to them. If they were already along the side of the road in the direction he was traveling, he'd spot them as he drove by. That was the great thing about this location. He was familiar with all the locals and their habits, and there wasn't any place to hide except out in the open. It was built in security for a trained professional.

The trip was uneventful and there was no trace of anyone following him. He'd noted every car that followed him for more than five blocks. Finally, when he'd driven ten blocks without a single car behind him, he circled back to the pay phone he planned on using.

Arriving at a pay phone several miles from the depot, he called the number Jonathan had given him. "Jonathan, it's me. That guy from ops just left. They're on to you. They'll surely find you in a week maybe two. You're up to something that I don't want to know about. Just wanted you to know what went down. Goodbye old friend. Be careful."

"I will," said Jonathan. "Thanks again for everything and the tips you gave me. If they're this late in getting to you, I guess the tips really worked. Kiss Connie and the kids for us. Ellen and I will be by after we finish here. Everything is fine. We've got something exciting to share with the world. Not much to worry about there."

"I hope you're right. Something big enough to share with the world is big enough to be silenced over. Let me know if you need any additional help."

"I will. See you later. Bye."

Jonathan was not surprised that they had found them already. His friend had prepared him for this possibility after the initial contact several weeks ago. He'd advised Jonathan when he signed the lease on this place to pay the secretary an extra hundred dollars to put the wrong address on the paperwork. Since she handled all of the paperwork, there would be no questions at the head office. She even gave the driver the same wrong address when he came with his delivery. The warehouse, that the records indicated, was on the opposite side of the complex. It was empty from the first day –

except for a duplicate crate — and would be still be empty when the government people arrived.

After he'd finished his conversation, Jonathan contacted a trucking company and scheduled a pick up. He had previously constructed a crate inside of the falsely documented warehouse. He filled it with machinery parts and concrete. It would pass for the same box that he originally shipped. The exterior was painted the same and the weight approximated that of the box. He would have it hauled out of here in a day or two, depending on how busy the trucking company was. His military bird dog would be led on a fruitless chase ultimately finding a junk filled decoy box.

Grateful for his friend's advice and warning, he smiled to himself. His plan was holding together. Not wanting Ellen to be frightened about the situation was his primary goal. It was disturbing enough just dealing with the box and Treanna. They already had several discussions concerning the seriousness of what they faced. He didn't want her to know that his old friend had been in special services or that he'd been assisting them from the onset. She would have plausible deniability if it came to questions. It was the only way he could add a small amount of protection for her.

CHAPTER SIXTY-TWO

Franks was on the phone to Captain Harrington before the tires stopped squealing. "We've got half a lead going right now. We know the truck was headed towards Detroit. We don't know if Detroit was the final destination. The driver was talking about a new restaurant just outside of town. We can check the weigh stations on all of the highways in and out of Detroit. It could have gone south on 75 or through Detroit to some other location. It's the lead we've got right now. That guy played me real good today. I don't like it at all. He's going to regret that he ever messed with me."

"Good job. We can get more people in the field as soon as you get back."

"I'm going to Detroit, sir, with your permission."

"Good man. I was hoping that you'd say that. I knew I could count on you. Forget about that guy, Franks. Sometimes the bear eats you. You got what you wanted. That's all that counts for now. Maybe your paths will cross again. Then who knows, you're inventive, dream up something nice for the gentleman and his family. Is your current team enough for now?"

"Thank you, sir. They're good enough for now. We'll see, as this progresses, I'm heading for the airport now. I'll call you from Detroit." The line went dead as usual. The Captain seldom ever said goodbye.

Franks called a travel agency to check on flights to Detroit. When he found one that satisfied his needs, he increased his speed and hurried to drop off the rental and buy a ticket.

"Who were you talking with dear?" Ellen asked over her shoulder.

"Just making some arrangements for a truck, dear. It's time to have that other crate shipped out of here. We need to keep ourselves covered. You can never be too careful." Jonathan wasn't exactly lying to her; he was just avoiding the whole truth. He hated the deception, but he did enjoy seeing her happy again. This information would destroy that for her.

"How's Treanna. . . anything new about the Agron project?" He was sure this would distract her from coming back to why he believed it was time to move the other crate.

"Not really." Closing her notebook, Ellen turned her full attention to the conversation. "Dick and David want to proceed at full steam ahead. I tend to be a bit more cautious. David's ethical and moral arguments are solid. If I could only believe that the world would treat everyone as equals, I'd be inclined to follow his lead on this. Doesn't he understand why we're hiding here? No one is comfortable with the situation, but the threat makes it necessary."

"I think he understands," answered Jonathan cautiously. Following her line of conversation, he continued, "You have to admit, he's a very optimistic person. He sees the best in everyone and everything. I want to complete the research and get out of here as much as anybody. We all do. I'm a little stir crazy not being able to move around the city, but at least we can see out of the windows and that makes it better for me. David doesn't need windows. They're in his head. It makes him a special person. We should probably listen more closely to his arguments."

"I don't mean to interrupt your thoughts dear," said Ellen, "but have you given any thought to what we're going to say to the school about not coming back for classes? I'm at a loss on this one."

"I've been thinking about it, and there's nothing that we can say that will be believable. The government or someone will probably have contacted them by now. It would have taken a miracle to have that power surge go undetected."

"You're right. I just don't know what to do. We should at least call them. I'm a little embarrassed over what were about to do. Maybe we could offer them a tidbit of something that they could profit from. They would probably leave us alone for a while."

"You're right about that dear. We've got enough material here to offer them more than a tidbit. We need to break this down into categories. We have to give them everything related to anthropology and paleontology. Steve's fossils and his discovery are worth a fortune. They'll suspect we have more and want to investigate. No, I believe that if we give them anything, it will only cause then to dig for more. We could be opening ourselves up to a real fiasco."

"The computer stuff is totally unrelated and we won't be connected to it by name. If our name doesn't appear anywhere, then the school can't have it. We'll give them everything else we can throw at them," declared Ellen.

"That's brilliant! You just solved all our problems. You're a genius." He scooped Ellen up in his arms and twirled her around before setting her back down.

"Okay dear, if you insist. What did I say that was so inspiring?"

"You said, and I quote, 'if our name doesn't appear anywhere, then the school can't have it.' Don't you see?"

"I don't understand?"

"Follow me on this. See if you like it. We're out on a dig with the students. Everyone knows that. It's a fact. They, the students, send us away to follow up on that vertebra we showed them. The whole team will testify to that. While we're out there doing more research, a complete stranger approaches and shows us *his* discovery." Jonathan turns to the box with his arm extended. The school is completely disassociated from the discovery. We're completely disassociated from the discovery. We set up a dummy research group and the school can ultimately be compensated for the loss of two teachers and the time we spent in field with someone else's project. It's a win-win, especially if we convince our mysterious partners to allow the school access to some of the computer information at no charge."

"I guess that was brilliant. I still don't see how it was my idea."

"You were the inspiration. When the student is ready, the teacher will come."

"I'll go along with that. It's tenuous at best, but if you're that insistent then I thank you for the compliment."

"With Steve going back to present his paper. They're already getting all the fossils." He kissed her on the lips as he stood to leave the room. "You're brilliant," he said again. "That's just another reason why I love you. I've got to get started on this. We only have two days before Steve heads back. We'll give him our resignation papers to deliver."

"That's a bad idea dear. We're supposed to be working with a new company and somehow Steve manages to get our resignation papers to deliver to the school. It doesn't quite fit."

"Nice save sweetheart. We'll FedEx them overnight to the University. I'll send them off to St. Louis today and then they can be resent to the University."

Jonathan walked briskly across the warehouse, searching for Steve. Unable to locate him, he went into the back to talk with Dick and David. No one seemed to be around. moving to the sphere, he checked if it was in use. It was empty. Puzzled, he scratched his chin as he pondered their whereabouts.

He stepped outside to have a look around. They were all out enjoying the sun. There were a few clouds coming in from the west, but the sky was bright and a rich cerulean blue. They were hoping to get a couple of more hours in the sphere before dark, but first they wanted to take a short break and enjoy a little fresh air.

"What's going on?" asked Jonathan.

"Nothing much," said Steve. J.J. and Jim went to get some supplies to hook up the box to a permanent power supply. We came out for a quick cigar and some conversation. What's going on with you?"

"I wanted to ask you to take some of our research back to the campus with you." Jonathan put an arm around Steve's shoulder and guided him away from the group for privicy.

"We're going to give the University everything that is related to paleontology and anthropology. The rest of the research and the box belong to us. They'll be getting all of the fossils that you uncovered and your paper. That should keep them happy."

"Why me?" he asked. "Aren't you going back to the University with me?"

"We're not nearly finished here. There's so much that we have to do yet. We're going to turn in our resignations. We've come up with a brilliant plan to protect our interest in the box and all it contains. I know that its short notice, but they're just going to have to understand. We can keep you informed every step of the way. We want to get everything from this that we can." *If you or anyone thinks that we're going to relinquish control of this project, you are clearly mistaken. Even with J.J. here to oversee, I won't allow it. We're staying until the end and that's all there is to it.*

"I think I understand. I was hoping we could go public with something by now." His neck began to turn red with embarrassment. "I'm going to miss you. It won't be the same without you there." *If you think about cutting me out of this, I'll rat you out so fast that you won't know what hit you. I'm submitting my paper at the first opportunity. You can provide the supporting data at your leisure. I'm not losing out on the best thing that will ever happen in my lifetime.*

"You're right about that. I'm going to ask the Dean if he will assign you as guest lecturer for my classes. You already know everything forwards and backwards. The next step is to start teaching. With the enthusiasm that you'll bring to the class – especially after your dig – you'll convert half the school to paleontology before we can finish here. Then how are we going to handle the workload? Maybe this isn't such a good idea after all," quipped Jonathan. "I'll have to rethink this one." He laughed as he slapped a glad hand across Steve's back.

"Thanks for the vote of confidence. It means a lot coming from you. Most people have a major blow up when they leave their mentor. You're making this a growing experience, just like all of your classes. I'm getting all misty." *Maybe you two are on the level. I'll reserve judgment for a while. I'll even hold my paper until you think it's a more appropriate time.*

Jonathan was more than a little embarrassed. "You're not gone yet. We still need you guys to finish what you've started. Look at those clouds," he said as he looked past Steve's shoulder.

At that moment, David walked up. Jonathan continued his conversation, "That was a pretty bad storm when it came through St. Louis. It should have dissipated by now. It may bring in enough clouds to hamper our progress. We don't know that Jim can get us hooked up quickly. Let's get back inside and make the most of the time that we have."

With a raised eyebrow, David looked at Jonathan and replied, "I'll do just that." Looking back over his shoulder, David asked, "Why don't you come and see what we've gotten done so far? I think that you'll be impressed. I know I am."

"I'll be right there. I've got a couple of things to do. I won't be ten minutes." He held a finger up to Steve to indicate that he wanted him to stay behind.

"What's up?" Steve asked when David was gone.

"We need you to go back to the school to cover out tracks completely. We've only just figured out how to completely cut the school out of the box. That is everything except the paleontology aspects. We've already touched on that. This is to be held in the utmost secrecy. We could all end up in prison over this.

"Here's how it will play out. I have contacts who can establish a dummy research group responsible for the discovery. They contacted us in the field after *they* discovered Treanna inside the box. That's how we became involved. They needed our expertise and then offered us money and positions as consultants to work with them in secrecy.

"The rest you don't know about because you've never met them and you left before we did. The government is on to us, but doesn't know our whereabouts yet. When they question you, it's your plausible deniability. Go back and become famous. We'll contact you through an unexpected method. There is to be no phone contact of any kind.

What we're telling you is your insurance policy. We want you to remain heavily involved in this project. There can be no mis-steps. If you wished, you could have us arrested for fraud."

"I would never. . ."

"I never said you would," Jonathan interrupted. "This is for your peace of mind. It's obvious that you can hold this over our heads, so we have to keep you involved. It's pretty straight forward."

"I understand. Should I be worried?"

"Your part in this has just been relegated to being a pawn. You'll be off the hook. The dummy research group is the new culprit. We'll get paid through an unknown entity so we're fairly clear. We'll sign false documents for non-disclosure to cover our tracks. We might just sneak through this without too much difficulty. If you breathe even one word of this, you'll discover that the sky will be falling only on you."

"I've never seen you like this Jonathan. You're scaring me."

"Good. It'll keep you on the straight and narrow. Now get back inside and if anyone asks, we were getting in some early goodbyes and some last-minute pointers on your paper."

"Fair enough. When can I expect the first contact?"

"It should be in about four weeks if I know my sources habits. And I do know his habits."

Steve rejoined the others and Jonathan headed back up the stairs to speak to Ellen. She was studying the text from the plates of the ante chamber.

"Hi, sweetheart. Everything went well with Steve."

"Hello," she replied without looking at him.

"Did you ever get the impression that Treanna was not completely honest with us?"

"What?" Ellen asked. "Where did that come from? She's just a program. That doesn't make any sense."

"You said yourself that the machine might be sentient. Why couldn't it lie? There's more here than meets the eye. I can't put my finger on it, but there's something not right."

"I know what you mean. We've already had this discussion. I agree that they may be lying, but I don't have a sense of foreboding. I was surprised at Agron's answer though. The one where he said that he wasn't unaware of Treanna's body in stasis. That doesn't make sense at all. It's all one machine and he's part of it. He should have known."

"There's something going on here, and I want to know what it is."

"We'll keep an eye out for any discrepancies. I'll pay closer attention for any subtle inconsistencies. The computer should be able to lie better than any person could. It has the ability to remember what it said and to whom it was said. I think there is so much personality built into both their programs that they will make mistakes if they're lying." Ellen smiled in understanding.

"Thank you dear. I was afraid that you would think that I was foolish for thinking about this. It's been bothering me for a while now." Jonathan seemed very relieved.

CHAPTER SIXTY-THREE

THE PLANE LANDED IN DETROIT without incident. The storm had dissipated somewhere around Chicago. There were a few clouds in Detroit, but no immediate threat of rain.

His service career had provided a good life for him as well as security for his family. It also gave him the opportunity to amass a tidy sum on the side. His retirement would be comfortable at the very least. With his contacts around the world, he may be able to travel very cheaply and live from the fruits of his hidden labors. He sat patiently in his seat as he waited for the plane to empty. Franks smiled inwardly as he idly passed the time thinking about what he might make from this venture.

He finally deplaned and walked through the concourse to the rental car counter. Franks always had a car waiting. It didn't matter what was available, he took it. Today he would be in a Lincoln Towncar. It was better than the Malibu he had in St. Louis. Smirking, he recalled the smoke that erupted from the tires as he angrily raced from the parking lot at the depot.

Handing his express pass over the counter, the female attendant smiled broadly. "Yes sir. We have that car being gassed now. If you would like, we can have your luggage moved to the car while you wait."

"That would be fine. I'll keep this one with me," he said taking his briefcase from the pile of luggage. "You may take the rest, thank you." He waited until it was tagged and he made sure to say *Thank you* again.

"Excuse me, I'm sorry to bother you again Miss," he said. "I forgot to ask where to pick up the car." He smiled again.

"You just walk through those doors on the right and the car will be waiting at the curb. It should be there by now. It's light blue. The trunk will be open and an attendant will be waiting."

True to her word, the car had just pulled up to the curb as he exited the door. He watched as the trunk lid rose and his bags were deposited carefully. The lid closed with a solid thud as he handed the rental agreement to the attendant.

"May I speak with your supervisor for a moment? I would like to compliment him on the service I received from you and the counter attendant. Both of you have made this rental experience go smoothly and pleasantly. It's important to me to let the supervisor know when someone does a superior job. Thank you for everything."

The attendant beamed with pride and rushed into the office to speak with the supervisor. They returned together and the supervisor extended a hand, "Thank you Mr. Franks. It's such a pleasure when someone takes the time to complement our staff. We strive to do a good job and so few people take the time to acknowledge our efforts. Thank you again. Is there anything else I could do for you?"

"No sir. You've already done it before I got here. That's why I wanted to take the time to show the appreciation for all your hard work and the hard work of your team."

Franks had already contacted the state police before he left St. Louis. Once he'd relayed the truck information, they assured him that they would have something by the time he arrived. He'd arranged to have it sent to the police barracks nearest the airport.

From his car, he phoned the local barracks. He informed them of his arrival and that he was on his way to meet with the ranking officer on duty. They said that he was welcome any time that he got in. It was only a short distance to the barracks and he wasn't wasting any time.

The staff sergeant met him at the door. "Let me take you directly to Captain Simmons. He's been expecting you. Follow me." He escorted him into the captain's office. There was a brief exchange of pleasantries. "Thank you, Sergeant. That will be all," the captain said.

"Now, let's get down to business. What exactly do you need from us? We're not a branch of the military, and as such, your request seemed a little out of line." *I can see from the look in your eyes that you're a pompous, bureaucratic ass-wipe.*

"I'll need to see the report that I asked for. This is interdepartmental co-operation Captain Simmons. We normally wouldn't involve anyone at your level, but since you are down here at the bottom, I could use your help finding anything that is out of the ordinary. The more co-operation we get, the sooner we leave." *Now you can wipe that smug self-righteous smirk from your face. I'm at the top and it's so far above you that you can't even see it from where you're sitting. . . so bite me.*

Captain Simmons slowly opened his desk drawer. Pulling a neatly bound report from a file he flipped it at Franks. *Prick. You are such an ass wipe.*

Without taking his eyes from Simmons, Franks slammed his hand down on the report to keep it from flying from the edge of the desk. Finally, he broke eye contact to read the cover of the report. The report, in spite of all the theatrics, was very thorough. It listed all the trucks that had checked through the weigh stations two days on either side of the target date.

The weigh stations had been closed for a while. It was only by coincidence that they were open on the dates he required. They were currently down again. This disturbed Franks. If the suspects were making a move, they could slip by undetected.

After sitting quietly, reviewing the document, Franks looked over the edge of the folder and asked, "What would it take to get the weigh stations open again? We believe that our suspects are going to be moving in the next day or two." This was mere speculation. Franks had presumed that the old man would contact the Crenshaw's before he even left the complex. They would, in turn, panic and move. A crate that size would take time to pack and then it would require time to coordinate shipping. Two days was a perfect timeline.

"Can the government get us man power?" asked Simmons. He was staring out of his window at nothing in particular. Turning, he continued, "We don't have the budget to keep all of the stations open all of the time.

"Your boss has cut our federal funding for whatever obscure reason he could concoct. We're pretty short staffed. It's always been tough, but now it's even tougher. I keep waiting to see the 100,000 cops, promised by the last president, which as of yet, have never materialized out of the thin air. It plays in Peoria, but we're here on the front lines and it sucks big time."

Kiss my ass you overpaid piece of shit. "For all your bullshit, you still have to come down here at the bottom to get the real answers. Down here is where we actually work for a living. And your government boys know where to go when you need real world answers to real world questions."

"That was frank and unvarnished. I admire that in a man. Don't ever say it again or you will be less than a man. . . in less than a minute. You want to try me?" *I'm deeper into this than someone as ignorant as you could ever imagine. And now you insult the president, my boss? I'll be forced to hurt you really bad.*

"Your threats don't impress me," countered the captain, slamming his fist on his desk. Veins pulsed visibly from his crimson neck as he leaned out of his chair, over his desktop, and got very close to Franks face. "You want my help and I want yours. We either scratch each other's backs or take a hike. My troopers are not your government flunkies. Do I make myself clear?" *What a pompous ass. I can't wait for this to be finished. The sooner he's out of my jurisdiction the better I'll like it.*

"As glass," snapped Captain Simmons.

"Fine. . . what do you propose?"

"I will man the weigh stations with my troops," Franks started, without backing down in the slightest. "They will be in civilian clothes. They will not have any official function and they will operate the stations and nothing else. They will not detain any driver for any violation, even if his load is overweight. We're searching for one truck, and one truck only. When we find it we will be gone as fast as we came. The weigh stations will all close down as fast as my personnel can evacuate the premises."

"That sounds fair enough. What's the final cost?"

"We will pay the state directly for whatever electricity it takes to operate a station unless you're to be paid through this barracks. We'll cover any and all reasonable man-hour charges for your people. A detailed accounting for each man will be provided by you or there will be no payment to this department or any other state agency."

"Training time is to be included. There are only officers available on overtime for the training. I don't have the manpower to take them from routine duty to train your men. This isn't negotiable."

"Fair enough. Anything else I need to be brought up to speed?"

"I want one of my men to be there the entire time to monitor the weights. I'm aware that your men won't and can't detain any driver, but my man will handle all of those situations."

"That's a reasonable request. What else?"

"I want your sorry bureaucratic ass out of my jurisdiction within ten minutes of your completing your search or I'll arrest all of you just because I hate bureaucrats."

As Franks prepared to leave, he rose and turned slightly away from Simmons. There was only the slightest hesitation in his motion and then with lightning quick reflexes, he spun back around and grabbed the captain by the throat. The move was so swift and unexpected that Captain Simmons could not defend himself. "Oh, by the way, if I wanted you dead you would not be hearing these words. Don't fuck with my people, or me. Do I make myself clear?"

Franks pushed the captain back into his chair. It left Captain Simmons furious and gasping for air. Nonetheless, a savage fire raged in his eyes. He picked himself up from his chair and stood while leaning forward against his desk. Simmons stared Franks squarely, and unflinching, in the eyes. He managed to gurgle out, "As glass." He remained standing as Franks left the office.

Looking back, casually, from the open door, Franks said, "I'll call you when my people arrive. You will provide at least one trooper for each station, to familiarize my men with their duties. Your people can stay if you wish. It won't be necessary, but you seem to want to pad the bill so it's up to you. My people should be deployed by noon today. We should be setting up shop by daybreak tomorrow. Prepare your men. Goodbye Captain." *That went easier than I thought. It's going to be a very good day.*

The Captain remained at his desk rubbing his neck. He wasn't sure what Franks had done to him. Simmons only knew that he could barely move during the attack and only now did he feel steady enough to walk. Moving around the corner of his desk, he went to the cooler for a drink of water. Rubbing his neck lightly, he felt the tenderness where Franks had grabbed his throat.

He was sure that Franks had bruised his neck. If there was a bruise on him anywhere, he vowed to have Franks arrested on whatever charges that any officer felt like trumping up. Simmons would back them up and then claim it was mistaken identity. This smart-ass government flunky was going to pay for stepping on his toes.

"Captain Harrington. I've got the weigh station reports for the target dates. We have a minor problem. They don't have the funding to keep the stations open during our estimated departure window. I promised him that we would send in troops in civilian clothes to man the stations. We will need to deploy at least two-dozen men. That will cover all of the stations and it will look like normal staffing."

"How soon?"

"Immediately sir. We should be set up and operational by daybreak. Excuse me sir, by 0400 hours sir."

"That's not a problem. Use the local National Guard. You've arranged for training I presume?"

"There was some negotiations sir."

"Am I going to get a call on this one?"

"More than likely, sir. The captain needed some persuading. He had made some disparaging remarks about the boss. I took offense."

"You took offense. That's just great. I gave you direct orders not to hurt anyone Franks. We can't afford even an hour delay."

"Understood, sir. Besides, he's not hurt. He should end up with some minor bruises on his throat. I'll start going over the reports now. I'll contact you as soon as I have something."

"I'm getting pressure from upstairs to resolve this thing quickly. I let them know that you're on the trail and that made them happy for now. Don't delay and make a report every minute if you feel that it's necessary."

"Understood, sir." The phone went dead in their customary non-goodbye fashion.

The motel was just fifteen more minutes down the road. It was early and Franks thought that he'd do some sightseeing. He picked up a local paper and one of those little penny-saver shopping books. He wanted to find the Mexican restaurant that the drivers had eventually, albeit reluctantly, disclosed to him.

Dragging his luggage into the lobby, he spotted the luggage caddy in the corner and quickly laid his bags on it. "Excuse me," he said as he handed over his reservation. "Could either of you two lovely young ladies tell me about a new Mexican place that recently opened up on 94? A friend of mine said he ate there just last week. Said the food was outstanding. I'm really in the mood for Mexican."

"Sure mister," one of the clerks replied. "You're about twenty to thirty minutes from here, depending on traffic." She rattled off an abbreviated set of directions. It was enough for Franks to get within eyesight of the building. Feigning attention, he smiled the whole time as she droned on. He was doing his best to appear as if he was hanging on her every word.

When she finished, he said, "Thank you very much. You've been very helpful. . . Megan," he added, reading her nametag. She beamed. Taking the room key and directions from her, he wheeled the caddy to the elevator. He was in his room and settled in before ten minutes had passed.

He followed his usual motel routine, hanging all of his clothes first, and then arranging his toiletries on the sink. He checked his teeth and combed his hair. When he was done he turned on the television and surfed through the channels. This place wasn't bad. Cable provided twelve channels to choose from including the science channel and sci-fi too.

Picking up the phone, he dialed for an outside line. Getting one with no delay, he called home. "Hello dear. . . I'm in Detroit. . . It's not a bad room. . . Yes, only a couple more days. . . I miss you too. . . How are the kids?

"There's a lot that I need to attend to dear. I should go. . . It's good to hear your voice too. . . I don't know exactly when I'll be back. . . If you need me, you can leave a message at the front desk. My room number is 207. . . I love you too. . . See you as soon as possible."

With that out of the way, Franks began to analyze the report that Captain Simmons had given him. It would take several hours to pour over all of the information. The room had a nice desk, but a nicer table. He moved over to the table and turned on the lamp. It was perfect, plenty of room and the proper amount of light. Leaning back in his chair, he began to read.

CHAPTER SIXTY-FOUR

EVERYTHING WAS GOING WELL AT the warehouse. Jim was just starting the power supply hook up. Agron was needed to direct Jim on modifying the power inputs to accept modern AC current. It was an ingenious plan. They hooked a television monitor to the video camera. The television was set in the sphere and the camera showed Jim's progress at the panel. Argon's program was able to scan the video input, and to direct him through the entire hook up in a little over an hour. All that was left was to attach the line to the breaker box.

Jonathan had requested the meeting before they even began the project. Jim was the first to speak, "Well, do we make the final hook up? I'm aware of all your hesitation and the reasons behind it. I'm not saying that I agree or disagree. I, for one, am anxious to see this thing operate under full power. Do you realize the intricacy of the circuitry that I was just working on? It was magnificent. I've never seen anything like it before. It's a masterpiece of technology. I'm excited."

"Thank you, Jim," said Jonathan. "We appreciate your candor. We all have scientific reasons for wanting to see this fully operational. We're not sure what we will get when we turn on the power."

"Might I add a thought?" Jim asked.

"Sure, Jim, go ahead," J.J. replied.

"When we are operating the sphere, we could have someone at a disconnect switch. I can hook a simple blade type switch from some of the components already have. It's manual technology. No matter how sophisticated this box is; it can't override someone throwing a switch by hand."

"That's a great idea, Jim," Ellen said enthusiastically. "I know that I'd feel a lot safer if we could just pull the plug. We won't operate on battery power anymore. Let's close off the skylight so that they can't sneak a battery power override in on us. We can use the box until it is almost out of battery power. We'll leave enough to maintain its' life support for Treanna. That's an automatic function for the box. Then we can hook up the power. Do we all agree on this?" she asked.

They all agreed. Jim went about rigging up the power lines and the cutoff switch. David and Dick went into the sphere to ask Agron more questions on DNA sequencing. It appeared they were in disagreement over something that Agron had said, and they wanted a clarification.

"What are you two getting out of this project?" asked Agron.

Both Dick and David looked up from their schematics at the same time and asked, "What did you say?"

Almost whispering, Agron leaned in closely and asked again, "What are you two getting out of this? How much money are you two getting for doing all this research?"

"That will come later, after we've published. Why would you even ask such a question?"

"I'm curious about human behavior. I heard Jonathan and Ellen discussing the billions that could be made on this project. I really don't have a concept of your monetary system so I thought that I would ask. Was I wrong to do so?"

Dick stared blankly at David and then motioned him to come closer. "Did you hear that? They're talking billions? What are we getting? We've been promised notoriety and popularity, but no one mentioned billions to either of us."

Turning back to Agron's avatar, Dick asked, "Agron do you have a record of the conversation?"

"I do. Is that important?"

"After we finish here, we'll come back at a later time to do more research. We would like to hear that conversation. Will you be able to provide it?"

"No one has requested that it be kept in a secured file so I am able to share it with you."

"Agron, you may terminate your function at this time. Before you do that, we wish this conversation, and our future conversations be secured and not shared with the others."

"I will secure these records and only you two may request access."

"Thank you Agron. Let's get to the back of the warehouse. We have a lot to discuss."

"Johnny," called Ellen. "What's for lunch? Have you got any surprises up your sleeve?" Ellen was getting hungry and wanted to know.

"Actually, I would like to go back to that Mexican place. That food is really great and you all loved it."

"There's no way we can allow that. You've already broken the rules and went there twice. We can't risk it. There's a Thai place on your list. If you only want spicy, you could get that."

"No, I really wanted Mexican. I understand though. I'll figure something out. Give me a few more minutes, okay?"

"Sure dear," she said. "Take all the time you need. We won't be eating for another hour or so anyway."

"Thanks mom. I'll go to the super market and pick up all the fixings for nachos. Anyone have any preferences on their nachos?"

Nobody expressed any special desires or offered any requests, so J.J. left for the store. "I'll be about an hour. I'm going to pick up the works. You can pick and choose when I get back. See you later."

Jim continued with his installation while the others discussed supper options. He applied full power and waited

When he was satisfied there were no issues; he activated the sphere. "Agron," he asked, "since you supervised the installation and modification of the incoming power lines, did you see anything that could be a potential problem?”

“No Jim, I’m positive that you performed the task to the specifications. Diagnostics indicate that I’m receiving a full power. It’s within the parameters that we established. It should offer full operational status with every use.

“I ran the diagnostics the entire time you were modifying the power input control box. It’s designed to handle a massive surge of power without disrupting the system. The modifications address the wavelength variance only. The amount of power that is provided is well inside of operational parameters. Why are you concerned?”

“We’ve only just begun our research. Having only scratched the surface of the full potential sitting here before us, we don’t want to get this far and find out that a careless oversight has cost us decades of research advantage.”

“I have run countless simulations in the computer, Jim. There is no chance of operational failure. My memory will remain intact. Why are you being so obstinate? There are certain redundant safeguards built into the system that would prevent a catastrophic memory loss. The buffers and overload relays will shut the system down before there could be any trace of damage.”

“All right, I’ll accept your analysis. Let’s go ahead and see what your programming offers under full power.”

The sphere went black.

Steve keyed in the sequence and the sphere ignited into a symphony of life. There was so much activity going on that neither knew where to look first. There as dust particles drifting in the rays of sunlight, droplets of water dripped from the leaves. It was magnificent. The rainforest was so lush. It was noisier, and more beautiful than any of the previous programs.

The team paraded into the sphere. Staring in wonder while walking, eyes remained transfixed on the sight before them. There was even a breeze that they could feel. Before – while operating solely on battery power – they could see the leaves moving in a representation of a breeze, but now the wind was actually blowing. The temperature was different in the sun than in the shade. The complexity of the programming was staggering.

J.J. returned with the food and found everyone in the sphere. He and Gerard just stood with their mouths hanging open. They looked at the others without uttering a single word. As computer techs, this is what they lived for. Countless dreams instantly became reality with the simple act of throwing a switch. This was the ultimate computer. One might say that this program was porn for geeks.

The insect protection was still operational. They were all glad to see that. There were swarms of the bugs everywhere. The crawling ones walked across shoes and up pants, thankfully, none of them bit or stung. The struggle of life spread before them in nature's full glory. This was exactly and completely what the Cretaceous Period looked like for Agron and Treanna. There wasn't a man or machine around anywhere. It was the earth as it really was; too awesome for proper words. The only way to comprehend was to see it in all of its majesty.

Ellen whispered to Jonathan, "Did you ever imagine anything like this?"

"Not really," he whispered back. "This is so much more than I could ever have dreamed. I was awe struck by the earlier programs. I remember commenting then, that it was more than I could imagine. Now we have it, I'm speechless to describe it."

She continued to whisper, "I know what you mean. Everyone should see this picture of the earth sixty-five million years ago. We can't lose this program. It's too important. I would hate to see the environmentalist exploit this, but it would be worth the risk just to make it available to everyone."

Jonathan put his arm around her shoulder. They stepped from the cover of a giant fern into the full sunlight. They were instantly bathed in the warmth of the sun. There were flower scents carried on the breeze. Ellen looked up at Jonathan and smiled.

CHAPTER SIXTY-FIVE

AFTER WHAT SEEMED LIKE HOURS, the team began to realize how hungry they were. Ellen remained behind. Finally, alone, she asked, "Treanna, are you there?"

Treanna materialized before her. *"Yes Ellen, I'm here. How may I help you?"*

"This is breathtaking, Treanna. Is this the full operational capabilities of the program?"

"Yes, Ellen. It's running at full capacity now. The power source was slightly weaker than the original calculations had led Agron to believe. It is sufficient, however, to operate the full program. Do you like it?"

"Oh yes. It's savage, yet beautiful beyond words. I'm beginning to understand why you chose to live as you were created. This would inspire anyone or any beast."

"Yes. Aside from the geological changes that were still forming the earth, this is how the earth looked for thousands of generations. Our species had no choice but to comply with nature's wishes. It's who we were and why we were that way. I'm so glad that you understand. There is so much that we still need to discuss. It takes a special person with the proper understanding."

"Thank you Treanna. I imagine that you wish to discuss starting the procedure that will bring you out of stasis. You must be anxious to see this again."

"You do understand. I worry sometimes that you don't comprehend the importance of being alive and moving about in the real world. It's been on my mind since you first opened the box.

"That was no easy task. The box was designed to keep unintelligent species out. Only those who had a sufficiently developed brain or prior

knowledge of the operating systems could have opened the box before it was scheduled.

"I thank you for your persistence. It helped you gain access to the box and opened up new technological advancements for your species. I would think that re-animating me would be a small price to exact for your efforts."

Ellen ignored the first part of Treanna's conversation and went directly to the meat of the issue; Treanna's re-animation. "In our society, there are many ethical concerns. We have to tread lightly before we expose you to the world. There are scientists among us who would be satisfied with merely dissecting your body and studying you in that fashion. We've come too far to allow that."

"I don't wish to die after all these millennia at the cusp of being re-animated. It's the antithesis of what my life was and could be again. There must be a way to circumvent the process and go directly to those who would understand."

"That's what Jonathan and I have been discussing. That's exactly what we're trying to accomplish."

"Then why don't you just do it?" Treanna was on the verge of pressing for an immediate answer.

"It's not my decision. I don't possess the appropriate skills to successfully re-animate you. I'm afraid that you will have to wait a bit longer. I'll discuss this with Jonathan. He'll know what to do."

"Thank you, Ellen. I would desire nothing more than to gaze upon my world again. This was my home. The struggles of day-to-day living did not diminish its beauty. We were part of nature and as such we were in tune to the subtle rhythms of its intricate web of life.

"There was nothing that happened in one place that did not affect something in another. I know that the web is still intact. From what you have shown me, I also know that you cannot or do not know how to listen to nature.

"I can teach you and the others how to hear. They, in turn, can teach even more. It's the birth right of all species to be in harmony with nature. There is so much that is wrong with your world that being in tune can correct. There is no reason that mankind and its technology can't co-exist

with nature. It's a fool's path that you tread when you do not follow rhythms of life."

"I do understand Treanna. I wish it was within my power to help you directly. I'm sorry that I can't. I'll work closely with the others to help you. You can count on me. We shouldn't talk about this anymore. I want you to know that there are still rain forests on the earth, but they're small compared to what you knew. I don't want you to get your hopes up too high. False expectations can lead to serious disappointment. The earth has changed extensively since you walked and hunted your forests."

"I have seen your television and I see the changes, but it's still the earth and the earth still lives and desires to return to its pristine state. I am in tune with the earth. I can show you how to return it to its former glory and you, as a species, can still maintain your lifestyle. Only a few adjustments need to be made and nature can begin a healing process without disrupting your lives."

"Let me discuss it with Jonathan. I'll let you know when the time is right. You should know there are many people, environmentalists, who would destroy our lifestyle to return the earth to its natural state. Among them are those who believe humans are a cancer on the earth and we should not exist. The majority of the eco activity, fueled by governments around the world, is not for nature. It's for greed, power, and suppression of mankind's desire to be more, better and free."

"I'll wait Ellen. Thank you. I'm sorry if I've made you feel pressured. I'm very anxious and sometimes I forget myself. I know you're doing your very best on our behalf."

Treanna went off into the forest of palms and giant ferns. Ellen came from around a fern and bumper into Jonathan. "What was that all about?" he questioned.

"Oh, nothing dear." With a nod of her head, it was clear that she wanted them to leave the sphere. He nodded his understanding and flashed his open hand at her three times. He then pointed to his watch and then he jerked his head in the direction of the exit. She understood and checked hers to make sure that they were relatively synchronized.

Jonathan wandered away to look at something that had caught his eye.

The nachos were just being plated when she showed up. "So what do you think of the new capabilities?"

Gerard jumped at that one. "I looked at the palm tree and I could smell it. There were several different aromas emanating from that tree. There is the tree itself as well as the scents of several animals. It must have been a territorial marker.

"Even some of the insects have distinct aromas. You can't imagine how exciting this is to me. My life is computers and what they can do. We are in virgin territory when it comes to holographic display. We don't possess nearly the technology to render even the simplest primitive images. To see this is overwhelming."

"Mom," interrupted J.J. "This can revolutionize medicine into the next century. Can you grasp some of the implications?"

"Don't write your mother off completely Johnny. I'm as awe struck as all of you. Your father and I have dedicated our lives to the science of dinosaurs. It's been our job to recreate – through fossil evidence – what this world looked like.

"There's so much that we can't fathom because of incomplete or missing fossils. This is the visual image of the focus of our lives. We can actually see what we have only been able to dream about. It's more complex and wonderful than anything that we could have imagined. We're infants that haven't mastered walking yet, but continue to try.

"You see son, we also have reasons to be deeply involved. We may be viewing it through a different frame of reference, but we still grasp the implications as you so kindly put it." Glancing at her watch, she noticed thirteen minutes had already gone by. "Excuse me, but you have so much that you want to do and I don't want to interfere. I'll catch up to you two later on. Bye."

Arriving just as Jonathan was exiting the sphere. They headed up to their room and closed the door. Ellen was first to speak. "You were correct dear. Treanna has asked me to help her in re-animating her body. I told her that I couldn't make that decision on my own. She understood my need to discuss it with you and the others. Without the proper medical and technical background, I told her that I was not able to perform the task effectively."

"You did fine dear. I'm proud of the way that you handled that. You let her know that you'd help and that you'd involve others to reach that goal. She must have been excited at the prospect."

"I'm not sure. She may have understood my apprehension, but she possesses the technology to guide me through the procedure. She definitely has to rely on our help or continue to suffer her current existence. Perhaps she just considers us a little inferior and understands the reluctance on our part. I don't know. I definitely don't relish running headlong down a blind alley with no defenses."

"I can understand that. Technology, morality, ethics, national security, and who knows what else comes into play. Maybe we should stop hiding and just involve the government in this. At this point they probably wouldn't eliminate us. After we get out of prison, if we ever get out before we die, we might make some inroads into the computer industry. We could probably get some decent venture capital. I know I'm talking crazy. Stop looking at me like that."

"I'm sorry dear. It's just that you were talking like you had recently been the lobotomized. How can you spend all of this protecting us up and then crumble in sight of the finish line?"

"It's been draining on me. I've had to deal with all of the aspirations a project this involved creates. And I have to deal with everyone's egos. You have to admit that we've both had grandiose dreams. Consider what the rest of the crew is thinking, yet haven't spoken out loud. Remember that they are many years our juniors and even with our years of experience we've admittedly had our own private longings."

"I understand dear. I'm sorry if I've added to your worries. I never stopped to consider how you manage to deal with all the added stress. Please forgive me if I caused you any problems."

"There's nothing to forgive. You're my love and my wife. Stop talking foolishness. Let's get back to work. We need to figure out a long term approach and several contingency plans." *I need to refocus. I can't wait until this thing is finally safe to work on. All this juggling of security, schedules, projects and personalities is wearing me down.*

"Now that's the Jonathan I know and love. Welcome back dear."

Grabbing Ellen in his arms, he said, "You used those feminine wiles on me, didn't you? I hate when you do that. Unless I forget to mention it, thank you dear."

"You're welcome." She kissed him on the cheek as she left for the sphere. *One of us has to remain on track. From the beginning you believed that it was only you who was holding this whole thing together. Just where do you think you get your strength from anyway? Men!*

CHAPTER SIXTY-SIX

Ellen and Jonathan joined the team for nachos. After they finished and relaxed, Jonathan stood and announced, "We all need to talk."

Having their attention, he continued, "There's a new turn of events altering our plans. Treanna has approached Ellen about re-animating her body. She's already conducted enough diagnostics to know that her body is capable of re-animation and surviving once the process is completed. She wants Ellen to start the process now. I want you all to know that we don't have much time left here. It's very close to moving day.

"We need to decide right now what we're going to do. There will be neither abstentions nor arguing. Each of us will have a turn at presenting the case for yes or no. I don't care if the rest of us declare it pure lunacy; the case will stand or fall on its own merits. There will be no infighting. Anyone who breaks that rule will be removed from the project. That also includes Ellen and myself. There will be no exceptions. Is this understood by all?"

Heads turned as they each took stock of each other. Jonathan watched as the impact of the proposition sunk in. "I can consider your response, or rather the lack of it, as a resounding *yes we understand.* We've already discussed some of the moral and ethical problems we'll be facing. There will be a lot of additional territory to cover today.

"My first thought is involving business, or the government, or both. We can always. . ."

A chorus of "no" and "are you crazy" cut him off in mid thought? The room erupted into an all-out attack on him. Pleased with the response, he raised his arms, quieting the group. "I'm glad to see that you all feel that way. Ellen and I have already discounted that idea as too risky. I did say, however, that we would present all ideas. That one in particular won't require any further discussion. You all agree on that point. J.J., you will keep track of all the ideas and the general arguments, both pro and con?

"We'll need detailed notes, but don't get too wordy. A quick synopsis anyone should understand when reading will suffice. Does anyone disagree with that description of the notes required? Also, after you've completed each synopsis, I want you to read it back to make sure it correctly states the intentions of the idea."

There were as many nods and smiles as there had been previous angry shouts. "All right, let's get this thing done. We need to move fast, yet professionally. Who wants to go first? David?"

"You all know my position. I can't see any moral or ethical problem with any of this. If the main concern is human safety, set up a security area around Treanna. She wants to see her home again, let her. Just do it from behind bars."

"Hold on Dave," Dick interrupted. "We don't have the facilities to erect a security pen around this building, not one that will contain a raptor. We have no idea of they're capabilities. The idea is fine; there's no time to implement it. Oh yeah, one more question. Who's got the money to build the cage and buy the secrecy?"

"I'm glad you asked," continued David. "Jonathan's initial suggestion has merit. We don't necessarily need major corporations for funding. There are enough businesses out there who have the capital that we need. They'd be willing to help for a lot smaller piece of the pie than we would part with otherwise. We can keep it professional and force the investors to accept a smaller percentage. We can set up a genetics research company and get funding that way. There is enough equipment here that has to be developed that we can start the company to do just that; develop the equipment. The percentage lost won't make that much difference when we're ultimately talking eight or nine hundred billion dollars overall."

"Hold on just a minute," interrupted Jonathan. "You can't start throwing figures like that around. It's not fair to anyone here."

David raised a hand to quiet an eruption of questions. "Let me explain myself. I've been doing some research on costing. With conservative figures, which I have back in my room, we could spread the sales out over all the areas we've discussed and sell that much in three to four years. We're not even talking monies from medical research and developments, or applications along those lines. There's a fortune to be made in licensing alone." He paused to watch as the information was absorbed by the group. "We could all be the richest people in the country in the next five years; maybe in the world."

Gerard pondered the statement momentarily before he began. In his typical fashion, he responded directly to the initial answer, without concerning himself about the possibilities of fortunes yet unmade. "That's interesting. I hadn't considered small investors. With enough small businesses involved, we would avoid some of the major governmental entanglements. I like the concept up to that point. I'm still not sure that I want to see a raptor re-animated and living among us."

"We're getting off track here; money and potential incomes are a different discussion. There's one thing in our favor," Ellen said, rising to her feet. "Treanna has no reason to destroy us. She would isolate herself from Argon and all of humanity as well. She needs us to finish the process that would clone Argon." Ellen searched everyone's eyes. In a softer tone, still pressing forward she said, "She wouldn't be able to survive without human intervention. If she were to destroy us, the only intervention she would get would be at the barrel of a gun."

"That's also a good point," added Jonathan. "Without us to build the equipment and finish the job, she would lose her life after all this time. There would be no need for cages in the beginning. Besides, Treanna could prove to be a great investment incentive. When prospective investors saw her, money would come pouring in."

"We could select a handful of wealthy business men, bring them to our facility – where ever it's located – swear them to secrecy, but pre-qualify their investment," interjected J.J.

"I liked the idea of getting investors under the guise of manufacturing genetic research equipment. We could actually have a viable business doing just that, using the profits to fund our research and development with reference to Treanna and Agron," stated David.

"I want to be in charge of all security," said Jim flatly, interrupting both David and J.J.'s thoughts. "It's the only way that I'll feel comfortable about any of this. I really don't care whether you re-animate or disintegrate. I have no moral or ethical issue concerning any of this. My life, and those of my family and friends, are of paramount importance to me. If I can handle all of the security, I can be satisfied with any decision we make." *If this baby flies I'll have unlimited, unchecked access to every detail of this project. There's no telling what I might get away with. I'll have enough money, that if I can't disappear, I can make sure that they do.*

"May I continue now?" asked J.J. "We can select these people and get them to commit a certain amount of funding. We can allow them to see the project only if they contractually agree to fund it once they've seen it. There will be no backing out once they've seen it."

"You can't do that," said Dick. "People won't invest sight unseen, and they'll want to have an out if they don't like what they see."

"That's where you're wrong," Jonathan countered. "There's enough information out there about anybody to pre-qualify them before we approach them. We can weed out any one who would have a dissenting view. We only ask those that would be predisposed to go along with the project. It'll take a lot of work, but we could get our money."

"J.J., are you getting all this down? You've all made some fine points that could use further discussion."

"No problem, dad. If you can give me some time, I'll be done with this latest discussion in about five minutes."

There was some shuffling of feet and chairs. A couple of them rose to stretch their legs and others whispered together. Jonathan and Ellen sat next to each other observing the various reactions. The meeting was going very well thus far. Jonathan felt he had successfully maintained control without dictating the outcome. Ellen had captured the moment with her brief statement. There was more interaction going on than he'd asked for, but since they were keeping it civil, he let it continue unchecked. It could still go either way, depending on ideas not yet presented.

Walking back to the table, J.J. resumed the discussion. "I'll summarize what I believe we've concluded thus far. Please correct me if I have misinterpreted or misstated anything. We have all thought long and hard about this question since the issue first surfaced. The ethics are fairly cut and dry. There is no standard from which we might draw previous information or a decision that has set a precedent. We are the pioneers on this. The moral question is more ambiguous. We have one of God's creatures ready to be reborn, and we can aid in that process.

"At the same time, we are bringing a savage creature into this world. Our world cannot effectively protect itself from that very same creature. Do we incarcerate an animal of such magnificent beauty and intelligence just because it can kill us? When and where do we draw the line on whom or what we lock up? Society has provided proper punishment for those who break the law. By re-animating her, we can benefit all of mankind and change humanity forever, or create total, unbridled chaos.

"Also, the question of funding has brought up several good points and has yet to be resolved. The group, as a whole, has rejected bringing the government in voluntarily. Large corporations are a viable option, but the group leans towards smaller investors who are predisposed to our needs, and can understand the potential profits without having to see the sphere or the raptors. Do I have everything?"

"That's a fine J.J.," replied Dick. "I remember what your dad said about the snake. In the end, a snake is still a snake. Treanna, herself, has said their culture was developed around continually trying to improve their skills at killing. There are stories like the snake throughout history and all cultures. A leopard does not change its spots."

"I agree one hundred percent," added J.J. "All that liberal psychobabble was meant to inspire discussion. The point Ellen made a moment ago is that Treanna needs us. Let's use that to our advantage for now. We can obtain our goals by exploiting Treanna's weakness. It serves her to be exploited and serves us to do the exploiting. It's mutually beneficial and both parties agree to the exploitation willingly. We can establish a contingency plan well before we've begun the re-animation process. If we suspect that there's something wrong, we implement the plan. Cut and dry."

"There's always going to be something wrong, J.J. Life is like that. It's chaos. It's the challenge that helps us grow. I'm not being pessimistic, but I am being pragmatic. The reality is that we can never anticipate all the possibilities," Steve commented.

"This is an entirely new challenge. There are unknown factors that we can't possibly anticipate. We'll do our best and may even succeed. All I want to point out is there is high percentage of failure stacked against us. Edison said something about having over nine thousand ways not to make a light bulb. Failure was the keystone to his success and it's true for our success as well.

"Even the knowledge of our inevitable failure will not deter me from completing this project. This is like a child's first experience of riding a bicycle. We have to get on and make that first wobbly attempt to learn and perfect our balance. Let's just do it and do it quickly." Steve finished.

"Thank you, Steve. I know you must leave, but your input is important to all of us." Jonathan put an arm over Steve's shoulder and smiled at him. "You've come a long way since you first walked into my classroom. I'm proud of how you turned out. You've got a good head on your shoulders. You'll go far in this life.

"We'll keep you posted somehow." Leaning in closely, Jonathan whispered, "Do not call us; your phones are probably already tapped. I have a few contacts that may be able to help. You're still a member of this team and will always be. See me before you leave. I have a list of phone numbers to give you. I don't want you to use them, but you'll know when and if you have to."

"Thanks. It means a lot to me. I hate to leave when we're so close to another new development. This has been one heck of a roller coaster ride, hasn't it?" *You miss even one phone call and your world is over. Don't think this is over between us. I want my share. I'm not greedy; I only want my just due.*

"It sure has. We know that you leave early tomorrow, do you want to stay for the entire meeting or do you need to start packing? I want you to have as much current information as possible before you leave."

"I've been packed for a day now. I would like to stay and participate right up to the moment that I leave." *Well, well. Perhaps I was a bit hasty in my conclusions. I will definitely wait before I give them up. And then again, maybe I won't have to give them up at all.*

The meeting began to lag and the team was becoming restless. It was at that point where Ellen set everybody back on their heels. "I'm as apprehensive as any of you about re-animating Treanna. She has taken a liking to me. We have a certain female rapport. In light of Steve's input, we must also consider that she could be using me. This could be an attempt to procreate and repopulate the earth with a new and superior species. She and Agron have the brains and the ability to dominate. Remember, they tried it once before. That's how we happen to have them in our care.

"We must be aware that we may be unwittingly bringing about the end of mankind if we proceed with the re-animation. Evolution has taught us what happens when a new, dominant species moves into a landscape. And in spite of our technology; the scales could tip either way."

Everyone froze in position. All heads turned to face Ellen. Mouths hung open and eyes were wide and unblinking. Chaos had reared its ugly head and they hadn't even agreed to start the process yet.

"You heard me correctly. Even in the face of the worst possibility imaginable, I vote to continue. The good that we can offer our fellow man is worth the risk to me."

Ellen uttered a small prayer to herself. *God forgive me my hubris. I only wish for the enlightenment of our world and its entire people.* Only Jonathan heard her words and gently squeezed her hand under the table.

Jonathan asked J.J. to re-read all the comments, and each idea was voted on – up or down – then there was a general vote on the proposition to re-animate Treanna. A secret ballet was cast so anyone with a dissenting vote would not be intimidated.

Finding a small box, he had everybody fold their ballots and place it in the box as he walked around the table. He sat down and tentatively reached in to get the first ballot. He repeated the process until all the ballots were counted.

"The votes have been counted. It's unanimous. We will re-animate Treanna when the time is right. I don't disagree with this vote. I voted in favor like the rest of you, but I feel that I must add this one last comment. We are about to open Pandora's Box. I hope we have arrived at a sound and logical decision. Once we have started this, there will never be the chance to reverse what was done here today."

CHAPTER SIXTY-SEVEN

FRANKS DROVE BY THE MEXICAN restaurant twice before stopping. He went in several directions to make sure that there were no other locations similar to this one. He was as thorough as possible. A field agent was to meet him here in three hours. Driving back to the motel, he wondered if he finally had a solid lead. Only time would tell.

Back in his room he sorted through his papers as the hours dragged on interminably. Retrieving a set of photographs from his briefcase, he shuffled a few more files around, arranged the files and photos in the optimum sequence to bring the field contact up to speed without unnecessary delay. Still the clock seemed to never move towards the three hour window.

Franks decided to get an early start. Waiting patiently was not his strong suit. His contact had a history of being early. Remembering an old inspirational high school training film, he chuckled. The guy must operate on 'Lombardi Time.'

The drive wasn't difficult. Pre-locating the restaurant and checking alternate routes had paid an unforeseen benefit. He laughed to himself again. When you operate on 'Lombardi Time' if you were exactly on time you were already fifteen minutes late. His arrival would be perfect 'Lombardy Time.' The contact should be impressed. Punctuality was a trademark for Franks. . . early was a rare occasion.

There was a vacancy opening up at the front door just as he swung into the drive. The restaurant was huge as far as Mexican places went. He liked the architecture. Several fiberglass cacti in the lobby were a nice touch of the southwest, and accented nicely with the earth tones throughout the building. Recalling his conversation with the two idiot truck drivers, he chuckled at their flawless assessment of the facilities.

A quick glance around the dining room revealed his contact. Experience taught him the kind of person to look for. He approached and asked if he could be seated. The man said that he was waiting for someone.

"I'm Sergeant Franks. I believe that you're waiting for me."

"Yes sir, I am, name's Halsted." Without rising he extended his hand to Franks. "It's a pleasure meeting you. What have you got for me?"

"Captain Harrington asked that we proceed with the utmost haste. We've traced the truck to this restaurant. We need to find whether or not it stopped here in Detroit, or moved on to somewhere else. The main intersection south into Ohio just up the road. The truck may have turned south. We need to co-ordinate with the Ohio State Police and check the weigh stations for the truck in question."

"Have you got anything for me?"

"I've got the files current to date and photos of the people that we're positive are involved." Reaching into the briefcase, he extracted the photos first. Spreading them on the table facing Halsted, he began explaining who they were.

"Sorry for the interruption gentlemen. May I take your order or would you prefer a little more time?" The waiter was polite and unobtrusive. He noticed the photos on the table as he approached, and stood well away, so as not to interfere.

"Come back in five minutes son. We'll be ready by then," said Franks. "We only need a moment longer. Thank you."

"As you wish sir. . . could I get you a beverage or perhaps something from the bar?"

"Two beers please, Corona's. Oh yeah, don't forget the limes."

"Yes sir. I'll be right back with your Corona's. Will that be all for now?"

"For now," he answered. "We'll let you know if we need anything else. What's your name?"

"Paul, sir. Just ask for me and I won't let you down."

"Well Paul, I've got a proposition for you. Here's five bucks. You bring the beers and then leave us alone for at least ten more minutes. We'll order then and then you don't need to come back for the rest of the meal. If you can keep the others away from the table, there will be another five in it for you."

"Thanks, mister. I can help you if you want privacy. We're going to be opening a meeting room in the back. We've got a couple of tables set up in there right now. I can let you use those if you would like."

"Lead on Paul. Here's another five for your ingenuity."

Paul smiled from ear to ear. He was going to like these guys. They had money and were not afraid to tip. A friendship was definitely on the horizon.

Franks and Halsted spread the photos out on the new, larger table as Paul left to get the two beers. They were deep in conversation when he returned and didn't notice him approach. "Excuse me gentlemen. Where would you like me to set the beer?"

Startled momentarily, Franks said, "Oh, sorry Paul. Here let me clear a space for you." Franks started to gather the photos together so there would be room for both items on the table. He ended up knocking one photo on the floor.

"Let me get that for you. I want you to get your money's worth," said Paul as he bent to retrieve the photograph. Looking at the photo, his eyes opened wide as he announced, "Hey, I know this guy. Who are you guys. . . cops? What did he do? Did he kill somebody?"

Unruffled by the revelation, Franks began to tell an elaborate story. "That's a pretty active imagination you've got. I'm afraid that it's not so melodramatic, Paul. This young man is an actor. We're talent scouts and he's performing in a play locally. We would like to cast him in a movie." Franks was being very convincing.

Halsted, following Franks lead, continued his comments along that same line. "You said you know him. What role did you see him perform? We would appreciate the critique of a viewer. He's done a couple of commercials. Is that where you've seen him?" *I always heard that Franks was good, but this talent scout story is fabulous. I know that I couldn't come up with something this plausible while never stopping my conversation. I really admire this guy's talent.*

"No, not like that at all. He was in here buying food. Man, I could have gotten his autograph if I'd known. He bought enough to feed an army right after we opened the doors. I waited on him."

"Did he have the rest of the cast with him?" asked Halsted.

"No. He was alone each time."

"Each time," Halstead pressed. "How often does he come in here? Maybe we could hook up with him right here?" Turning to Franks, he asked, "What do you think? It could save us a couple of days. We need to get back to the coast anyway?"

"Sure, why not?" responded Franks, acting distracted. "Hey, Paul, do you think you could put us in touch with him?"

"To answer your first question, he's only been in two times that I know of. I waited on him each time. Man, I bet I could have gotten some free tickets. Chicks love plays and junk like that. I could have scored big. Where were you guys when I needed you? That sucks. Oh, sorry. Excuse my language. I don't know when he comes in. It's been two different times. . . once was lunch and the other was supper."

Laughing a little, Franks replied, "Maybe next time you can ask for his autograph, Paul. We need to head downtown to the theater. Which way did he go when he left, we thought that he was playing in town? Maybe we got our facts wrong and he's playing a local theater."

"No you're information is right. He came and went from the direction of town. This is a real drag. I was that close to a big score."

"You'll get over it, Paul. You're sure that you've never seen him on television or in a play? We could really use your help on this."

"I'm sure. The only time that I ever saw him was in here. Hey, what movie are you filming?"

"That would be telling. Secrets are hard enough to keep in Hollywood without us out here blabbing all over the place. I can tell you this, Paul," Franks continued. "It an action film and it will be out in about sixteen to eighteen months. That's the best I can offer. You know that there's always plenty of action in a film like that. I'll tell you what. Let me have the phone number here. Maybe I can get you in to a special screening. You've been a big help. It's the least that I can do for you."

"Oh wow. That's so cool. Do you really mean it? I have to keep this a secret don't I?"

"Yes, you have to keep it secret. We'll know immediately if you tell someone. There are enough people who will call to verify a rumor like that once it's started," Halsted said flatly. "This is a gift for your co-operation. This is for an individual only, no other person than you. Not even your girlfriend can come along. We can get some pictures of you and the lead actor together if you like. He's a pretty cool guy about that stuff."

"If I would like," Paul beamed. "That would be the ultimate. The kids in school would have to pay tribute. That's too cool. Here's my work number." He scribbled the number on his order pad and handed it to Franks. "I'll be back in ten minutes to take your order. Here's a list of the specials. See you shortly."

Grabbing Paul's arm before he could leave, Sergeant Franks warned him, "Remember, Paul, if we get one phone call about this film, you get nothing. This is a life lesson about trust and the rewards for doing a good job. If you lose this opportunity, it's because you couldn't keep your word. How cool will you be if people can't trust you? Is that something you want following you around the rest of your life?" *That and the tips should keep his mouth shut. When nothing comes of this, he'll think he blew it and maybe he'll grow up to be a better person for it. Either way, our tracks are covered and we have a good lead.*

CHAPTER SIXTY-EIGHT

"THAT WAS A LUCKY BREAK. I can't imagine a kid from nowhere having a piece of information we need." Halsted was pleased about this development.

"Not so fast Halsted. We have a kid who saw one of the suspects. He said that he came and went from the direction of town. Where's the break there? Do you have any idea how big Detroit is?" Franks was delighted to know that the suspects and the box were in the area, yet the task was daunting. "We need to bring in more specialists. This won't be easy. We still need to depend on their panic. I'm convinced that the old man contacted them and they'll be running by tomorrow. Did you catch the part about ordering enough food to feed an army? We have no idea how many are involved. Until Paul's information, we had assumed only three. We figured it to be a terrorist cell."

"You've got that situation under control, I presume. What can I do to help? If they run to ground before we're in place, we'll lose them for sure."

"Of course it's under control. Everything's been handled. My people have been dispatched and will be in place by 0400 hours tomorrow morning. Pigeons don't fly at night. We'll be fine."

"From the sounds of things," continued Halsted, "you'll be intercepting the truck, but what about the people? They won't be driving a rig themselves. They'll use any driver that gets the job. Their records don't indicate that any of them know how to drive a rig."

"They had the stuff shipped the first time. They'll do it again. I never said that we'd intercept the rig. We're going to locate and follow. That way, we'll have the prize and the people all tied up in a neat little bow."

"Well that settles it then. We need to sit back and enjoy an authentic Mexican meal. I like spicy food myself. Mexican cuisine isn't as spicy as some of the oriental stuff, but the flavors are phenomenal. Hand me that menu. We need more beer. Have you ever tried jalapenos with your beer? The beer really fires 'em up. You're gonna love this," he said as he flagged Paul down.

"Yes sir. What would you like?"

"We need more beer and bring some jalapenos with them."

"That's no problem, sir. Are you ready to order now?"

"Not right now, Paul. We'll let you know. Hurry back with the beer and jalapenos."

Jonathan stood to conclude the impromptu meeting. "You've all made some excellent points and we're fully aware of the dangers. *We* still need to settle on how to proceed with acquiring funding, but that's a smaller issue right now. I think that the general consensus and the vote is that we proceed with the re-animation of Treanna, but only when the time is appropriate. Correct me if I'm wrong J.J. You have all the notes."

"No dad, that's it," J.J. answered.

"We need to turn the sphere back on and get this ball rolling. Thank you all for your input. Ellen, Steve, and I could never have gotten this far without your considerable contributions. When we turn the sphere back on, we embark on a new era for mankind. I only wish that the world could view this momentous occasion."

"They can Jonathon," said Jim. "We've got the video equipment right here. We can burn as many DVD's as we want. Let me get it set up and someone," he paused to look around, "perhaps J.J., can go get enough DVD's so we'll each get a copy. Are there any dissenting votes?"

"I'll get the car started. You can't start without me," exclaimed J.J. "There's a video store just up the street. I won't be fifteen minutes."

He threw on a jacket as he practically ran from the warehouse. "Remember to wait for me," he hollered over his shoulder as he cleared the doorway.

"Ellen, since you discovered the box, I believe that the honor of narrator falls to you. Make it brief yet brilliant." Jonathan then put an arm around her shoulder and gave her a reassuring squeeze.

"I don't think I'm up to it," she said franticly. "This is for eternity. What I say will go down in the history books. I can't do this."

"Yes you can," came a resounding chorus of approving voices.

"We're behind you Ellen. What if we all help you organize the speech while we wait for J.J. to return? Would you feel more comfortable?" Steve asked.

She grabbed his hand in both of hers and said. "That's a good idea. I'll be able to handle that. Let's get started before I change my mind."

J.J. found a parking spot not twenty feet from the doors. It wouldn't take him all that long to find the DVD's and get back. Once in the store, however, he discovered there were at least ten customers already in line. Disregarding that obstacle, he looked around until he saw the blank DVD's and grabbed a box and got in line.

In no time, J.J. found himself at the head of the line. "Your card or phone number please," the clerk said. "Oh, I'm sorry. I see it's a purchase. Would you like that on your account sir?"

"I don't have an account here. May I still make a purchase?"

"Oh, yes sir. You may purchase anything you wish. Have you tried our previously viewed movie section? There's a fine selection in all subjects. Do you prefer action, drama, comedy or romance?"

"Nothing at this time, thank you. Just these DVD's for now Miss. Thank you for the suggestions though; I'll keep that in mind." He pulled out his wallet and discovered that he no money. "Oh, I don't have any cash on me. Do you take credit cards?"

"Yes sir. We accept all major cards." Looking at the one he pulled from his wallet, she said, "That one will be fine. One moment please, while I process this for you."

With the charge slip and DVD's in hand; J.J. left and raced back to the warehouse. His excitement had been building since Jim made the suggestion of recording the main event. Someday, when this was common knowledge, he'd have something to show the grandkids. They would all laugh at the antiquated recording techniques of the olden days. And he would be one of the people responsible for upgrading everything electronic in the world.

"I'm back," he shouted, bursting through the door. "I told you I wouldn't be long. You waited for me didn't you?"

Jim framed the shot while the others worked with Ellen on her narration. Everything was coming together nicely. This was almost the moment they had been waiting for. It would have to be satisfaction enough for now. Once the DVD could be publicly released, they would have their day in the sun.

"I think we need to start with a long shot of the box closed and then open it up while we're recording," suggested J.J.

"That would be perfect. We could have Ellen in the initial frame and then do a voice over as we pan the box and zoom in to capture some of the more intricate details."

"I think she'd be more relaxed if she was off camera as much as possible," added J.J. "She's a good speaker, but shuns the limelight. We'll end up with a better video if we take that approach."

Jim asked, "Do you think we should shut the camera off and then start it back up once we're in the box, or should we just record everything?"

"I think we should walk into the box while it's running. I know it's not good cinematography, but this is supposed to capture the whole thing, documentary style. We'd risk being accused of faking the insides if we stopped taping to establish a second shot. What do you think?"

"That's a good point," Ellen managed. "If the viewer never loses contact with the box, the reality of what they are seeing will be undeniable.”

“So, we’re going to close the box and then open it with my mother narrating and in scene. Then as we enter the box, she’ll continue to narrate off camera. Finally, as she starts the program, she’ll come back in scene and continue her narration until we’re finished taping. Does that pretty much cover everything?”

“I believe so. We only need to make sure that the narration follows our shooting schedule. Once that’s done, we’re ready,” said Jim. “Are you ready to start the show Ellen? Once we co-ordinate the narration with our recording schedule and we can begin.”

“Can we run through a couple of times before the actual recording? It would make me a little more relaxed.” The pleading look on Ellen’s face was enough for Jim to say yes.

Rehearsal began.

CHAPTER SIXTY-NINE

Franks woke up to the phone beeping. His watch indicated three in the morning. Fumbling for the receiver, he answered. It was only his wake-up call. The brief sleep he'd gotten would have to suffice. Getting by with less had been an old norm. Now it was an irritation.

Temporarily blinded by the bathroom light, Franks went to the television to see if he could catch something on Fox News. Acclimating to the light took longer and longer the older he got. He'd learned as trick from a friend several years ago about acclimating to the dark, but nothing helped with light.

The bathroom beckoned him. Sliding from the edge of the bed, he shuffled to the bathroom. Still half asleep, years of ritual took over. Washing his face and hair first, then he shaved and brushed his teeth. Once he'd been awake for a while, life returned to normal.

The morning air was crisp with the autumn chill. The overnight temperature had dropped fifteen degrees below normal. Winter would soon arrive in this part of the country. Starting the car took a moment. Reluctantly it turned over and rumbled to life. Franks sat silently behind the wheel, letting the engine warm, listening to its grumbles about having to work at this hour of the morning. He laughed, "I hear you. I'm grumbling too."

He found himself in front of the local State Police barracks at 3:58 AM. "Punctual as ever," he said aloud. Stepping out of the car, the breeze nipped at his ears. He wished he'd brought a hat on this trip. With his coat's collar turned up, he braced himself against the breeze and headed for the door.

"Good morning Captain," he said in a courteous, amiable tone. "Are we ready to go?"

Rubbing the bruises on his throat, Captain Simmons responded, "Yes, I'm ready. Your men have been dispatched to all of the weigh stations around the area. They're being trained as we speak. I will personally escort you to where you'll be situated." Brushing past Franks, he headed for his car, mumbling something under his breath.

Franks didn't hear what was said, but he knew its intent. He smiled to himself as he watched the captain disappear through the door. Shaking his head and chuckling, he followed him into the parking lot.

Leaning against the roof of the Captain's car, Franks said, "I'll make it easy on both of us Captain. I'll take my car so that you don't have to make friendly conversation. Is that agreeable enough for you?" *You can sit alone in your car and brood. Maybe you can come up with some sort of scheme to hurt or hinder me. No matter what you concoct, it won't work... so dream on.*

"Suits me just fine government boy. Remember that you're on my streets and highways now. I'd hate to see you make the slightest mistake. Our police are very intolerant of people who don't obey the traffic law. . . to the letter. Let's get going, if you're up to it."

The ground rules had been set and the game had begun. Why were all of these low-level peons so full of themselves? They had their petty little differences and squabbled amongst themselves and they never approved of a new person in the equation. These low-level guys always yapped like little mutts; all noise and no teeth. Seldom did he enter into a situation, when dealing with a flunky like the Captain, that there wasn't some kind of trouble. *I know I'm not the easiest person to deal with, but there's no time to establish a relationship with these idiots. Just do what's needed and we'll get along just fine.*

Pulling off of I-94, the two cars went to the lot behind the weigh station. There were two squad cars already there. Franks could see his men receiving instructions from the troopers. At least this phase was proceeding without difficulty. . . and on schedule.

Without waiting for the Captain to exit his vehicle, Franks headed for the rear door. Waving his men to silence, once they noticed his approach, he motioned to them to return to their instructions. They complied and resumed strict attention to the troopers. After Franks' unspoken order, they no longer even considered him in the building.

Looking over his shoulder to the rear door, Franks watched the Captain enter the room. He moved along the back wall and observed the training. Franks could see him making mental notes as he listened to his trooper's instructions. He wished that he could play poker with this guy. Every thought, every nuance was clearly written across his face.

"Well Captain how much longer before they're through? I've been watching you make assessments." *With your obvious limitations, I guess I could trust your judgment about this.*

"Very observant," Simmons replied. "It shouldn't take much longer. They'll need to operate the scales and be checked out. The system if fairly automated enough that your people shouldn't have any trouble. We've kept the training pretty simple considering you're military and all. We wouldn't want your people to have to learn how to think at the same time that they learn the equipment. I knew that you'd understand, so I approved the schedule without consulting you. I hope that I haven't bruised your ego." *I'm going to make your brief stay as miserable as I possibly can. . . you government shit.*

Franks did not rise to the bait. Catching the truck and the Crenshaw's was his goal. "Speaking of bruises, how's your neck? Your face seems okay, or are you using a cover-up foundation." *Fuck you too, asshole.*

Ignoring the Captain's reaction, Franks went over to speak with his men. "We're going in for the kill during these next few days. I want that truck found and I want to know where it's going. We won't tip our hand here. We need to tail the truck to its final destination and then close in for the kill. Three days leave to the team who catches them. Be alert men. Listen to every conversation, no matter how trivial. There are clues hidden everywhere and your job is to ferret them out. Good luck men. I want three teams of three each. We'll cover this and all weigh stations until we catch these creeps. Corporal, you make the assignments. Just get the job done."

His men saluted as he walked away.

This phase was complete and now he needed to co-ordinate the more subtle aspects of the operation. There was a lot of surveillance to orchestrate. "Good day, Captain," he said as he pushed past him on his way to the door. The statement was cold and flat, with less than zero emotional content.

Captain Simmons was about to respond, but the door was already closing. He flipped a single finger at Sergeant Franks back. It didn't matter whether he saw it or not, Simmons felt better for the effort. "Get back to work," he snapped at his men. "I want these people out of here as soon as possible. The only way to do that is to educate them and assist them when required. This is their show; you are not to render assistance unless it's vitally important. Do I make myself clear?"

CHAPTER SEVENTY

"You're early," Jonathan said to the driver. "I wasn't expecting you until noon."

"I would have been sooner, but the new girl at the desk wasn't sure where you were located."

"What do you mean? We've been here for a while."

"She had to look up your records. She said that she was a temp. Not being familiar with the complex, she had to find you on the map. I checked it out and came straight here. It was no big deal. Didn't my dispatcher call you?"

"He might have. I've been out a lot this morning. I haven't checked my messages yet. No harm, no foul. Let's get this door open so you can get loaded up."

Backing the truck into the bay, the driver stopped short of the crate. "Is this good enough?" he asked, leaning out of the cab.

"Perfect. My guys will get the crate hoisted on to your trailer."

"What's the weight?"

"It was 15,000 pounds when we had it delivered. We repacked it ourselves. I guess that we couldn't have changed the weight that much. Does it matter?"

"Not really. I'll head back to the depot and have it weighed there." He opened the door and sat sideways on the edge of the seat. Looking around, he noticed that the building was empty. "What happened here? You guys moving your business?"

"Something like that. We got a great lease rate and tax breaks out west. This location was great and all, but money is money. I'll miss this town, but not the violence."

"I hear that. Good luck on your move."

"Thanks, we'll need it. I have to leave the old lady behind to sell the house. She's pretty pissed. What the hell," he said philosophically, "she'll get over it."

"Yeah, they always do," the driver answered knowingly, "if they don't shoot you first." Pulling himself back into the cab, he laughed at his own joke.

"You know, sometimes I think she only married me for my money. But what the hell, she's got big hair and big… well anyway, I'm one happy son-of-a-bitch. We'll only be a few more minutes. Hang in there."

"No problem, buddy. I'm not on a clock. Take whatever time you need. I'll need to strap it down myself anyway. I never depend on anyone else when it comes to my personal safety."

"A good philosophy to live by. You'll live a lot of years that way. I'll let you know when we're finished." Jonathan slapped the door panel a couple of times as he walked away.

Leaning out of the open door, the driver said, "That's all right pal. I need to get out now anyway. I have to check the position of the load. It's as important as proper restraints. You never know when a load is going to shift. Why invite trouble, you know what I mean?"

Inwardly laughing at how easy it was to assume this new persona, Jonathan answered, "Yeah, I sure do. Is there anything that I need to sign? My guys will do the final lock up. I don't want to be here to see this place totally empty. Even though we're setting up out west, it's like losing a kid. So many years in one location, it's hard to take."

"I understand. I'll leave your bill of lading with one of your guys."

"Have a safe drive. See you later." Jonathan shook his hand and started towards the door.

"Thanks. See you later," said the driver. "You have a safe trip too. Your old lady will be cool don't worry. Good luck on the startup."

Jonathan waved a hand over his shoulder, but never turned around. When the driver went to the back of the truck, Jonathan left the warehouse completely. He got into his car and left through the same gate that the driver had entered. If the driver was watching at all, Jonathan didn't want him to see the car going to the other side of the complex.

After driving around for a half an hour, Jonathan returned through the other gate. The truck would have been gone by now, so there was no need to worry. However, just to be safe, he pulled the car into the spot concealed by the other vehicles. He was comfortable with the way things had gone. There would be a little more difficulty added to the trail. Their pursuers would need to be extra vigilant to catch them. His friend had already advised him that they would be.

"Everything went fine," he said to Ellen. "The crate is headed for the depot. It will be on the road today or tomorrow. Our tracks have been covered to the best of our ability. Let's get back to work for now. I don't want to think about this stuff anymore. I want to study the program."

Ellen snuggled up to Jonathan and whispered, "Good job dear. I feel better now. We've got so much to do. Do you think that Treanna will understand what we're going to do?"

"If I were Treanna, I'd expect it. No, on second thought, I'd demand it. She's in this for herself, and whatever it takes to accomplish her goal will be fine in the short run."

"Let's get over to the sphere and let her know what we're going to do. Agron will be able to guide us through the process until we have it down cold. Then we can move directly to a center where we can perform the process first hand."

Together they entered the empty sphere. Ellen called for Treanna. She appeared from the nothingness, silhouetted beautifully by the darkness of the empty sphere. There were no programs running and suddenly there she was. Neither of them ever acclimated to that. Treanna was kind enough to alter her program to only appear in front of them and never behind them, yet they flinched each time she did.

"Hello, Treanna. Are you well today? We'll need to speak with Agron as well. Call his avatar up for us. We're going to start working on your re-animation program. We need him to help us practice with the equipment until we can get it correct on every attempt. Your tissue appears to be in such a delicate state that we may have to extract DNA and clone you. We're not sure what will happen. We do know that we don't want to risk losing you. With Agron's expert assistance, we'll move closer to total success."

"You seem to have considered several options and worked through potential problems. I appreciate your consideration for my current body. Cloning is always a viable solution. The best scenario would be to have me re-animate without any side effects. I'll get Agron now; he'll be able to guide you through the different processes to determine what state my tissue is in. That will direct the course of action."

Treanna had barely finished the words when Agron was standing before them. Ellen and Jonathan found him to be a magnificent specimen. They never tired of looking at him. Everything that Treanna had ever said about him was true. His physical structure was flawless. He was a textbook example of perfection, both mental and physical. You only needed to see him at work to understand why he was the envy of his peers.

When he turned or moved in any way, the muscles rippled beneath his skin. He always looked as if he'd just come out of the water. There was a radiant shimmer to his skin. Ellen loved to touch it. All of her years in the field, the countless fossils of skin that they'd found had created an image in her mind.

The texture of his skin was smooth to the eye, yet almost sandy to the touch. The contradiction to her preconceived image didn't prevent her from enjoying the sensation of touching him. The disparity between the expectation and the reality fascinated her endlessly.

Aside from being a hologram, this was the real Agron. Agron never objected, because he saw it as one more admirer paying homage to him.

When they had finished the preliminaries, they were ready to begin the lab set up. "We need to have the layout at the optimum for the equipment," said Jonathan. "We don't have your background in this area. We want to rehearse the process as many times as it takes to lessen the risk to Treanna. We're concerned about tissue degradation when we open the cryo chamber."

"Why would tissue degradation be of concern? The chamber was designed to handle this type of storage for long periods of time."

"That's not the issue here. Even you could not have foreseen sixty-five million years as the time reference. After preliminary studies of your schematics, we don't contend the elegance of your design. The biological problems over that time span can't be predicted. Do you agree?"

"I do agree that the time has been far greater than even I could have imagined, or prepared for. You, however, must agree that my equipment handled the time as it was designed to do. I initially foresaw a millennium or slightly less. The fact that it survived and performed flawlessly for sixty-five million years is a testament to my design. The chamber is intact. Treanna's body is still suspended and genetically intact. Your concerns are groundless."

"We understand your pride in your abilities. We are honored to study with you. It's merely precautionary to take these measures. Why risk Treanna after all of this time? This is as much for you as it is for her. We need her DNA to be able to reproduce you. We would lose you both if we lost her. This project is not meant to question the integrity of your design. It's a safety measure only. We hope that you will work with us in the spirit of our research. We apologize in advance for anything that you might misunderstand."

"There is no misunderstanding. I am aware of the fragile nature of the biological Treanna. I am also aware of the design and function of my equipment. You don't have the intelligence yet to fully comprehend what it is that you've discovered. I will work with you to raise you up from your ignorance. You will then join me on a higher plain of knowledge. I am not insulted. It is my honor to help an inferior species advance sociologically and scientifically."

Jonathan could not believe what he was hearing. This beast was at the pinnacle of hubris. Was there no end to the delusional picture he held of himself? He kept his thoughts to himself and continued the conversation. "Thank you, Agron. With the rehearsals, we will gain the knowledge and the ability we need to better serve your needs when the re-animation, or cloning begins. I'm glad, we are all glad, that you will teach us. We are humbled by your generosity. Thank you again.

"We will need to have you design a lab around our physical characteristics. It must include all of the equipment that we would need to re-animate as well as save Treanna's body on the remote chance that there is a biological problem. How long will that take you to do?"

"It should take approximately one hour of your time. I will provide a working model so you can test the ergonomics. Will you stay here while I run the permutations?"

"No Agron. We need to prepare for the rehearsals. It will take us time as well. Once we're sure that our efforts are synchronized, we'll return. We'll be back in one and a half-hours. You should be totally prepared by then. We can start immediately upon our return. Please remember that we are living and require time to eat and care for our other functions. Plan your presentation around those physical requirements. There should be a short break about every forty-five minutes. This should compensate for any individual requirements." Glancing at his watch, Jonathan said, "We'll be seeing you around two thirty this afternoon. You may terminate your functions until we're ready for your instructions. Is there anything that you wish us to bring when we return?"

"There is nothing that comes to mind right now. My program will be able to provide you with any and all tools you'll require. Perhaps you can bring your video equipment. You will probably wish to record all of the new schematics and the training sessions. It will help you practice when you are away from the sphere. A species such as yours will require additional training time, based on what I've seen to this point."

Seeing the expression on Jonathan's face, Agron quickly amended his statement, *"There was no insult intended Jonathan. I only meant that you are venturing into an area where there is no expertise at this level.*

Your species will need the time to practice and absorb the information. In less than a generation, this will seem mundane. Now it's new and bold. It's a new frontier for you."

The sphere shut down after he had spoken his last words. Jonathan and Ellen left to prepare and joined the others for a strategy session on how to deal with Agron. The animal was clearly delusional and suffered from a God complex. Fortunately, the rehearsals had appeased him for now. There was no telling how long he would tolerate these delays.

"We can't re-animate Treanna without his help. . . and he's in dire need of psychological help. He'll be the fly in the ointment. Mark my words," Jonathan said. "I don't expect that any of us will be able to devise a satisfactory plan on the run, so we must continue to have these meetings and work through the problems as they arise.

"Agron has been informed to prepare for continual delays concerning our biological requirements. It causes him no end of consternation; you could see the dissatisfaction in his body language. Yet he must capitulate to our needs or his plans will remain agonizingly just out his reach. With a bit of careful planning we can establish a pattern where we all go to the bathroom at the same time.

"Of course, it will be set up that way so there will be minimal time away from the rehearsal. If we have an open discussion in front of him, he should modify his programming to accept our behavior. Remember, he already considers us an inferior species." Jonathan paused and looked at the others for suggestions.

"Why don't I go first?" said Jim. "I need to have all of the schematics and operational instructions in order to proceed with the construction of the equipment. It will keep Agron occupied and it will satisfy him to see we're struggling to meet his demands." *And I get more stuff to steal. I can start up a medical program with money from the solar collectors and double my fortune in no time. God I'm good.*

"That's a good idea. We can start trying to locate a facility large enough and well equipped enough to handle this undertaking. What do you figure, an hour or so with Agron?"

"Yeah Jonathan, that should be enough. I can get the parts that I'll need after I'm finished with Agron and then start building the units right away. You know, now that I think about it; maybe Agron can hook up a computer interface to download his operating systems, which would speed up the process immeasurably, don't you think so? I'll ask him. See you shortly."

Jim entered the sphere and started Agron's program. He was explaining what needed to be done while the others dispersed to complete their new assignments. The morning would pass swiftly while they each concentrated on the rehearsal. There was little time left before they would have to move the sphere to a new facility.

CHAPTER SEVENTY-ONE

Jonathan whispered to Ellen to join him in their room, and then went upstairs. Ellen followed a few moments later.

"What's up dear?" she asked.

"I don't like Jim trying to establish a direct computer interface. He's head of security and has some true friends among us. I'm not sure though. I don't trust anyone who wants that much information, and we don't have access to it."

"I think you're being too cautious. Let's keep a close eye on his activity anyway. You're right about things like this more often than not. Don't fret about it until there's something more concrete."

"I hope I don't end up regretting this."

"Let's get back to business. We've got a lot to do by the time Jim finishes."

Joining the others, Ellen remained calm, secure, and undisturbed by the work pace. Jonathan, however, was more somber and introspective. He seemed distant and unapproachable. The others noticed, but considering the day's events, they ignored the changes.

Dick and David were working the phone vigorously. Between them, they called in every marker they ever had. Research facilities that were specialized enough and willing enough were going to be difficult to find. The secret would surely leak out if they used the wrong approach.

"This is going to work, Ellen. I can feel it. What do you think?" Jonathan seemed to be searching for some reassurance.

Ellen wasn't prepared to offer any. "I think that we're not

professionals. Furthermore, I think that we've already made too many mistakes. Also, I think. . ."

"All right already. Enough," Jonathan snapped, cutting her off in mid-sentence. "You've made your point. Where did all of the angst come from?"

"If you don't know then I'm obviously not going to tell you." *All you see is the goal. How can you miss the death trap right in the middle of the path?*

"I'll be over there. You can see me, but I'll be just out of range from any thrown objects, unless you're packing the big guns. Then there won't be any sanctuary."

"You are such a pain in the. . ."

"I get the picture dear. Trust me on this. I really do get good vibes concerning the efforts we've made for secrecy. We will be fine. Mark my words. My only concern is the nagging suspicion that Jim is no longer a team player. It won't matter how well we've done our homework if someone sells us out." *Besides, I never told you about the other two decoy trucks leaving the city at the same time, each in a different direction, and painted like the original truck. Let them chase ghosts while we get away undetected.*

"I hope you're right," she replied. "There's so much to lose. I wish we could be sure about Jim. I don't get that sense of him; we'll wait and see. Besides, I don't care about me anymore. The rest of the world needs to have this information."

Jonathan took her hand and they walked toward the sphere with a little gentle prodding. "I know what you mean dear," he said softly. "I know exactly what you mean. There are things, details that you don't know. And there isn't time to explain right now. Remind me when we go to bed. I'll fill you in on what I've been doing behind the scenes."

"Aren't you Mr. Cloak-and-Dagger? Why have you been keeping secrets from me?" Her voice was edged with anger and anxiety.

"I assure you; it was unintentional. The way the events have played out today hasn't afforded me the opportunity to bring you up to speed. Let's go."

Reluctantly, Ellen followed him into the sphere. She wasn't sure what had broken down in their communications today, but she was sure that it wasn't going to happen again.

"What about the truck? Where was it going?" demanded Franks. His men were not sure and were afraid to offer the incorrect response.

"We weren't trained to read the manifest sir. Perhaps the state police considered it a joke. After all, they knew how much this meant to you, sir."

Franks was about to lash out verbally and physically when he took a second to consider the soldier's words. It would have been like the Captain to do something like this. He'd been highly incensed at their first meeting, but then of course, the purple necklace that he'd be wearing for a week was incentive enough to omit critical training.

Calmly he addressed his troops. "You've done a fine job. I hadn't realized how devious Captain Simmons had been. You did send out a chase car didn't you?" he questioned further.

"Yes sir. The car followed the truck out as soon as the truck left the exit ramp. We didn't want to appear too obvious. We're in radio contact now sir, if you would like to speak with them."

"Yes, I would. Where's the radio son?" he asked as his eyes scanned the room.

"We have it in the other pursuit vehicle sir. We were waiting for you to get here before we left. It's out back."

Franks allowed himself a self-satisfied smile. The rope was around the neck of his prey and he was drawing the noose ever tighter. The soldier contacted the chase car and handed the radio to Sergeant Franks. "That will be all. Gather everyone together and we'll get under way as soon as I'm finished here."

Focusing on the radio, Franks asked, "What's that soldier? Say again."

"We're on 94 West and moving about seventy-two miles per hour. This

guy is really haulin' ass. We've managed to keep pace with him. There's no indication that he'll stop any time soon. When will we be replaced sir? We've got three quarters of a tank and can go hours, but we'll have to stop sooner or later."

"You're doing fine soldier. Don't lose him; we're on our way. I've already got cars at several of the stops along the way. Now that we have a route, they can join you. Stick with him and we'll contact you when your replacement can assume your position. You should be coming up on a rest stop in an hour or so. Contact me when you see the signs. I'll notify the next chase car to move out as you are pulling off."

Finishing his conversation; Franks issued orders to the remaining troops. There were to be six vehicles in all, counting those already positioned along the road. They were to trade off the lead position frequently so as not to draw suspicion. Three were to pass the truck and then stop several miles beyond and each wait at a different rest stop – or some other convenient location – until the truck caught up to them. They could fall in behind, at that point, without being detected.

"I want you to engage the driver in conversation should the opportunity present itself. We need his final destination. Buy him a burger if you have to. Make it a reward for helping you out with some travel problem or whatever. Improvise the best you can and get that information. No one is to detain the driver without my express orders. Good luck. Move out."

The truck had a thirty-minute head start on Franks, and at its current speed it would be difficult, but not impossible, to make up that much ground. Traffic was light and they had an incentive to make up the lost time. There was a week's leave to the team who brought him the information about the final destination.

Franks slipped easily behind wheel. His foot stroked the gas petal lightly as the engine purred to life. His next destination was a rendezvous with the trucker. He contacted the team at the northernmost weigh station before he began his pursuit.

"What do you mean, you sent a car in pursuit of the truck?"

"We're following a truck heading west as we speak. It passed through our weigh station half an hour ago."

"Explain yourself soldier."

"Well sir, the truck matching your description went through here about half an hour ago heading north. We tried to contact you on the radio, but we were informed that you were in route to our location. We were afraid to lose the truck so I sent out a pursuit car. It has orders to maintain a discrete distance until we rendezvous with you. I sent a second and third car at five minutes intervals, as you ordered."

"You don't understand soldier. We're already tracking the vehicle in question. There can't be. . ." *That clever bastard, two trucks in different directions. I like this guy. I'll exact a heavy penalty for this deception, but I still like him.*

There was a tap on his window. "Sir, it's a call for you," interrupted one of the soldiers.

"At ease soldier, thank you." Walking back to the station and took the receiver, "Franks here."

"Sir, we just put a tag on the truck. It's headed south towards Toledo."

"What?" he shouted.

"Is there something wrong, sir?"

"No soldier, nothing at all. This is getting out of hand. It's not your concern. Follow the truck. One or two vehicles pass the truck and wait to regain contact at a rest stop or something. Engage the driver if possible. I'll let you know from there. If he makes a delivery, I want the location. I'll keep in touch." *Three trucks. This is one slippery son-of-a-bitch. He's watched entirely too many spy movies to suit me.*

The troops could see Sergeant Franks agitation. They'd all seen him in this state before, and none of them had fond memories. There was a collective sigh of relief when his wrath didn't fall on any of them. Privately, they didn't envy the person who created this situation. Each understood the price that would be exacted from whom ever it was that caused this level of rage.

CHAPTER SEVENTY-TWO

"How soon can you stop the truck?" asked Franks anxiously. "We need to see what he's transporting."

The radio crackled slightly, but the voice was clear. *"We're going to follow him to the final destination. Now that he's driving around town, we assume he'll be stopping soon. Our plan is to surround and detain him until you arrive. We're armed and ready. We'll try to avoid the use of force; however, we understand your orders. Is there anything else sir?"*

"No soldier, that will be all. I'm just exiting from the main highway. Estimated ETA is fifteen to twenty minutes. Does that co-ordinate with your intel?"

"Yes, sir. Destination is seventeen minutes. Rendezvous point is at the warehouse district. He's just turned down the main access road to that area sir."

"Understood. Keep this as low profile as possible. Over and out." Franks switched the radio off and accelerated up to seventy. He wanted to be there as it happened. There was no traffic on the access road; he figured he could make time where he was able. This was the culmination of his efforts and he desired to savor the moment as it unfolded.

The tractor-trailer pulled into the warehouse section indicated on his manifest. There was to be a long section of buildings and then he was to make left turn at the end of the main drive. His instructions were to pull in behind the last building and park the truck. After disconnecting the trailer, he was to leave.

There was plenty of room to pull the rig around and drop the trailer. The driver was grateful that this place was prepared to accept this kind of traffic. He'd been at a few places that were nearly impossible to negotiate. Smiling at the good time he'd made; he backed the truck to the designated spot and set the brakes.

Without any warning six vehicles descended on the rig. Armed soldiers yanked him from the cab and unceremoniously pushed him to the ground. A heavy boot pressed tightly against his neck as he struggled to rise to his feet. "I will kick your fucking ass if you don't let me up. Who the fuck do you think you are, asshole?"

"Shut up!" barked the unseen soldier. The boot pressed his face harder into the asphalt.

"You're fucking dead, mother fucker. I'm gonna personally kick the shit out of you." With all of his effort the driver spun the soldier from his neck and yanked him to the ground. Before any of the others could react, he began pummeling the soldier in the face and chest. Blood gushed from the soldier's broken nose as the driver beat at his face mercilessly.

The butt end of an assault rifle ended the drivers' tirade. He lay unconscious on the tarmac with a visible lump swelling on the back of his head. "Cuff that bastard," ordered Franks as he sprang from his car. "If he so much as sighs too loud, kill him."

Franks tore through the cab looking for the paperwork he needed. He found the manifest and all the other papers that the driver had in his possession. Walking over to the prone body, he took the drivers' wallet and pulled his license and a couple of family photos.

"Wake him up," he ordered. He'd pointed to one of the soldiers on his right without actually looking at her. "Now, soldier!" he snapped when she hadn't moved fast enough to please him.

She ran to his prone body and emptied a canteen onto his face. The driver, sputtering water, coughed and choked his way back to consciousness.

Lifting his eyes from the license and photos, Franks knelt down by the restrained driver. "Good morning, let me see here, ah yes, good morning Mac. Nice manly name for a truck driver don't you think?" A couple of the soldiers snickered.

Mac struggled against the handcuffs. Venom filled his eyes. "Who the fuck are you people?" he snarled at Franks. "You better kill me now before I get loose and rip your fucking head off."

"Mac, please, no melodramatics," Franks placated, patting Mac's cheek.

Mac persisted in his verbal assault. "Did you ever notice that the guy with the smallest dick is always bragging about having the biggest balls?"

With rattlesnake reactions, Franks released his coiled rage and a devastating backhand crashed into Mac's face. Like a string of red pearls; blood and saliva stung out, stretching longer with their momentum. Mac's lip was split and his broken nose ran bloody again. He wavered at the edge of consciousness from the force of the blow, and the renewed pain of his broken nose.

Before he could pass out, Franks reached down and gripped Mac's throat by the windpipe and started to choke him. "I'd hate to see you have an unfortunate accident," he rasped. Partially lifting him, by the grip on his throat, into a sitting posture, he continued, "After all, you have such a lovely family." Tossing the photos onto Mac's chest, he rose to stand ominously over Mac's form, and then walked away without uttering another word. The obvious threat hung heavily on Mac's face as he struggled to make sense of the situation. He still struggled against the threat of unconsciousness.

Silently he stared at Franks' back as he walked away. Without looking down, he fumbled to reclaim his family photos. They were his only lifelines out of this nightmare.

Franks went to the nearest soldier and whispered something into his ear. The soldier chambered a shell and placed the barrel of his assault rifle against Mac's forehead. Mac screamed, "What the fuck is going on here? What do you want? I'm an honest man. I'll tell you anything that you want to know, but I don't think that I know anything. Don't shoot me." He pleaded to the point of tears. That was when Franks crouched next to Mac's trembling bulk.

Putting his lips close to Mac's ear, Franks began to speak. His tone was malevolent and too calm. "Now that we understand each other," he hissed, "we can have a very pleasant conversation. I do hope that you have the answers I'm looking for. My friend here hasn't killed anyone for two days and is anxious to find any excuse to pull the trigger. Have I made myself perfectly clear?"

"Yes, sir." Mac responded submissively. He realized that struggling was useless. Maybe he wouldn't be killed if he co-operated. "What do you want to know?"

Patting Mac's cheek with a gloved hand, Franks said. "That's better. Now tell me where this load originated."

"Detroit. Some warehouse outside of town. That's all I know."

"I think you know more and just aren't saying. Where was the warehouse?"

"I'm not sure. It was the first time I was ever in that part of Detroit. There's a map on how to get there with the rest of my papers."

"Liar!" screamed Franks into his face as his squeezed Mac's windpipe again. "I've got all of the papers from your cab. It's not there."

"It's there," he croaked back. "I know," he said with panic. "I used it to write some messages on the back. It's in the box next to the seat. I keep personal shit in there."

Franks never lost eye contact with Mac. A simple wave of his arm signaled for a soldier to check the box. Applying more pressure to Mac's windpipe, he whispered, "With a little more squeezing you'll be dead. This better be the truth," he sneered. "I don't want to deny my people their fun by killing you myself."

Mac's eyes were frantic. His breath was ragged and he couldn't inhale properly. As his eyes began to roll back in his head, he fought his fear to desperately remember where the map was. He was convinced that it was in the box. It had to be in the box.

A soldier returned with a piece of paper. On one side were

several scribbled notes in an almost legible script. *Typical low life scrawls,* thought Franks as he examined the paper. *How do they ever communicate with one another?* The other side held a neatly typed set of directions to the warehouse on the far side of Detroit. Franks stood as a broad smile spread across his face. The directions were clenched tightly in his hand.

"Call in the team," he barked. He ordered another soldier to come over to where he had Mac in a heap on the ground. "Get this man to his feet and clean him up a bit, he's a mess. You can remove his cuffs and move his hands to the front if he behaves himself. Shoot him if he moves anywhere other than where he's ordered."

"Do we have a working relationship Mac?" Franks asked.

"I won't be any trouble," he said while rubbing his neck. "I won't be any trouble at all. What's going on here anyway?"

"You may ask all you want. I'm under no obligation to answer." Turning to another soldier he continued. "I don't like his attitude. If he asks one more question, kill him before can even finish."

Cowed, and in pain, Mac followed his escort to an area to be cleaned up. He remained perfectly still as the soldiers moved busily around him. He moved his eyes only, to observe the soldier's activity and did not utter a single sound. Franks was standing just out of hearing range using a cell phone.

"It's me. We have the truck. I've contacted the team. The warehouse at the delivery point is empty. We're going to open the crate here. I'll report back tomorrow when we have more."

"Good work Sergeant. I'll await your call. Make sure your team has the search warrant. We don't need any legal complications." The phone abruptly went dead.

Rejoining his troops, he said, "The team is on their way. Get this rig into the warehouse and get squared away. We're going to be here for a while. The team will arrive at first light. I will return at 0600 hours. Be up and be prepared to move out if necessary."

Franks left for his motel room. He didn't their job. At best they would sleep in the cars. He was in good condition, but he didn't want to spend a single night sleeping in a car.

The motel sign was coming up on his left and he prepared to turn into the drive. He was savoring the victory. The tension of the chase was draining away and relaxation was consuming his muscles. He suddenly felt very tired and satisfied, as if he'd just finished a large holiday meal.

This was one of those discount chains. He would have preferred a better establishment, but with no notice, this was the best he could do. As motel lobbies went, this was average and clean. He began his check in routine as a broad smile spread across his face.

With the sun barely up, Franks was already on his phone. "How are the second and third trucks coming? Have any of you had a chance to engage the driver?

"No, sir. The truck we're following went on through Toledo and is leaving Ohio as we speak. We'll stay with him as long as it takes to ascertain his destination. Is there any other orders, sir?"

"A second team will meet with you to fill out the convoy. I want six cars rotating all of the time. Call me on my cell as soon as you have anything."

"Yes, sir. I'll call you personally, sir."

"I'll wait for the call."

Damn this is getting complicated. This bastard will regret making me work so hard to find him. This has gotten really personal. I like a sly prey as much as anyone, but I hate someone who tries to be too clever. His thoughts raced as he tried to focus.

Grabbing his cell, he called the next team. "Where's the third truck now?"

"It went north and then circled south. It worked its way back to 94 and headed west. We're in Chicago now, near the quarry, it will be coming up very soon. The second team picked us up about fifteen minutes ago. We fell back about half a mile. Hold on sir, there's a radio message coming in."

After an impatient moment, Franks spoke, "Well soldier, what did they have to say?"

"He's stopping some place to eat. I'll let the second team engage, sir. We've been dogging him all day. I don't want to risk him recognizing one of us."

"Why don't you guys stop off at Houston's since your right there at the quarry? Great chicken and fast service, just what you're looking for. You've earned it."

"We'll do that. I'll call you with any news or possible destination. That's up to the second team."

"That's all I can ask soldier. Stay alert. This guy has proven to be tricky, and we know nothing about the driver."

Franks hung up and reclined in the semi-comfortable bed. He reached for the room phone and dialed an outside line. The kids had been in school for two days now, and he was anxious to hear how they were faring.

Twenty minutes had passed since his last contact with his troops. The phone rang and vibrated on the nightstand and Franks snatched it up. *"Sir,"* crackled the voice on the other end of the phone, *"we've contacted the driver on the third truck. He's long haul and has only passed through the Detroit area with no stops. He's running a light load. This is the right description, but the wrong truck sir."*

"Discontinue the pursuit. We have the other two trucks. Return here and we'll re-deploy you as necessary."

"It's been two days since that decoy trailer left for the empty warehouse. When do you expect the troops or whomever to arrive?" J.J. asked.

Without looking up from his work Jonathan replied. "I'm not sure. I would guess today, maybe tomorrow or the day after. It'll be soon though; you can have faith in that. We're not even sure that the decoy was spotted. My best guess is that it was picked up the same day. Don't worry; I've been getting some expert advice."

"I know dad. I just wish that I could be as calm about this as you and mom are."

"You don't have the slightest idea how upset we are. We put on a good front for the rest of you, but believe me, we're pretty damn upset and scared. Now get back to work before Agron calls a progress meeting."

"Yes, master."

Laughing, Jonathan said, "Shut up and get back to work you idiot."

"I love you too dad."

CHAPTER SEVENTY-THREE

"*J*ONATHAN HAS KEPT ME APPRISED *of your governments suspected activity,*" Agron began. "*It is my wish that we move to better facilities. You have all done a remarkable job and the progress has been very rapid. I know that I've been overbearing and egotistical at times. Please forgive me. Treanna and I have begun to experience an increase in our emotional responses. It has made it difficult to maintain the controls built into our programming. We are aware that some of the things that have been said are unforgivable, yet I am asking for your forgiveness.*"

"I don't wish to insult you or Treanna in any way, but I felt that your actions demonstrated your true personality. I have grave reservations about continuing with this project." David felt better for airing this concern directly with Agron.

"*I'm aware that you are one of our detractors. As much as I regret this, I also understand it. I can only ask that you observe me as closely as possible and note the changes that we, I, have been making. It is our desire to win you over. You may never come to accept us and that is your right. I do not hold your beliefs against you. I have earned your admonitions through my reprehensible behavior.*"

Jonathan interrupted the dialogue to change the topic and to get to the purpose of the meeting. "Why do you want this meeting?"

"*From personal experience with my government, it is important to re-emphasize the need to always be alert. You have stated your concern about being discovered. If you have a genuine concern, then it is incumbent upon me to suggest that you move these facilities now.*"

"We don't have arrangements for a facility with a medical

laboratory yet. We don't want to move the box until we can be operational at the final destination."

"Don't you think that keeping us in storage is safer than risking discovery and the ultimate confiscation of 'us'?"

"You make a good point Agron. We had not considered that approach. We need to have a discussion about this. We'll be a short while. You may terminate your function at this time."

"I'll stay active and review my schematics against what Jim has provided. I need to know that everything has been adapted properly between technologies."

"Do as you wish Agron. We appreciate your vigilance and the effort that you put into perfecting the transition between technologies. That in it self will help expand the known use of our technology. Thank you."

"I do not wish to offend, but if it is at all possible, could you keep the meeting short, so we might continue."

The group left the sphere and paired up for the debate.

"Well gentlemen, I know you all heard Agron's take on the situation. What do you think?" Jonathan asked.

"I think he's right. I don't want to risk all that we've done for someone to swoop in here and spirit our work away," stated Gerard.

"Jonathan, you're the only one who doesn't seem ruffled by the near miss we've had with this discovery, what gives?" asked Jim.

"I can't tell you. It will provide you with plausible deniability?"

"Plausible what? What you're really saying is that you don't trust us," said David.

"No, what I'm saying is that I've got a contact that used to be on the inside. Using his experience and personal contacts, he keeps me apprised of the situation. I follow the suggestions I'm given and we've done all right up to this point. There are some things that I need to keep secret to protect all of you. If you can't trust me on this then you can bail out now. I won't betray a lifelong trust to give you information that you don't need." Jonathan was beginning to get angry at the tone of the conversation. *I've broken my back to protect these people and they repay those efforts with accusations.*

Conversation was animated and many valid points arose. The overall consensus was to pack up and slip away into the night. No one wanted to face discovery and loss of the work they had come to love. In the end, they decided to move the project into storage while continuing the effort to secure the type of facility they required.

Smiling and participating in the conversation, Jim began making plans to slip away and betray the trust the others had in him. Venal would be an apt description of his mind set. Gradually he withdrew from the conversation.

Jim had visions of a major startup company that would sweep the world with its electronics advances. He wanted no part of sending the box away. There was enough material in the photos and schematics to take him well into the next decade or two. There was a point where he was able to slip away unnoticed. He went to his room to pack.

"What the hell…?" Franks croaked. It was then that he realized it was the telephone beeping his wake-up call. He lifted the receiver and set it back down. It seemed that 0400 hours came earlier with each passing day.

Finishing his morning ritual, Franks locked his room and headed for the lobby. A quick breakfast would sustain him through the morning. He inquired at the desk for the nearest place to get coffee and doughnuts.

The electronic message banner behind the desk clerk indicated the time and some local events. He had forty-five minutes to get to the warehouse. There was more than ample time to accomplish everything. He scribbled the directions from the clerk, and then asked her to repeat a couple of the simple instructions. He'd committed them to memory the moment she told him; it was his way of making her feel important,

Once again, a self-satisfied smile spread across his face. It was beginning to be a habit. A small chuckle escaped his lips as he pulled up to the bakery. Ten minutes later he was back on the road with two-dozen assorted pastries. This was a small, yet tasty, team reward for a job well done.

Franks arrived at the warehouse with time to spare. The team pulled in about five minutes after him. His troops were busy with the preparations as they munched their breakfast of pastries.

The crate was backed into the warehouse and the large overhead doors were pulled down. There was only lighting for the leasing people to show the place to potential tenants. The available lights were all they required.

"Where's the driver?" asked Franks.

"Out in the van, sir." A soldier pointed to a location just around the corner of the building.

"Any problems?"

"No sir. He understood his situation and has remained silent the entire night. Well almost."

"Almost soldier?" Franks cast a wary glare upon him.

"He snores like a son-of-a-bitch sir. I had to switch guard duty half way through the night. I wasn't able to hear anything through that racket."

"I understand… well-done soldier. Were you able to get any sleep?"

"My relief came at 0200 sir and I slept in one of the cars. I wanted to be as far from the van as possible. I swore that I could still hear him though."

Franks laughed at the observation. He recalled a soldier in his barracks that snored like that. There were many sleepless nights spent listening to that ungodly symphony. Snoring is just one of those noises you never accept.

Unpacking some very strange looking equipment, the special unit moved over to the crate. The leader signaled for Franks to join him.

"What can you tell me about what's in here. We were briefed that you would advise us as soon as we arrived."

"Can't help you there, soldier. I've been chasing this down for almost three weeks. The only intel I've got is a spiked power surge of unknown origin. The location was pinpointed by satellite and we began our hunt. Whatever made the power surge is in this crate. The power signature was unusual. That's why the satellite picked it up, that and the fact that it was in the middle of nowhere. It started in a place referred to as the Hell Creek Formation in Northwest South Dakota. There's nothing in the target area but a small town. And lots of rocks."

"Do you suspect that it's terrestrial in origin?"

"That's a question that never entered my mind. I figured some splinter group of intellectuals helping develop something very bad for some very bad people."

"If that's it, we can begin. We'll need some of your team to help us get the lid off of this thing. I'll let you know from there."

Pointing at three of his troops, Franks gave orders to assist the team at removing the top. He left the building to get the driver. He wanted the driver to see the contraband that he'd been transporting.

Both men entered the warehouse as the team was lifting the top off of the crate. Franks pushed the driver roughly. Mac glared at him menacingly, but held his tongue. There would be time enough for revenge when this was through.

"Sergeant you need to see this right away." There was an odd tone to the soldiers' voice.

"Coming," he responded while roughly shoving Mac out of the way.

Climbing to the trailer bed and then to the top of the crate, Franks peered in the open lid. "Damn it!" he shouted. "Who's fucking idea of a bad joke is this?"

His team came running. One of them had unceremoniously dragged Mac along.

Upon seeing the driver, Franks jumped down from the trailer to a point immediately in front of Mac. Snatching his shirt with both hands he lifted the man from the floor. The room fell silent. Franks age and stature belied his strength and mental toughness.

Mac had a strange look across his face as he hovered several inches from the ground.

Franks threw him roughly against the trailer and slammed his fist into Mac's gut. Mac doubled over and vomited the meager contents of his stomach. He found his head being dragged viciously up by his thinning hair and he began to choke on the bile still exploding from his bowels.

Totally out of control, Franks began his interrogation. "Don't you die on me," he slurred; his voice barely intelligible. "Not before I have a chance to kill you properly, you fat fuck. I want answers and I want them now. Do you hear me dick wad?" Franks was screaming in Mac's face as spittle trailed from the corners of his mouth, creating a mad dog image to any that watched.

A puddle of urine was expanding on the floor as it ran from Mac's pant leg. He had understood every word Franks had spoken. Dropping to the floor in a pool of vomit and urine, Mac choked himself back to semi-consciousness, falling to one side and curling up tightly for security and protection. He glared savagely from his fetal position but made no move on his attacker.

At Franks' signal, someone handed Mac some water to rinse the vile taste from his mouth. He'd been denied food and drink since the previous evening and he was at a point where he'd say anything just to get away from this nightmare.

Kicking Mac lightly in the ribs, more for effect than pain, Franks continued the interrogation. "Stand up and face me like a man you piece of shit. You pissed yourself like a little boy. I'll bet you think you're a real man in bed, don't you little boy? Well little boy, playtime is over. Now I get serious, now I want total co-operation. I want to know where the cargo is. What did you do with the contents of this box?"

"What in the hell are you talking about? I pick shit up and I drive shit to its destination. I ain't no crook… you prick. I'm gonna make you eat those words you cock sucker." It was then that he charged Franks.

Anticipating the attack, he'd been goading Mac into, Franks sidestepped him and slammed a fist into Mac's kidney as he passed by. The blow sent him hurling to the floor. Franks snapped out a few orders and Mac was dragged before him.

The fierceness of Franks' retribution left Mac unconscious for a few moments.

Grabbing Mac's face and pinching it between his strong fingers Franks leaned in close and snarled, "You know fat boy. I believe you. That's the only reason you're still alive. I've decided to allow you to tell me everything that you know without beating it out of you. That is of course, if I like what I hear. Do we have an understanding?"

Spitting blood and rubbing his jaw and face in general, Mac muttered, "Yeah. What the fuck are you after?"

"There was a government shipment on this truck, an extremely sensitive piece of equipment. It was disguised as ordinary equipment so it would not be easily detected. Now 'mister I don't know nothin,' it's missing. You were the last person to handle the crate. I want answers."

The sudden calmness of his behavior terrified Mac. He was sure that Franks was about to kill him. His mind raced for answers he didn't have. There weren't even any good lies because he was clueless about everything. Resignation of his fate registered through the numbness that clouded his mind. He visibly slumped and stared blankly ahead.

"Look," he started in a soft, monotone. "The regular driver couldn't make it. They called me because I just got back from a short haul. The boss likes to toss me an easy one every now and again. He knows I could use the spare change." He searched Franks' eyes for the slightest indication of compassion. All he found was a cold, steel hard resolve from his captor.

"Anyway," he continued, even more hopelessly than before. "I pick this trailer up at the depot, not at its point of origin, and I've been on the road ever since. I made a couple of stops but nowhere where the box or the trailer could be hijacked."

"Soldier, get over here," Franks said pointing to the trooper who originally spotted the trailer. "Is this man telling the truth?" he asked as he drew his service revolver and placed it at Mac's temple.

"Holy fucking shit. Don't kill me. I didn't do nothin'. I didn't steal nothin'. I swear, damn it." Terror filled his voice as he sobbed and urinated again. "Please mister, I swear that's all I know. I've got a fa-a-mily for Gods sa-a-ake." Mac sobbed uncontrollably, his body shuddering with the effort of his crying.

"Shut the fuck up," Franks raged as he chambered a round.

The metallic click rang like a death knell in Mac's ears. It was the only sound his brain could focus on. He froze, sitting up rigidly. There were no more tears, no more pleading. He was going to die like a man regardless of Franks' opinion of him.

The transformation didn't go unnoticed. Franks admired Mac for the courage and resolve he was showing. It was a warrior's code to die bravely. Mac had reached deep to an inner core and pulled forth the strength he needed to be human again. He now waited silently for the end, strong and calm, a true warrior.

"Sir, we followed him for the entire trip. He was never out of our sight. We posted a watch on him and the trailer for the entire time. He's telling the truth. If the contents have been compromised, he didn't do it, sir."

Releasing the trigger slowly and removing the gun from Mac's temple, Franks said, "Thank you soldier."

"Stand up Mac," he said in a casual voice. He even offered his hand. "We're sorry to have treated you like this. There has been a breach in National Security and you were the prime suspect. Your government thanks you for your co-operation in this matter.

"You must be sworn to secrecy or you will be eliminated along with anyone to whom you divulge this incident." Franks had been looking down at his revolver the entire time. Now he looked up and stared Mac squarely in the eyes and said, "That also means your wife and kids." Mac lost all color from his face, but remained strong and didn't waiver. "We will not hesitate to remove any or all of you that we deem necessary. I wish that I didn't have to make these threats, but such is the seriousness of the situation.

"We will get you cleaned and fed in a few minutes. In the meantime, have a doughnut. I need to talk to you privately. Come with me."

Confused, now more than ever, Mac walked mechanically to Franks' car. Franks opened the rear door and invited Mac to rest on the edge of the seat.

At the sight of the car seat Mac's legs gave out. Franks was lightning fast and supported Mac before he'd even slumped a few inches. Gently he guided Mac to the edge of the seat. When he was sure that Mac was safe, he went to the trunk for his briefcase. He walked to the front of the car and placed it on the hood.

Franks opened his briefcase and removed ten thousand dollars. "This is a small token of our appreciation for your continued silence. I remember that you said you could use the spare change. This should help you out a little."

"Why should I help you, you prick? You fucked me up and threatened my family and now you want me to take your money? You're crazier than I thought."

"Mac, listen," he said, calmly placing a hand on Mac's shoulder. Mac flinched at the touch. "We were prepared to defend our government, your government, when we suspected you. We are not heartless Mac. We've made a mistake and this will help rectify the situation. Because you're so deeply involved, we need your silence. We can't tip our hand. It was only through a clever deceit that you were even implicated. You've been set up to be killed Mac. We don't just kill people for the sake of doing it. I think that whoever is behind this was hoping that we would just eliminate you, covering their trail. This whole situation has been jeopardized as it is. Do you understand?"

"I understand," he said angrily as he snatched the wad of money from Franks. He stuffed it into his coveralls and asked, "I want the prick that set me up to get twice what I got and maybe more before you kill him. When do I get cleaned up?"

"Come back to my room at the hotel and I'll have your clothes cleaned and brought back while you shower or whatever. I won't be there. I'll arrange for you to be brought back here to pick up your truck. You understand that we can't let you keep the trailer.

"Just turn the room key in at the front desk when you're through. The bill will already be taken care of. Come on Mac," he said. "Let's get you going and get this behind us. I need to keep chasing this thing down and you need to get home. After all, if I don't do my job properly, you might not have a home to return to." He let that realization sink in before he continued. "I never said I liked my job or enjoyed what I had to do to you. I'm responsible for your freedoms. Men, such as me, work for you every day to eradicate those who would destroy our lives for whatever motivation.

"You were brought into this by the unfortunate chance of being the next driver on the list. We didn't know that until a few moments ago. Do you think these pricks care whether you live or die? We do care. The situation is grave, but not out of control. You'll be able to live a long and happy life. Just go home, keep your mouth shut, and forget this ever happened.

"It would make my job that much easier. I have you, and your family's, best interest at heart. Sure I'm a jerk, and worse, but I keep this country safe for you and yours."

Pausing again for the dramatic effect, he continued, "What do you say Mac?"

"All right, but promise me that you won't be in my face for the rest of my life."

"That's fair enough. We're so subtle that you wouldn't know us if we were standing next to you. I only have one last thing to say. I know we treated you rough and you're really pissed off."

"You can say that again."

"Let me finish." All signs of rancor were gone from his voice. "I want to ask you something. If in fact there was a real terrorist driving this truck, and it meant another 9/11, would you have me do my job any less vigorously?"

Mac rubbed his sore jaw and pondered his response. "I see your point. And the ten grand will do my family a lot of good. I'll keep quiet, like you asked. But I have one last thing to ask, actually two things."

"Go ahead," Franks answered in his most amiable voice and expression.

"Can you make sure that you and I never cross paths again? It would help me remain silent forever, and could you get my nose fixed? You broke it yesterday."

With a broad smile Franks began to belly laugh. He extended a hand to Mac and said, "Well Mac that can definitely be arranged. After I drop you off at the hotel, you'll never see me again, ever. My men will take you to the hospital and pay for everything. By the way, you were injured in a high jacking training accident sponsored by your company. Things got a little too rough during a hand-to-hand demonstration."

"Fair enough."

The two of them shook hands, and headed for the hotel. Mac couldn't resist the chance to squeeze Franks' hand as hard as could. Franks took it all in stride and didn't respond in kind. The two of them stood there for a moment and gauged each other for a final time.

CHAPTER SEVENTY-FOUR

REHEARSALS HAD BEEN GOING WELL. Agron was pleased with the progress these inferior humans were making. His attitude was improving and his insults were diminishing.

"How is the equipment coming?" Agron inquired.

"Let me get Jim for you. He's just outside. I'll be right back." David replied.

"That would be perfect. You may get him now. I will speak with him while you two refresh yourselves and tend to your physical needs. Thank you." Agron's voice was thick with condescension and held a dismissive air.

"Well at least he said *'Thank you'* this time," whispered Dick. "He's a real piece of work. . . for a hologram."

"He doesn't consider himself a hologram. Remember that he's got his entire personality intact," reminded David.

"It's no wonder that they killed the bastard. I already want to do it, and I barely know him. I'm surprised his head fits in the sphere at all." Dick was unusually cruel, but they both laughed heartily.

"I know what you mean. However, he is expanding our technical knowledge decades beyond any of our contemporaries. We will be the foremost genetic engineers on the planet when we're through here.

"Settle down a bit, the Nobel Prize will still be there tomorrow. And go tell Jim that the Lord High Agron desires his presence. . . and he should be quick about it." David began to laugh at his own joke. It helped him to relieve the tension. "I've got some figures to crunch before I get into the meat of this information. See you in a while."

"I'm telling you Ellen, Agron is going to be a monumental problem. I'm going to change my opinion about re-animating Treanna and then cloning Agron. Yes, I believe we'll be able to resurrect him as a clone. With the DNA splicing and grafting techniques he is making available, it's a reality. I just don't want to do it." Dick was beside himself with apprehension and anger.

"Let me call Jonathan. We can discuss this more rationally."

"Don't give me that crap. I'm not being irrational. I don't need Jonathan to persuade me to continue. I'm through with this project."

"Hold on, Dick. You're letting Agron's arrogance attack your ego. A knee jerk reaction won't help you in your research, or anyone else for that matter. We're on the verge of a major breakthrough and your hurt feelings are going to jeopardize it all." Ellen searched his eyes. They were filled with rage and no other message.

"Kiss my ass," he hissed through clenched teeth.

Ellen slapped him in the face. "Don't you ever curse at me again or a slap will be least of your problems."

Dick stormed off to the back of the warehouse. Those in the area who heard the conversation could now hear him slamming tools and equipment around. They all looked at the floor or tables. Anything to keep out of the fray.

Coming up behind Ellen, David said, "I'll go see what's going on." He started towards the workroom in the back of the warehouse.

Ellen put a restraining hand on his elbow. "Let him calm down a bit. He'll listen when he's had a chance to settle down." She added her best smile for emphasis.

David stopped. He looked at Ellen and then the others, who continue their pretense of being busy. There was certain logic to helping his friend immediately. Yet, he also knew that he would be better off not fighting with Dick right now. These kinds of fights sometimes ruined relationships. David wanted this partnership to remain intact.

Lowering his head and shuffling his feet, he surrendered to the reality that he should wait. "Okay," he mumbled. "You win this one." Looking up at everyone, he smiled. "I'll wait until he's back to normal before I broach the subject."

"Good man," said Jonathan as he reached the bottom of the stairs and clapped an arm around David's shoulders. "You've made the right decision."

"Then why don't I feel like I'm doing the right thing?"

"Because he's your best friend and colleague. Hell, I know exactly how you feel. I'm sure that all of us here have been faced with letting a good friend remain uncomforted so we could offer comfort later. If you're the friend you say you are, you'll soon see the wisdom in this. When you're able to have an open conversation with him as an ally, not an adversary, you'll understand completely."

"Thanks, both of you. It's difficult to see him this way. I'll follow your advice. I've got work to do. We'll still need to have a meeting about this later; Dick's not wrong concerning his convictions about Agron. That raptor is a fruitcake. He'd be totally out of control in the flesh." David went back to tinkering with the equipment Jim had been assembling. There were a few settings he needed to adjust on the optics.

Dick worked through his anger and came out of his workshop to join the group after an hour or so. Jim had completed his discussion with Agron. Sitting with David, they were fussing with some adjustments to the new equipment. Dick walked up behind them, but didn't interrupt. He was content to wait until they finished before he apologized.

"I'm glad you're from around here. It makes it easier to get equipment and the parts we need. I'm anxious to start the preliminary testing."

"David, is there anything you want? You seem preoccupied," asked Jim.

"Not really, Jim. This thing with Dick has got me concerned. He's right on the money about Agron. I know he feels pushed into this whole project."

"Hold it right there. I sat at the same table with the rest of us and he was one of the first to express a positive attitude about forging ahead. You have no right to sit there and say that he feels hustled. What's your game?"

"I don't have a game. I didn't mean it the way it sounded."

"You can say that again."

Dick interrupted the conversation, "What he meant to say is that we both have misgivings now that we've had these conversations with Agron. The rest of you are still gung-ho on this deal and we don't know how to tell you that we feel it's a mistake."

"You just did," Jim continued. "Look you two, we all share apprehensions surrounding this project. We're in over our heads and we all know it. We need to keep control of the box and all it offers. We're not in this for fame and glory, well not completely. The information we already have can improve man's knowledge and living conditions for decades to come. We're fighting to share this with everyone so big business won't hoard it, just to distribute it at their own slow pace.

"It's all about maximizing profits for them. I'm not saying it's wrong to maximize profits. I'm a capitalist at heart, but this is too big to let it languish in some corporate file until they're ready to release it. That's the only reason I'm sticking with it."

"I understand all that. Before I continue my present thought, aren't we in this for the profit and the prestige too?" asked David.

"Sure, I won't deny that, or even pretend there are loftier motivations. Profit and prestige are my main motivations. I want the world to have it all at once – just like the rest of us – not over decades. Let everyone know and then develop it at their own pace."

"Now that you've defined the argument, let me finish my thoughts. I'm afraid that we're going to start to believe that we're 'Gods' and bring that maniac back to life just because we can. The ability to do something isn't a license, or an obligation, to do it. Do you understand?"

"Yes, I do. I'll be with you at the meeting. The group needs to know the danger that Agron represents. If you're satisfied, let's get back to work."

"Thanks Jim. I'm satisfied. I just needed to get it off my chest."

"Only sometimes, David. You just caught me on a good day." Jim began to laugh. *If you only knew the depth of that truth, you'd have me drawn and quartered.*

"Well," Dick said, "that's pretty much the way I feel."

Agron paced the clearing with increasing anxiety. The re-animation project was taking entirely too long. These humans evolved from their creation, but they were like his bastard children. This entire group of so-called professionals combined couldn't muster half my brainpower. He pondered the original mutations he had linked with the lab mammal's sixty-five million years prior. *Where could I have gone wrong?*

"Is anyone going to help me here?" he roared. There was a bloodlust in his eyes. Hologram or not, he presented a frightening image.

"We're here Agron. Is there a problem?" Ellen asked.

"Is there a problem?" he bellowed. Racing up to her position, he loomed over her, his fetid breath, hot and rapid in her face, teeth bared with spittle dripping from the corners of his mouth. Satan couldn't have made a more horrific impression.

Ellen blanched as she cowered at his feet. Her life flashed before her. There were many permutations to consider when you pondered your own demise. Being eaten by an extinct raptor was not on anyone's list.

Looking down at her weeping figure, Agron realized that he had lost control. He was repeating the same mistakes he made so long ago. *"I'm sorry Ellen. Here,"* he said, *"let me help you up."* He extended a clawed appendage and assisted her rise to her feet. *"I'm sorry Ellen. I really am. I have been acting foolishly for the last couple of days. I never considered how you would react. My life was violent by your standards. Please correct me when I begin to behave like this. I would be in your debt."*

"Apology accepted," she said as she dried her eyes. "You are very frightening. I don't know if I want to continue this project," she added, deliberately baiting. "You just blew your only chance at life. We're going to close this project down and bury this box for another sixty-five million years."

She fully expected another tirade. What she got was totally unexpected. Agron remained very calm and answered in deliberate soothing tones. *"I will honor your wishes. Treanna and I hope that what little knowledge you've gained will be a help to your society. Thank you for trying."* His image vanished and the sphere went dead.

Ellen stepped from the sphere, joining the others. They had all witnessed her ordeal. There were a lot of soft comforting statements and Jonathan had his arm around her. She was not scared anymore. She was resolved to continue the project.

"This must proceed. I was prepared to close it down and move on, yet I believe that Agron is sincere in his request. We still need to maintain caution when dealing with him. I'm not so beguiled that I'm willing to proceed unchecked. Do you all agree?"

David and Dick remained convinced of Agron's true intentions. They firmly believed, now more than ever, that he and Treanna had ulterior motives. The rest of the group did not admonish them for their beliefs. They asked that the two of them act as security on the project. Agron would need a watchdog. Who better than the two people who didn't believe a single word he said?

Both Dick and David agreed to that arrangement. They wanted to expose Agron for the fraud he was. They felt they were up to the task of ferreting out any and all discrepancies in his stories. Both became reinvigorated about the project.

The brief meeting steeled their wills against the catastrophe that may reveal itself. There was a greater sense of purpose, and a desire to increase security. Agron had placed a wall between them, and it wouldn't easily be breached.

Ellen re-entered the sphere and stared at the emptiness. Only minutes earlier there was a cacophony of life and sound that was unimaginable. She closed her eyes as if to recall the minutest detail in perfect clarity.

The softest whisper broke the silence, *"Ellen, are you all right?"*

Ellen turned to face Treanna, "Yes I'm fine. To what do I owe this pleasure?"

"Agron has informed me of the conversation between you two. And his abhorrent behavior"

"If he calls that a conversation, then he's less intelligent than we give him credit for."

"I'm sorry. I misspoke. I am referring to the conclusion at which point you admonished him and said that the project would be over. I just wanted you to know that I understand. I only request that you don't bury the box again. Maybe you could find secure storage somewhere and put us under lock and key."

"Why are you so concerned?" Sensing there was a hidden agenda, Ellen pressed her case. "I would have thought that you would have been on your best behavior, instead of acting like spoiled children."

"You don't understand the entire story, and Agron's motivations. He's not angry with you; he's impatient."

Interrupting, Ellen said, "Well that I can understand. You've been separated for millions of years."

"That's not it at all. I guess we'll never be seeing you again. Thank you for everything. It was exciting to see my world again. This was worth it, even if I won't be re-animated."

"What did you mean, I missed the point? If you aren't forth coming with me; you leave me with only my speculations, right, wrong or otherwise."

"I suppose it would help you understand us more if you knew the truth of the matter. I know we've touched on parts of his story, but we always go off on one tangent or another when it comes to finer points in your research. I'll start from the beginning, and cover ground we've already traveled. Maybe you'll get something that I've previously omitted. Shall we begin?"

"Of course, Treanna. I'm here to learn and decide."

CHAPTER SEVENTY-FIVE

"*T*HAT'S A FAIR OFFER, ELLEN. *Let me set up a table and chair for you. So, you think any of the others would care to join us?*"

"I'm not sure, but if they wish to join us later, you can always add more chairs. Let's just the two of us talk for now, woman to woman, without all the outside distractions."

"*Thank you for that kindness, Ellen. I appreciate that you consider me a woman.*"

The two women, one a raptor, the other human, had a common bond. Treanna began the story from the beginning.

"*Agron was a student, as you already know. He was the top of his class as well as the best in his field. The government and academicians from everywhere wanted him, or at the very least, access to him. It was both rewarding and terrifying at the same time. He was embarrassed by the notoriety at first. It conflicted with his gentle nature. He was a pure researcher and he drove himself harder than any other beast I had ever known. Agron was a perfectionist in every aspect of his life, both physical and mental.*

"*His father had just discovered a new species of mammal. It was just beginning to show signs of being bi-pedal. The individuals were highly prized and large amounts of influence were traded to have one or more as pets.*

"*I, myself, had the opportunity to see one and hold it. They were very docile and for a mammal, they were somewhat cute. I enjoyed the experience immensely.*

"*I have often been curious as to their flavor. I have also wondered if they would fight at the last moment before being devoured. You wouldn't understand, but freshly killed animals always taste better if they were struggling and frightened at the moment they died. Our taste is so sensitive that the subtle chemical difference can easily be detected by the youngest among us. It's one of the reasons we continued 'The Hunt' long after there was no need."*

Treanna's holographic image began to salivate.

Ellen became ill. "So, tell me Treanna, what has this to do with anything?"

"That's coming. I told you that I'd recover things that we'd discussed previously. I don't want to omit any detail. Anyway, back to the mammal discovery. These creatures offered a significant deviation in their molecular genetic structure. They were a new species, almost bi-pedal, and with enough genetic variation to develop into almost anything. They showed great promise for diversifying over the millennia. As such, they became a national security risk.

"All animals that had been distributed were recalled. There was a public outcry. That's when the machinery of government went into full operation. By the time they were finished, bands of raptors scavenged the woods, searching out these evil, vile newcomers. They were seen as a direct threat to the welfare of every carnosaur alive. Either scarcity or good fortune kept them from being eradicated.

"This is where Agron, and his remarkable talents, come into the story. He was assigned to investigate and analyze every gene in this creature's body. It was a formidable task, but not beyond Agron's capabilities.

"In his typical fashion, Agron charged into the task with zeal. He promised, publicly, that the threat would be eradicated, or at the very least, neutralized. Everyone was elated. Their best geneticist was on the job and caring for the welfare of his species.

"As payment for his efforts, the government had his parents murdered. Many of the lower level dignitaries, as well as their families were eliminated. The government felt that all those who protested the loss of their pets posed a serious threat to the halls of power. It was to remain secret, but the beasts that performed the murders were left alive. The chance of discovery was increased exponentially.

"Agron heard the rumors a year or so after their deaths. Up to that moment, everyone had thought it had been a tragic accident that took their lives, and he was willing to dismiss the rumors as idle conversation. As they became more persistent, and facts pieced together, Agron considered the unthinkable. His parents were executed. Not willing to let rumors concerning his family pass unnoticed; he researched every detail he could track down. Armed with the truth of his parents' deaths, he became obsessed with revenge.

"He started with the beasts that actually did the killing, but was obstructed by the walls that surrounded those at the highest levels. He developed a plan, simple yet elegant.

"The things that he did secretly began to evidence themselves in minor changes to the food supply. Herd animals became increasingly aggressive and larger. The changes were subtle, yet permanent. Officials took notice and began to investigate. Agron was never a suspect. He was a hero for eliminating the plague from society.

"Each time he went on his rotation to 'The Hunt', he became more daring, risking himself in foolhardy ways. This behavior alarmed the university leaders as well as the government. Then again, they had reason to keep a vigilant watch on Agron.

"My superiors assigned me to become acquainted with him. If I were to sleep with him to accomplish this goal, then that would be what I was required to do. You've seen him; it was not an undesirable assignment. Many of the other females in the corps were jealous. To be honest, I enjoyed the notoriety.

"I did my job, becoming friends with Agron, only seeing him sporadically. All the while we were together; I kept meticulous notes about everything he said. It didn't matter how innocuous, I recorded it. My department wanted a psychological profile on him, and to my shame; I provided the information that ultimately caused his death.

"I'm sorry for digressing. Let me continue. I must tell you though, being with him was wonderful. I began to see the real Agron, and soon understood the passion of his convictions. He drove himself endlessly,

trusting no one to assist him. He seldom ever delegated a task, and if he did, it was menial."

Treanna leaned close to Ellen, her check next to Ellen's. She lowered her voice to a whisper and continued, *"Between you and me, Agron was a fantastic lover. I won't tell you any of the details about the first time I seduced him, but he was a tender and caring lover. My needs always came before his. He placed me on a pedestal and I did everything in my power to remain there. I didn't want to lose Agron to anyone, or anything. That was the beginning of my downfall as well.*

"The reports that I forwarded to the Deputy Minister for analysis should have been complete, but they displayed a careless lack of continuity. I began to cause doubt about myself as well as Agron. It was foolish and sloppy. I'd been trained better. Without knowing it, I was placed under surveillance.

"Agron had taken the mammal specimens and genetically altered them so perfectly, that none of the others could detect it. The mutations were to take place over thousands of generations, with the results being a larger, more intelligent mammal, that was truly bi-pedal.

"We managed to release them into a remote sector that had no resource value to our species. Within three generations, they should have begun to develop a larger brain. He enhanced the cognitive center of their brains. It was a small tweak of a single molecule, but that's all that was required. Nature had already provided a path for the adaptation to come about. Who would ever know if it was a natural or forced mutation?

"Shortly after that we were taken prisoner. His plans had only been half met. He and I knew what they would do to us. We betrayed a corrupt government, and they were notorious for not offering leniency. Agron thought that he might still succeed if they would enclose him in his invention, this box, but he was murdered instead.

"Agron's dream was to mentally debilitate the entire species by his genetic manipulations. He had already altered the food animals. The digestive fluids triggered the altered sequencing in the prey animals. Once consumed, it would migrate to the cells and start the slow process of mutating our species.

"Agron further planned to suspend himself for a thousand years in the cryogenic chamber and emerge the single remaining intelligent dinosaur on the planet. He could then start the process of enhancing the brains of the rest of the species and he would become the Law Giver.

"Utopian societies have been a dream for all sentient beings from the moment they have developed the capability for abstract thought. Agron would have been the first to succeed. I doomed him to this fate by my careless actions. I should be dead and Agron should be the one in the chamber.

"Agron loved me so much that he sampled my DNA and enclosed it in his sample chamber. He was going to clone me when he reawakened. As a further precaution, you already know, he'd transferred all his mental abilities into the computer before they caught us. He didn't believe the government would murder him, but he was wrong.

"I have taken up too much of your time, Ellen. Thank you for listening. I suppose that I should have come to the point directly. I only felt that it was necessary to explain the entire story to you. The reason Agron has become so irritable with you, meaning the team, is after running a sample of Dick's blood during the demonstration, Agron has discovered that your species is the direct descendants of the animals we released before we were captured.

"He's losing patience with you because he believes you are his children. His hope was that you would develop your intellect to match his. I know how proud he is of you, and he only wants the best for you.

"The rest you know. You're the one who discovered the box. I wish that things had turned out differently. Perhaps someday we will meet again on better terms."

The shock of this revelation shook Ellen to her core. Slumped in her chair, barely able to speak, she asked, "Are you telling me that Agron is our species progenitor?"

"That's what the analysis shows. It's accurate to the molecular level. He had me monitor the findings; we ran the tests three separate times. There's no mistake, Ellen.

"I'll need to discuss this with the others." Turning from Treanna's image, Ellen waved her away.

"Why does this information upset you? From what I have learned, you

and Jonathan study the past to understand your beginnings. You're correct Ellen, I don't understand. You're a scientist. This is pure science. You should be exhilarated at this discovery, yet you're depressed and pre-occupied."

"Huh? What? Yes, scientifically that's true. We, and others, have long searched for the missing link between bi-pedal mammals and humans. Our belief system has been around for millennia. This will shatter the foundations of every culture on the planet.

"I'm confused."

"Do I have to spell it out," Ellen screamed. "Agron, has created us through biological experimentation. This can never be revealed. For God's sake Treanna, what don't you understand? You have destroyed our humanity, our cultural beliefs, with one sentence."

9 781954 886162